Girl in the Rearview Mirror

Girl in the Rearview Mirror

A Novel

Kelsey Rae Dimberg

An Imprint of HarperCollins*Publishers*

FIRST HARPERLUXE EDITION

ISBN: 978-0-06-291209-1

HarperLuxe™ is a trademark of HarperCollins Publishers.

Library of Congress Cataloging-in-Publication Data is available upon request.

19 20 21 22 23 LSC 10 9 8 7 6 5 4 3 2 1

For Greg

You see, Mr. Gittes, most people never have to face the fact that at the right time and the right place, they're capable of anything.

—NOAH CROSS, *CHINATOWN*

There's the cold in your stomach, but you open the envelope, you have to open the envelope, for the end of man is to know.

—ROBERT PENN WARREN, *ALL THE KING'S MEN*

Girl in the
Rearview Mirror

1

Yesterday had been the hottest day of the year, and today was even warmer. Arizona seemed to be moving closer to the sun. If only we'd stayed inside. Instead, I escorted Amabel Martin through the holiday festival.

It was one of those endless summer afternoons when time seems to bend back and repeat itself, like taffy stretched and pulled over the elbows of a giant machine. Amabel and I wandered the midway for hours, buying an invisible dog on a stiff leash, losing a yard of tickets playing games, and drinking cup after cup of lemonade. Heat pressed over the fair as though the striped tents were made of wool. Already five people had collapsed, and a line of ambulances idled behind the grandstand, waiting for the next. Volunteers distributed bottled water compliments of "Senator Martin—*Your* Senator!"

All afternoon, Amabel had fixated on the Tilt-A-Whirl, nagging to ride until I gave in. Her head just cleared the height requirement. Gloating, she raced to a cart, and now sat impatiently, kicking her legs. Her cheek sparkled with a painted flag, stars rendered in silver glitter. At four years old, she was already a beauty, with a bossy, charming face and strawberry blond hair.

On the sidelines, one of Senator Martin's men—a Snoop, as Amabel and I called them—chewed his gum impassively, like a man at a bus stop. A curly white cord snaked from his ear down the stiff collar of his polo. Amabel waved at him with her arm stretched straight. Snoops had shadowed her all her life; the Senator had been in office for decades.

With the scream of a guitar riff, the Tilt-A-Whirl jerked into motion. The seats lifted and began to glide, first in one direction, then the opposite, still slowly enough for the dizziness to feel pleasant. A breeze swept our hair.

Amabel wriggled beside me, giddy, as we waltzed by other carts. Then, abruptly, she gasped and tried to stand, pushing at the lap bar.

I snatched her waistband. "Sit down!"

She pointed, jabbing the air. "That girl—she's following me!"

Our cart spun, more quickly now, with a sick zip of acceleration.

"What?" In the direction of Amabel's finger were two carts, one holding a trio of boys, the other with its back to us.

"The one with the red hair!" Amabel's voice was shrill.

The second cart spun, and I caught a glimpse of a young woman—maybe a teenager—with long bare legs and bright hair. She was riding alone.

"Don't be silly, Ammy," I said.

We sailed backward and slammed into a turn. Amabel squealed. The force of the spin pressed her legs into mine, and her face was flattened and distressed.

I squeezed her hand. "It's almost over."

Amabel scowled, resenting being babied. She craned at the carts sailing by, a hectic impression of shirt patterns and white faces. The music was so loud it felt physical, like someone breathing on my neck.

Finally, the song ended and the ride drifted to a stop. The slouching attendant began releasing the safety bars. People streamed away.

When our bar was lifted, Amabel darted to the exit.

"There she is!"

She pointed to a teenager moving with the flow of disembarking passengers. The girl was striking. Bright, tomato red hair fell down her back, contrasting with her milk-pale skin. She wore a short white dress and aqua cowboy boots. We reached the exit at the same time she did, and she stepped back to let us go ahead, smiling blankly, though Amabel was gaping. An intricate tattoo of flowers climbed her bicep. No—face paint, with a heavy dose of glitter, like Amabel's flag.

We filed down the stairs and I took Ammy by the shoulders to keep her clear of the crowd. The midway was packed, people carrying corn dogs and typing into their phones and pointing at Uncle Sam striding past on stilts. Around us, spinning rides filled the periphery of my vision with color and motion. The racket of shouted conversation and tinny carnival music thickened the air like soup.

My head pulsed, and I knelt beside Amabel to ask what she wanted to do next. Her lower lip shook.

"Sweetie, what's wrong?" I asked.

"You didn't believe me." A fat tear rolled down her cheek, blurring the flag.

"About the girl?" I glanced around, but in the chaos, the redhead had vanished. "We ran right into her, and she didn't notice us."

Amabel sniffled, smearing her hand across her nose. She was imaginative, always inventing stories in which she played a starring role. Being followed, being kidnapped, being rescued—these were her current obsessions, influenced by a library of princess movies she knew by heart.

I pulled a napkin from my pocket and dabbed at her eyes. Her skin felt feverish. "Why don't we take a break?"

We bought Italian ices and settled at a picnic table in the shade of a striped tent. Misters sprayed a haze of water that evaporated as it hit our skin, deliciously cooling.

"Now," I said. "Tell me about the girl. Is she a spy?"

Amabel shook her head, giggling. In a stage whisper, she told me the redhead had trailed after us all day: had her arm painted as Amabel got her face painted, rode the Ferris wheel with us, stood behind us at the puppet show.

"It's probably a coincidence," I said. "Do you know what that means? It's when something seems important, but really just happened by accident."

Amabel frowned. "No! She was staring at me."

"She was looking at your beautiful flag." I touched her cheek. Her skin had cooled. I unfastened her ponytail and gathered the loose hairs.

Ammy squirmed. "I saw her before. At the restaurant," she said, pronouncing it *rest-oh-want*.

My hands slowed. I leaned to see her face. It was smooth, innocent, her lips faintly parted.

"At your dad's restaurant?"

Sensing she had my real attention, Ammy knelt on the picnic bench and shimmied. "Yep!"

"Sit still," I said, arranging her hair again. "When was this?"

She shrugged. "We were eating ice cream."

I looped her ponytail through the elastic band and patted her to sit back. I scooped the soft, slushy layer from the top of my lemon ice. Its tartness puckered my mouth. In the blur of summer, I couldn't remember when we'd last visited The Grove. I hadn't noticed any girl. Maybe she worked at the restaurant, but I knew most of the waitresses, and she'd seemed too young.

Amabel tipped her cup back and swallowed the last drops, coming away with a sticky mustache of juice.

"Do you remember when we talked about knowing when to stop playing a game? It's okay to tell stories as long as you stop when we ask you to."

"I'm not! It's not a story, Finn." Her eyes were wide.

"I still think it's a coincidence. But if you see her again, you tell me right away. Promise?" I held out my hand, and she latched her pinkie in mine.

"We'll see her again," she said. "She's following me."

I scanned the tent, packed with heat-strained adults and riled kids. I didn't see the redhead girl, or anyone else, watching us. The Snoop stood a few yards away, legs planted wide.

Ammy must have had a rough morning, scolded and rushed, the Martins tense about the long day ahead. She was just jealous of the attention the Senator was getting.

"We have a little time before the fireworks," I said. "Let's do something fun."

Amabel ran to the carousel and climbed onto a purple unicorn. As we circled, the ride bobbing gently, mothers held their palms out, ready to catch their children if they fell. The only danger here was artificial, like the slingshot ride across the way, currently shooting a pod in the air that plummeted to earth, bouncing and tumbling on its bungee. Delighted screams fell down to us.

Over the last year, Amabel had begun to lie. Mostly harmless fibs, and obvious, since she told them in a pleased, sly tone. But once, she managed to fool us.

Last fall, she'd started ballet lessons. Three months in, she announced she was going to be in a recital with the older classes. I was surprised; her movements were comically clumsy. It would be cute to see her onstage. The studio sent a glossy invitation to its "annual evening of music and motion," and Marina bought her the pink tutu she'd been coveting.

On recital night, Amabel and I left Philip and Marina in the auditorium and found our way backstage. Girls much older than Ammy rushed about, stretching and slicking on lipstick in mirrors. They were graceful and sinewy, dressed in black, hair swirled into lacquered buns. I panicked, wishing I'd checked with the teacher about what to wear. I didn't even notice Amabel was crying until she grabbed my hand with both of hers and tugged me to a stop.

"I don't want to see Miss Eva," she whispered. Her face was stricken.

It had been a lie. Another girl in her class had been chosen to dance in the recital, and Amabel, jealous, blurted her story to me, not realizing how it would grow: the invitation, the tutu, her parents dressed up, big girls all around her, anticipation thick in the air.

I carried her out, and we drove home, Philip and Marina stonily silent in the front seat, Amabel holding my hand tightly in back.

After I tucked her into bed, I went to say good night to Marina. She sat by the pool, dangling her legs in the water. Her white swimming suit glowed in the twilight.

"She didn't mean it," I said into the quiet. "She must have expected one of us to catch her."

Marina stretched her legs in front of her, appraising her toes, a delicate-stemmed wineglass beside her, near the edge of the pool. "They say lying is a sign of intelligence in children." Her voice was flat and cool.

Amabel refused to return to ballet, so she switched to horseback riding lessons. For a while, she was sober and remorseful, but soon enough the fibs began again.

Pink clouds, pale on top and glowing neon below, blanketed the wide desert sky. A white rocket shot into the air and popped with an authoritative boom, signaling that the show would begin soon. Heads tilted up, and the general tide shifted to the field.

Amabel danced in place, the mysterious girl forgotten. She begged for a piggyback ride, and I indulged her.

She squeezed my hips with a vise grip.

"Boy, you're strong. Must be those riding lessons."

Awkwardly, happily, we strolled to meet her family.

The Martins were using the festival as a rallying event. They were cordoned off from the crowd, surrounded by folding tables piled high with Senator Jim swag and plenty of staffers to solicit donations and distribute yard signs. When Amabel and I crossed the security barricade, the volunteers were packing up, faces tired and sweaty. They wore matching navy shirts printed with the slogan we'd all heard a thousand times already, though the election was still months away: *Senator Martin—Your Senator.*

The Martins were easy to spot. Look for the nice clothing and perfect posture; look in the direction all the faces are looking; find the center of attention. Marina and her father-in-law, the man himself, were yacking with a gaggle of white-haired ladies. Tall and rangy, the Senator towered over them. Like teens, they held out a selfie stick and he stooped into the frame.

His son, Philip, leaned against an empty table, listening to an excited middle-aged man in a garish bright suit, like a caricature of a used car salesman. Though Philip was polite, I could sense his desire to open a beer and be alone.

I knelt to Amabel. "Go give your dad a kiss." She scooted over. He set his palm on her scalp like a cap. Catching my eye, he winked. His golden hair was etched with a clean part, like that of a young Robert Redford. He wore navy, khaki, and boat shoes, giving off an aura of nonchalance. If the Senator was the success, and Marina his cheerleader, Philip was the most popular, the easiest to like, quickest to laugh, the only one who chafed at the stiff, stuffy importance of the Martin name.

Marina had spotted me, too, and was heading over with a scary smile. Worry about the campaign had made her frenzied in her enthusiasm.

"Amabel!" she called. "Let's get you in a picture with Grandpa."

Amabel went warily. The Senator placed a hand on her shoulder. It sat heavily on her thin frame. Cameras flashed. The picture might soften his image, remind people that, in spite of his decades in Washington, he was a family man.

All of us had paused to watch the photograph—the volunteers, the old ladies, the car salesman. Our faces turned toward the Senator like flowers to light. He didn't miss the opportunity. Smiling, benevolent, he lifted his chin to project his voice.

"It means a lot to be with my granddaughter today. This is a day to celebrate our oldest values. The beliefs that haven't changed—what we fight to keep from changing. This day helps me remember what I'm working for." In spite of his age, his voice was deep as a drum and syrup smooth.

Amabel twisted, but his hand pinned her in place. I gave her a sign to be patient.

The Senator went on, patriotic, proud, rallying. He drew people in with his rhythmic cadence; suddenly he amplified his voice, belted out a crescendo that could raise goose bumps in the desert heat.

"Today I don't want to talk about what needs fixing, though everyone knows there's plenty of work to do. I want all of us, every one, to celebrate and give thanks for the best thing we have. Freedom!"

We burst into authentic applause, and the Senator's smile seemed authentic, too; his face gleaming, his shirt damp at the collar.

The campaign was faltering, though none of the Martins said so aloud, not around me anyway. The Senator had struggled in the primary against a Tea Party candidate who energized crowds with talk of border walls and bucking big government. The near-loss rattled Jim, made him a little bit resentful and very tired. He'd taken a vacation, thinking the worst was over. He'd underestimated his Democrat rival, who kept the anti-establishment fervor going; people were angry about the economy and the housing market, and Latinos were turning against him in droves.

I couldn't imagine him losing. The Martins were pillars of this place, as much Arizona to me as the dry heat, the red rocks, the scorpions.

Another rocket popped, and a voice crackled over a loudspeaker, "Take your seats for the firework extravaganza!"

The reporters left and visitors decamped for their seats. Abruptly, we were alone. In the sudden privacy, the Martins' collective exhaustion was laid bare. The Senator shook a handkerchief from his pocket and mopped his face. Philip rolled his neck. Marina passed around hand sanitizer. They'd been on their feet for hours in that scrubby patch of grass, the sun beating down, shaking hands, memorizing names, smiling smiling smiling, sneaking off one at a time to a nearby RV to use the bathroom or just sit in the cool air for a spell.

Amabel stood forgotten by her grandfather. I went to rescue her.

At my approach, the Senator came out of his daze.

"Finn," he boomed. "I'm sorry I didn't say hello earlier. How are you?"

"Senator. I'm well, thanks. And you?" I was embarrassed by my artificial tone, the pretentious *well*, delivered in a rush like the manners of an obedient child.

"Please, call me Jim." His eyes drifted over my forehead and hardened. "No news, I hope?"

Bryant Dewitt, a top aide of the Senator's, had arrived. He must have come from another event, as he wore a formal suit. Though short and slim, he was classically handsome, with thick, wavy dark hair and a lilting voice. His mother was Colombian, and he spoke Spanish fluently, if with a scholarly accent. The Senator dispatched him to any event that anticipated a Latino crowd.

Bryant was jocular. "No news. We're all set for the email blasts to go out at nine."

"Excellent." The Senator dropped a hand on his back and they strolled away, heads together.

I knelt to Amabel. "You were nice to stand with your grandpa while he gave his speech. Do you remember what happened on July fourth in 1776?"

She rambled about Christopher Columbus while I spread a picnic blanket over the trampled grass. We settled down, Amabel leaning heavily against me in spite of the heat. I watched as Philip and Marina set out lawn chairs, Marina bending to brush the seat with a palm.

Bryant joined us. "Hello, ladies."

Amabel adored him. She wanted to tell him all about the fair. We sat side by side, his fingers resting lightly on my wrist even as he asked Amabel teasing questions that made her giggle. As I gazed at the sky, a feeling of peace settled over me. I was really here, this was really me, with Bryant, and my darling Amabel, and the senator of Arizona. Details stood out in stark, specific richness: the lumpy hard ground under the blanket, my thin shirt sticking to my back, a breeze sweeping over my bare legs, the bruise-colored sky above. *Remember this,* I thought.

With a sputter, a recording of the national anthem began to play. The crowd staggered to its feet. The music was crackling and out of tune, but a brave voice began to sing along. The Senator's baritone joined, then Bryant's. Amabel contentedly sang nonsense to the melody. Marina's smile shone at us. Our ragged song fell behind tempo and finished a few beats late. Still, a collective cheer rose from the field. The Senator waved triumphantly. Behind him, a Roman candle ignited, a white flash that lingered when I closed my eyes. Then the show began in earnest. Fireworks bloomed and burst, throwing robes of smoke that drifted away. The smell of powder and fire remained.

"That went well," Marina said softly to Philip as we drove home. Amabel was absorbed in the movie on the headrest TV, each of us listening through one earbud.

"Sure did," Philip said. "They spent enough on it."

"Jim did well, I thought. He shines in natural situations."

"He hasn't been in a natural situation in twenty-five years," Philip joked.

Marina shook her head, gently chiding, "I've never seen him so worried."

Philip shrugged. "People are frustrated. They like to get fired up, hear someone say it's not their fault."

"Exactly," Marina said. "That's exactly it."

"The media loves controversy. Jim's losing is more of a story than him winning. In the end he'll be fine. The majority of voters like the way things are going."

"How can you be so—"

"Honey. Worrying about a Democrat beating Jim is like worrying about a snowstorm in August."

The Martins only used terms of endearment when they were annoyed. Marina's hand jerked up to toy with her necklace. Then she must have remembered I was there because she shook her shoulders and said lightly, "I wish I had your confidence."

It was an open secret that Philip would run for his father's seat the next term. He'd been an Arizona boy forever, a football star at ASU—everyone knew his name. He was handsome and young, for a politician, with a fertile network: his own business and real estate ties, art connections through Marina, political through his father. His restaurants staffed mostly Latinos. He was perfectly positioned. But first, Senator Jim had to hold the course.

"I'm just saying," Marina said a few minutes later, into the silence. "We shouldn't take anything for granted."

Philip let her have the last word.

After Ammy went to bed, I found Philip in the kitchen gazing out the glass doors to the balcony. The Martins lived in Ocotillo Heights, a neighborhood built up the side of a mountain, with sweeping views of the city in the valley. Its lights glowed like fireflies.

"Amabel settled in all right? Long day for her." Philip held out a pack of Oreos to me. He had a tumbler of whiskey in his other hand.

"She's asleep." I waved away the cookies.

"You see our coyote yet?" His arm grazed mine. He'd unbuttoned the top third of his shirt. His skin gave off a minty soap smell.

I held still so we stayed close, but not touching. My reflection in the dark glass was ghostly.

"A couple times. He was pretty far out."

"I saw him run last week. Maybe a rabbit. That's when I got the binoculars out." The binoculars sat, heavy as lead, on the counter by the espresso machine.

"I try not to draw attention to him. Coyotes are dangerous. Amabel might think it's a dog."

He studied my reflection, tilting his head.

"You think I'm being paranoid," I said.

"Are you off to see that boyfriend of yours?"

The kitchen light came on.

"Finn. I didn't realize you were still here." Marina blinked at us. She'd changed into yoga pants and drawn her hair into a ponytail. Frowning, she opened the wine fridge and bent to rummage through it. From the back, she might have been twenty. Her shirt was cut to show off her lean, muscled shoulder blades, the result of hours of Pilates.

She selected a white in a fluted bottle and opened it with a practiced twist of her wrist. Her glass sang as it hit the marble counter. "I'd offer you a drink, but I know you have to drive home."

"We were just talking about the coyote," I said. "He's dangerous."

"The dog? Why? He's beautiful. He's a desert animal, he won't come up to us."

I decided not to mention the time their garbage cans had been tipped into the street, bags ripped, trash everywhere.

"Finn worries Amabel might think of him as a pet."

Philip set the cookies on the counter and topped off his glass with water at the tap.

Marina sealed the cookies with a clip. "You and your junk food habit. Those are for Amabel and Finn." But her voice was teasing.

I said good night and left them as allies.

As I drove down the tight curves of the mountain road, Marina's words lingered in my mind. The coyote *was* beautiful. His fur held all the tones of the dusty hills, so he was impossible to spot unless he was moving. His gait was sporadic. Now trotting, now sniffing, now still, ears up and body tense. Then he'd relax, lift his leg to a shrub. Through the binoculars, I'd admired his trim snout, comically large ears, the patina of gray and red and brown on his coat.

Once, when he came closer to the house, I saw him in more detail. He was gaunt. In the heat, his mouth was open, tongue lolling. A yellow undertone to his fur made him appear jaundiced. He stared right at me, or so it seemed through the binoculars. His eyes were perfectly round and black, inexpressive. Not a tame thing after all.

2

Red, white, and blue spotlights lit the façade of the club. The party was on the rooftop. Bryant was already there, at the invitation of Rick Leach, the entrepreneur who owned this club and half the others on the street. At twenty-four, Rick had intuited a demand for a Vegas-like strip in Scottsdale, where tourists could go at night after spending the day golfing, watching spring training, or tanning by the pool. Now Rick was thirty-two, rich, and developing an interest in politics.

Tonight, the club's long line gave the impression of exclusivity, as did the row of refrigerator-wide bouncers checking IDs. Mirrored elevator doors swung open, and the already-buzzed crowd pressed in. Women tilted on high heels, grabbing at each other for balance. Cologne choked the air.

A guy behind me bent over to mess with something at the level of my ankles. I shifted my knees together.

He stood, holding out a lipstick. "You drop this?" He was frattish, blond, and smirking. Chunky plastic glasses gave him the look of a superhero's alter ego.

"Don't think so." My purse was zippered.

"Sure?" He pressed it into my hand. It was mine, "Wild Child" red in a lacquered tube, a $30 splurge.

"Thanks." Returning it to my purse, I ran my fingers across phone, keys, cards. Everything seemed accounted for.

The elevator doors opened, releasing us into the hot night. An insistent beat pulsed, bass notes registering as a buzzing pressure in the air. Searchlights panned the sky. In the crowd milling on the rooftop, the dominant theme was skin: bare shoulders and plunging necklines, dresses that barely skimmed thighs. Teeth and tans. Drunk girls swayed to the music, but most people stood still, shouting over it, hearing nothing.

I was tired, and not in the mood for a party, but Bryant had insisted. He was close to securing Rick's support; he needed me.

We made a successful team at his gatherings. My first events, over a year ago, had felt foreign, awkward, daunting. I'd studied the popular women in the group and built a wardrobe like theirs, learned to talk and laugh like them. I felt sure Bryant had done the same, years earlier. Between us, I had the easy job. Nobody expected me to persuade them of anything. In fact, it was the other way around: men liked me best when they were coaxing me—to sit beside them, to laugh at their jokes or try a bite from their plates, to have another drink, to dance.

I wasn't ready to face them just yet. I ordered a vodka tonic from a bartender in a star-spangled bikini. The drink came in a thin plastic cup and tasted like sugared hand sanitizer.

I leaned against the bar and took the lay of the land. At the perimeter of the rooftop were rows of cabanas: gauzy white tents concealing private couches and those rich enough to reserve them. Bryant was in one, I knew, his suit and smile impossibly fresh.

The centerpiece of the party was a shallow pool, lit up yellow-blue. The water was crowded with slim women and men ranging from buff lifeguard types to older, fatter guys with gold rings and money. Belly-deep, they mingled as nonchalantly as if on dry land, holding their drinks clear.

In between pool and cabana was the no-man's-land of the patio, where people milled restlessly, longing to be obscured by the tents or ogled in the pool.

Someone tapped my shoulder. "You here alone?" The frat boy from the elevator. He must have wandered after me. Up close, I saw that his glasses had no lenses.

"I'm meeting someone."

His smile cut dimples into his cheeks. "Not yet, huh? Come on, keep me company." He rapped his knuckles on the bar and ordered a beer.

He was a typical Scottsdale clubber. Beach blond hair carefully gelled to appear tousled. Rolled sleeves showing off hours of quality time with dumbbells.

When his beer arrived, he sucked the inch of foam off the top. "So, where you from?"

In Phoenix, this was the default small-talk opener.

"Chicago," I said reluctantly.

"No shit? Me, too. Well, suburbs." He threw out a name—Lincoln Woods.

"I've never been." I tipped back my cup. The plastic cracked and split under my thumb.

"What brought you to A-Z?"

"Summer." I signaled for my bill.

"Right?" He laughed. "God, those winters were brutal."

I hummed in reply, digging for cash.

"Finn!" Bryant put his hand on my back. "Here you are." He sounded happy.

"Here *you* are." I kissed him a bit longer than usual. "Sorry I'm late."

"You must have been thirsty." He tossed a ten onto my bill. Then he noticed my company. He put his arm around me and held out a hand. "Bryant Dewitt."

"Guy," said the guy, shaking. He winked at me. "Thanks for hanging out."

On our way to the cabana, Bryant asked why I was laughing.

"A guy named Guy," I said. "I can't explain."

He gave me a forgiving smile. "You've had a long day. We won't stay long."

We ducked behind a curtain. The cabana reeked of booze and was packed with people I didn't recognize. Rick jumped off a couch, scrambled over several pairs of knees, and kissed me wetly on both cheeks. He was short, fattish and soft, with curly blond hair shorn like lamb's wool and a rosebud mouth. He looked like a seedy toddler.

"You wore this dress last time I saw you." He ran a finger down the strap.

I said something silly back, embarrassed, and reached past him to shake hands with his latest girl,

Meg. She said hi and stuck her Ring Pop back in her mouth. Her eyes were dark holes in her doll face.

I settled between her and Rick, Bryant opposite us. Rick launched into a spiel about his new "concept" for Tempe, a country-themed club where girls would dance on the bar. He spoke incessantly, and the others in the tent treated it like background noise, getting up for drinks and tripping over each other and laughing hysterically when things spilled. Only Bryant and I listened. Rick would be a big feather in Bryant's cap. Bryant found Republicans where they weren't supposed to be: backstage at the theater, the university administration, Rick's purple-lighted clubs.

At last a firework shrieked and popped, and then another, and another. Bryant cranked back the cabana's fabric ceiling. A couple slipped in, and through the opening in the tent, I thought I saw Amabel's redhead again, a slim silhouette in cowboy boots strolling languidly across the patio while everyone else craned up at the sky.

I stood, but Rick grabbed my wrist.

"You can't miss the show." His breath was sweet with booze.

I sat back down. I didn't see the redhead again, if she'd been there at all.

"Where do you think Rick meets his girls?" I called to Bryant. We were at his condo. He'd changed into basketball shorts and sat on the terrace outside his bedroom, smoking a cigar. I still wore my dress, which Rick's comment made clear I'd have to retire for a while. Already, I was mentally budgeting for a new one. If I put my electric bill on my credit card, I could probably swing it.

I sifted through Bryant's records until I found a cover I liked, poppy orange and yellow. I managed to get the complicated subwoofer turned on, and the sound of a saxophone poured into the room like a plume of smoke.

I joined Bryant outside. "Did you see that lollipop?"

"She was high." He tugged me down to sit on the arm of his chair. "Thanks for your help tonight. You were perfect."

I bit his ear, trying not to grin. "Did he contribute?"

"Only a matter of time."

I unclasped his watch and held it in my palm, cool and heavy as a roll of quarters.

"Amabel told me a funny story today. She said a girl was following her."

He cocked his head.

"She pointed her out at the fair. A redhead. Young, like sixteen or seventeen, maybe. I didn't think anything of it, but later, at the party, I thought I saw her again."

"Maybe she's following you." He ran his fingers up my leg.

"You don't think it's strange?"

"That Amabel made up a story to get your attention? Isn't she always pulling stuff like that?" He stubbed out the half-smoked cigar and stretched. "Speaking of, I found out Rick's a bit of a liar. I had this idea that he was self-made. A young success story. Turns out his dad's in oil. They're rolling in it."

He obviously expected me to be as surprised, and disapproving, as he was.

"Maybe he wanted to start fresh."

"But to lie?"

My pulse jumped in my neck, tense as a plucked string. "Maybe he thinks he's being private. Not lying, like malicious lying, that affects other people."

"That's semantics."

"Isn't that your job?" I said, trying to sound teasing. "Anyway, once he donates we won't have to see him so much, right?"

He shook his head. "I just can't understand misrepresenting yourself like that. It's so hollow."

I pretended to lose interest, standing and wandering inside to undress. I was glad when he followed.

3

It was a fluke that I found the Martins at all.

I grew up in a far-flung Chicago suburb and spent the last year of high school exiled with my dad in rural Indiana. When I turned eighteen, I escaped, moving to Arizona to attend the university in Tempe. Driving down Route 66, familiar farmland gave way to windswept Oklahoma prairies, empty Texas desert, pine-topped New Mexico mountains. As the speedometer ticked, I shed history. By the time I arrived at school, I realized I could start over. I introduced myself as Finn, my middle name, and it stuck. Within months, my first name sounded foreign. Natalie was the girl in the rearview mirror.

People, like Bryant, read into lies, as if they're somehow more revealing than the truth. But I was hardly alone in wanting to be different, new. On campus, the thrill of anonymity was airborne. Everyone tried on personalities for size. The California girls in fur Uggs, the guys falling off skateboards doing tricks on the library steps, the grad student TAs behind tortoiseshell glasses. It was rumored that even the dreadlocked bums panhandling outside the Mill Avenue bars were actually rich kids from San Diego, augmenting their allowances for pot money.

The spangled palm trees and sparkling pools intoxicated me. I spent a few delirious months playing with possibilities: cutting off my hair and hanging with the art kids, studying Chinese and inking a tattoo onto my shoulder blade. Finally, I settled on interior design. A woman I'd admired back home was a designer who'd worked on penthouses in Chicago. In her own house, every object had a story, from the antique French chaise to the blown-glass lamps. The beauty had been a revelation to me, like eating fruit after a diet of bread and water.

In design, I saw a key to transforming the basic shell of whatever you were given. Demolishing walls, rerouting plumbing, ripping out the bad decisions of the past and revealing something fresh.

I forged a new self: mature, reserved, artistic.

I didn't go home. Over winter break, I savored the deserted campus with its funny lit-up palms. Summers, I adapted to days so hot you sweated through your clothes, while the indoors were so air-conditioned you needed a jacket. I liked the perpetual blue sky, the shiny newness of it all. People weren't as friendly as they were back home; they were cooler, and vainer, which appealed to me.

After graduation, my friends left, many moving right back into their childhood bedrooms. The market was still recovering from the crash, and demand for new grads was low. I submitted my résumé to dozens of job postings. Not one of the companies so much as sent me a rejection letter, let alone called for an interview.

I finally got work as a waitress, hoisting platters of ribs in a dining room decorated with wagon wheels and fake license plates, the smell of greasy smoke on me all the time—the sort of job Natalie would have taken. I was lonely and felt like a failure.

My shifts ended after midnight. I'd lie in bed sleepless, keyed up from the physical work, the lifting and chatting and especially the smiling. Eventually I'd get up and switch on my desk lamp. I built a series of model rooms. I told myself I was filling out my portfolio, but the rooms were too personal. I re-created my old bedroom, under the eaves, with its canopy bed and toile wallpaper patterned with foxes. I made the glassed-in sunroom with the cane lounge set; the living room with the stone fireplace; the kitchen and separate butler's pantry complete with tiny marble sink.

By July, I'd rebuilt the whole house. I stacked the boxes against a wall and lived with the display for weeks, until one night, drunk and melancholy, I lit a fire in the courtyard grill and threw them in, one by one. Better not to remember. The bits of glue and polyester turned the smoke greasy and black, and bright, shiny fragments lingered like wreckage in the grate.

Summer passed.

In September, a professor emailed me about an internship with a developer's office. It was unpaid, so I'd have to keep waitressing, but I'd get real experience. The firm constructed luxury homes in planned neighborhoods around the city. My first day, I wore a new pencil skirt and a real silk blouse. My boss, John, took me around to meet the architects and designers.

By nine-thirty, I was unceremoniously led to a desk heaped with files. John's secretary hadn't returned from maternity leave, and I took her place. His department divvied up parcels of land into lots, fitting in as many houses as possible without losing the illusion of exclusivity. Nothing to do with design, but I kept the job. It filled my hours.

I was hunched over my desk, trying to locate a particular permit among a stack of fat folders. I'd gone for drinks after my waitressing shift the night before, and a headache stuck its hammer and chisel into my temple. I tugged at my skirt, which kept riding up over the leather seat, and the papers slid off my lap.

The door rattled open, and a big man came in, whistling. Big as in tall, with broad shoulders. He wore the nicest suit I'd ever seen, the color of new straw. He was handsome. Thick blond hair, and a face lovingly chiseled by time. Laugh lines framed his pale blue eyes, and a two o'clock shadow peppered his square jaw.

One of my papers had drifted to his feet. He picked it up for me with a gallant gesture. He asked for John, and I buzzed him through.

He was back again two days later: navy suit, green tie flecked with tiny white dots. He became a regular visitor. While he waited, he'd toss an idle comment my way, casually as a match to the sidewalk. The drought, the World Series, the light rail.

One day he remarked that there wasn't another person outside for blocks. It was eerie. He told me his favorite city was New York, with its bustling sidewalks.

I said I loved Chicago. He was intrigued. "Cold country, huh? I've never been."

His name was Philip. He came around once or twice a week. Sometimes he brought me iced coffee, always with a mound of sugar at the bottom that zipped up the straw and crunched between my teeth like tiny diamonds.

At the office manager's birthday party, I asked what his story was. We were all packed into the break room tearing into a sheet cake like children. My coworkers were mostly middle-aged and pasty, as if their skin had absorbed the sickly fluorescent lighting. They were over-worked and competitive, many still scarred from being laid off after the crash, but today Pam was talkative. She was turning fifty, and exuberant from everyone's teasing.

"You don't know who Philip Martin is?" she said. "They're right, I really am getting old! When I was your age, he was everybody's dream. A football star. So good looking." She paused for a bite of cake, holding her hand in front of her lips while she chewed. "He's the Senator's son. You know, Jim Martin."

The Senator I knew—in college he was reviled by students for his conservativism, although he was a generous donor. One of the buildings was named for him, his portrait hanging solemnly in the hall.

"We all thought he'd do something major after school. Become a movie star, or go the big-time in football. He was really something. But there was some kind of scandal." She tapped her fork against her lip. "He left the limelight then."

I asked what had happened, but she didn't remember the details.

"Landed on his feet, of course. His type always does. He owns a ton of land. He's working with John on some mixed-use development. Restaurants, condos, the whole 'boutique living' thing." She flashed air quotes. "I shouldn't scoff. It's keeping us in paychecks."

"I assumed he was a lawyer," I said. "Working so closely with John."

"Funny, isn't it?" She winked. "He has been dropping in a lot lately."

"Please. You know John won't return a phone call if he can help it." But a giddy sugared feeling buzzed through my body.

A few weeks later, Philip was holed up in a conference room most of the afternoon. At quarter to five a sleek blonde came in carrying a little girl on her hip. They looked alike, their fair skin flushed from the November chill, dressed in white cotton sweaters, the woman's a slouchy kimono, the girl's embroidered with sheep. Frowns puckered their foreheads as they stepped into the stuffy office.

"We're here to meet Philip," the woman said. "Is he ready?" She brushed a strand of hair from her forehead and I saw a clutch of diamonds on her left hand.

I offered to take a message in, but she said not to bother, giving me a tight smile. She put the girl down and settled into one of the transparent plastic chairs in the waiting area, pulling out her phone.

The little girl sidled up to my desk and poked at the sculpture I'd set there: a wire figure holding a barbell with a metal sphere at either end. I showed her how it worked, pulling it off kilter and letting go. It bobbled back and forth, first violently, then slower and slower before coming to a stop in perfect balance. The girl laughed, a loud burble.

I asked her if she wanted to try.

She nodded shyly. Her teeth were tiny and white and spaced out, like pieces of candy. She told me her name was Amabel.

The next time I saw Philip, he asked if I might be interested in babysitting. I'd made a big impression, he told me, smiling.

I wore a new blue dress, but Philip wasn't home. His wife, Marina, showed me around their incredible house. I wanted to peek into every room, touch the surfaces, but Marina gave off an air of elaborate boredom, which I emulated. She was dressed for a formal dinner in a silver gown that clung to the saber-like contours of her body.

She opened a massive refrigerator and pointed out a meal someone named Eva had prepared for Amabel and me. Bottles of champagne lined the door, and a purple radicchio sat like a fat purse beside a ceramic bowl of eggs in a dozen shades of brown.

"You'll find everything, I'm sure." Marina played with the clasp on her bracelet. Her cell number, not Philip's, was on a Post-it note centered on the otherwise bare refrigerator door.

Amabel had been coloring in the kitchen during my tour, and now she jumped down from her seat. She shouted, "I wanna show Finn my fox," and darted away.

"Don't run up the stairs." Marina's voice was deep and flat, so she sounded as if she couldn't care less. She looked me over. "Thanks for coming out. Kids get these crushes. I'm sure it'll pass."

Making Amabel fall in love with me turned out to be easy. She led me to the playroom and proceeded to chatter for hours. She surprised me by preferring cheap plastic toys to the beautiful carved wooden ones on her shelves. Her particular favorite was a disturbing set of dolls whose heads snapped off and reattached to bodies in different outfits.

I was enchanted by the four-story wooden dollhouse that opened on hinges like a jewelry box. Its rooms were elaborately finished with wallpaper and furniture and tiny knickknacks: an etched vase on the mantel, a goldfish bowl with an orange fish inside. I lifted the hinge of the toaster, and a piece of toast popped up.

Amabel took it out of my hand. "You'll be Jasmine," she instructed, giving me a doll without a mouth.

I was back the next Friday night, and the following Monday, and then Philip asked if I'd consider a more full-time gig. Marina wanted to focus on expanding the museum, he explained, though I'd never heard of any museum.

"And Amabel adores you."

Absurdly, I felt triumphant. I tried to control my smile, so wide it stung my cheeks.

I had to provide my real name for the background check. It was six days before Philip called to say we were all set, his voice an unaltered purr. He asked me about Natalie, and I said, "I prefer Finn," and something in my clear, curt answer must have stuck, because I never heard that name from them again.

The next week, I went along on a trip to their house in San Diego. While the Martins hustled to massage appointments and dinner parties, Amabel and I played on the beach, the wind ripping through our hair. I ran along the ocean, seeing it for the first time. I'd expected it to be like Lake Michigan, wrinkled and gray. Instead, the ocean was a force, a roar in the deepest hollows of my ears. It was more alive than anything I'd ever seen. I felt like I'd found a door into a new world, bright and beautiful and flush with pleasure.

I kept the tiny fishbowl with its goldfish on my nightstand, a talisman from the dollhouse. I told everyone the job was temporary. But I fell in love with Amabel, and with the Martins. I met the Senator, and then Bryant, and soon my friends were Bryant's friends, the people I gossiped about were the Martins' people. The few hours a week I spent alone, at my apartment or talking to my parents on the phone, my life felt faded and ill fitting, like the molting skin of a snake.

4

Popular wisdom says Arizona heat is tolerable because it's dry. It's true that back in the Midwest the summer air was so heavily damp you didn't so much stroll in it as press through it, wearily. But this July, the Phoenix temperature rose to 110, 115, relentlessly, day after day. Exposed to the sun, skin grew taut and stinging, sweating from places I'd never known could sweat: shoulders, wrists, ankles. People took cover in the slim, slanting shadows of streetlights and stop signs and palms.

The Tuesday after the Fourth of July festival, I was trapped in traffic, twenty minutes late to pick up Amabel from her afternoon enrichment camp. Heat shimmered in oily waves between bumpers. The sun had sunk to an angle impossible to block with a car visor. Light drove into my eyes like wind or rain.

My dying air conditioner wheezed and spat warm air. Traffic crawled past blocks of upscale strip malls. A stucco Starbucks, a restaurant called Egg, designer outlets. Behind me, a Hummer reared onto the sidewalk, careened through a parking lot, and elbowed back into the street a few cars ahead. Horns blared.

Finally, I came to my turn. Amabel's camp was held in a private school, a low building surrounded by an appealingly ramshackle garden. The parking lot was empty, where usually there was a line of parents. I dashed out, leaving my car running.

The doors were locked. Kids' flag paintings were papered over the windows, stripes wavering and psychedelic. The lights inside were turned off. I yanked futilely at the door handle.

"Hello? Amabel!"

The day was mockingly peaceful. They wouldn't have let Ammy go anywhere on her own; they were strict about sending kids out one by one as the moms' cars arrived. Maybe they'd called Marina when I was late. Or she'd come to get Amabel for some unexpected reason, which had happened once, when Marina's father had had a heart attack and they'd gone straight to the airport.

I called Marina. No answer. Panic began creeping over my body, even as I tried to stay calm.

Then I heard a squeaking sound. And another. Rhythmic and repeating.

I heard, or hallucinated, a laugh.

I hurried through the gardens toward the playground. The path wove romantically and inconveniently around prickling shrubs and raised beds of protuberant cacti and the swollen tongues of succulent leaves.

Amabel's voice, clear and bossy, shouted, "Higher!"

I rushed around the last bend to the playground. Amabel was on a swing, safe, happy, her hair streaming behind her as a teacher pushed her high—too high, it seemed.

"Amabel!" I shouted, sick with relief.

"Finn!" She waved.

The teacher was tall and thin, wearing a floppy sunhat and flared white sailor pants. Strange outfit for someone dealing with kids.

"Thanks so much for waiting with her," I called.

The woman turned. She tugged the rim of her hat so it sprang into a parabola around her face. A face I recognized. Catlike and small under a frame of red hair.

It was the girl from the fair. The redhead.

"Hi, there," she said. Amabel's backpack was slung over her shoulder.

Amabel swung between us almost comically, thrashing her legs to slow down. I snatched at the swing's chain, jolting my arm. Amabel screeched. I hardly heard her. When I lifted her onto my hip, my shoulder flamed with pain.

"It's her!" She squirmed. "I told you!"

I let her down and grabbed her hand. She wriggled brattily, and I tightened my grip on her wrist, making her squeal.

I knelt to her level, breathing hard. Pink blotches of indignation rose on her fair face. "Are you okay?" I searched her for signs of harm, but she seemed fine, apart from her wrist. Her lip jutted.

The redhead observed us, arms crossed, and I swore she was smirking. She was older than I'd guessed at the fair, early twenties, maybe. Even in the shadow of her hat, her skin was pale, almost opalescent. Against it, her hair was bright as a flag. She looked me up and down, assessing my pastel shorts and black tank top, my practical outfit suddenly childish. She stretched the red bow of her lips.

"Is your shoulder all right?" Her voice was high and breathless.

"What are you doing with Amabel?"

The woman's head tilted, as if perplexed. "I was visiting with your daughter? Amabel was telling me about her school?" Her voice rose at the end of every sentence. "I'm thinking of sending my own daughter here. It's magical, isn't it?"

Around us, the gardens were as quiet as if the busy afternoon traffic, the bustling shops, didn't exist. Birds shrieked and rustled invisibly in the daylilies. Their droppings pocked the spongy ground under the swings. Amabel's hand was hot and damp in mine.

"How old is your daughter?" I asked, skeptical. She was beyond thin; her body was wiry, lean muscles running tensely along her bones. Blue veins curled up her wrists.

"She's four?" She tugged at Amabel's backpack strap.

"She wasn't at the fair with you. We saw you there, last weekend."

"You mean the fireworks? She's afraid of noise."

"Amabel said she's seen you before."

That laugh again. She crouched to Amabel and her hat brim hid her face. "Have we bumped into each other before? How funny. We must be neighbors."

Amabel grinned up at me. "Her name is Iris."

The woman clapped. "What a good memory! You must be very smart. I am Iris. And you are?" She held out a hand to me. Her nails were curved like talons.

"We need to get going," I said, pulling away. "I'll take her bag."

She shrugged off Amabel's backpack and held up her hands in surrender. She seemed amused.

I felt I'd made a mistake, like I'd missed something. I tugged Amabel away.

"Break a leg, sweetie!" the girl—Iris—called after us.

Adrenaline surging in my limbs, I walked too quickly, Ammy stumbling to keep up. Tomorrow night, her camp was putting on a play to celebrate the holiday. She must have told this woman.

When we reached the parking lot I glanced back, but the path to the playground was empty.

As we drove, I scrutinized Amabel in the rearview mirror. She had no marks on her, her clothes weren't askew, her feet were tightly laced into her princess sneakers.

"How long were you with that woman?" I asked.

"I dunno. After the other kids left. You were late."

"What did she want?"

Amabel kicked the back of the seat, her face stiff with an expression of regal hurt.

"I'm sorry I was late. But you should have stayed inside. Who let you leave without me? Huh?"

Amabel stubbornly clenched her lips together.

I pulled into a McDonald's. My hands shook as I unbuckled her.

Eventually—after four chicken pucks rattling in a cardboard box, chocolate milk, a Strawberry Shortcake doll in a plastic bag—Amabel talked. It was too good a story to keep to herself; she told it proudly, aware that I was acutely interested.

She'd been in the school lobby, peeking through the artwork to watch for my arrival. Most of the other kids had gone. When she saw a car just like mine—silver and "little"—she called, "She's here!" and scooted out. (I felt a flash of righteous anger at her teachers' negligence, a momentary relief from my own guilt and fear.)

When Amabel ran up to the car, both she and Iris were startled.

"She was smoking," Amabel said reluctantly, knowing it was naughty. "But she threw it away."

Iris was friendly. She asked Amabel if she wanted to play.

Amabel was enchanted. Up close, Iris looked like a movie star. She laughed softly at everything Amabel said. She wore a green ring, and when Amabel admired it, she slipped it off and gave it to her. (Amabel reluctantly brought the ring out from her pocket and set it on the table. The metal was warm, greasy with lotion; the inset was faceted green glass.) Iris asked where she lived, and Amabel described the big house with the pool that Iris could come visit.

Then I'd shown up, angry and mean, hurting Amabel's arm.

"You were rude," she accused, spitting the word—Marina's cardinal sin.

Exasperated, I shook my head. "Being polite doesn't mean talking to strangers, going off with them by yourself. That's not safe. You know better."

She gaped at my unfairness. "She wasn't a stranger! I knew her."

"No, you recognized her. That's not the same thing."

She shrugged, whacking her plastic-wrapped doll against the table.

I took it away. "Did she ask you anything about your parents, about your family? Did she do anything to you? Touch you at all?"

Amabel was confused. "She pushed me on the swing."

I bit the bag to unwrap her doll, tasting floral chemicals in the plastic. Amabel was safe. Nothing had happened, really. But my pulse drummed as I ran through the scene again, Iris's artificial, girlish voice, her long fingernails, her costume-like clothes. Even the birdsong was unsettling and strange in my memory.

She was lying about having a daughter. A mother would have taken Amabel back to school, instinctively.

And she'd spoken to Ammy in the deferential way of someone not used to kids.

Lurking outside the school, smoking a cigarette as the children were picked up. What did she want? She wasn't concerned when I showed up—as if she'd wanted me to catch her.

I was twisting the plastic toy wrapper. I dropped it and began sweeping our debris onto the tray. "We're late to meet your mom."

"You're not gonna tell her, are you? Please, Finn."

A bright dollop of ketchup had spilled on Amabel's collar. I dabbed it with my napkin, and it bled across the fabric. "Why shouldn't I?"

"She'll be mad at us."

Her face was like a doll's, perfect and innocent. Marina would be irate—at me.

I hedged. "If you see that woman again, tell me right away. Don't talk to her. Promise?"

Amabel nodded, petting her doll's red hair. "I promise."

Marina had asked me to drop Amabel at the museum. Formally, it was the Native American Art and Artifacts Center of Scottsdale; Marina, who served as director, called it "NAX," hoping it would catch on. Next Friday, the museum would host the annual Black and White Gala, the event of the summer. For $500 a plate, guests enjoyed the satisfaction of supporting a cultural institution. They might also hope to rub elbows with the Senator, who made a brief appearance every year. Mostly, it was a networking event for wealthy Phoenicians, business owners and financiers and lobbyists and university officials, who rarely used the memberships included with the price of a ticket.

Amabel and I parked in the underground lot and ascended to the lobby in the elevator. Through its glass walls, we admired a vertical stretch of sand studded with artfully buried artifacts—wedges of broken pottery; the skeletons of small, tailed animals; arrowheads and spears; an uncannily human-looking shoulder blade. Everything clean and polished and pressed insistently against the glass, the sort of bloodless, charming archaeological dig Disney would design.

At this hour, few visitors milled about the sun-drenched lobby. Marina stood behind the admissions desk, talking on the phone. She held up a finger at us.

Window washers were squeegeeing the huge panels of glass spanning the far wall. Amabel darted over to make faces at them. Dotting the hill outside, hook-armed saguaros stood over long, thin shadows.

"There you girls are." Marina glided over as smoothly as if on wheels. She wore a cream-colored suit, nude stilettos, invisible makeup. Enveloped in her mineral fragrance, I might have dreamed Iris. Mysteries did not happen in Marina's ordered world.

Her phone buzzed, giving me a moment to consider telling her. *A woman on the playground, probably nothing, but*—Marina's brow would pucker, her stylus hover over her screen. She'd be impatient with the vague threat of Iris and focus only on my tardiness.

"Amabel!" she called, sliding her phone away. "Come give me a kiss."

Reluctantly, Amabel stopped waving at the window washers and joined us.

Marina inclined her cheek to Amabel's peck. "Did you have a good day? What did you learn at camp?"

Amabel shrugged. "Can I go see the Frowning Man?"

The Frowning Man was a face in a totem pole between a lizard and an eagle. His brows arched angrily, and his black eyes pointed crazily in different directions. Amabel was half terrified of, half delighted by him.

"Not tonight," Marina said.

"Please?"

"Amabel, your mom asked about camp," I said. "Tell her what you learned."

Amabel clamped her lips and looked at the floor.

"Can you go wash up for dinner, sweetie?" Marina said.

Amabel dragged her feet as she headed for the bath-room.

Marina frowned at me. "She seems off. Did she get into trouble today?"

"She's tired, I think."

Marina's fingers moved to squeeze her earlobe, her one nervous tic. "She's been so moody lately. Maybe she needs more exercise. I spend all day dealing with issues here"—she gestured around us—"and when I get home, I want to spend time with a cheerful daughter."

"Amabel has her moments. I'm sorry if there have been more than usual lately." Even I could hear the defensiveness in my voice.

Marina sighed. "Don't get all upset. I'm sure you're doing your best. But I need you to be focused this month. I know you've been getting more involved with your boyfriend, more interested in socializing. I need one hundred and ten percent from you until the gala is over."

I blushed clear to my chest. "Of course."

"Good." Her phone buzzed, and at last her exacting attention dropped from me.

"I'll get Ammy." I escaped to the restroom.

It was empty, as I'd expected. Before I went to find Amabel, I washed my hands with the fragrant almond soap and pressed my damp palms to my hot face. I gave my cheek a sharp slap and hurried out.

I found Amabel whispering to the Frowning Man.

"You need to listen," I told her, taking her hand. She rolled her eyes like an older child, and for a nasty moment, she reminded me of Iris.

5

The next afternoon, Amabel and I spread a sheet over the kitchen floor and I dusted her hair with cornstarch, working it into her scalp with my fingertips. When it was sufficiently white, I pinned it into a stiff, puffy mushroom.

That evening, under the stage lights, a fine cloud of starch drifted up from her head. In her blue velvet coat—an old blazer of mine, cinched at the back—she looked more like a tiny old man than a founding father. She delivered her perfectly memorized lines with a proud, goofy grin. Philip nudged me with his elbow, and even Marina leaned forward to beam at me.

I couldn't concentrate. I kept turning to scan the audience. I didn't see Iris among the familiar faces behind me, or with the stragglers at the back—bored siblings crawling on the floor, mothers calming infants.

Only when the show ended and the lights came up did I relax. While the Martins circulated, I went backstage to collect Amabel.

When I hugged her, she whispered, "Did she come?"

"Who?" I said, playing innocent.

"The girl! Iris."

I put my hands on her shoulders. "Ammy, that woman is a stranger. I don't want you to worry about her anymore."

She shrugged, downcast. Marina's old words surfaced. *Kids get these crushes.*

I brushed starch from her forehead. "You were great tonight. I'm proud of you."

In the parking lot, I helped Amabel into the car and stepped to the front window to say good night to the Martins.

"Finn, why don't you join us for dinner?" Philip said.

"Thanks, but you don't have to."

"Of course you should come," Marina said.

I was worn out, but I agreed. It might be a chance to smooth things over with her.

Eating at Philip's restaurant was an event for most people. The Grove had been featured in travel sections of major newspapers, recommended in guidebooks, and voted Most Romantic Dining in Scottsdale four years running. Its gardens were lush with roses and figs and flowers thin as tissue paper, kept alive with an underground irrigation system and ingenious canopies, narrow and slanting like pirate's sails, which blocked the harshest sunbeams. Wedding receptions in the garden photographed beautifully, and Philip charged accordingly. In the dining room, the deep booths often hosted pro athletes and movie stars. The chef cooked classic Roman food: pounded salted meats, homemade pasta black with squid ink, and challenging seafood, things with tentacles or shells. While Philip's days were spent on broader interests—real estate development, board meetings, political work with his dad—the restaurant was his pet project, and he spent a couple afternoons a week ensconced in the office upstairs. Sometimes he stayed into the evening to buy rounds of drinks for important diners and circulate, glad-handing.

The hostess led us to a table in back, and before we'd even sat, the waiter brought over a bottle of wine and a wire basket of grissini, knobbed and crisped breadsticks Amabel liked to pretend were wands.

We toasted Amabel's performance. Giggling, she hoisted her Shirley Temple to clink with us, splashing maraschino pink onto the white tablecloth.

I'd hardly seen Philip since the night we'd talked about the coyote. He was home when I arrived in the morning, but he stayed in his study, murmuring on the phone, and left in a hurry, calling goodbye from the foyer, not even coming upstairs to kiss Amabel. Bryant, too, had been preoccupied—a new attack ad had come out against the Senator, its slogan maddeningly catchy. But Philip seemed unusually stressed, especially considering he'd just assured Marina his father would win. He was staying out late. I'd heard Marina's disappointed half of their phone calls, saw her clear his place off the table Amabel and I set, tossing his unused napkin into the laundry.

Tonight, Philip seemed his normal self. He gushed about Amabel's play, making her beam and wriggle under the heat of his pride.

"What are you hungry for?" I asked her.

"Chicken nuggets!"

"How about macaroni?"

She blew a raspberry. Marina's jaw tightened. Did she realize Amabel was being silly, not bratty?

Philip boomed, "You insulting your dad's food?" His face shone. He'd drained his wineglass and was filling it again, ignoring Marina's pointed look. Possibly they were fighting; they'd barely spoken to each other, hiding it behind talk to Amabel.

"She's being goofy," I said. "Lots of excitement today."

"I hope you'll behave next weekend," Marina warned.

Amabel slouched to slurp her straw.

"We're looking forward to the gala, aren't we?" I lied. I was trying to keep Amabel from getting excited. She'd be dressed up and paraded through the party, shushed when she chatted, and hustled home after the photo op.

"At least one of us is excited." Philip winked at Marina.

"This old act?" She addressed the inside of her glass. "You pretend to hate parties, but once you're there, you enjoy yourself more than anyone."

"Years of practice." He spoke normally, pretending not to notice her tone.

"Did you sit through a lot of parties when you were Amabel's age?" I asked.

"Did I!" Philip leaned over Amabel and said, "How old are you again?"

She bounced, knowing he was teasing. "Four and three-quarters."

"Let me cast back." He put a hand to his forehead. "A hundred years ago, I was four. My parents had wild parties. I'm talking, people dancing, singing, going swimming in their fancy clothes!"

Amabel's eyes widened at the idea of going into the pool in her lacy dress.

"People had dance moves then. I watched my mom do the Mashed Potato with my best friend's dad." He pumped his fists to show her. "They always put me to bed, but I'd watch from the top of the staircase. You know, I didn't see a single business card."

"You were too young to notice," Marina said. "Too busy watching the drinkers."

He wagged his finger at Amabel. "Your mom doesn't know! Those were the good old days. There won't be anyone having too much to drink at our party."

Marina sighed. "It's a fund-raiser. People can kick up their heels at the Everlys' tomorrow."

"That's this week?" Philip said.

She lifted an eyebrow.

He ran a hand through his hair. "I had . . . Nothing. I'll make it."

"Good." She sat back in her seat, one arm over her stomach, the other holding her wine aloft. Definitely a fight.

Amabel was kicking under the table.

"What should we do tomorrow?" I asked her.

Abruptly, Philip stood. "I forgot something for Victor. I'll be right back." He hurried away, heading toward the kitchen.

Marina snapped a grissini in half and chewed mutinously. When the waiter appeared, she opened her menu, resigned. "Let's not wait for Philip."

After we ordered, she folded her hands on the table and asked Amabel what her favorite part of the play had been. I idly watched the hostess flirt with the bartender, who swiped a white towel across the marble bar, his eyeteeth sharpening his smile. I remembered, suddenly, Amabel's claim that Iris had been here.

I excused myself, dropping my napkin on the table, and went after Philip.

The kitchen doors swung open as a busboy barreled through. Line cooks hunched over a prep table, chatting in Spanish as quick as their flashing knives; waiters waltzed in and out; the chef monitored a stockpot. No Philip.

I slipped through the double doors to the back room. Compared to the dining room, with its antique wood and weathered brass, the utility area was stark. A frayed carpet ran down the middle of a cement floor to a metal staircase. Industrial shelves held massive jars of olives, tomato sauce, tuna; plastic bags of bread crumbs, spices, soda syrup; takeout boxes stacked to the ceiling. From this vantage, the restaurant was unglamorous, and I was always surprised Philip didn't try to fancy it up.

A coffee can bristling with cigarette butts propped open the door to the loading dock, letting in a fuzzy warm breeze. The chef's beat-up Acura was parked by the Dumpster. No one was outside.

Upstairs, a banquet table and some folding chairs formed an ad hoc break room. A baseball game played on TV with no one to watch it.

The hall outside Philip's office was dark and smelled of cigarettes.

"You've put me in a terrible position." Philip's voice came through the door. "We have to take steps."

I hesitated. Then his voice dropped, and I couldn't hear his next words. A vivid picture of Iris came to me, sitting on Philip's desk with her legs crossed, a cigarette dripping on the floor. Already I hated her smile. Defiant, I knocked.

"What is it?" Philip's voice sounded tired.

Someone began to cough, wet and hacking.

I cracked the door open. The room was smoky and dim. "I'm sorry to interrupt. Are you all right?"

Philip sat with his elbows on his desk. "Come in and shut the door, Finn." He rubbed his chin.

A man sat across from him. Skinny, slump-shouldered,

riding out the end of his cough with a frustrated, moist hock.

Unease settled greasily in my stomach. I stepped forward to see him better. In spite of the cough, the man took a drag from a cigarette. His face was leathery and loose, framed by stringy hair past his shoulders. He wore a checkered shirt buttoned to the throat, and his chin kept jerking back, resisting the choke of the collar.

Philip stared at him coldly. A current of tension hung in the air.

"I didn't realize you were with someone." I fumbled for an excuse. "You missed the waiter. We all ordered."

"I didn't expect this to take so long." Philip wore his polite face, impossible to read. His angry tone could have been about their conversation or my interruption.

"This?" The man made a sound, and I realized he was laughing. "Bad manners, Martin." His eyes trailed over me, his gaze thick as smoke blown over my skin.

Philip tilted his glass back and impatiently banged it on the desktop. Empty. I was planted awkwardly in place, glancing between them.

Slouching, the man crushed his cigarette against the leg of his chair. His shoulder blades jutted like wings. "If the lady's going to stay, she should pull up a chair."

"I'll meet you down there, Finn." Philip picked up a pen and began clicking it rhythmically, staring at the desktop.

"I'm sorry." I backed out, shutting the door behind me. I stayed a moment, but heard nothing more.

Marina didn't look up when I returned to the table. She was cutting Amabel's spaghetti with a steak knife.

"Want me to do that?" I offered, folding my napkin over my lap.

Marina kept slicing. Her watch was loose and jangling on her wrist. She pushed the plate to Amabel. "Eat up, and we'll stop for a frozen yogurt on the way home."

"I'm sorry," I said. "I got caught in a conversation with the hostess. I had no idea I was gone so long."

Marina swept her hair back, her diamond earrings catching the candlelight.

"Your dinner has a face!" Amabel taunted me, sticking her tongue out.

I'd ordered the fish special, and the head was indeed still attached, lips fixed in a sad gasp, jelly eye wide. I squeezed lemon over the silver scales, took up my knife and fork, tried to chew and swallow.

"Is that smoke?" Marina sniffed.

"Of course not." I lifted my water glass and gulped.

Amabel wriggled up onto her knees and leaned over my plate, balancing a sticky hand heavily on my elbow. "Let's call him Herman!"

I shushed her. Sulky, she lifted her glass of milk in both hands and drank.

"There are my girls." Philip sank into his chair with a sigh. "Looking cranky, I'm afraid." He gave me a fleeting glance, and then leaned back in his seat, assessing his plate. Mussels jutted up from a red broth, like tiny traps. "I'm sorry. The kitchen's going wild."

"Your food will be terrible." Marina refilled her wineglass, shaking the last drops from the bottle.

"I'm not hungry." With his fingertips, he pushed the bowl away.

"Browsing in the kitchen again?" Marina used her light tone.

Philip rubbed his lips. "What gave me away?" He leaned toward Amabel. "Food in my teeth? Sauce on my lip? I know! Do I smell like garlic?" His forehead was sweaty, feverish.

"Ew, Daddy, stop!" Amabel squirmed, and her milk tipped over and poured into her lap.

Marina sighed at the ceiling.

"I'll get her," I said.

As Amabel and I headed to the bathroom, I saw Philip set his hand on Marina's shoulder. She stiffened at his touch.

I sat Amabel on the counter and wiped her legs with wet paper towels. She grabbed a tampon from a basket, peeled the wrapper back, and tugged at the string. "What's this?"

"That's for when you're older."

"But what's it for?"

"Much older," I said.

She stuck her lip out, pouting, but seemed comforted by the routine adult refusal to explain. In the pink lights, the blush I'd applied to her cheeks that afternoon was pronounced against her fair skin. Her hair still held traces of cornstarch.

"Carry me," she commanded. She wrapped her arms around my neck and rested her head on my shoulder. I kissed the part in her hair.

When we got back to the table Philip and Marina were already standing, Marina rolling lavender oil over her wrist. Seeing Amabel, they both hoisted their lips into smiles. Neither quite looked at me.

At their car, as I buckled Amabel into her seat, Philip watched me in the rearview. Our eyes met, and he shook his head sharply. A warning. *Don't ask*. Marina had her phone out and didn't stop texting as she said good night.

Their taillights glowed away into the purple twilight.

Now it had been nearly two days, and I hadn't told anyone about Iris.

6

The commercial began with a still image: a close-up of the Senator's face, looking secretive, eyes slanted away, lips pressed together. A gravelly male voiceover said, "Senator Martin likes to call himself '*your* Senator.' But how hard is he really working for you?"

Cut to a clip of the Senator on a golf course, shouting over the wind, "Three times a week when I can get away with it." The last four words echoed for a few seconds.

A stock image of a businessman boarding a jet filled the screen. The voiceover resumed. The Senator had spent over 200,000 taxpayer dollars on charter flights, and taken six weeks of vacation, including two at a luxury resort in Hawaii. "How did he get there? Charter flight, of course."

Back to the unflattering portrait. "Senator Martin: too good for first class. Not good enough for Arizona."

This ad was relatively kind. Another, in Spanish, accused the Senator of discriminating against Latinos—he'd supported the controversial S.B. 1070, which allowed police to demand papers for any (or no) reason.

The Senator's challenger, Marco Gonzales, emphasized his Latino heritage. His peppy blue yard signs read, LET'S GO WITH MARCO! A University of Arizona law school alum and the son of a popular minister, he had an appealing backstory. His grandparents had come to the U.S. with nothing and climbed into the middle class—shining examples of successful immigrants. Marco was interesting and fresh, with a broad potential base, and the Senator was nervous. His own ads highlighted his experience. Showed him, sleeves rolled up, pointing at an audience. Shaking hands with President Bush (Senior—no one spoke of Junior). Montages of the Martin family waving under a shower of balloons after his last victory. Tradition, he promised. Integrity. Family values. *Your* Senator!

The night after my dinner with the Martins, I went over to Bryant's place and found him lying on the couch, takeout pizza perfuming the room. His condo had gorgeous bones: high lofted ceilings, living room flowing into a concrete-and-stainless kitchen. But the furnishings were thoughtless bachelor standbys: vast leather sectional, TVs mounted on every wall.

Bryant railed against Gonzales.

"Is it the new ad?" I asked.

"That cheap shot?" he scoffed. "Gonzales is digging for dirt. He's obsessed with the university land. It's old news, but he's going to bring it up at the town hall."

I kneaded his calves. My official position on the land deal was neutral; privately, I hated how it made Philip look, but I didn't agree with the righteous anger the Senator, Bryant, even Marina were piling on him.

Last winter, Philip bought several hundred acres west of Phoenix. They weren't worth much, but he was betting that sooner or later the city would swell out that way. He made that sort of purchase routinely, parcels of land here and there, some slated for immediate development, others held until the value rose. But this particular lot didn't sit as long as he expected. Instead, in the spring, the university bought it, announcing plans to develop a campus for green technologies.

Philip profited enormously from the sale. He swore it was dumb luck. But it was hard to believe it was a coincidence. Senator Martin, after all, was a major donor to the university, Philip a powerful alumnus.

For weeks after the deal was announced, local papers wrote grumbling editorials. There was no hard evidence of wrongdoing, but the whiff of corruption was unmistakable.

Now, Gonzales's team was working to spin the land sale into something bigger, a pattern of privilege. "The conspiracy theory," Bryant called it, dismissive but furious. I knew he blamed Philip for making a badly timed mess.

"I wouldn't worry," I said. "I don't think people are paying attention."

"That's because you adore them," he said testily. "You don't realize the climate we're in. The public doesn't trust powerful people. They think wealth is a sign of bad character or something. It's sick."

I dug my thumbs into his thighs. "I pay attention."

"I'm sorry. I know you do. I'm just tense. It's getting to me. I shouldn't let it." His eyes were red and hazy. Lately, every morning he dissolved a vitamin C tablet in water; at night he chewed antacids like candy. Sometimes he winced when he talked about work, as though the pressure were a vise tightening around his chest.

I'd never realized how grinding a campaign was on the inside, the torrent of judgment and scrutiny over every little thing. At the beginning of the summer,

Bryant himself had been swept up in controversy, accused of racism when asked why, as a Latino, he didn't support Marco; he'd replied that he considered himself more than just Latino.

Just Latino. People were disgusted.

After his public flogging, I'd gone over to his place, found him nursing a bottle of bourbon, scrolling through photos of his childhood trips to Colombia. He told me about the food; the sojourns to the beach; his grandmother's Christmas tradition of setting up a model village complete with rivers and trees and animals. And people were treating him like a few words negated his whole life!

My job, until the election, was to be the calm one, the cheerful one. So tonight, though I'd wanted to tell him about Iris, and the strange man in Philip's office, I decided to keep it to myself. He didn't need the extra worry.

I ran my thumb over his anklebone, thinking up a new topic. "I've been meaning to tell you, I'm studying for the GRE."

"That's big news." Bryant gestured for me to pass his drink. "I've been wondering what you planned to do . . . you know, long term. What do you want to study?"

I shrugged. "I'm still deciding. Maybe art history, or even education. It might be fun to be a teacher."

"You're certainly good with kids." He squeezed my arm affectionately.

I sighed, suddenly melancholy at the idea of a life away from the Martins. "I can't believe Ammy will start kindergarten in the fall."

"Time flies," Bryant said.

"I used to think they might have another kid." In fact, I'd vividly imagined it. Picking Amabel up from school, an infant sleeping in a car seat. I'd make Ammy a snack and she'd tell me about her day.

Bryant laughed. "I think not." He sounded certain.

"It's not impossible," I said, annoyed.

"Well, they're on a certain track now, aren't they? Six years goes by fast. That's where their minds are now. Trust me, no more babies." Seeing my face, he laughed again. "Sorry to disappoint you." He swung his legs off my lap. "Let's go to bed. I've got an early flight to D.C."

We met at the Senator's birthday party, about a year and a half ago. Marina had had the idea that a dinner party would be cozier than a restaurant. But the intimate guest list ballooned into thirty, forty heads, and she hired a half dozen staff to help out.

Guests began arriving shortly before sunset, and rooms filled with conversation and the smell of wine and salty food. The sky was putting on its show, right on schedule, yellow and orange and pink, and even the sophisticated company couldn't resist drifting over to the windows and touching the glass with awed fingertips.

The Senator arrived last, to applause, and his abashed response was convincing. (Really he knew exactly how many people were coming, and exactly who.)

Ammy and I kept out of sight, watching movies in the playroom. After she went to bed, I snuck downstairs for a bottle of water. The kitchen was sealed off with tapestries hanging over the open doorway, Japanese-style. I ducked in. The staff were busily cleaning a mountain of dishes. I retrieved an orange and the water and hurried back out, still new enough to working for the Martins that I was afraid of breaking protocol. Slipping through the tapestries, I collided with a man in a suit, my water bottle releasing a jet that splashed spectacularly across the floor.

As I apologized, he laughed and took me by the wrists. "My fault entirely," he said. He was young, with a dancer's compact, energetic body sheathed in a simple black suit.

"I'm sorry," I said again. "I was just grabbing water. I didn't want to interrupt."

"What are you interrupting?"

"The party?"

He leaned forward as he spoke, a tall man's habit, though he wasn't tall. "I can't think of a party that wouldn't want you to interrupt it."

The line made me groan, which made him smile.

"We'd better mop this up." He ducked into the kitchen and came out with a towel. He touched the hem of my skirt. "Silk? Did it get splashed?"

I laughed again. "Are you going to clean me up, too?"

"Don't mock. I attend these things for a living. I know how to deal with every kind of stain. You wouldn't believe how messy those tiny appetizers can get."

"Thanks, but it'll be fine. My company is usually messier than me. Since she's three."

"Ah. You must be Amabel's new nanny."

"Do you know the family?" I asked.

"You could say that. I've worked for Jim for . . . oh, eight years now, I guess. Bryant." He had a nice hand-shake, dry and cool.

"Finn."

"Very nice to meet you." His eyes lingered on mine.

Under the focus of his attention, I felt sloppy. I'd pulled my hair back into a ponytail and my lipstick had faded ages ago.

"I should go. I'm supposed to be watching Ammy."

"Ammy," he repeated. "I like that. I've never heard it before."

I nodded and turned down the hallway with more decisiveness than I really felt. The noise of the party entered my ears again. Jazz music, a woman singing in French, the Senator's booming voice reaching a punchline, and the braying reception.

Bryant tracked down my number and called the next day. Dating him was exotically formal, very by the book: first dinner and drinks, then a movie, sleeping together on the third date, a gravelly old record on the sound system and martinis on the nightstands. I knew instinctively to dress up, rolling sheer tights over my legs and curling my hair. I knew to let him make the moves, to wait for his call or text, though I could always count on it.

Early on, he gave me his official autobiography: father in sales, mother at home; older brother and younger sister, both now married; a childhood outside Los Angeles; a vacation house in Flagstaff; four years at Princeton, two interning in D.C. before he started with the Senator.

His openness startled me. I was used to keeping my past past, revealing as little as possible. It didn't occur to me to mention to Bryant that my name was actually Natalie—I wore Finn comfortably by then; it was my name. Mentioning Natalie would only lead to questions.

I never meant to lie. That is, I never wanted to. At first, I gave him only the barest details, all true. I was from a suburb of Chicago. My parents had divorced, and both remarried. I had two younger brothers.

But he pressed for more. I had to tell him something. And the drab reality wasn't an option. My mom worked as a nurse's assistant. My stepdad was in tech support. They married late, when I was thirteen, and had my brothers one after the other, as if rushing to redeem a coupon before the expiration date. We lived on the border of a nice town, a calculated snatch at the school district. Our rented ranch had been built in the sixties and updated with the worst of every decade since. My mom's life had so thoroughly rerouted to accommodate Ted and my brothers, I felt like a hitchhiker along for the ride. We were already drifting apart, and then I got into some trouble. Everyone was relieved when I went to Indiana to stay with my dad. Then I moved to Arizona, and the break between us ossified.

We still talked on the phone every few Sundays, my mom directing the conversations as formally as a pollster armed with a clipboard. After we covered the weather, we moved on to their updates. My stepdad played sand volleyball on weekends. Caleb and Kyle were occupied with an assortment of sports and study groups and music lessons. I imagined my mom kept them busy, hoping to prevent another bad teenage experience.

We were polite, but the call never managed to be pleasant. It didn't sour so much as stale. When I hung up, I was wrung out, like the spent orange husks heaped on Bryant's counter after he made his morning juice. For a few hours afterward, I felt uneasy, like I was being sucked back into my old life, like I hadn't left Natalie safely behind.

How could I explain any of that to Bryant, when everything about him was perfect? His family could have been in a catalog, with their ski holidays and summer reunions where everyone gathered on the porch for a photograph, their raucous games of Ping-Pong in the sprawling "cabin" in Flagstaff, and the nights around the dinner table, everyone chiming in on inside jokes and stories of this prank or that trip.

So I lied.

I said that my mother was a designer and my stepdad was a lawyer. I showed him a photograph of a big, Swiss-style house, cream with crisscrossing brown beams, a brick chimney running up the middle like a nose, a leafy maple out front. In the photo, I stood under the tree, dressed in shorts and a borrowed linen blouse, holding a cocktail glass in both hands. I was sixteen. My hair was the dull color it had been, my face gleaming in the heat.

Bryant had laughed and said I looked like the gardener. He probably thought it was a strange picture to keep. It was the only one I had of myself alone with the house.

I rarely spoke about my past, trying to limit my lies, but I knew with a mix of triumph and unease that Bryant believed my life was like his.

Now and then, I thought he might be suspicious. The first time he saw my apartment, for instance, shabby and in a fringe neighborhood. But he assumed that I was too stubborn to take money from my parents. To my shame, he said he admired that.

Our relationship accelerated. We spent a weekend in Flagstaff. I met his sister when she came to visit. Over a long weekend, we flew to Mexico and stayed at a cheesy resort: private beaches, unlimited cocktails, the Gulf chlorine blue as a swimming pool. I began sleeping at his place more often than at my own. When he went out of town, he let me use his car. I picked him up at the airport, his favorite fast food in a bag on the dash. He brought Amabel and me souvenirs, kitschy postcards from small towns, key chains, trinkets encased in plastic spheres from bubble gum dispensers. I went along when he shopped for clothes, and weighed in on the fit of jeans and blazers while a piano player serenaded us. We jogged together along Tempe Town Lake. I did my laundry at his place. On our anniversary, we exchanged keys.

With every step forward, my excitement was tempered with dread. It seemed inevitable that Bryant would find out I was lying. He'd want to know when he could meet my family, or at least why I never went home. Or I'd make a mistake, contradict some part of my story.

Yet even as I was afraid, and guilty, it was exhilarating. Becoming Finn for him. Walking into a party on his elbow and thinking that no one knew me, nobody realized that I didn't belong. Fixing my hair in the mirror at some five-star restaurant, I felt I'd come so far I'd never go back.

Sometimes, laughing together in bed, or meeting his eyes at a party over some inside joke, or seeing his face loosen when I entered a room, I thought: I can tell him. He'd understand. But more often, his upright code of proper behavior made it clear that he wouldn't. It was too late. I couldn't tell him the truth now.

7

Friday morning, the sun was shining for the 165th time that year. I dropped Bryant at the airport and sped away in his BMW, the car leaping at the slightest pressure of my toes. Air-conditioning poured from the vents, luxurious as cashmere.

The Martins lived on a red rock mountain that curved around the valley like a hand cupping a bowl. In college, my friends and I had hiked it, not realizing the land was private. Fenced yards stymied our progress, and halfway up we ran into a patch of brush and couldn't go farther. The view was still incredible. At the horizon another mountain, humped like a camel, book-ended a quilt of low buildings stitched by roads. The sunset was stunning, as if the red rocks had steeped in the sky, releasing clouds of syrupy color.

I always felt a thrill when the heavy iron gates to Ocotillo Heights swung open for me. The narrow, twisting road was lined with dense hedges. Here and there a driveway allowed a snatched glimpse of a garden, a turret, a cantilevered roof. For these residents, privacy was the ultimate luxury.

The Martins lived at the apex of the road. Beyond them, the mountain made its final ascent—steep, pebbly, treacherous—to a blunt peak. Lizards, snakes, scorpions, and the coyote made homes in the dry dirt and foliage there. Afternoons, dust rose, filming the air.

Their house appeared in *Dwell* after they built it, ten years ago. It was a stout white bunker from the front and a sheer, sparkling ice cube on the other sides. Tiered succulent gardens ascended the front yard; at the top, a tree with olive green branches and silvery leaves stood in elegant silhouette before the blue front door.

Inside, the rooms were boxes of light. Marina's aesthetic was warmed-up minimalism with global touches. In the living room, whitewashed bones and tribal masks hung over a white sofa with slim silver legs. In the kitchen, reclaimed wood from church pews in India topped the table, while domed overhead lights recalled an operating room. The *Dwell* spread showcased a younger Marina, hair extravagantly long down her back, rinsing a bowl of lemons in the sink, lighting the fireplace with a long match, gazing at the pool from a balcony, the living room curtains billowing like skirts.

I parked in my usual spot in the driveway. Landscapers were pruning the citrus trees in the side yard, releasing a smell of lemon Pledge. I punched in the garage code, hung my purse in the laundry room, kicked on the slippers I kept there.

In the kitchen, Amabel sat with her stuffed cocker spaniel, Patrick, wearing her princess nightgown and drinking a glass of milk. Marina clattered in heels from fridge to blender, shaking a green smoothie into a jar, talking nonstop, *don't forget the check for the stables, could you work late next week, we need to set up a playdate with Tonya.*

"The playdate is Tuesday. And I'm totally available next week." I kissed the top of Amabel's head. "How you doin', Ammy?"

"She might have a bug. Feel how warm she is? Lay low today. Call me if it gets worse. That camp is a germ factory."

"I'm sure she'll be fine. We'll have a movie day."

"You're the best! I'm out the door!" Marina bent to give Amabel an air kiss.

I sliced an apple while the espresso machine warmed up. When I asked Amabel if she wanted to foam the milk, she shrugged. Her workbooks were stacked on the table, which I took to mean Marina expected her to do them regardless of the bug.

Every six months or so, Marina took Amabel to a child development specialist. I'd come across the reports by accident, when I was looking through the file cabinet for Ammy's vaccination records. I flipped through the doctor's notes, righteous and incredulous. Her latest review indicated strong results on communication and fine motor skills, but a below-average attention span. Now we did exercises out of a concentration workbook every morning.

After we finished our page, I set up a movie in the playroom. Amabel settled into a beanbag with Patrick, so sleepy she seemed about to suck her thumb.

The doorbell chimed once, and again a few seconds later.

"Eva must not be here yet," I said. "I'll be right back."

The stairs were sharp-edged and slick, not easy to hurry down. The bell rang impatiently, three, four times.

Muttering, I swung open the door.

Iris was on the other side, thumb pressed to the bell.

I froze, and she rushed by me into the house, trailing perfume like sticky candy. She wheeled in the foyer, taking it in. Soaring ceiling, curving staircase, light fixture like a hundred slashing raindrops frozen midflight. She was a frenzy of color, red hair, yellow dress, blue heels. She tottered to a console table that always held an elaborate floral arrangement—today peonies, pure white—and crushed a flower between her fingers. "Are these real?" Petals showered to the floor.

Once, a bird flew into my apartment. Soared through the patio door and crashed into a mirror. Dazed, it flapped wildly, a panicked dervish of feathers and fear. I'd stood paralyzed, hands gathered to my chest, as if I might be hurt. The bird hit the ceiling fan with a horrible thump and dropped to the floor.

I dropped my hands. "Iris? What are you doing here?"

She threw me a defiant glare. "Are they home? I know he isn't, but is she?"

"Who do you mean?" I thought of Amabel upstairs, snuggled into her beanbag.

"Her. The wife." Iris spat the words like hunks of gristle. Her heels grated on the floor. A clump of peonies still in her hand.

The fear that Amabel might hear made me do the opposite of what I wanted. I took Iris by the wrist and pulled her farther inside, away from the staircase, into the living room.

She strutted to the windows over the backyard. The pool sparkled on the deck. "Does anyone swim out there?" Her nose touched the glass.

I crossed my arms. "You shouldn't be here."

"Look at this place." Her voice was harsh and dismissive, but she was obviously envious. Her eyes darted over everything. The white rug, the marble fireplace. The only color in the room was a Saarinen womb chair, siren red. An enormous canvas hung over the couch, white with a white rectangle in one corner, the exact shade as the canvas, yet it appeared to hover over it. Iris, seemingly mesmerized, touched it.

"There's a security system," I warned. "I could call the police."

Her hand snapped back. "Don't." She bit her lip, tears in her voice.

The alarm was over the light switch; I could reach it from where I stood. But I didn't. I was curious, I realized. I wanted very badly to know who she was. Amabel was safely upstairs. The Martins weren't due home all day.

"Will you sit down?" I said.

She covered her face. "Oh, God. What am I doing? Shit!"

"Quiet," I said sharply. "Sit. Please."

"You must think I'm insane." She perched on the couch, her knees bouncing, jittery. "I just needed to see where he lived. I could never picture it, his house. His stuff." She pressed her hands into the upholstery. "I pictured him living in a hotel. She picked this out, right? He wouldn't do anything like this."

I straightened my shoulders, imagined myself as Marina. Calm, cool, superior. "Why are you following me?"

She gasped. "I'm not—"

"You knew you wouldn't find Philip or Marina here this morning. Or at school."

She mumbled into her lap.

"Excuse me?"

She looked up. Her face was wet. "He has a daughter. He has a family. I knew it but I never really knew it."

Alarm lifted its wings in my stomach. She made the pronoun sound as intimate as a nickname.

She pulled a pillow into her lap, tortured its embroidery with black fingernails. "I thought it would be easier to accept if I saw."

I gripped the back of the red chair, my palms damp. "You knew he had a daughter. You've seen her."

"You didn't tell them about me. Did you?" Iris dropped the pillow and stood. Relaxed suddenly, as if she'd won some concession. She opened an ivory box on the mantel and retrieved a pack of cigarettes and matches, smoothly, as if she knew they'd be there. "He hides them at work, too. She must be strict. It doesn't pay to be strict. They do whatever they want anyway."

The match didn't light off the pack so she pulled it between her nails. The spark sizzled. Exhaling smoke into Marina's purified air, Iris sat and stretched an arm over the back of the couch.

I nudged a shallow ceramic pot across the coffee table toward her. Not an ashtray, but it would do. I wasn't about to leave her alone for a minute.

"They have weird taste. I've only seen the restaurant and that's . . ." She tilted her hand: *so-so.* "It doesn't really seem Italian." She flicked ashes in the general direction of the dish.

Her abrupt shift from tears to bluster unsettled me. Her voice was gossipy, as if I'd lean in eagerly to hear more. I remembered once Bryant had told me to be careful: the Martins brought out strange reactions in people. Just knowing a Martin made some people think they deserved something.

"So you know Philip from the restaurant?"

Iris nodded. "I thought you might recognize me. I didn't work there very long." Another drag and she crushed the cigarette out. "I've been trying to quit, but it's hard. I'm so anxious lately, smoking is the only thing that calms me down." She clamped her hands between her knees. "I can't sleep."

"I don't understand," I said, cutting off her dramatic, breathy voice. "What do you want?"

She shook her head. "You know. You knew the other day, when I saw you with the little girl. The way you looked at me . . . you knew." She bit her lip, watching me closely, waiting for me to say something. When I didn't, she said, "I'm pregnant. I'm pregnant, and it's his."

My laugh was as involuntary and harsh as a cough. "You can't be. You must weigh one hundred pounds."

She rested her hands on her flat stomach. Her nail polish was chipped and gnawed. "I've been to the doctor. I'm seven weeks along." Her mascara had blurred down her cheeks. "What should I do?"

It was my turn to go to the windows. String lights hung over the patio from a dinner party last week. Marina had worn a lime dress, Philip a white polo; she'd fussed over his collar. I'd stayed to watch Amabel and was reading in the guest room when they came upstairs. Marina whispered something I couldn't catch, and Philip replied that he wasn't tired and was going to the poolroom for a bit. She'd gone into the bedroom alone, and after an hour or so, the light under the door had gone out.

Iris set a cold hand on my wrist. "I don't know what to do. He won't talk to me."

She was so gaudy, so emotional. I couldn't imagine Philip attracted to her—even tolerating her.

I couldn't look at her. "If you're telling the truth, how can he not talk to you? You must have some sort of relationship."

"You don't believe me."

"It's none of my business. I'm not sure why you're even telling me all this."

"I love him. I thought you'd understand."

Anger swelled in my veins, and I slapped her. I'd never hit anyone before. It was more of a rough tap across her cheek and mouth. Lipstick came off on my hand.

She blinked, startled, and then began giggling. I tried to hush her, but she doubled over, giddy, gasping, shaking. Collapsed in my arms, her body was warm and sharp. She was taller than me, and I struggled to brace her. Touching her bare, bony back felt queasily intimate.

The garage door rumbled.

Iris snapped up. Her face was splotched red. "Shit!" She grabbed the ashtray and shook it into the fireplace. Ashes dusted the floor.

"You have to go." I ushered her out of the living room, toward the foyer. I could hear someone coming in through the kitchen.

"Is it her?"

"It's probably the housekeeper." But I was nearly jogging, tugging her along.

Petals were still strewn across the foyer floor. There was no sound from Amabel upstairs. We went out the front door. To my relief, it was only Eva. Her car was parked at the top of the driveway, and she'd gone in through the garage, as usual.

Iris had parked on the street. She drove a silver sedan, similar to mine, but with a white panel over the hood, obviously a cheap fix for a collision. I was surprised. Her clothes looked expensive.

"I want to give you something." She reached into the glove compartment and withdrew an envelope. She shook it at me. "Open it."

I glanced back at the house. Was that a face in a window, watching us? "I have to get back to work."

She yanked a picture from the envelope and held it in front of my face, so close I couldn't see it.

I took it. It was an ultrasound. The cartoonish outline of a guppy body, a patchy constellation in a galaxy of dots and smudges.

"There's the head." She traced it. "And a little fist."

"You need to leave."

"You really don't want to believe me." She was amused again.

"He has a family. Remember?"

Her smile faltered. She chewed a lip. "He talks about you."

My chest rushed like a sail caught in the wind. Pleasure so startling I had to suspect it. She was flattering me.

I still held the ultrasound, shiny paper catching the sun. Maybe it would melt in the heat. Vanish.

"Meet me later. Please? Just once. I need to talk to someone who knows him."

Later, as I set up the air purifier in the living room and Windexed the smudge her nose had left on the window, I realized I could be fired. Easily. I'd talked about the family's private business with a stranger. Let her into the house. Left Amabel alone.

Iris had begged for my phone number. She wouldn't leave without it.

Seven weeks pregnant, Philip the father. This lodged in my head like a jingle. It wouldn't be so un-usual, really. The Martins' parties buzzed with gossip over affairs, separations, messy divorces. Of course, if

Philip and Marina split, the Senator might suffer in the fallout. His hope of a legacy for Philip could be lost.

As Iris drove away, arm hanging out the window, cigarette smoke streaming, I'd felt sticky with dread.

In the playroom, Amabel sprawled on her stomach. She kicked a heel at me in greeting. I felt her for a fever, and she squirmed away.

My phone buzzed. Iris already, asking me to meet her for dinner.

I sank into the beanbag chair. The Little Mermaid had become human and was brushing her hair with a fork. *Seven weeks pregnant . . .*

Restless, I went downstairs to check the house again. Everything was back to normal. In the kitchen, Eva unloaded groceries. She was a small woman, plump and neat as a sparrow. She turned to say hello. "Beautiful day. You two should get outside before it's very hot."

I stretched over the counter. The cool marble kissed my skin. "Amabel's not feeling well."

Eva made a sympathetic face without pausing in her methodical work. She could somehow lift a gallon of milk and two Greek yogurt bins into the fridge all at once. A case of Diet Coke, frozen spinach for Marina's smoothies, parsley she propped into a glass. She frowned at me as she took the garbage out, obviously wondering why I was staring. But she didn't say anything.

When she returned to scrub her hands at the sink, I said, "I had a friend drop by this morning. She was only here a few minutes. I'm just mentioning it in case you saw her car outside and wondered."

She glanced at me over her shoulder. Her brown eyes were inscrutable. "I didn't notice. You finished?" She swept a water glass marked with my lip gloss into the dishwasher.

No matter what she'd seen, Eva wouldn't tell the Martins. I envied her aloofness. She was distant even as she wiped the Martins' plates, cleaned their toilets, picked up their prescriptions.

"All set—yes? See you Monday."

On her way out, she passed my shoes in the mudroom, my purse on the hook, my swimming suit pinned to dry beside Amabel's.

As I drove out of Ocotillo Heights that evening, I passed Philip heading home. He saluted me. My car veered from its lane as I stared. Sunglasses, white collared shirt, probably classic rock on the stereo. Everything as usual. He'd never seemed so remote.

8

Iris stood outside the restaurant, balancing on the curb. When she saw me, she tossed her cigarette, accidentally dropping her cell phone along with it. "Shit." The case was bedazzled in pink crystals, and several had broken off onto the blacktop. She squatted to collect them. "I was never clumsy—before." Her eyes slid away from mine. She'd piled her hair in a bun on top of her head and changed into yoga pants and an oversized tunic, as if to conceal a swollen stomach.

She'd suggested a Chinese restaurant that smelled of bleach and orange chicken. She expertly slid her tray along the buffet, piling her plate and stashing a fistful of soy sauce packets into her purse. I was embarrassed, but the cashier was watching the doors as though willing customers to enter. The red vinyl booths were empty.

At our table, Iris crushed a fortune cookie in her fist and salvaged the paper from the crumbs. "'A journey is more than its steps.' Funny, huh?" She ate quickly, spilling rice over the tablecloth. "God, I'm starving. I've been driving around all day."

The broccoli stems were tough. I sliced them with a tarnished knife, relieved for an excuse not to eat.

"Listen. I feel bad about this morning. I shouldn't have come over like that."

"No," I agreed. I stared past her, at a mural on the opposite wall. Robed figures wandered among mountains, pagodas, and dragons. Kites hung from the ceiling, strings shining in the slanting afternoon light. Kitschy, but pretty. Like Iris.

She didn't seem eager to meet my eye, either. "I wanted to see how they lived."

"They're happy there," I said, though that wasn't quite accurate. *Successful* would be a better word. "Like you said, they're a family. They have a daughter."

A vein flickered down her temple, and she looked furious. But just as quickly, her face smoothed into an artificial calm, lips drawn into a pout. "I'm going to have a baby, too. What about that?" Her voice was sugared. She frightened me.

"I need water." I went to the soda machine, found a tray of glasses still warm from the dishwasher. I filled one and drank, shards of ice rushing to my teeth.

Iris followed. "You should have taken soda. They never check." She helped herself to Diet Coke, plucking a lemon from a plastic dish with her fingers.

"How did you even meet him?" I asked, incredulous, but she squeezed my wrist gratefully.

"I've been dying to tell someone."

We returned to our plates, hers wiped clean, mine barely touched. She leaned across the table conspiratorially as she spoke.

She'd been hunting for a job as a waitress. At The Grove, she handed an application to the bartender, and a man in a suit called out from a booth, "I'll take this one."

Philip led her up to his lonely office. At first, she didn't think anything of him—a middle-aged guy, pretty wife, cute kid (he kept a framed snapshot on the desk). He said he liked her face and gave her the job.

During lulls, Philip taught her things. How to pronounce the menu items in Italian, pour wine without spilling, wipe glasses with newspaper for the clearest finish. He name-dropped famous diners, unlocked the cabinet with the most expensive bottles of wine. Iris rushed to explain that he wasn't showing off the money behind everything, but his expertise, his knowledge.

As she spoke, I thought: Of course. Marina and the Senator had never admired the restaurant Philip built from scratch. They acted as if it were an eccentricity to be tolerated. To brag to someone who showed an interest would be irresistible to Philip.

Iris rested her chin on a hand and gazed into the middle distance. For someone pregnant by a married man who was avoiding her phone calls, she didn't seem bitter. Her voice was caressing, even proud. One night, she said, he was there late when she had to close. He stayed upstairs. She pretended to leave with the line cooks, and snuck back in through the service door. She waited for the bartender to close the registers and lock up. Then she climbed the back stairs, so excited it felt like sickness. Philip was at his desk, a bottle of booze glowing amber in the light. She went to him and he touched the hem of her skirt, just above the knee, and said they were both making a mistake.

My hopeful kernel of doubt was gone. I knew the Philip she described. I knew how his attention rested on your face like a touch. I understood how he could maneuver her, as though he were being pulled along in spite of himself, as though she were in control.

"Weren't you afraid you'd get caught?"

"Who would catch us? We went to my apartment or hotels." She dropped her napkin on the table. "I knew he was married." She picked up her fortune and twisted the paper into a ring around her finger. "Talk to him for me. Please? Tell him I'm not upset. I just need to see him."

"He won't leave Amabel." I tried to sound certain.

Iris rolled her eyes. "You can love your children more than anyone else. But you never really love them more than yourself. And it's for himself that Philip will leave." She patted her belly. "Not even for my baby. But because he wants me."

"If that's true, why is he ignoring you?" I was having trouble concealing my dislike.

Her chin quivered. "Ouch." She pressed her fingertips to her cheeks, catching phantom tears. "I obviously understand it's not easy for him. I don't mind waiting. I just need to hear from him."

"Why should I help you?"

"Because you're smart. You know he's stupid to avoid me. If he doesn't want me, I won't want him, either. Or his baby. I can say that, because I know it won't be true." She was radiant. Defending her love had brought color to her cheeks, and tendrils of her hair floated free of her bun as if electrically charged.

Right now, the Martins would be in their living room. The evening news on. Philip reading the paper, ankle on a knee. Amabel chattering about her day. Marina sipping wine, making brittle comments at the TV, shushing them when the Senator's ads came on. Philip staying quiet. Reading the words on the newspaper page? Or staring at the margins, thinking of Iris?

Maybe he'd slept with her once or twice, and lost interest. Or he'd gone back again and again, each time telling himself it would be the last. I wanted to shake him, slap his face.

"I'll talk to him," I said, and Iris reached across the booth and locked my pinkie in hers.

9

Since my earliest days of working for the Martins, I was fascinated by Philip. I sniffed out information about him: his history, his interests, likes and dislikes. No detail was too trivial. Evenings, jolting along on the broken elliptical machine in my apartment's gym, I'd go over my findings carefully, like a magpie arranging shiny scraps.

Philip was the second son in the Martin family, born to James ("Jim") Martin IV and Lillian Martin (née Park). The Senator's webpage provided a bio of the first James Martin, who made his fortune in railroads. In a sepia portrait, he was a frowning, reedy man with a face like a worn baseball glove, a testament to the hardness of his time. In one of the Senator's famous speeches, he'd speculated as to what James Martin I would think if he could see Arizona now—sprawling cities, crystalline swimming pools, the miracle of air-conditioning—an oasis attainable by anyone willing to work.

Philip's older brother, James V, inherited the family name. The Senator's biography mentioned James lovingly. A good son, a patriot, Eagle Scout, National Merit Scholar, West Point graduate summa cum laude. His photograph showed a handsome kid in uniform. I recognized it with a jolt. The same portrait was framed on Marina's dresser.

One afternoon, I hit a jackpot, an old photo album on a shelf. Amabel and I sat on the couch to flip through it. Ammy was soon restless, but I was fascinated. Philip's childhood, captured in gaudy Kodak color. Jim, unbelievably young, with a full head of hair. Philip's mother, Lillian, a chic brunette with a penchant for dangling earrings. Philip was exactly the same, blond and charming, with a ready grin.

There was another boy, older, dark-haired like Lillian and large-eared like Jim. James. Blowing out birthday candles, swinging at a ball on a tee, dressed in a Scout uniform. He stood two heads taller than Philip, but they were obviously close, pictured together digging in the sand, tossing a football, James driving a Mustang with Philip riding shotgun.

"What are you two doing?" Philip came in, sunglasses on his head. I feared that the album might be off-limits, but he seemed wistful, not angry. "That's me and my brother, James." His voice was warm and casual.

"I didn't know you had a brother," I lied.

"I want a brother!" Amabel shouted.

Philip gestured for me to pass him the book and flipped through it slowly, telling little stories. "James loved camping. He was an Eagle Scout. I hated it. Look at my face . . . Here's my trumpet concert. I was terrible. James was the talented one. I was always getting into trouble, and James, never. Well, once, he tried to teach me how to bike and I broke my arm . . . Look there. That must have been the summer before he left for West Point. See how he cut his sleeves? Showing off. He spent the whole summer doing push-ups." He laughed.

I watched Philip's face as he looked at his big brother, frozen decades younger than he was. I wanted to say I was sorry for what had happened, but I couldn't without betraying my knowledge.

Philip shut the book. "Swim?" Amabel cheered.

I put together their childhood in pieces: the album, the anecdotes Philip let slip, Bryant's longer knowledge of the tension between Philip and his father, and something else—a feeling I had of knowing Philip.

While James was disciplined, diligent, inclined to pleasing others, Philip enjoyed what came naturally to him—math, gym, friends—and avoided anything difficult. Their father (alderman since Philip was three, county supervisor when Philip was nine) ran a tight ship. Church every Sunday. B average, minimum. He signed his son up for football hoping to instill discipline, but Philip slacked off, hating the drills. By thirteen, he was openly rebellious, smoking pot, dating girls, sneaking out at night.

Meanwhile, James excelled at West Point, graduating with honors and completing military training enthusiastically. When he came home for two weeks' leave, he was an adult, strange to Philip.

Jim was exploring a run for Senate, and he treated James as an equal with Lillian, the three poring over procedures and guidelines at the dining table, analyzing the expenses and the messaging, the time commitment and the odds. Philip glazed over, bored, forgotten.

In late summer, James was deployed overseas. Jim and Lillian worried. There was talk of war in the Middle East. They took comfort in the news anchors' refrain that the fighting wouldn't last more than a couple of weeks.

Philip was oblivious. He'd never even heard of Iraq until James went to fight there. On TV, jets shot across the sky with a ripping sound, and tanks rolled over gray sand. It was like a movie, but boring. Philip imagined his brother in a bunker somewhere, perhaps standing over a huge map, moving pieces around, like a game of Risk. It never occurred to him that James was not remotely safe.

The news came on a Wednesday. Philip was pulled out of gym class and sent home wearing his smelly uniform. His mother wrapped her arms around him and clung. It was the first time an adult had ever hugged Philip to get comfort for themselves, and the pressure made him quake.

The family reeled. Lillian went to bed; Jim haunted the house. At the funeral, James's girlfriend, their pretty blond neighbor, broke down and was escorted out by a throng of wet-eyed girls. Later, at the house, she showed Philip a pinprick diamond ring. They hadn't told anyone their plans; she was only eighteen. Philip found letters in a box under James's bed and returned them to her. He didn't see her again for over a decade.

Jim rallied first. He threw himself into the Senate race. He spoke eloquently about losing James, his sorrow and pride. He earned a reputation as someone who had sacrificed. A patriot. A family man.

He won.

Things changed quickly. The family moved to a big house surrounded by a high fence. Philip's new school had a standout football program. At tryouts, instead of blowing it off, he worked. He woke early for conditioning runs. He threw until his arm moved seamlessly. He did drills up on his toes. In his uniform, he was camouflaged: just another player, no longer the Senator's son, whose brother had died in an exotic war. He felt good hitting, and being hit. At the end of the day, he slept without dreaming.

He made the team. At practice, his mind ground down to a fierce blank into which no thoughts of James could intrude. He was aware of every muscle in his body, first because they ached and eventually because they were strong. His coaches singled him out with praise; his teammates loved him with an easy vulgar banter. Girls adored him. He kept up his bad habits, learned to vault the high fence to meet an idling car at midnight.

The Senator was wrapped up in work, but in Philip's senior year, he attended a few games. Already he seemed awkward outside of a suit.

When Philip graduated, his parents bought him a

red Jeep. He'd landed a place on the football team at ASU, Jim's alma mater. At a celebratory dinner, the Senator spoiled the mood by warning Philip to focus on classes over the playing field. Dismayed, Philip felt the heavy mantle of the Martin family legacy settling onto his shoulders. He missed his brother in a new way, as not only a lost companion but also an imagined adult, the man who might have kept their parents happy, married his girl, had children, followed Jim into politics.

High school games, their piddly bleachers and tinny marching bands, hadn't prepared Philip for college ball. He ran onto the field beneath a mountain of fans. Fireworks flashed and boomed. Cheerleaders whirled in red and gold. The crowd booed and cheered, the noise inhuman in its magnitude.

The first game, Philip was dazzled. Then he learned to shut it out. He kept getting faster, stronger, better. There were moments when he felt sure he couldn't fail, when everyone else on the field was laughably slow and the ball spiraled in a big, beautiful arc he knew would connect even as his heart flew through the air with it.

I liked to imagine Philip then. He was at his strongest ever, physically, and he'd abuse his body as kids do, exercising all day, drinking and smoking all night. He was beautiful, almost too good looking, the sort of handsome that made people shy. He walked with a swagger, because he was the leader of the football team, because he was Philip Martin. His skin was covered in bruises and little cuts; his hands were calloused from lifting weights, tugging ropes, throwing. After a game, he shuffled into the shower and stood there like a penitent, steam pounding his back and water catching the fine golden hairs down his chest.

People asked him his secret. Found excuses to touch him, his bicep or his back, like he was a lucky rabbit's foot. He felt twenty feet tall. He was happy, purely happy, as if he had escaped the quiet cold house of his childhood forever.

He hadn't, of course. He was invited to dinner every week, and even though he was frequently out of town or at practice, or invented another excuse, he still had to go, sometimes. The sad gloss of Lillian's violet eyes compelled him. They ate in the frosty, silent dining room. The Senator carved, Lillian passed the plates. Her brittle, quivering anxiety both held the men in check and set them more on edge. They were usually polite, but then the Senator would make some condescending remark (*He's just a boy, he doesn't know what he wants*), and Philip would snap. He accused the Senator of wishing Philip was James, and the Senator accused Philip of selfishness.

———————

Falling in love with Tina settled Philip's anger, gave him a glimpse of a different future.

They met when he was a sophomore, she a freshman. Tina was a cheerleader studying to become an accountant. She laughed at Philip for not knowing what he wanted, when he had everything. She said she'd been lucky to get a scholarship. This was her ticket to a *good* job, the adjective emphasized and underlined, the way she'd grown up hearing her working-class parents say it. (The way I still heard my parents say it: *When will you get a good job?*) She danced in the mirror as she lectured Philip, and he didn't believe she meant a word of it. Just watch how she moved, her whole body taken up by the music. She couldn't be trapped behind a desk, bending her pretty face over a calculator. (Philip still didn't believe he'd end up an adult, either.)

They argued about everything: the proper amount to tip a waiter, how fast to drive, did they have time before class to make love, should she dance with other guys at bars, could he be trusted while on the road, would they end up together forever, did he really love her, was he just using her to get back at his father?

Because, from the very start, the Senator hated Tina.

Lillian brushed it off. *They're young, don't make it more serious than it really is.* But it nagged at him.

How wrong she was for him, clearly—and he for her! When she came over for dinner, he was sure she gaped at everything, stunned by the niceness of it. Whenever Philip looked at her, she flashed a manipulative bright triangle of teeth.

"Not everyone," the Senator warned Philip, "is Martin material. Not everyone is up to the challenge."

And Philip fired back, "Including me."

In Philip's junior year, the Senator's pressure intensified. He took Philip out to dinner. Spoke of law schools, maybe out East.

Philip ate with a thudding anger in his chest. He concentrated on the bustle beyond their table. The waiters who appeared and vanished like genies, the bartenders' rhythmic alchemy, the useless beauty of the food's vertical arrangement on the plate. The conversation between father and son remained polite, as if the heavy linens absorbed their tension, and the rich sauce stuck harsh words in their mouths.

Back at school, Philip worked out until an exquisite exhaustion knitted through his limbs, an endorphin high, a feeling of worthiness. James hadn't been the only good son, the only talented one.

My first months working for the Martins, I'd go to the university library on weekends and dig out Philip's old yearbooks. The football team's candid photos spanned several pages. Philip posed with a football, elbow drawn back to throw. His blond hair was long and wavy, his face smooth and open. He seemed sculpted from gold. A shot of Tina, jumping with her knees bent and white sneakers kicked up, poms spangling in the air. Her legs, slim and bronzed, stretched for ages, vanishing under a skirt the size of a dinner napkin. Her dark hair was cut in a thick, bouncing bob. (In the background, the other cheerleaders' ponytails hung like ropes.)

On the computers, I found a database of old college newspapers. Philip's name appeared often, in gushing recaps of victories. I was scrolling through these when I came across a different sort of headline: STAR QUARTERBACK BENCHED AFTER ACCIDENT.

Suddenly I was holding my breath.

In the *Arizona Republic* archives I found more details.

SENATOR'S SON INVOLVED IN FATAL ACCIDENT ON SOUTH MOUNTAIN.

STUDENT DEAD AFTER FOOTBALL TEAM PARTY.

SENATOR MARTIN PLEDGES FULL COOPERATION IN INVESTIGATION OF "TRAGEDY"

D.A. ANNOUNCES NO CHARGES IN FOOTBALL PARTY FATALITY.

Grainy old photographs, backlit by a white desert sky. A Jeep tumbled on its side, windshield shattered.

I read the stories rabidly, with a morbid excitement.

The next time I saw Philip, I felt ashamed, dirty. After all, I kept my own history a secret, tamped deep down.

Still, I had a vivid picture of the accident—as if I'd been there.

Saturday in October. An afternoon game won by a hair. Philip was drained, unable to shake off frustration at his own mistakes. Now a senior, he felt reality breathing down his neck. The calendar pinned to his fridge listed all the games he had left. How many minutes was that? How many plays? How many more times would he have the moment of agonized stillness when everyone lined up and waited for the snap? How many more wins, the glorious rush of being a hero?

That night, the usual crew was heading out to party. Philip almost skipped it. But then he remembered the ticking clock, the end of everything approaching, and he took a cold shower and headed out.

The party was on South Mountain. Philip drove Tina in his red Jeep. The mountain rose ahead, ugly, like a vast heap of dirt, brown and unevenly shaped.

It was a state park, left largely wild, one paved road branching into dozens of slender, twisting dirt roads. No guards, no gates.

The party was waiting for them, guys from the team, girlfriends, cheerleaders, a couple of the more attractive band geeks, the coach's nephew who was always hanging around. Music pumped from a car's souped-up sound system. People danced, unsteady on the pebbly ground.

Dusk fell quickly, smoothing the uneven, rolling terrain into a stretch of darkness. A bonfire lent the party flickering light. Smoke hung overhead, thickening the air.

Philip lingered on the fringes of the action, going over the game again, erasing every mistake. Thinking about football too much was his problem, and also his balm. He felt dizzy, standing near a sharp drop. The stars floated above the city as though communing with the lights below.

Tina was exhilarated. Her favorite games were the up-and-down ones, the rush of jumping into the lead, the tension of falling back, the final thrill of a win. She wanted to dance, and tugged him into the group. Her body was warm, crackling with energy.

After midnight, Philip and Tina snuck away, spread out a blanket, and made love in the dark. Gradually, the party broke up. Philip and Tina stood, brushing themselves off. The fire had died to embers, and the park was in near-total darkness.

Here was the Jeep. Philip drove, and Tina stood in the backseat behind him, arms around his shoulders. Another player rode shotgun, though I hardly considered him; he was a blank, an extra, outshone by Philip and Tina, and the tragedy that awaited them.

The sides were open and the cold night air blew in. Philip started down the mountain. The going was more difficult than he remembered, sharper turns, steeper descents. He'd expected a short drive, that's what he remembered, but it went on and on, the road an eel before him.

The wheels left the road with a startling grinding noise and Tina hooted into the night. Philip sped up, wanting to make her shriek again.

Or maybe Tina leaned forward to kiss his ear, and his attention drifted, and he loosened his grip on the wheel.

Or he was drunk or stoned, and he fell asleep, just for a second.

For whatever reason, Philip took a turn too fast. For a horrifying moment, the Jeep skidded as if on ice, two wheels lifting off the ground and hanging in midair, and then the car tipped onto its side, spun shockingly fast, and struck a rock wall with violent, deafening force.

The noise of the crash rang in the night. Philip and his teammate were breathing loudly, quickly, unmistakably alive. The driver's side was on the ground, and Philip's mouth was against rock, which tasted of blood. He panted, laughed, swore. Shock delayed his reaction. Then he realized Tina was gone.

After the accident, after Tina's funeral, after the indignant editorials and palmed whispers, after the end of his football career, after sitting stock straight in classrooms with eyes crawling over him, Philip graduated. He left. He spent two itinerant years in Europe, where history hung thick as ivy over the buildings and streets, and Arizona's lemonade light and gleaming boulevards seemed not just distant but alien. He spent less time pacing museums and pondering art than he spent reclining on thin European mattresses and coughing through cigarettes at pubs and cafés. His brooding silence and hefty muscles inspired people to call him cowboy, to trot out clumsy John Wayne accents. Philip didn't explain himself. Didn't bother learning any languages. In every city, even the smallest, there was a group of Brits and Americans hanging around, familiar with the topography of the night, accustomed to passing weeks and even years doing nothing more than drinking and seducing women and getting worked up over the local soccer team's fortunes on a fuzzy bar TV.

Eventually, the Senator cut off Philip's spending money, and so Philip moved to New York City, another place with nothing in common with Arizona. Ten years passed.

At thirty-five, he was featured in a *New York* magazine profile of prominent city transplants. I paid $9.99 for digital access to the article and found it disappointingly brief. Philip was a partner at a developer's office. He'd grown up. He still had that golden glow, but where his face had been bright and open, it had settled into a guarded expression, competent and inscrutable. He was engaged to a woman he'd known back in Phoenix.

A year later, Philip married Marina at the Fairmont Princess resort in Scottsdale. She wore a white gown with a long slit up the leg and not an ounce of frill.

They moved back to Arizona after Philip's mother died. Marina insisted that his father needed family nearby. She'd always liked the Senator, and vice versa, even back when she was a teenager and dating perfect, too-good-for-anyone James.

The years moved fast. The net tightened around Philip. Once he said yes to attending a party, hosting one was only natural. After he agreed to serve on his father's eponymous scholarship committee, sitting on a few boards of directors was just good business sense. When his real estate projects sailed through red tape with ease, Philip couldn't deny that his name had helped him, even if he preferred not to think about it.

No one could remember who first suggested Philip might run for office himself. The idea seemed to arrive fully formed, not merely a possibility but a plan. The Senator clearly felt it was natural and right that his son follow him; Marina desired it with a nervous energy; and Philip . . . Well, he went along with it.

I thought I knew Philip well. I'd built up his story in my mind, so when he drifted to the outskirts of a party, or went suddenly quiet at dinner, I imagined he was thinking about what might have come out differently.

I wanted to confide in him about my own past, the ghosts I saw in the mirror when I dressed to go out with Bryant, or woke to my dark apartment and felt for a panicked moment as though I were lying on rising and falling water, the noise of a crash echoing. Sometimes, Philip's voice in my ear, his hand on my hip, watching his profile as he drove his car, I felt as if our secrets bound us together more tightly than our formal, public bonds.

It had never occurred to me that he might have this effect on plenty of women. After my dinner with Iris, a litany of possibilities ran through my mind. The bartender with the peroxide hair, the sleek contract lawyer, the willowy interior designer, Marina's sculptor friend with the boots up to her thighs.

And Iris.

If anyone found out about her, it would be the end of Philip's secondhand ambition.

10

Because I skewed my own truth, invented and omitted and pretended, I thought I knew about lying. I believed Iris had had an entanglement with Philip, that they'd slept together, maybe more than once, but I didn't buy the love story. Maybe he'd said, *You're special, wonderful, amazing*—words to placate, not to commit. I pictured him turning away, standing and pulling on his shirt, if she said she loved him, if she sleepily reached for him, asked for more.

After my dinner with Iris, I wanted to do something, go somewhere, forget. But what would I do with Bryant out of town? So I went home. I hung my dress over the shower, took off my jewelry, washed my face. I climbed into bed, just a mattress on the floor surrounded by a plush white rug. My apartment was mostly negative space. Bare walls, a few ceramics on a shelf, design books piled on the floor. A potted jade plant sat in front of the sliding glass door to the balcony, surrounded by a confetti of dead leaves.

The apartment was more than I could strictly afford, almost half of what I made in a month. After electric and cable and internet and food and Target and student loans (the $95 monthly payment adjusted to my income), I usually had about $100 left, if I was lucky. Just enough to make one of my strategic clothing purchases, usually a new dress or shoes for an event. If Bryant minded paying every time we went out, he didn't say. If I stayed in, I ate eggs or salad from a bag. My frugality was hard learned. For the first months working for the Martins, my paycheck had seemed generous compared to what I earned as a waitress. I'd gone a little crazy spending, on what I couldn't even remember. My credit card bill was still swollen, interest ballooning the balance every month even though I was so careful.

I lay back and stared at the ceiling, where fifty-seven origami swans (painstakingly folded under the instruction of a perky YouTube star) hung in a bristling orb, concealing an ugly light fixture. Images of Iris and

Philip scrolled through my mind. Stealthy meetings, cheesy dialogue, tawdry lingerie. His eyes on her. Her self-conscious poses.

By the time I called him, I was furious. His cell went straight to voicemail. I tried The Grove, but the hostess said he wasn't there. Her tone was knowing, as if women called him all the time. I couldn't risk Marina answering at the house. I left a second, strained message on his cell asking him to call me, and then I waited.

I was glad Bryant was in Washington for the weekend. I didn't know how I'd keep this from him, though I instinctively knew I had to. If I told him, he'd tell the Senator, and this had to be a secret so buried no one else would ever know.

The weekend passed slowly. I went for aimless drives in Bryant's car on the smooth freeways north of the city. I drained the tank and filled it, anxious that I was using the wrong pump, startled by the price of premium unleaded.

Sunday afternoon, I still hadn't heard from Philip. I drove to Starbucks. I spread my GRE book on a table and tried to concentrate. *If Ron, Matt, Sarah, and Lisa have birthdays in March, and a particular set of facts is true, who is youngest? If Dana must walk nine dogs, and follows these arbitrary rules, how many walks will she take? If a handsome, successful middle-aged man commits adultery, is he more likely to leave his family or his mistress?*

I shut the book. My temples ached. The espresso machine hissed violently. People streamed in and out, never removing their sunglasses. The barista's shouts were pointed as darts. *Myra! Felix! Isaac!* Names that, for an instant, sounded like Iris, like Philip.

So when Philip pulled up to the drive-through window, I thought I was imagining things. Then the barista laughed, frothy and flirtatious, and I knew it was him. I grabbed my purse and went out the door, waving wildly.

But Philip didn't see me. He paused at the exit, consulting his phone, then turned right.

I hurried to the BMW and swung out of the lot. At a red light, I was caught a few cars behind him. I called his cell. It rang and rang, but no answer. Impatiently, I waited for the people in front of me to turn. Philip got onto the freeway, heading south.

I followed.

For several miles, I was trapped in a flock of slow cars. Philip darted from lane to lane, tailgating so closely he continually had to hit his brakes. Not how he drove when Amabel and I were with him.

By the time traffic thinned, we'd passed all the exits I expected him to take, beyond the familiar territory of our lives. It might have meant nothing; his business carried him all over. But it was a Sunday afternoon, when Marina dropped Amabel at riding lessons and had her spin class, and afterward they went for a treat. A time Philip was routinely alone.

The freeway split, and he headed south on the 10. I could have swung around and gone home. Instead I stayed behind him.

The suburbs thinned, restaurants and big box stores replaced by convenience stops, McDonald's, Kum & Go, Circle K, Holiday Inn Express. The road kept getting emptier and emptier. Philip's gleaming coupe stayed resolutely in the left lane. I kept five or six telephone poles behind.

The land opened up. Flat bare fields, baked dry. The highway was a straight ribbon you could see down for ages. Now and then a low hill rose at the horizon, the dip before it flooded with water. It was an optical illusion: heat made visible in a shimmering haze.

After we'd been driving an hour, I wondered if I was wrong, if Philip was going to Tucson on campaign business. I imagined him listening to Springsteen, drumming his steering wheel. Oblivious. Already wisps of sherbet orange striped the sky.

Stray buildings began to appear, widely spaced then denser and denser, as a town gathered itself. Abruptly,

Philip veered over and barreled off the exit ramp. I followed, narrowly cutting off a semi. Its horn bellowed accusingly.

Philip drove slowly, as though he wasn't familiar with his surroundings. We passed a plaza with a shuttered red-roofed Pizza Hut, a liquor store, a boutique selling candy-colored quinceañera dresses. Past a one-pump gas station, he turned into a drive marked with a faded wooden sign, THE SUNSET MOTEL, the o drawn as a setting sun. A red placard nailed to a corner spelled VACANCY in acid yellow letters.

The motel was a crumbling stucco wedding cake. Three stories, white, with a scalloped tile roof and balconies edged with elaborate cast iron railings. A boy in denim cutoffs trotted down the winding staircase and slipped through a gate to a greenish pool, where a chubby couple floated like dumplings. A DANGER sign affixed to the gate rattled as it slammed.

Philip parked in the last row, so I pulled into the front, facing a sun-faded Coke machine. He lingered in his car. Maybe performing some preparatory ritual, removing his wedding ring, chewing a mint. Maybe she'd come out, he'd take her to dinner, stop by the liquor store on the way back to the room.

My chest felt heavy, as if pressed under a lead vest.

One of the motel doors opened, a few yards from

my parking spot. I tensed, but instead of Iris, a man emerged. Bent and squinting, like a mouse from a hole. He paused as if stunned by the heat. Thin, colorless hair hung like Spanish moss over his shoulders.

It was the man from Philip's office.

He crossed the lot, swinging his gaunt arms. I watched in the rearview as Philip got out and shook his hand. Sunglasses concealed his expression. He handed the man a white object—a folded paper, or an envelope—then glanced over his shoulder.

The next minute, Philip was back in his car. He must have left the engine running, because he swung out of the spot immediately, tires squealing.

The man had tucked the envelope away and was coming toward me. He passed by my passenger window, so close I could see the pinched skin of his elbow. I froze, expecting him to lower his face to mine. But he kept up his slouching walk back into the room. Number 107. The door slammed behind him.

I stopped at the dinky gas station. It took me ages to scrub away the bugs stuck to Bryant's windshield like eggs to a pan. The place was deserted, the squeak of my squeegee the only sound.

Philip had come all this way to hand a man an envelope. No conversation, nothing. I assumed he'd gone north, back home; I didn't try to follow him again. Frustrated, I worked over the car until it was perfectly clean. As the air cooled, heat rose from the ground like steam.

When I got home, I texted Iris. Have you heard from him yet?

She replied immediately. No, why? Did u talk to him?

Later, she wrote again, Hello? Whatd he say?

I can't reach him. I'll text you later.

I was lying in the sun. Water splashed me. I opened my eyes. Philip was in the motel pool, though the building and the parking lot weren't there; we were in an open field. He beckoned to me, then leaned back into the green water, sinking out of sight.

I wanted to go to him but the sunlight soaked heavily into my skin, pinning me in place. I heard breathing behind me, and the coyote sauntered past. His fur was thin, bristled and sticky in patches where he'd gnawed at fleas. His ribs swelled and receded as he panted. He went to the pool and drank.

Philip surfaced and swam to the edge. I wanted to warn him, but before I could, he reached out to the dog and ran a hand down his flank. The coyote jumped over the water and loped into the horizon, vanishing. Suddenly I was sitting on the side of the pool, Philip's hand on my ribs. A whisper soft in my ear said, *Jump in.*

I woke, desire thrumming between my hipbones. I shut my eyes against the cottony dark of my room and pretended to myself that I was going back to sleep.

11

When I arrived at the Martins' the next morning, Marina wasn't rushing around the kitchen as usual, but sat at the table gazing out the glass doors to the balcony. She wore a white dress with a white cardigan over her shoulders, matching the pristine white kitchen. When she turned to me, her face was bleached with tiredness.

"What a terrible weekend," she said. "Did you hear?"

My arms froze in the act of pulling a water glass from a cabinet. I shook my head, not trusting my voice.

"Gonzales? The town hall? It was horrible. I wasn't ready for it to get ugly yet." She shook her head sadly, her gold earrings catching the light.

I eased the cabinet closed, relieved. "I'm sorry. What did he say?"

"Oh, he went on and on about the land deal. Suggesting we're out of touch. Too—" Anxiously, she smoothed her crisp collar. "As if we're different from anyone else. We work hard, don't we?" She blinked at me. Her fumbling fingers had raised a red flush on her throat; her skin was so delicate, so thin.

"Of course." All I could think was, *She has no idea.* "You work harder than anyone I know."

I'd overcompensated, sounded sarcastic. I turned and rummaged in the fridge for a grapefruit. I sliced it in half and began carving each segment with a little curved knife.

Marina sat stiffly, embarrassed. "We have help, I know. But we give back. We're part of the community."

"People won't listen to those personal attacks," I assured her. "They're tacky." But I'd said the same thing to Bryant, and he'd scoffed, told me I was wrong.

Marina rolled her shoulders. "You're right. I shouldn't pay attention." She stood and set a teacup and saucer out on the counter. "Would you mind staying late tonight? Tonight I've got a dinner thing, and Philip had to rush up to Flagstaff this weekend."

"Really?" I tried to sound casual, but the grapefruit

knife slipped. It was too dull to cut me, but the slice stung. "When did he leave?"

"Yesterday. He's helping Jim rally. Of course it's important, but the timing couldn't be worse. The gala is Friday, and he might not get back until Thursday. I have three dinners this week, so I'll need you to be available."

The shriek of the kettle interrupted her. She poured boiling water into her cup, one hand unconsciously massaging an earlobe.

I filled the coffee grinder with beans. The motor's roar nicely filled the silence. Flagstaff was two hours north, in the mountains. "I can work all you need. Is there anything else I can do?"

Marina shook her head. "Luckily the caterers seem with it this year. Jim will be there, so we'll have to set up some security. I can't make everyone climb through metal detectors so we'll have to figure something else out. It will be an ID-only event, so don't forget yours." She sipped her tea, wincing. "Hot. I don't know why I made this anyway, I've got to go." She dumped it down the sink. "Once I start to list, there's more to do. Typical of Philip to leave." She gave a bright laugh, as if she were joking.

The doorbell rang, and I dropped the pitcher of cream on the counter. It clanged but didn't crack.

Marina frowned. "You aren't yourself today, Finn. What's the matter?"

I scrambled for an excuse. "I get like this when I'm getting my period. It'll pass." A humiliating lie, the most effective kind.

Her lips thinned in irritation, but she believed me. "You should take an iron supplement. Can you get the door? I've got to run."

I trailed behind her to the driveway. The laundry truck idled by the mailbox.

While I hauled the cloth sack of dirty linens down to the deliveryman, Marina backed out her Range Rover, nearly running us over.

"Sorry about that," I said, passing off the bag. I headed back up the drive.

"Miss?" He held out the bag of clean things.

I took it, apologizing again.

He wiped his gleaming forehead with the back of his hand. He wore a shiny soccer jersey, murder in this heat, but he was grinning. "You've got something on your mind. Smile! You're a beautiful girl and it's a be-you-tiful day."

The week Philip was gone didn't resemble the usual march of weekdays. While Amabel and I kept to our routines—Monday, camp; Tuesday, playdate;

Wednesday, riding—the days were long, the hours thick as gravy. I found myself leaving Amabel on false pretenses, to answer the phone or make a snack, and I wandered the house, checking the locks, looking out the windows. The sun glared brightly, and the blue sky was flat as plastic, unchanging as the set of a play.

Though Marina was gone for twelve, thirteen hours a day, I still found traces of her everywhere, as though she wasn't sleeping, either. Unfinished cups of tea, biscotti nibbled and abandoned. She left jewelry lying around at random—a turquoise ring on the mantel, gold earrings on the windowsill above the sink, a diamond tennis bracelet in the pocket of her robe. Eva wouldn't touch them, so I gathered them and returned them to her dressing table.

Late at night Marina would rush in the door and tap me on the shoulder where I drowsed on the couch. "Good night, thank you, I'm off to bed, stay in the guest room if you want." Her neck was strung with tension, her eyes bloodshot. I hoped my thoughts were as opaque to her as hers were to me. I didn't stay over, though I usually took any chance I got to sleep there. I drove through the black night to Bryant's, too tired to speak. I felt such relief when we made love. This was under control, at least.

Bryant was also tense, in a busy straightforward way. I asked him about the town hall, about the polls, but he told me everything was fine. He fell asleep instantly and snored quietly in his throat. At dawn, I woke feeling as if I'd just shut my eyes.

I didn't hear from Philip. I called once, and when he didn't answer, I was almost relieved. I fielded dozens of texts from Iris, replying as minimally as possible, keenly aware that anything I said could get me in trouble, but afraid of what she might do if I ignored her entirely. The ellipses when she was typing seemed to flicker for an eternity. I was afraid she'd threaten to make her story public. But she'd only write how she missed him, or, worse, how grateful she was for my help.

Wednesday afternoon, Iris texted me a picture of another ultrasound. On my little screen I couldn't make out a defining shape in the white specks, and when I compared it to the other ultrasound (stashed in my purse like an unlucky charm), I couldn't tell whether anything had developed.

Otherwise, the day was perversely peaceful. Marina called, cheerful, to say Philip would be back tomorrow, and she'd be home by nine.

I settled Amabel in for her nap, sitting on the side of her bed to tell our usual story.

"Once upon a time," I said, "a girl lived in a big old house on the edge of a forest."

"A princess," Ammy interjected, as she always did.

"Her bedroom was at the top of the house. It was winter. It snowed more than it had for a hundred years—piles of snow, taller than you!"

I asked if she'd seen snow, and she shook her head.

"It's heavy, and very wet. Imagine you're in the swimming pool, up to your knees. But the water is thick and heavy and cold. Freezing! And when you walk, it's hard to move your feet through it. You step on top, and sink in."

Amabel fidgeted, resistant to the artificial dark of her closed blinds.

"The princess was stuck inside for days, watching at her window. Soon her dog's house was buried under snow. The path to the woods vanished. Even the birds shivered.

"Then a polar bear walked through the yard, heading for the trees. So she got dressed in her boots with the fur inside, and her coat, and her mittens. And she went outside into the snow."

I went on, improvising. The princess followed the bear, but he disappeared, and she met instead a wicked witch who wanted to keep the snow falling forever.

Our story always began with the girl in her high

bedroom, and the woods below. After I'd been telling it awhile, when Ammy was three, I showed her the photograph of the Swiss house. It was bent from being carried in my wallet.

"This is the castle from our story. And that's me," I told her, tapping the teenager under the maple. Amabel obediently studied the picture.

I showed her another, this one of the flagstone patio out back, a thick cluster of rosebushes, and a treehouse perched in a low, spreading mulberry. I'd carefully trimmed away one side of the snapshot.

"That's the princess's hideout," Ammy said, rolling the word over her tongue like candy. The hideout featured in many stories.

"That's right." I tried not to be hurt that she wasn't particularly interested in my reveal—I'd lived here; the princess was me. But for her, the big Swiss house wasn't a castle, and the girl in her shabby outfit no princess. Ammy was starting from a different perspective than I had, the Martins' glass house, which would have been a castle to Natalie, and still was, even to Finn.

Today, after we finished our story, I shut Ammy's door and went into the Martins' bedroom and idly sifted through the drawers, and the hamper, and Philip's pockets, hunting for signs of Iris. Nothing was out of place.

12

The next morning, the day before the Black and White Gala, Philip was in the kitchen when I got to work. I stopped in the doorway, a Starbucks Venti steaming in my hand.

He stood at the counter reading the newspaper. Toast crumbs showered on the business section as he took a contemplative bite. He looked refreshed. He wore a pale aqua shirt buttoned halfway, revealing the tan landscape of his chest. His hair was wet and combed back, and he was cleanly shaven, cheeks pink from the razor.

He glanced at me, shaking out the paper. "Planning to paint my portrait?"

The coffee was burning my hand through the cardboard. I clumsily stepped forward to drop the cup on the counter.

"Ouch," he said. "You all right? Here, sit down. You want some toast?"

Coffee trickled down my palm. I brought it to my mouth. "Did you have a nice trip? Where'd you go, again?"

"Nowhere half as nice as home. You can't get anything but *USA Today* at these hotels." He popped two slices of sourdough into the Dualit toaster.

I perched on a barstool. "I need to talk to you."

"You sound very serious." He rinsed his mug. "Do you want a raise? No, I've got it—you're getting married?"

"No."

"Good. It's too early in the morning for either topic. I've got to run. We'll chat after the party. How's that boyfriend of yours, by the way? Gotten too serious for you yet?"

I opened my mouth, shut it. I was disoriented; was he acting strange, or was he always like this? Iris's story had dropped a filter over my eyes, making everything appear queasily different.

Philip laughed. "I'll take that as a yes. Have him take you to Mexico some weekend. That's the kind of thing you need to do when you're starting out with someone."

"Do you ever wish you could start out again?" I asked recklessly.

Philip waved my question away. "Oh, Bryant's not so bad. I'm teasing you."

"I meant you."

The bread jolted out of the toaster.

"Is that a proposition, Finn? Don't tease a man." Philip reached to flip the slices over. "Hot!" He put his fingertips to his lips and checked his watch. "I'd better get moving. See you tonight." He slipped his briefcase over his shoulder, then leaned in close, his face inches from mine, and grabbed a manila folder from the counter behind me. I smelled the balsam of his aftershave. "Ciao," he said, dropping the word into my ear, soft as a kiss.

I called Iris from the living room.

The phone obviously woke her. "Finn," she rasped. "What's up? Did you talk to him?"

"I couldn't. He's been out of town."

"Out of town? You didn't tell me." She sounded genuinely annoyed, like she hadn't known.

"I thought he might be with you."

"I told you, I haven't talked to him. If I'd seen him, why would I keep texting you?"

"I don't know." I was out of energy. Out the window, a haze of brown dust obscured the valley.

"Listen, I can't wait forever. I was thinking I'll tell his wife."

"Believe me, Marina is the last person you want to talk to."

"The only person I want to talk to won't talk to me." Her whine burrowed into my brain.

"I'll talk to him, I promise. Tomorrow."

"He'll be home tomorrow?"

"If not Marina will kill him," I said, unthinking, then cursed to myself.

"Why?" Iris said, suddenly fully awake. "What's tomorrow?"

"Nothing," I backtracked. "Some party they have to go to. It's no big deal."

"I don't have forever, you know. The doctor said it's developing really fast."

"Do they develop at different rates?"

"Jeez, you don't have to snap at me. It's not like I did this to myself."

"Sorry," I said, trying to mean it. "Hey, have you ever been to the Sunset Motel?"

"Maybe? There were so many places, it's hard to remember."

"This is about an hour south of the city."

"Really?" Her voice was sharp. "How'd you know about it?"

"I heard him mention it."

She hummed. "I doubt it. We wouldn't spend that much time driving." Her breathy laugh was like acid in my bloodstream.

I unclenched my jaw. "I've got another call," I lied.

"I'll call you tomorrow." She hung up on me.

The next morning, the day of the gala, Philip had gone by the time I arrived. Marina was rushing around the kitchen, smelling of lavender oil. "I've got to run some errands, and then get my hair and nails done. I'll be back around three. If anyone from the catering company calls, tell them they should already know what to do. Don't let any guests cancel. If Philip calls to say he'll be late, call me right away." She put a hand to her forehead. "What else? I think that's it."

"Party! Party!" Amabel chanted. "I want to put on my dress!"

"I hope you're this excited tonight," Marina said in a warning tone.

Amabel and I were only making an appearance in order to get a family photo. Then I'd take her home and stay overnight. After Marina left, Amabel ceremoniously unrolled a Disney Princess sleeping bag on her floor and told me grandly that I could have her bed.

The day puttered along, the threat of Iris's call like a wasp hovering nearby. Amabel, having heard about the party for so long, was giddily energetic. Wound up, she was in danger of melting down, which would certainly be blamed on me. I hustled her from activity to activity, stories to games to the swimming pool.

The water glittered. Sitting on the side, Amabel rested her feet on a kickboard and pumped it in and out of the water. Waves rose around her, first small, and larger, until the entire pool roiled. "It's a stormy sea!" she yelled.

I swam over and grabbed her. We paddled on a leisurely circuit. She liked to play in the water, but was fussy about swimming, hated to have water splash her face.

"You know, the Little Mermaid loves to swim," I said.

She stretched her arms back and thrust her chest forward. "I'm Ariel!"

"Finn!" Marina's voice sliced through the afternoon. She'd appeared on the deck, arms crossed, unsmiling.

"Mommy, I'm a mermaid!" Amabel called.

Marina ignored her. "Finn, I need to see you right away. It's time for Amabel to take her nap." She headed back up to the house. The pool gate slammed. Amabel shrieked in protest.

Leaving the mess of toys and towels, I got Amabel upstairs, into her pajamas, hair combed. These tasks always took an inordinate amount of time. For once I was glad for the delay.

After I shut her bedroom door, I stalled in the hallway. I could hear Marina saying my name in her clear, cold voice. It didn't have to mean Iris had talked to her. Something had gone wrong with the party; she was annoyed to find the clutter by the pool; her manicurist had chipped a nail.

When I went downstairs Marina was in the living room, standing at the window.

"I'm sorry about the mess out there," I said. "I'll clean it up."

She didn't answer. A vertical groove etched between her brows.

"Is it the coyote?" I scanned the backyard, searching for the movement that gave him away. Nothing. A plane trailing a Geico banner made its sluggish way across the sky.

Marina's eyes flicked at me. Red marks dug into her nose where her sunglasses had been. Her nails were unpainted, I realized. She looked close to tears.

"What's the matter?" Cautiously, I touched her wrist.

She snapped away. "What time is it?" She spun to check. "After three! Sit down."

I perched on the couch. The air-conditioning turned on with a gentle sigh. Cold air rose from the carpet and encircled my ankles.

"Is Amabel asleep?" Marina held her elbows in her thin fingers. Her collarbone curled forward.

"She should be."

"How long did you swim?" Her voice was flat. She kept staring out the window, as if in a trance.

"Is there anything I can do to help with the party?" I asked.

She flinched, as if rudely woken, and dropped her arms to her sides. "I'm not going to the party." Her voice was low and utterly calm. "I'm going out of town." Pulling her shoulders back, she went to the bar cart and righted a glass. She touched the row of liquor bottles one by one, lifted the vodka, and poured out a few fingers.

I found my voice. "You mean the party's canceled?"

"Something has come up." She tipped the drink back and studied the glass as if surprised by its sharpness. She touched the corner of her lip. "Amabel will need clothes for a week. Pack extra underwear. And a toothbrush. You know what to bring."

I twisted my wrist in my hand. "You're going away? What happened? Marina, you seem—"

She slammed her glass on the bar. Her eyes were cold and expressionless, like the coyote's. "Really, Finn. Your job is to do what I ask." She poured another drink. The bottle's neck rattled against the glass. She set it down and flexed her fingers.

"Let me." I went to the bar. I could smell the eucalyptus in Marina's hair spray as I opened a tonic to top off the vodka.

She cradled the drink in her palm. "Thank you." She cleared her throat. "I heard from an old friend. I need— They've had some troubles. I've helped them in the past."

"Did you cancel the party? Does Philip know?"

She shook her head. "Pack Amabel's things and then wake her. You don't need to explain anything."

"I'm happy to watch her if it's inconvenient to take her," I said stupidly. Of course there was no friend in trouble. She was leaving Philip, and taking Amabel with her.

"My daughter is not an inconvenience to me." She overpowered my curious gaze with a disdainful, reprimanding stare. But the anger I'd expected, the accusation, wasn't there. So Iris hadn't mentioned my part.

I dropped my eyes first. Marina still wore her stack of diamond rings. Engagement, wedding, anniversary.

She handed me her empty glass. "I'd love to be leaving in half an hour."

Amabel sat cross-legged on her sleeping bag, murmuring to Patrick.

"Did you get any sleep?" I knelt to hug her. She smelled of chlorine. "Your mom has a surprise. She's taking you on a special vacation."

"And then the party?"

I began opening drawers, pulling out leggings and shorts and tiny tank tops. "The party was canceled. It's not going to happen anymore. I know it's disappointing." I brushed her hair from her forehead. "Can you go to the bathroom and wash your hands?"

She left, stomping her feet.

Marina would never miss her own party. She wouldn't retreat from Philip Martin and let Iris have him. Yet that's exactly what she was doing. I laid out a sundress and sandals, added sneakers to the bag. I concentrated on neatly folding the clothes. Packed Patrick and a singing guitar that would drive Marina crazy. Books, paper, crayons. Marina would have her phone, so Amabel could play games.

I could tell her I knew about Iris. Offer to help. But knowing of my involvement would make her quiver. If she found out I'd known for days, she'd fire me on the spot.

Where would Marina go? What would I do, if I were her?

I wouldn't have lost Philip in the first place. I'd never have been so cool to him.

I added a windbreaker in case Marina took Ammy to their house in San Diego. The backyard opened onto a strip of windy beach, where I'd first seen the ocean. From there, Marina could conduct an entire divorce. Shop, surf, eat sushi, find a boyfriend. She'd hire a new nanny.

I tasted iron. The inside of my lip was raw.

Amabel came out of the bathroom without having flushed the toilet or run the water for her hands, and I led her back in and helped her. She refused to put on the outfit I'd picked for the car. "I want to wear my dress!"

"We'll pack it." I eased the lacy dress off its hanger and tucked it into the suitcase. Its price tag was still attached—half a month's rent.

It was quarter to four by the time we went downstairs. Philip would be getting ready to come home.

He'd stall, not dreading the party itself but the anxious preparation preceding it. He'd go out of his way driving home, stop by the inexpensive gas station that stocked his favorite candy bar. He ate these on the way home, toffee crumbling onto the seat, winking if I teased him, offering me a bite.

Amabel's suitcase looked pitifully small in Marina's trunk. Marina had tossed in a leather duffel for herself. It flopped over as if empty. The smell of new car blew out when I shut the trunk.

Amabel wore her star-shaped sunglasses. "You aren't coming?" She twisted in her booster seat.

"Not this time. But you'll be back before you know it."

"When?"

I took her hand. We counted down from ten on her fingers. "See? It'll fly by."

Marina came out and slung her purse into the passenger seat. Orange prescription bottles showed through its opening. I remembered her vodka drinks and was seized with anxiety. "Do you need me to drive you somewhere?"

"Finn, you're fussing." Marina glanced in the rearview. "Are you ready to go?"

Amabel nodded at me instead of her mother's reflection. Her eyebrows twisted into an anxious frown that would have been comical on her miniature features if it hadn't wrenched my heart.

I kissed her. "Draw me a picture of what you and Patrick do, okay?"

I shut her door. The tinted window reflected my worried face. I forced myself to smile and touched the glass, like a blessing.

The front window lowered. Marina was polishing her sunglasses on a cloth. "Tell my husband not to call me. I'll call him."

"Can I tell him where you're going? He'll be worried."

She laughed. "Do you think so? I think he'll be angry. Well. If you're right, tell him we're fine and I'm calm." She slipped on her glasses, as if to give merit to her lie.

The window rolled up. The car glided away. I went to the end of the driveway and stood barefoot on the scalding pavement, staring after them.

Tell my husband not to call me. Philip was not disowned, then, but firmly claimed.

A gritty breeze swept my bare legs. The sun had shifted to a lower perch in the sky. The party would start in three hours.

13

The house loomed, large and empty. In the kitchen, dirty dishes were piled in the sink, down to the cheese sandwich Amabel had abandoned. Every twenty seconds or so, the faucet dripped. I began to wait for it, the suspension between drips achingly silent and expectant.

I dug out my phone and dialed Iris. When she didn't answer, I waited through her voicemail's robotic prompt, but after the beep, I couldn't find sufficiently withering words. I threw the phone onto the island and ran my hands through my hair, pulled it into a ponytail in my fist. *Think.*

Marina had left her blue leather notebook on the island. In it were lists of errands, tasks, calls, meetings. Everything done on paper before it was entered into her phone, locked into her calendar. The rough draft of her guest list spanned a dozen pages. Important people, who might already be getting ready: picking up the tux at the cleaners, fixing their hair, steaming the wrinkles from a gown. And I was the only one who knew the hostess had left.

Here was the seating chart, a timetable, a list of outfits slashed impatiently with her pen. I imagined her doodling in the margins, leaning against her upholstered headboard, Philip downstairs shooting pool alone, or away at the restaurant, or in his car with Iris, his hand on her knee.

I went upstairs. Marina had shut the bedroom door. I grasped the cool silver handle and went in. The bed was unmade, wrinkles pressed into sheets, intimate hollows in the pillows. Marina's laptop blinked on the dresser. I opened it, but when the password prompt came up, I tried Ammy's birthday, and Philip's, then gave up.

Marina's dresser drawers were full. In the bathroom, her makeup bag was gone, but her shampoo and razor remained in the shower, eye cream in the drawer. Her jewelry was still arranged on its enameled tray. Here were her favorite pieces, the slim watch, diamond studs. My favorites, the citrine hairpins, the sapphire cocktail ring, the hammered rose gold bangle.

No note, nothing for Philip.

Why not leave tomorrow morning? Surely Marina had enough self-control to get through one night of artificial smiles by Philip's side. But she'd left as though the gala meant nothing to her.

I sat on the foot of the bed. I pulled out my phone again.

Bryant answered right away. "How's the party house?"

Tracing the weave in the linen sheets with my thumb, I said, "There's a problem, I think. I'm not sure what to do." My voice was tight.

"Hold on." The phone made a scratching sound, and Bryant's voice was muffled. After a pause, he came back on clearly. "I just stepped outside. What's going on?" He was calm and serious. I imagined him handling the Senator's calls in such a tone. *Philip's made us look bad again: gotten into a car accident, pulled some dubious land sale. Knocked up a girl.*

I said, "Marina's gone. She just left. All of a sudden."

"She left," Bryant repeated, his tone still neutral.

"Yes. She took Amabel. She's not coming to the party."

"Start over, Finn. Tell me step by step."

I told him how she'd come home midafternoon, earlier than expected. "She was upset, but she wouldn't say why. She told me she was going away to help a friend."

"With Amabel? What friend?"

"She didn't say. I don't know if she was telling the truth." My face was hot. I shook the hem of my shirt, cooling my skin.

"When did they leave? Where were they going?"

"About four," I said. "I packed some clothes for Ammy. Marina didn't seem to take very much. Her suitcase looked empty. She said she'd call Philip."

"Where'd they go?"

"I have no idea. They drove away, down the hill."

"All right," he said. "I've got to make a few calls here. Just hang tight, okay?"

"Should I call Philip? Or the museum?"

"Don't do anything for now. Stay there. Call me if they come back."

He hung up.

I wandered downstairs. My legs moved heavily. Spiky purple flowers bristled in the vase on the foyer table. I opened the front door and looked down the empty road.

I cleaned the kitchen, soaping everything by hand instead of loading it into the dishwasher, because it would fill more time. Then I went outside and tidied the pool area, bringing an armful of stuff up to the house. Still no word. Maybe Bryant had been swept up in damage control and forgot he'd told me to stay here.

My hands were brittle and stiff. I hadn't told him about Iris. I wanted to forget I'd ever talked to her.

I was in Ammy's room, pinning her latest artwork onto her bulletin board, when Bryant called back.

"Can you meet me at the museum before the party? As early as you can?"

"I was getting worried. What's going on?"

"It's too late to cancel the gala. I'm going to play host until the Senator or Philip arrives."

He paused. I was staring at Ammy's drawing of a princess and a polar bear.

"What did Philip say?" I asked.

Bryant cleared his throat. "Jim will handle Philip. The gala is my priority now. I don't have to tell you how important it is."

"But without Marina, how can there be a party?"

"We'll explain that there's been an emergency. She had to go away unexpectedly, but the museum still deserves a fund-raiser—doesn't it? I'll head over there on the early side, make sure everything's running smoothly. I was hoping you'd join me."

I worried the ends of my hair, stiff with chlorine. "I wasn't even meant to attend the gala, really."

"We've had plenty of practice at this point. It'll be like any other event. Right?"

I found myself agreeing.

Already, an hour had passed since Marina and Amabel left. I made Ammy's bed and went through to the bathroom. My reflection was anxious and tired. My dress hung over the bathtub. A knee-length, machine-washable black sheath meant to blend in. It wasn't within a mile of what I needed if I was attending with Bryant.

I went back to the master bedroom. I paused in front of Marina's dresser. The framed snapshot of James—was that a goad to Philip? Did Marina miss him, particularly when she had to nag and maneuver Philip into behaving? I took it for granted that Philip still thought of Tina, though there wasn't a single picture of her in any of the places I'd searched. People didn't need photographs of memories they kept in their minds, fresh as filmstrips.

I showered in the master bath and wrapped myself in a robe. Their closet was the size of my apartment. Marina's pastel wardrobe seemed to huff at me. I sank my hand in the pocket of one of Philip's blazers, the capaciousness surprising, swallowing my wrist. At the bottom, a slice of Big Red gum had gone dry and stiff in its silver wrapper. I folded it into my mouth and slowly chewed it to softness.

Marina's party dress hung in plastic. A white gown in buttery silk so fine you could have drawn it through a wedding band. Marina was counting on most of the women to wear black. More slimming, less likely to stain or make your complexion ghastly in photos. Only Marina could wear white without ever blemishing it; only Marina with her honey hair and perfect tan outshone the white.

I wasn't bold enough to wear her dress. I found a comparatively simple black gown, calf-length with a full skirt and cap sleeves, backless.

In the full-length mirror, I looked unlike myself. The dress draped beautifully, making every movement sensual and fluid. It transformed me, as a cape transforms a magician. I tilted my chin and assessed my hair. Waves, I decided. I stood barefoot on the bathroom rug and worked Marina's hot iron back to front. The wet strands sizzled against the paddles, puffs of steam releasing as I twisted my wrist. I was jumpy, energy fizzing under the surface of my skin. But I was also weirdly calm. The hands that painted a liquid black line around my eyes were perfectly still.

As a last touch, I stepped into a pair of slingbacks. I didn't dare borrow any jewelry. I texted Bryant that I was on my way.

14

Marina's desk was a clean expanse of glass shaped like a teardrop, her computer in the fat swell, a row of carved statuettes along the pointed end. A stack of lilac stationery towered at my elbow. It was serious paper, heavy, soft. I shook out my wrist and copied Bryant's words again.

Welcome, I wrote, in a fair mimicry of Marina's tidy, slender cursive. *Thank you for attending this year's gala!* On it went, gushing and grateful, a tone not very like Marina's. The idea, Bryant said, was that Marina had prepared these cards in advance. Picking one up at the door, guests would feel her graciousness, even in her absence. At the corner of the card stock, a white orchid clung to a dainty gold pin, for men to wear on their lapels and women to fasten to their updos.

Bryant had closed me up in Marina's office. Its windows overlooked the sculpture garden, where the party would proceed after dinner. Totem poles bordered a patio, where three blond women set up a bar. A fountain stood at the center of the patio, a circular platform like a lily pad springing up in the middle, rinsed endlessly with water. Beside this, a wooden platform already held a drum set and a tangled carpet of cords.

Bryant was bustling around the museum, organizing the caterers, going over the schedule with Marina's assistant, confirming details with security. I flipped over another card and began again. At last, dozens of cards stood in stacks on the desk. I packed them into a box and carried them to the lobby. My heels rang across the polished marble. Here were men unloading leafy tropical plants from a cart, arranging them to screen off the ticket counter and gift shop. Here was the coat check, where someone might drop off a shawl or handbag. Here was the sign-in table, swag bags choked with tissue paper. I fanned out my forged notes. I felt efficient and authoritative. This was going to work, I thought. The gala would go on, the Martins wouldn't be embarrassed, and Marina would come back when she'd cooled down. She'd have to thank me, for carrying on so well.

I pinned a flower to my dress and followed the hum of activity into the ballroom. Tuxedoed caterers moved in tight circles, setting vases on tables. More slowly, a young woman in a white shirt and white suspenders hunched over, dealing cutlery beside plates. Another trailed with a ruler, setting each piece right. I left them to it, wandering through double doors to the utility area, where banquet tables were laden with chafing dishes. The greasy smell of meat drifted in the air. Bryant stood with a clipboard, addressing a troupe of college kids in white gloves. Professionally, he didn't acknowledge me until he was done with them.

He touched my elbow in lieu of a kiss. "T-minus thirty minutes."

"The ballroom's just about set up," I said. "And the cards are ready to go."

"Perfect." In his tux, Bryant evoked Cary Grant. His demeanor was confident, if tightly wound. He set his hand on my back and ushered me toward the door. "I'm off to handle the sound. Let's reconvene in the lobby at quarter to. Not that anyone should get here early, but you never know, the older guests . . ." He trailed off as we entered the ballroom. He snapped his fingers, and a caterer rushed over. "These flowers are too high, you see? They'll block the person opposite. Trim them down." A dip of the head, and the guy was off.

Bryant picked invisible lint off a chair and sighed.

"Is the Senator arriving early?" I asked.

Bryant looked surprised. "Why would he?" He squeezed my elbow. "There's no need to be anxious, Finn. Just smile, and have a good time. Okay? I'll see you in ten."

The galleries were empty and bright. Marina had arranged the objects with plenty of space between them, as in a boutique. Fringed ceremonial gowns, drums with stained tops, wood carvings splintered with time. Placards beside each piece described not only its origins and significance but also the lengths to which the museum had gone to acquire and restore it. I could see Marina typing out the cards, landing on a tone both self-congratulatory and serious, her new reading glasses standing on the very tip of her nose as if she hardly needed them.

I imagined her at the airport, glasses on, reading a magazine at the gate. But she'd be attending to Amabel, which she rarely had to do; she'd be tired and edgy, the party a nagging buzz in the blare of her thoughts.

Or maybe she wasn't thinking of the gala at all. Probably all she could think of was Philip with Iris. Iris's garish bright hair, her sweet voice, her cat's smile.

I went to the Frowning Man, friendly territory for

my phone call. I dialed Philip's cell, and when there was no answer I called the house. I was sure it would ring through, but then Philip picked up.

"Finn?"

"You're home." I felt dumb, my tongue thick.

"Did you expect something else?" His voice was cool.

"Is your dad with you?"

"No." I heard ice cubes hit glass. "He let me know. If that's what you called about. Marina's . . . emergency." I imagined him in the living room, in front of the bar cart where Marina had stood earlier, her hands shaking as they poured vodka in the middle of the afternoon.

"Have you heard from her?" I asked.

Philip grunted. "I assume she didn't tell you where she went."

"I tried to call you." After I said it, I realized it wasn't true. I tugged my earlobe. "I didn't know what to do. I'm at the museum now. Everything is all set for the gala."

"I don't give a damn about the gala." He sounded as though he'd be angry if he wasn't so tired. I wondered what he'd told the Senator about Iris—whether he'd confessed, or pretended to be innocent. More likely, he'd said nothing at all. Told his father it was none of his business.

"Are you going to be here soon?" I asked.

He laughed. "I doubt it."

Now he'd be sitting on the couch, or slouched in the womb chair, digging a toe into the carpet and wishing his empty glass could refill itself.

"Philip." My voice was a whisper. "I know about Iris."

His reply came back sharp and clear. "What's that?"

"She came to me. She told me what's going on. She asked for my help."

There was a click like a caught breath. Philip said, "Are you the one who told Marina?"

"No!" I said quickly. "Absolutely not. I've been trying to talk to you, but I couldn't find how to bring it up, and then Marina left, and that has to be why."

The line clicked again. "Jim's calling. I have to go."

"I just wanted—"

"Don't tell anybody anything. Don't say a thing."

The Frowning Man had a hooked nose, brown skin tinged red—was that original, or an effect of the paint's aging? His smooth black hair lay in a clean line above his grim scowl. He stared fiercely at a fire extinguisher mounted on the opposite wall. I ran my hand over his brow, knowing it was forbidden. Smooth as driftwood.

Suddenly a male voice rang through the room, followed by a bubbly lounge beat. Speakers were mounted discreetly in the corners of the ceiling. The music was much too loud. The ancient statues and ritual masks seemed to wince.

A dismayed laugh came from my chest like a hiccup. Everything was absurd. The museum, the party, the Martins, and especially me—wearing Marina's dress, carrying Iris's ultrasound in my purse, an absolute impostor. I smoothed my skirt and shook the feeling away. How many times had I plunged into a party, even when I wasn't in the mood, and easily found my groove: flattering and teasing and flirting and listening, the sense of my power buoying me up? Bryant was right—tonight was for the party. Philip would see when he got here.

A man entered the gallery, baggy white shirt unbuttoned and untucked, probably a caterer arriving late, smiling flirtatiously at me. I spun around and headed to the lobby.

Bryant was waiting for me, a flute of champagne in each hand. We drank, lifting the glasses to our lips and swallowing more than we normally would. He bounced on the balls of his feet. Around us, servers waited in the shadows.

"I hope he's not too late," Bryant said.

"Who?" I adjusted the flower on my shoulder with damp fingers.

"Philip." He looked me over, for the first time since I'd arrived. "You look beautiful. New dress?"

I took another drink instead of answering.

Now the elevator light glowed with the first guests rising from the garage. Bryant planted his feet farther apart. I felt the clenched effort of my smile.

It was the Feinhorns: he a banker with combed-back silver hair, she a bottle brunette involved with the children's hospital. She came into the lobby with arms stretched out enthusiastically. She obviously expected to grasp someone she knew, but she gamely took my elbow and hovered her cheek next to mine. Her face seemed to have been washed free of its original features and new ones drawn on: steep black brows, brown lips, angular pink cheekbones.

"Hello, hello. We're the first, aren't we? We're always too early! I blame this man." She slapped her husband on the shoulder with her jeweled clutch.

Mr. Feinhorn, having already released Bryant from a python's grip, stretched his shoulders. "People are circulating, Winnie. Around and about."

"Please," I said, "take a moment to sign in." I gestured to the table. The Feinhorns ambled over, happy to ink their names in the book and admire the photo montages of last year's event. As they came back, pinning on their orchids, a caterer swung by with a tray of drinks. I set my empty down and picked up another. I'd have to pace myself, that first glass had slid away. Nerves.

"I know you, don't I?" said Mr. Feinhorn. "You work for Jim."

"Guilty as charged," Bryant agreed. "He'll be here, of course."

"Fashionably late," Mr. Feinhorn chuckled.

"But how exciting!" Mrs. Feinhorn said. "You must work around the clock. Of course, we don't even know the other candidate's name."

"Gonzales." Bryant sounded jovial, as though he couldn't help liking the guy. "He's got a lot of energy."

"I'll bet he does," said Mr. Feinhorn. "He snuck into this country and thinks he can tell us how it should work."

"He's from Tucson," I said, worrying Bryant would be offended.

They turned to me, mouths open. Bryant smiled, angry.

Mrs. Feinhorn held up a palm. "No politics. Marina would be scandalized to hear us talking politics at her party."

"My fault entirely," Bryant said. "There seems to be nothing but politics in an election year."

Mrs. Feinhorn laughed meaninglessly.

"Marina will be so happy you came," Bryant said. "You've heard, of course, that she's had to fly to Florida. Her aunt . . ." He trailed off, inviting them to fill in the gap. "You know how Marina is family first." Smiling winningly, he rushed on, "But here we are, keeping you in the lobby! Please, you could drop your coats— and there are canapés—and the galleries are open, of course."

He was persuasive. The Feinhorns hustled out of the lobby with drinks in one hand and shrimp skewers in the other, and roamed out of view into the galleries.

The elevator lit up again, and this time eight guests poured out, already mid-conversation, and Bryant and I welcomed them, my greeting coming more smoothly already. With a trickle and then a flood, the party began.

When I was with Bryant, the clusters of conversation opened and swept us inside. He flattered, he flirted, he wanted nothing more than *to share a word with you, Mr. Clark. And you, Mrs. Sherwood, may-I-call-you-Cindy?* The trick would have seemed cheap, but Bryant genuinely liked people, and he remembered everything, not only your name but that of your spouse, children, dog. He remembered the summerhouse with the flooded basement, the niece who'd won a Fulbright, the eagle on the thirteenth hole at the Stadium Course.

The crowd swelled. The rooms buzzed with chatter. None of the men cared much about the absence of their hosts. The women clucked their tongues sympathetically, smirking. They probably suspected the truth—marital problems, infidelity, a younger woman. On Bryant's elbow, I was accepted as an appropriate representative; they didn't recognize me as the person they usually saw in shorts and sneakers, rallying their children. I was dizzy with cheek kisses, hand squeezes, drinks pressed on me as my half-full glass was whisked away. I'd always been awed by these people. Up close, their insecurities were on display. Lenore Leland's white shawl shed feathers; Heather Clark's dress might have been spray-painted on. Mrs. Gilly had gotten another face-lift, but her neck remained crumpled as a paper bag. Jennifer Jensen, married to an oil contractor away in Iraq, found her way to Paul Huff, the professional golfer, and kissed him lingeringly on the cheek. Sweat and perfume mingled in the air.

Seven forty-five. Heels clicked; waiters collected empties, their red bow ties setting them apart in the sea of black and white. Philip still hadn't arrived. I left Bryant and checked my phone in the quiet of the ballroom. No calls, no texts. I dialed Philip again and was shuttled straight to voicemail.

Reentering the party, I felt shy. Bryant had disappeared among the men in suits. From outside the circles of conversation, backs and elbows created impenetrable hedges.

I drifted in the gaps between groups. The ivory blooms on every guest had a unifying effect, like activist ribbons, turning the crowd into supporters of Marina. I'd already talked to everyone I recognized. I stuck to the perimeter of the room, pretending to admire the artwork. It was absurdly hot. My throat was dry, my neck flushed.

While I studied a tapestry, a woman approached, holding her champagne flute tensely up near her chin.

"Beautiful," she said with a perfunctory glance at the art. Her lips twitched over her big teeth. "You're Finn, aren't you? I've been trying to say hi all night." Her handshake would have crushed a small mammal.

I didn't recognize her. She might be one of Marina's lower-tier friends, or one of the school moms who set up playdates for Amabel even though their children were much older or younger, angling to gain entry into the Martins' circle. She wore an unflattering dress that flared over her hips.

"How is poor Marina doing? She must be just crying about missing this."

"Family comes first for Marina." I'd repeated the line all evening, until it had worn out and frayed. I wondered how the Senator managed to say the same words over and over, and always make them sound forceful, like a fresh epiphany.

The woman nodded, scanning the crowd around us, and I was both relieved and offended to lose her interest. But then, to my surprise, she stepped closer. "I wonder if she's upset with Philip." She lifted an eyebrow.

"Oh, no," I said. "He'll be here any minute."

An impatient sigh. "Let me lay my cards on the table. I'd love to bend your ear—I'm willing to make it worth your while." My confusion must have been clear because she clucked and lowered her voice. "You work for the Martins? They're my job, too. I'm doing interviews . . . learning more about them. Nothing bad! Just: what are their habits, what's their daily routine, and so on. You've got a unique perspective—"

She was cut off when a man joined us. Young, blond, holding a glass of champagne as roughly as a can of beer.

"Some party." He was amiable, addressing both of us. An ordinary party guest, schmoozing before dinner.

The woman's lips pursed. I excused myself and slipped away, pushing through the crowd. I nudged the men, my palm on their shoulders or backs, and when they turned and saw me they ducked away, smiling with wet lips. The women didn't move; their heads spun with sharp eyes, like hawks'.

The room was loud, a roar more like a machine engine than human voices.

I finally spotted Bryant. His artificial laugh hadn't lost any of its gusto. I seized his hand, and he blinked at the eagerness of my hello.

Three men filed into the room, mundane as grooms on a wedding cake, except for the cords running from their ears to their collars. Snoops.

A whisper rustled through the crowd. Heads turned. The Senator stepped through the doorway. Funny how his famous face stood out even in the crowd of old white men. For an instant, it seemed everyone might erupt into cheers. He threw an arm up into a wave. The gesture sufficed to make everyone feel personally greeted. A smattering of applause, giddy laughter. The buzz restarted with twice the energy. The crowd pressed forward, but the Senator was flanked by two Snoops and made his way to Bryant and me. He nodded at this person and that, but when he reached us, his eyes glittered narrowly.

Bryant held out his hand. "You just got the party started, sir."

The Senator's mouth was curled upward agreeably, in a politician's photogenic smile that wouldn't widen or droop the rest of the night.

"And hasn't Philip arrived?" Surprisingly, he was addressing me.

"Not yet," I said.

His eyes hadn't dulled with age. They were critical and probing. The flag pin punched into his lapel had an aggressive air, like a sheriff's badge. From his stance, and the edge behind his question, I concluded that he knew it all—Iris's pregnancy, Marina's humiliated retreat, perhaps even my part.

"Haven't you heard from him?" I faltered. "He said he spoke with you earlier."

He pounced. "So you have talked to him."

Bryant took tight hold of my elbow, glancing between us like a man watching his horse lose.

"Only briefly," I said. "I called him after the party started, to see where he was."

"And where was he?"

"I assumed at the house. I'm sure he'll be here, though. He knows what it means to Marina." Involuntarily, my lips had spread into a desperate smile.

"Does he?" The Senator seemed irritated. He scanned the room over my head. "By the way, Marina sends her apologies. I heard from her on my drive over. She said she was embarrassed to have left you in the lurch. Apparently she was in too much of a rush to explain anything. But Bryant's told you, hasn't he? Her aunt is sick. Days to live. They were very close, apparently."

"She did leave in a hurry," I said carefully.

The corners of his eyes creased with apparent amusement. "Smart of you to call Bryant. It's always best to let a professional handle these things." He pivoted toward the room, as though he were referring to the party.

Bryant's grip on my arm relaxed, but anxiety remained wedged like a bone in my throat. The Senator must know I knew his story was untrue. He was warning me.

"Marina had planned every detail," I heard myself say. "It was simpler to carry it through than to cancel."

"Marina was devastated to think of canceling." Bryant gave me an adoring smile, as if he hadn't just bruised my arm.

"Was she? Then I should thank you." The Senator took my hand and lifted it, dipping his head in a courtly gesture. I was painfully aware that my palms were sticky with sweat. He lowered his face closer to mine. "You look lovely, Finn. I'd hardly have recognized you."

Before I could respond, he released me and inclined his head almost imperceptibly.

His assistant stepped forward. "The Albrights would like to say hello."

"Off I go," the Senator said. "If Philip does arrive and you manage to spot him before I do, send him to me."

The guests shifted like currents in a river as the Senator crossed the room.

"I didn't realize Philip wasn't here," Bryant said. "I should have been paying more attention. I'd better call him." He pushed off in his boss's wake, and the guests swirled, propelling me out of the gallery and into the hall, where a bell began to chime. Dinner.

15

The dinner: small plates. The music: Sinatra. The company: businessmen whose titles didn't offer any clues to the nature of their work, their wives, and Bryant's empty seat. The talk was of Italy, children's immunizations, a popular podcast. Wine poured freely; I never saw the bottom of my glass. The food was a success. Tiny clams glossy with butter, spicy steak, sweet potatoes flecked with cilantro, a mango crème brûlée. Marina had said she was so tired of custard, but it was the thing now, everyone would expect it. Better than lava cake, at least.

Bryant slipped into his chair midway through the entrée. "He's here." He snapped his napkin into his lap. Apologizing to the woman on his other side, he was sucked into a conversation about her powder room renovation.

I couldn't spot Philip. The room was crowded, and the black and white attire made everyone alike.

"Miss?" A waiter lifted my plate. "Finished?"

A microphone shrieked. Philip stood at the podium, tapping the mic. He was immaculate, hair smoothed back, tuxedo crisp. He wore his most charming mask.

"Ladies and gentlemen, friends and neighbors—I owe you all a sincere apology. You shouldn't be listening to me right now. You should be watching my wonderful wife, Marina, the heart and soul of this institution. You've done nothing to deserve the downgrade in the program, and I can only assure you I'll do my best to approximate her charms." He paused for a bubble of laughter. "As you know, this institution has been Marina's dear project for the last decade. But it's only thanks to you that it's grown from the valley's minor art museum to one of the premiere centers for the study and preservation of indigenous art and culture in the West. Last week, the guest book included names from California, New York, London—even China."

The speech continued, wrapping saccharine thanks in statistics of the museum's success, like the bacon-wrapped dates we'd had for an appetizer. After every thank-you, the guests applauded. Finally, Philip introduced the speaker, a professor from Mexico City. A thick gold bracelet cinched her bicep, offering a contrast to the staid wardrobes of the mostly white faces tipping up at her, listening, but also tapping their brûlées and stirring Splenda into coffee. She traced the story of the more valuable—*culturally rich*—pieces. Mostly things related to death: knives, spears, drums.

Philip had taken a seat behind her. The spotlight on the podium left him in shadow.

I touched Bryant's hand. "Where was he?"

"Not now," he whispered. "I should check in with Jim. I'll meet up with you later." He dropped his napkin on his seat, and a waiter swooped in and folded it into a pyramid.

"The knife handle depicts a coyote in the traditional pose, howling at the moon. Many cultures believe the coyote was present at the beginning of the world. The coyote is neither good nor evil, but simply wild."

Or beautiful, I thought, remembering Marina's words. The lean silhouette darting across the dusky backyard, furtive and starved. I ran my fork across the tablecloth, tracing random lines like the wake of a boat.

The woman was still speaking. "As important as preserving the pieces themselves—the clay, the fabric, or the ink—it's vital to preserve the stories the cultures told themselves to understand the world."

I finished off my wine and knew I'd had too much. I went to the restroom, unsteady in my unfamiliar shoes.

Golden lights bordered the mirrors and lit my skin with a healthy pink glow I suspected wasn't accurate. I reapplied my lipstick and listened to the gossip in the stalls.

"She's always been a cold fish. Do you remember when I sat next to her at the Clarks' Easter brunch? She didn't say a word to me."

"You know I had to make some calls just to get invited to this?"

"I bet she walked in on him."

"With someone younger."

"More flexible."

Cackles.

"Form a line, please," the attendant said. Women streamed into the lounge. The lecture must have finished. I stared in the mirror, surprised by the deep red tint I'd drawn on my lips.

In the ballroom, people milled around the empty tables. There was no sign of Philip. The perfume I'd touched to my wrists threw off a nauseating thick odor. I slipped out to the patio. A dance floor waited under strings of lights. The band had finished setting up, and the players were hanging around the bar, chatting up the bartenders I'd seen from Marina's window.

I sank into an uncomfortable wooden chair. The seat swayed like a raft.

The smell of smoke slipped into the air. A man ashed his cigarette into the fountain as he headed to the bar. He wore a loose white shirt with no jacket. Whatever he said to the bartenders made them giggle. Turning away, he held a highball in each hand and the cigarette clamped between his teeth. Sloshing booze with every step, he headed right for me.

It was the man who'd interrupted my conversation with the pushy woman. And, I squinted, who'd approached me by the Frowning Man.

"Give me a hand?" he said.

From politeness, I took the sweating glasses. He sat sideways in the chair next to mine, so his knees jutted toward me.

I passed him the drinks.

"Just one. I'm not greedy."

"No, thanks."

"Come on, keep me company." He shot a toothy grin, crunching on ice. "Nice party. They were giving away whole cases of Altoids in the bathroom." He held his glass out, admiring the heavy base. He lit another cigarette off an orange plastic Bic.

He seemed strangely familiar, but I couldn't place him. Maybe he was just a type I'd met too many of. His hair was combed back to add a couple inches of height to his face, and he'd stuck his orchid behind his ear. His shirt was baggy, a feat given that his shoulders were big enough to lift refrigerators. A gold chain glinted under his collar. His was definitely not among the names inscribed on Marina's satiny invitations. Probably he'd come as some woman's plus one, and she regretted her decision to bring him and abandoned him. He stood out like a tarantula on a dish of crème brûlée.

"So, what's a girl like you doing in a place like this?" He reclined, crossing his ankle over a knee, exposing an inch of skin fuzzed with blond hair. He wasn't wearing socks, and as he jiggled his foot I saw his shoes were golf shoes, spiked with cleats.

"I'm sorry?"

"I'm pretty sure you have to be geriatric to be in there. Or a trust fund kid."

"Which of those are you accusing me of?"

He drew from his cigarette and blew the smoke sideways. "So who are you, then?"

"I work for the Martins," I said. "Have we met before?"

He leaned until our foreheads were practically touching. "I'm single, if that's what you're wondering."

A flurry of activity kicked up on the bandstand, the players shrugging into their guitars and adjusting the knobs on amplifiers.

"So what's the nanny doing at the fancy party?"

Before I could reply, the musicians counted off into a song. The ballroom doors opened, and conversation and laughter preceded the guests onto the patio, like little dogs on leashes.

I took a gulp of the drink in my hand and winced at the medicinal sharpness. I should go find Bryant, or Philip, or a big glass of water. I was too dizzy to stand.

My companion was still smiling as if he hadn't noticed my inattention. "When does everyone get drunk and jump into the fountain?"

"Not in an election year."

The band's oldies tune wasn't ideal for dancing, but a tall man in shirttails escorted his partner out for a spin.

"So where are the big shots?"

"The Martins? Philip is here. You may have heard Marina had a family emergency."

He tapped me on the knee. "You can tell me the dirt—I don't care about politics like everyone else in here. Did she leave him?" He winked, jaws working over another ice cube.

I crossed my legs. "I don't know what you've heard, but it's not true."

"What about the little girl—the one you watch. Is she home snoozing?"

A vise tightened on my lungs. "Why do you ask that?" He only smiled. I stood, reeling dizzily, trying to spot a security guard in the press on the patio. "You shouldn't be here."

He gallantly took my elbow to steady me. "You really don't remember me, do you, Finn?"

I shook free and studied him again. His smirk tripped a wire in my brain, but it wasn't connected to a particular memory.

He docked my chin, infuriatingly possessive. "I'll save you. The Fourth of July party. We had a drink together. I'm Guy."

The guy named Guy. I scoured his face. Something was missing: a beard? No—glasses. He'd been wearing cheesy hipster frames. Without them, his eyes were narrow in his square face. Now I remembered that smirk, working his dimple. He'd had some line ready to go then, too.

"Were you even invited?" I wanted to jar loose his grin.

But it widened. "Nope. I came here to see you."

I backed away. Though I felt panicked, no one seemed to notice. I could hear whole lines of conversations, distinctive laughs, could tell which were fake and which real. And yet no one noticed Guy reaching for me.

He caught me, grabbing my shoulders and moving his face into mine as if we were intimate friends, drunk and sloppy together. I tried to stand up straight. Every time the string lights came into my field of view, the bulbs spread into dazzling yellow smears.

"Relax," he said. "I happen to know you through someone. Iris is my sister."

My heels wobbled. Guy didn't look anything like her. But their style was similar. The careful grooming meant to look good under bar lights. The flashy, inappropriate clothes. And especially the expression, satisfaction laced with bitterness.

"She's not here, is she?" I asked, afraid I'd turn and see her dancing with Paul Huff or whispering to Mrs. Feinhorn.

"Just me, I promise," he said.

"What do you want?"

He held up a palm. "I didn't come here to make a scene."

"Why are you following me?"

"Don't freak out. I've only seen you once before. It was my sister's idea to talk to you." He jerked his head at the crowd, his lip curled. "My idea is to stay away from these people. You see what they do to things they want? The art in there? Grabbed from Indians and put behind glass and turned into money and parties and bullshit?" He dropped his voice. "What do you think they do with the things they don't want?"

"Iris told me she didn't have anyone to talk to. She never mentioned a brother."

"She doesn't like what I have to tell her. Philip is dangerous."

"Did you come here to confront him?" I took his hand and pulled him onto the dance floor, where his voice would be muffled by the music.

"I'm here to confront you. Iris is hysterical. What are you promising her?"

"Promising? I told her she wouldn't get anything. Not a marriage proposal, not a father. It will ruin her life."

"There are laws. They've got a lot to lose." His gaze swept the patio.

"They might give her some money, but she won't get rich. They won't lose any of this." I kept my voice calm, but I was lying. The Martins could easily slip. Philip could lose his position as the assumed next senator, and another ambitious man—probably the religious one, Frank Grant—would snatch it.

"Did she leave him, though?" Guy said. "Marina? She must have taken the kid, or you'd be watching her."

"That's none of your business."

He wasn't used to dancing to old-fashioned music, and we swayed choppily, spinning too often. I felt sick.

"What's he like? Iris says you like him."

A loose laugh bleated from my mouth. "I could say the same for her!" People stared. I was making a spectacle of myself.

The band crescendoed to the end of a song, and the singer took a pull from a water bottle. The freshness of the night had been smothered. The heat of the patio came through the soles of Marina's shoes. Moving away from Guy, I reached down to adjust an ankle strap. The evening had become sleazy, the dance floor crowded with old men clinging to pretty girls. I thought I saw Bryant with a woman in black sequins, but it turned out to be a waiter, face fixed in a smile as the woman rubbed his shoulder.

A slow song started. Under the billow of his shirt, Guy's torso was warm. His hips slid forward, pressing into mine, and I stepped back, following his rhythm but avoiding his touch. He grinned mockingly and laced his fingers tighter around mine. His palms were calloused. "Will Marina pay Iris, do you think?"

"Pay her? Why would she?"

"Don't play dumb," he said. "They're in real shit. If this came out—"

I stopped, and the couple behind us collided with Guy.

"I thought you weren't threatening anyone? I'm done with this. Tell Iris, will you?" I pushed my way off the floor.

He caught up, snatched my wrist. "You're going to leave me all alone?"

"Sure. Don't break anything."

"That's him, isn't it?" Guy pulled me into him. In my heels, I was his height. Close enough to see the sweat at his hairline, the cracks on his lips, a knot of freckles on his nose. His body was tight against mine, his chest and arms and the hard clip of his belt. His cheek was rough. He hadn't known to shave before the party.

"What are you doing?"

He laughed and kissed me, slipping his tongue into my mouth. Juniper and smoke. For a moment my knees went hollow. Pulling away, I punched him swiftly in the ribs.

Philip stood a few feet away, talking to a woman with a gold cane. What he said made her laugh, and she turned to her friend to repeat it. Philip cut his eyes over to Guy and me, and I knew he'd seen.

Philip danced like he spoke, a teasing burst of energy and attention, then a gentle, disinterested waltz to the side of the floor, where he'd leave his partner. He did this with three or four women—in between greetings with men—before he stopped at the bar.

Guy and I didn't speak after the kiss. We returned to our seats like children awaiting punishment. I motioned for him to leave, but he shook his head. Took out a cigarette, filed it behind his ear, and finally pulled out his phone and busied himself.

When Philip came our way, Guy put on his signature smirk. "You must be Philip. Finn was just telling me about your lovely family."

Philip studied Guy as if scanning for weapons. With a wry smile, he shook his hand. "I don't believe we've met. I'm Philip Martin."

"This is Guy," I said. "We knew each other in college."

"I'm surprised you're still here, Finn," Philip said. "And impressed." He glanced pointedly at the glasses around our chairs.

"I've been wanting to talk to you," I said.

"You've had a long day." His gaze was steely. I knew how I looked, drunk, my hair uncoiling down my back, my ankles bending in my heels. "Should I find Bryant to take you home?"

"I'll take her," Guy said. "In fact, we haven't seen Bryant in a while. I guess we lost track of time." He stretched and gave Philip his empty glass. "Great to meet you. Best of luck to the museum and all."

"Finn, do you want to escort your friend out?" Philip said. He beckoned to a caterer and handed off Guy's glass, then walked away, a hand sunk deep into his pocket. The first group he passed drew him in, and he gave a boisterous guffaw nothing like his real laugh.

"Shall we?" Guy said. My purse dangled from his elbow.

I snatched it. "I'll walk you out, but only so I know you left."

"Again with the manners." He tutted.

The ballroom was abandoned. Lipstick-smeared glasses and stained napkins littered the tables. The caterers had gotten sloppy, paying more attention to each other than the guests. I felt a flash of irritation at Bryant for talking me into this only to abandon me the moment it began. This was preferable to my nagging worry that he'd seen me with Guy, and gone. The Senator had certainly left; he never stayed anywhere past ten.

Guests milled around the galleries, bleary under the lights, presumably sobering up before driving home. The energy had dissipated, burned away like scrap paper.

In the lobby, a solitary man sat against the wall, shoes kicked off, typing into his phone. His glasses shone in the blue light. Out the windows, the night was black.

"That didn't go very well for you, did it?" Guy said. "Though as an old friend of yours, I'm a little insulted at the brush-off from Phil."

The elevator doors opened. "Good night," I said.

"I think you should come with me. Iris wants to talk to you."

"Sorry to disappoint her."

Guy shrugged. His dimple cut his cheek. "She could come here instead."

I stepped into the elevator, pushed the button for the garage. The dark glass walls reflected my slouching outline. My hair wilted over my forehead.

In the parking lot, a valet trotted up, but I waved him away. "Where did you park?" I asked Guy.

"Let's take your car. You're in no shape to drive." He brushed my hair off my face.

"Don't." I flicked him away, my reflexes slow. My phone buzzed. Not Bryant. Iris.

Where ru guys?

"Come on," Guy said. "Let's get while it's good."

Guy reclined the driver's seat until he was practically lying down. Leaving the garage, he checked the rearview every two seconds.

"Expecting to be followed?" I asked.

For once he didn't have a smart answer. I remembered his whispered fear of Philip. Of what *these people* could do.

I hoped to see someone behind us. Philip, making sure I was all right. Bryant in his BMW, geared up to fight Guy. But no one followed, of course. Even as I'd walked past the guests I'd greeted at the start of the party, people who'd kissed me on the cheek or shaken my hand, no one had acknowledged me. Some of the men had glanced at my body, a quick assessing ogle, and turned blankly away. No one recognized me as the hostess I'd imagined myself to be, hours before.

16

On the road, Guy didn't stop moving. Now raking his hand through his hair, now drumming the wheel to some internal beat. At a red light, he lifted a hip and dug a cigarette from his pocket to hold, unlit, in his lips. If I were sixteen, I might have been intrigued by his bored bad-boy act, the careless grace of his movements, the angry twitch in his cheek.

I lowered my window and drank gulps of air like coffee.

We met Iris at a sake bar in downtown Scottsdale. The trendier the bar, the thinner the hostess, and ours had elbows sharp as knives. Diners with shiny hair and shiny clothes clustered around the high tables as though they were life rafts.

Iris waved us over. Her pleated dress flared around

her hips so I couldn't see her stomach. Eight weeks along now. When would it be too late to do anything? Twelve weeks? A topknot hovered over her face like a mushroom cloud.

She tilted her head at me in mock concern. "Feeling okay?"

I volleyed a fake smile back at her. "You didn't tell me you had a brother."

"How was the party? I hope he didn't ruin it for you." Guy punched her in the arm, and she hit him back. "Asshole."

A waitress appeared and set three porcelain shot glasses and three mugs of dark, foamy beer on the table.

"I don't want anything," I protested.

Guy dropped the shot into his beer and tipped it back in one long swallow, belching. Iris laughed at him and drank just as quickly. She wiped her mouth with the back of her hand, blurring her lipstick.

I pushed my mug away. "What do you want, Iris?"

She licked her teeth. "How is dear Philip? Since Marina left him, I mean."

"I didn't get to speak to him, thanks to your brother."

"Are you so sure he'd have confided in you? 'Oh, Finn, I need you,'" she moaned.

Guy smirked, standing stiff as a cardboard cutout.

"What do you want?" I said again.

"You have to talk to him for me."

Her intensity made me roll my eyes. "Talk to him yourself. Go over there tonight. Marina's gone. He's in love with you, remember? He'll be thrilled to see you."

Iris shook her head. "As if I'd go over there alone."

"What are you talking about? That's exactly what you've been waiting for."

Her artificial shock lifted her eyebrows a few inches. "He'll be so mad, Finn. I'd be crazy to be alone with him. Guy talked me out of it."

At this point I assumed everything she did was an act. Tired, I said, "Why did you tell Marina, then?"

Iris played with the pendant on her necklace, an elephant with red crystals for eyes. "I thought she'd help me."

I laughed, exasperated. "You're kidding."

She shook her head quickly. "It doesn't matter. Tell Philip he has to come see me, somewhere public. Tomorrow."

"He won't do it."

"If he doesn't, I'll publish the ultrasounds online. I'll tell everyone what he did."

"You have no idea what you're doing. You're going to ruin lives."

"How can you hate me and not him? It's his baby, too."

"Oh, shut up. You know you're going to get rid of it."

The words fell to the table. Guy whistled under his breath.

Iris curled her lip. "They told you to say that."

"Would you be surprised? No one's happy about it. Not even you. You're drinking, smoking. Why pretend? The longer you wait the worse it will be."

"Speaking from experience, Finn?" Her smile was sweet.

Guy upset the shot of sake into my beer, splashing the table. "Drink up."

I took a sip. The warm sake mixed with cold beer made me want to vomit. I pushed it away. "I'm leaving. Good luck with everything."

Iris grabbed my wrist, hard. "If I don't hear from you by Sunday night, I'm not going to keep it secret anymore."

I yanked away, jarring her off balance. She bit her lip, surprised. It might have been the first genuine reaction I'd ever seen from her.

"I won't see him before Sunday. You scared Marina away and she took Amabel, remember? I won't be going to work for a while."

She recovered her composure and sneered. "I know you'll think of something. You're probably even more desperate to talk to him now that he's seen you with Guy."

Guy had finished my drink and was tossing two of the shot glasses into the air, trying to juggle. He winked.

I drove myself home. It wasn't too far.

At my apartment I showered and braided my hair into a wet rope. Somehow it was after one. I felt a jet-lagged wakefulness and summoned an Uber.

Bryant's condo was frigid and dark. I tripped over his briefcase on my way to the stairs. As I stood it back up I felt his suitcase, too. He hadn't mentioned a trip.

I climbed the stairs, took off my jeans, and got into bed with him. After a moment, I could see by the green glow of his alarm clock. I held down the button; he'd set an alarm for four.

"Tell me you didn't drive here." His voice was clear.

"Good, you're awake," I said.

"Did you drive?"

"Of course not." I shifted over to lie beside him. He faced the wall. He was naked except for boxers. I traced his ribs.

He recoiled. "Your hair is soaked."

"I need to talk to you."

He didn't budge. "I have to get up early, Finn."

We lay in silence. His clock clicked, turning over a minute. He sighed. "Fine." He reached and switched on the nightstand lamp. Blinded, I put my hand over my eyes.

"I'm getting a glass of water," he said.

"No, stay." I opened my fingers to let the light spill in slowly.

"What is it, Finn?"

"I want to explain what happened at the gala." My voice was hoarse, as if I were still drunk. "I assume you saw me with Guy. Maybe you remember him? We met him at a party once."

Bryant didn't reply. His jawbone was tight as rope.

"You saw us together, right? That's why you left without saying anything."

"I have some manners. You were enjoying the party."

"Bryant—"

"Actually, I shouldn't have let you make a scene. The Martins don't need any more gossip."

"You're being harsh."

He pounded the mattress in a tight, angry gesture. "Come on, Finn. Don't pretend you don't know what I mean. You came with me and hooked up with some frat boy."

"I did not!"

"I have an early flight," he said.

"You don't trust me." I blinked back tears, furious.

"Not after you humiliated me in front of my boss. In front of our peers. No."

I'd been touching him, but now I drew back and hugged my knees to my chest. Guy hadn't gone to the party to talk to me. He'd gone to contaminate me.

Bryant glanced at the clock. "It's late. I'm exhausted. I have to be up in three hours. What is there to say?"

"It's not what you think," I said. "Guy has a sister. Iris."

"So?"

"Do you remember on the Fourth of July, when Amabel told me a woman was following her?"

"Not really."

I let that go. "Her name is Iris. She's been hanging around lately."

"What do you mean, hanging around?"

"She wants to talk to Philip. I guess they know each other. She told me—"

He snapped awake. "No, no, no. Stop."

His vehemence confused me. "I don't think you understand. It's a big deal. It could affect the election, the Senator."

Bryant's face—usually taut with interest, eager to

absorb any Martin anecdote I had to share—was serious and stern. "I don't want to know. Really. It's none of my business."

I was desperate to tell him, as if unloading onto him would take the pressure off me. "But we always—"

"No, Finn. Seriously." He shook his head tightly.

Perplexed, I sat back, chewing my lip. Bryant always wanted to know about the Martins, even small things. I wondered if the Senator had told him some part of the story, or warned him against talking with me.

The anxiety and guilt of the past week returned to me. Briefly, in the frenzy of the gala and the leering threat of Guy, I'd forgotten the reality of the afternoon. Packing Amabel's clothes. Marina grimly leaving Philip. Today was already Saturday. On Monday, what would I do? When would they be back? If only I'd talked to her about Iris, or to Philip, or even Bryant, earlier. Before she was packing her suitcase and driving away. I'd even washed her vodka glass at the sink, rinsed away her lipstick. As if I could make it so it never happened.

"You shouldn't get involved in the Martins' business," Bryant was saying.

"I didn't mean to," I said, defensive. "Iris brought me into it. I tried to warn Philip—" Seeing his expression, I wavered.

"Finn. The Martins are not your family. They're not your friends." He grabbed my foot and shook it. "Don't you see? These people are using you to get to them."

"I don't have a choice. If you heard her story, you'd know what I mean."

"I don't want to know. That's what you say. Sorry, I don't have access to their personal lives. When you saw her brother at the party, you should have called security to throw him out. Period."

"He would have made a scene. I was trying to keep him quiet."

"Come on, Finn. The Martins have lawyers on retainer. They don't need you to protect them."

His grip on my foot was too tight. I flexed, and he let go.

"I'm sorry. I thought you knew how to handle this kind of thing." Bryant got out of bed and stood in front of the balcony doors. From the back, he looked boyish, his hair pushed up from the pillow, boxers loose on narrow hips. "Philip will be mad, but he likes you." He scratched his scalp. "Here's what you do. First, stop contacting them. Iris and Guy. Never mention them again. Act like you never met them."

My drunken energy had evaporated. I wanted very badly to lie back and shut my eyes. "They'll find me."

"Call the police. Call me."

I imagined pulling out my cell phone and dialing Bryant. Iris would laugh. She wouldn't be put off.

"Finn?" Bryant said.

"What else?"

"Never mention any of it to the Martins. Don't even apologize for the guy at the party. Stay quiet for a while. Be unobtrusive. Polite."

"Marina's gone," I said. "It might be too late."

"She'll be back. Marina isn't going to let her marriage break up. Don't worry." He kissed the top of my head, then hugged me, pressing my face to his stomach. "I'm glad you told me. This could have gotten much worse." He brushed my hair back from my face. "I'm sorry I was angry. I didn't know what to think."

Through the thin cotton of his boxers, I felt him harden at the pressure of my chest. I kissed his belly button. He was so warm, alert, I felt like I was the one who'd been sleeping. I wet my lips and ignored my thirst. He rested his palm on the back of my neck and murmured to me. I wondered how Amabel had spent her day. Where she was sleeping. I wondered what Marina was doing. I wondered whether Philip was still awake, thinking about his mistress or his wife.

Bryant wound my hair around his fist and laughed.

After, I brushed my teeth and heard the TV come on. Sports shows always sounded the same to me, men's voices speaking over one another. I changed into Bryant's big Princeton shirt.

In bed, he reached for my hips and pulled me into him. I knew even though he was tired he wouldn't sleep until he could bring me off, too, so I slipped off the borrowed shirt. The cool air met my skin, and Bryant tucked me back into his warmth. His hand traveled across my stomach and his fingers curled into me, and for an instant I was back on the dance floor, kissing Guy. I closed my eyes and flipped through memories of sleeping with Bryant. In this bed dozens of times, dressed and undressed and somewhere in between; in his car at an empty park and a drive-in and once in the parking garage; at a hotel room in Tucson, leaning over the balcony railing in my dress while he stood behind me, an old man in a swimming cap traversing the pool below like a slow white manatee, gazing up bewildered at my sudden cry.

I succeeded. In minutes, Bryant's breathing slowed. For a long time I listened to the chatter on TV. I was thirsty but too lazy to move. Finally, I crawled out of bed and went down to the kitchen. The fridge was bare. I opened a bottle of orange Gatorade and hunted through the drawers until I found a packet of airline peanuts, digging into the oily bag and licking the salt from my fingers. I went upstairs and stood at the threshold of Bryant's room, watching him sleep in a curled shape, spooning no one. I felt sick with guilt, like I'd manipulated him. Except tonight I'd been honest. So why did I feel this way? Dirty and ashamed.

Eventually I slept. My dreams were terrible sharp fragments of the day, things I should have stopped or prevented: Marina leaving, Philip hanging up on me, Guy handing me a heavy glass. I wanted to do things differently, but they were fixed, unchangeable. I saw myself rinsing Marina's glass, setting the house right, curling my hair. My usual instinct to escape disaster by pretending it had never happened at all.

17

At noon, I sat on the Martins' front step and emptied my purse on the ground. I rummaged through wallet, phone, Band-Aids, crayons. On my shoulders, my hair hung heavy as a fur pelt; I impatiently scraped it into a ponytail.

My copy of the house key was gone.

I stood too quickly and saw black. My head ached so badly even my eye sockets hurt.

I rang the doorbell. Rang it again. I thought of Iris standing here last week, the house rising before her, mysterious and forbidden.

Philip opened the door. "Finn?" He peered behind me, to the driveway. "It's just you?"

"I forgot my keys."

He looked as hungover as I felt. His eyes were pink

and small in his face, as if they'd withdrawn to avoid light. His skin was dry and colorless. He wore a gold ASU shirt, deeply creased and tight across his chest, the devil mascot faded.

"You're letting the air out." I moved in past him and shut the door. He smelled like dust, and I realized his shirt was one Eva used for cleaning and kept folded in the laundry room. He must have grabbed it on the way to the door.

"I'm in the poolroom," he said, padding down the hall. "It's not so ungodly bright in there."

The room was as cool and dim as a bank vault. Wooden blinds sliced the sun to thin stripes. Where they fell across the Turkish carpet, they illuminated flashes of gold thread in the deep blue weave. A pool table stretched across the room like a bed, an overhead lamp spotlighting the plush wool. In the shadowed corner, a pair of leather chairs slouched. I followed the stink of bourbon to a broken glass in the sink.

"Have you been here all night?" I asked.

He grunted. "More or less."

The cue lay across the table amid scattered balls, mostly stripes. He'd been playing against himself. A bottle of beer sweated on the rail. I lifted it and dried the wood with my palm.

He took the bottle from me and tossed it into the garbage. "Want a drink?"

I declined and perched on the arm of a chair. "Have you heard from Marina?"

"You'll be the first to know." He went to the other side of the table. His movements were jerky, irritated. When he made his shot, the stripes scattered aimlessly. He vengefully ground chalk into his cue. "Grab me another beer, if you wouldn't mind."

The mini-fridge under the sink was well stocked. With my hands busy, I found I could talk. "I'm sorry about last night." I pried open the bottle. White smoke curled out. "I didn't want anything to do with Guy. He wouldn't leave me alone."

I glanced over my shoulder. He watched me coldly.

"Must be a common problem for you."

I laughed stiffly, as if he were teasing, and handed him the bottle. He tipped it back, silent, assessing the table. He leaned again and his shoulder shot forward. A ball sank into the pocket with a shudder.

I turned the bottle cap over, its teeth biting my palm. I wanted Philip to carry us along, as he always had. I wasn't used to being at odds with him, and I'd have preferred anger, an outright argument, over this chilly distance.

When I'd started working for the Martins, I'd been

enamored of Philip. Dressing for work, assessing myself in the mirror, I'd imagined how he'd see me. Driving to Ocotillo Heights, my car panting as I sped, I turned my music up and let the wind take my hair in its fist, because if he was there he'd find my wildness appealing.

He was rarely home when I came over, and when he was he didn't say much to me. But he watched me, I knew it. Then one morning, as I mixed pancake batter at the kitchen counter, he touched my shoulder. His fingertips grazed my collarbone as he lifted his hand away. I pushed the spoon against the bowl, the batter rippling. He poured a coffee and ducked onto the balcony. The sun nuzzled the folds of his shirt. Sipping, he gazed out at the brown and yellow valley. Maybe he saw the hidden flickers of green, as I did, undertones in the cacti's leather skin and the dusty palm leaves. I tapped my fingers to the faucet, wetting them, and flicked droplets at the frying pan. They sizzled and danced over the iron.

For a while, the flirtation, or whatever it was, continued. He touched the top of my head when I sat on the floor coloring with Ammy. Pressed the small of my back when we came to a doorway at the same time, cupped my hip to move me from a drawer. It felt at once rich with meaning and silly. Most days went by with nothing at all, but the anticipation was nearly as good.

Now, the bottle cap digging into my palm, the question—*Why her? Why Iris?*—wanted to blurt from my mouth.

Instead, I watched Philip reset the balls. I dug into the nearest pocket and brought up two solids, cool and clicking in my hand. He dragged the rack over the felt.

"You must have something to say, to bring you all the way out here with a hangover. And, I imagine, an angry boyfriend." He reached over and plucked the bottle cap from my hand, tossed it into the sink. "Why don't you sit?" He gestured to the low club chair.

I sank into it, the leather cool and springy against the bare backs of my legs. I'd worn a thin sundress, and now I felt conscious that I'd chosen it carefully, the flattering blue, the way it hugged my skin.

Instead of resuming his game, Philip leaned against the table and stretched his legs so his crossed ankles were just inches from my feet. I watched his face, tired and drawn and petulant around the mouth, but still golden, the noble nose, the athlete's grace. Still handsome, and more so because I felt I could slice through his courteous charm to the real Philip beneath, ironic, easygoing, obliging, hungry.

"I'm sorry about the party," I said. "I should have called you as soon as Marina left."

He passed me the bottle. "Your throat is dry."

The beer was sharp. I gulped it and covered my mouth with a palm, felt the kiss of carbonation.

"Tell me about Iris," he said. "That's what you want to talk about, isn't it?" He cocked his head and stared me down.

"I met her about a week ago," I said. "She said she used to work at the restaurant. I didn't recognize her. She's tall, skinny. Red hair."

He made an impatient jerk of his hand. "Go on, Finn. Who is she, what's the problem?"

"She's pregnant." I spoke in a rush.

His neck snapped back when I said it, and I thought he'd protest, but he only grunted, *Go on*.

Rows of metal studs dotted the chair arms; I ran my thumb over them. I told him Iris had said she was eight weeks along, that they were in love. I left out some details, like that she'd been at Amabel's school and the house.

"And what does she want from you?"

"She wanted me to persuade you to talk to her. I'd never have gone along with her, but I hoped I could talk her out of it. Having the baby, I mean."

"So you believe her?" His tone was light, as if he didn't care either way.

In my rush to get his forgiveness—for that's what I wanted, I realized, even though I'd thought I was angry with him—I'd blundered past this. I stared at his ankles, where the hair was thinned from dress socks. "Not at first. I thought she was lying. Just after money or attention."

"But you believe her now."

"She showed me an ultrasound." I dug the envelope from my purse.

He took it and turned to hold it under the light. His hands were still in spite of the hangover, in spite of the image he held.

"I'm sorry," I found myself saying. I shut my mouth.

He didn't reply. I wondered if he'd seen this hard proof before, or if he'd hoped Iris was lying. I wondered if he was remembering Amabel's ultrasound, the happier notice of life gathering itself. I wondered if he saw the white specks against the black as his duty, or an interloper to be wished away.

"I don't think it's too late," I said. "At first she seemed to believe you had a future together. But I saw her last night, and I got the feeling she'd get rid of it if you gave her a little money."

"And how does she look? Does she look pregnant?" He spat the last word.

"No."

"Still smoking every five minutes? Still going around half naked?" I could feel his contained anger, but I couldn't decipher his thoughts. He wasn't doing anything reasonable: denying everything, for instance, or crumpling up the ultrasound.

"Philip, she told me she was going to post this online if you don't talk to her. She said she'd tell the whole story—soon. She said she's tired of waiting."

"Come here." He pressed the ultrasound flat on the table. "What do you see?"

I instinctively wanted to avoid it, hide it in my purse. Focusing, I saw nothing, really. A froggish shape, perhaps a head.

"Where's the date? Where's her name?" He flicked it. "She can post this online all she wants. Some friend probably gave it to her."

I picked it up and sank back in the chair. He was right. The image was anonymous and flimsy, like a picture print from Walmart. Still, she carried it in her purse, a ticket into Philip's house, a pass to speak with me, Marina, anyone she wanted. Obviously it had some power.

Philip sat back against the table. "You aren't satisfied."

"I'm relieved." My skin was slick against the leather. "But then who is she? What does she want?"

"I never said she didn't know me. What did she tell you, that we met at my restaurant?"

I nodded.

"She wanted a job. She was young, but Vic liked her, so we gave her a chance."

I shivered. Goose bumps rose on my legs. I hugged my knees. "That's more or less what she said."

"She was refreshing to talk to at first. Like you. So one day we got a drink after work. No big deal.

"She had the idea to go to some club. We had a couple drinks, and I drove her home. The whole time we were in the car, she watched me. We got to her place, and she jumped on me. Stuck her tongue in my mouth. Next thing I know she opened my pants, pulled up her dress. I pushed her off. I was rougher than I meant to be." He rubbed the back of his head. "I would never tell this to anyone I didn't trust, Finn."

I nodded. The scene sounded unpleasantly realistic. I could imagine Iris's impulsive, dramatic gestures, her presumption of her power.

"She was mad as hell. She cussed me out and ran off. *I* was mad as hell. I had Vic fire her the next day.

"That's the whole story. I promise. I'm not saying I

was perfect. I should never have taken her out. Never should have had anything to do with her. But if she's pregnant, it's not from me."

"You could order a paternity test," I said.

He laughed bitterly. "That would imply I slept with her. All I can do is ignore it. You think I don't know everyone's whispering at work? That's been her angle all along. She calls me there. Won't leave a message, just tells them I'll know what it's about." He gestured to the ultrasound. "I'm surprised that never showed up in my break room."

"Why would she lie? Why would she track me down—and Marina?"

"Hell hath no fury," he quoted, sardonic. When I frowned, unconvinced, he scratched his chin, serious again. "Money, I'm sure. Unfortunately, it's not the first time someone has tried to extort us."

I was curious about that, and still not satisfied, but he leaned forward to take my hand.

"Finn," he said softly. "You know me. You know I'm telling the truth."

His touch was warm, like always.

He rubbed my palm. "I shouldn't have compared her to you. She's nothing like you." His thumb wandered up my wrist. "Will you tell Marina we need to talk? That she shouldn't stay away?"

The jolt of hurt was cold, like an egg cracked down my back. Of course he wanted his wife back, of course that's what his mind was on. I stared down at the rug. "I don't know where she is." My voice weak and bitter.

"She'll call you. She'll be tearing her hair out trying to watch Amabel. She's always needed you. We both have."

My back hurt from bending toward him. "I hope you're right."

"So you'll tell her?"

"If I talk to her. If she calls me. I don't know what she's thinking. What would you do, if you were her?"

"Let me worry about that." He helped me up and escorted me to the front door.

Stepping into the merciless afternoon light, we both squinted.

"Damnit," he said. "The caterers must have served cheap booze. I haven't had a hangover like this in years."

I was trying to dig my sunglasses from my purse, but they'd tangled in my key chain. I yanked them free, and they dropped to the driveway with a snap.

Philip stooped, clumsy. "Lens cracked. I'll have to buy you a new pair."

In fact, they had been a gift from the Martins last Christmas. Dolce & Gabbana.

Philip opened my car door, and I ducked in. Like crawling into a furnace. The metal clasp of the seat belt scalded my fingers. All at once, the heat, the headache pulsing in my forehead, my nausea and embarrassment, congealed into a physical anger directed purely at Iris. Her idiotic lie had ruined everything. I should be in the Martins' living room watching cartoons with Amabel while Philip and Marina recovered from the party.

Philip ducked into the window. "You'll call me if you hear from her?"

"Yes. Will you call me?"

"Sure." He reached out and shielded my eyes with a cupped hand. "You'll want to wear those shades anyway. Brutal out."

"I will."

"Take care, Finn." As he pulled his hand away, he brushed my hair, and it fell against my face like feathers.

After months, the shimmering energy of possibility became hard to sustain. I remembered the exact moment Philip and I changed course.

Amabel and I were in the pool. She was only three, and bobbing in her water wings. Philip came out the back door and made a running dive into the water, whooping. We hadn't known he was home, and the sudden large presence in our quiet afternoon was startling.

Once Philip surfaced, Ammy laughed. He dove under and lifted her in the air so she soared and fell with a splash.

"What do you think?" he asked her. "Should I boost Finn, too?"

"Yes!" she screamed.

He grinned. He looked so young right then, his shoulders bare and tan and his hair dark with water.

"No," I protested, but he'd already gone under.

He coasted underwater, his trunks a vivid green. He gripped my hips and kissed my stomach. The pressure of the air in his mouth bubbled into my skin. Then he lifted me, boosting us together out of the water. We fell backward with a slap. A splash washed over us, and Amabel's laughter was uncertain. It had probably looked violent.

"It's okay, sweetie," I said. "Your dad's just goofing around."

Philip went back to Amabel and tossed her again, and I swam across the pool. Underwater, I watched their legs, Amabel's kicking and uncertain, Philip's strong and still.

I surfaced and rested my elbows on the edge. Dust rose off the yard like steam.

"Finn!" At the other end of the pool, they were climbing out. "We're going for ice cream." Philip held Amabel's hand, walking slowly to match her pace.

It never happened again. The charged atmosphere between us gradually dissipated. We settled into an easy understanding. I was his ally, a relief from the demands of his family, his name. And in exchange, I got to know the real Philip, the one without his mask—flashes of the defiant younger brother, of the golden hero, of the man who'd loved someone like Tina.

I spent the rest of the day at Bryant's, watching movies and drinking water until the night before was reduced to an ache in my limbs. My nagging worry about Iris had quieted, and I felt clearheaded and cheerful, as if I'd just gotten over an illness.

It wasn't that I believed Philip entirely—he'd certainly downplayed the story. Maybe they'd danced at the club, or he'd touched her, concealing it as accidental in the crowded restaurant. But I did believe he'd recoiled at her insistence.

When Bryant called, I was tempted to gloat that I'd heard the real story from Philip, that I knew the family would be fine. Instead, when he asked what I'd done all day, I invented a trip to the gym, a nap.

"You should go out," he said. "Take advantage of the night off."

I hummed. Before I worked for the Martins, I'd hung out with other waitresses, or the suburban moms from the developer's office. Those ties, already tentative, easily slipped away when I began spending more time with Bryant. I had nothing in common with them anymore.

"I'm not in the mood," I said. "I'm not going to drink for a long time."

He laughed. "Poor baby. Listen, I've got to run to another meeting. Let's talk tomorrow."

I comforted myself with the fact that Bryant didn't have friends, either. Associates, yes, contacts, a social circle, but nothing intimate. Outside of me.

I took myself out to dinner at a fancy steak house in Scottsdale, popular with Bryant's crowd. I decided to eat at the bar, where someone might recognize me and stop and say hello. And if not, fine. I ordered a grilled salad and a glass of wine.

I speared a wedge of romaine and sliced it with a steak knife. The bartenders all looked like Guy, with varying hairstyles. I wondered if Iris had lied to him, too. If he knew she wasn't pregnant, he might tell her to drop it.

I glanced around the dining room, a flash of anxiety as if Iris might be there. The diners were mostly older couples in suits and flowered dresses, having dinner before a movie, as well as the inevitable tables of sunburned tourists, almost all men, still in the polos they'd worn golfing, their voices loud from drinking in the sun all day.

My phone buzzed.

Marina, the screen read. Marina calling. Slide to answer.

Though everyone else had expected this, I hadn't. I knew how she'd acted when she'd left. Her anger when I'd offered to watch Amabel.

I swiped the screen. "Marina?"

"Hello? Finn?" The voice on the line was nervous, sharp, fast. "Finn?"

"Marina?"

"Of course. Listen, are you available tonight? I need you. Hurry."

18

The Phoenix skyline was a cluster of bright lights that came to a disappointing apex in a row of tallish buildings, not skyscrapers made of stone, but featureless glass cubes reflecting the pretty lights back at themselves. Marina was hiding here, in a luxury hotel named for a letter of the alphabet, like a British spy.

When I was seventeen, I worked for the same hotel chain. The resort was on Reed Lake, a few hours from Chicago, and drew guests from the city like animals to a watering hole. They were rich, scribbling signatures on their bills without glancing at the amount owed. The men wore pressed chinos, shirts in sunny yellow or pure white. Their feet were bare in boat shoes. Mornings, they bought coffee in the shop off the lobby, read folded newspapers, skin throwing off the grassy smell of the hotel soap. The women walked in languid pairs to the spa or led children to the pool.

Afternoons, everyone went out on the water. On breaks, I walked down to the dock, hands plunged in the pockets of my khaki uniform, admiring the sleek motorboats bobbing at the pier, sides contoured like racehorses' flanks. Far off in the oblong oval of the lake, boats darted, slicing across the sparkling water and bouncing back through their own wakes. Sometimes a skier trailed on a rope, or kids on an inner tube, legs flailing in the chop.

At night, darkened with sunburn and hoarse from yelling through the spray, the guests gathered on the patio under strings of yellow lights and ate and drank more. They never tired or ran out of things to say.

Watching them, I felt awake, shimmering with energy. I coveted the impeccable polish of their veneer, their leisurely self-assurance.

My best friend, Erica Everett, lived in one of the grand old mansions on the lakefront. The Everetts had been visiting the resort for years, coming to dinner or for a round of tennis, usually motoring over in their vintage red speedboat and parking in the marina. The Everetts had gotten me the job, and liked to pop in at the front desk, Erica smirking at my white polo and pleated khakis, Mrs. Everett praising my work ethic.

After work, I walked over to their house. I often slept in the spare bedroom, with the toile wallpaper and ornate canopy bed that felt like my own. When I had to work first shift, I'd slip out early, before anyone was up, and walk the shore of the lake to the hotel, crossing the private beaches with my sandals in my hand, the calm early waves lapping over the tops of my feet. The feeling lingered even after I changed into my regulation closed-toed oxfords.

Tonight, I crossed the hotel lobby without slowing to take it in, as Natalie would have done. In the elevator up to Marina's room, I saw my reflection with a jolt of unrecognition. My hair was drawn back into a sculptural twist of wire, a style Mrs. Everett had worn.

I hadn't thought of the Everetts in a long time—not about those early, perfect days, at least. They were still as sharp as a film. The house, the family, their delight at my delight—*Natalie's never done this!* they'd exclaim. Tennis, sailing, waterskiing. Using a waffle iron. Eating lobster. Lounging in the sauna, Erica taught me to spit on the heating unit and make it hiss.

Shaking away the uncomfortable memories, I knocked at room 1715. The drone of a TV leaked into the hall.

Marina opened the door with a finger to her lips. A cloth headband held her hair off her forehead. Fully exposed, her face was pale and bony. She wasn't wearing makeup, and her features ran together, lips into skin, eyebrows hardly visible. She looked like her own ghost.

"Come in," she whispered. She crept back into the room, leaving me to close the door. She collapsed in an armchair and took up a glass of wine from the floor.

"Are you okay?" I asked.

She muted the TV. "Keep your voice down. She finally went to sleep."

The door to the bedroom was cracked open. I stuck my head through. Amabel was curled in one of two queen beds, breathing wetly, Patrick clamped to her neck.

When I turned to ask what had happened, Marina was absorbed in the Home Shopping Network, ignoring me.

I crossed the room to turn on a lamp, and the illuminated mess was startling. Empty glasses and wrappers littered every surface. Styrofoam packaging was strewn in a corner; wet towels trampled over the bathroom floor. The coffee table displayed the remains of dinner, a grilled cheese, one bite in each half, and fish that was starting to smell. I put the plates out in the hall and filled a glass with water in the kitchenette.

"Quiet!" Marina hissed. She waved the glass off. "Stop fussing." She pulled her legs under her, taking her slender feet in her hands.

I sat on the couch and was jabbed by a sword-shaped plastic toothpick. I rolled it in my palm. It was slick with grease.

On the muted TV, two women admired a gaudy gold necklace on a model's chest. Their witchy hands stroked the chain, and the model's chin clenched in a brave smile.

"I thought this would put her to sleep," Marina said. "Now I can't stop watching."

"We've been worried about you," I said.

"I hate when people speak in the collective," she muttered.

"Philip and me. The Senator. Your friends."

"Which friends?"

"The party guests."

"Philip went ahead with the gala?" She snorted. "I'd have expected him to be thrilled to get out of it."

Her sarcasm annoyed me. "Would you rather have canceled?"

"I suppose not." She pointed at the bottle on the floor. "Could you?"

I knelt to retrieve it, and she filled her glass messily. "What did you tell them?"

"That you'd gone to Florida to see your aunt."

A lazy laugh. "Who came up with that one? Jim?" She scratched her ankle. "Did he attend?"

"Of course," I said, surprised.

"He did," she murmured. "That was the least he could do."

I was taken aback—she'd never talked about the Senator in such a tone before—but she asked, casually, "How did it go?"

They talked about you, I imagined saying; *they laughed at you. If only you were nicer. If only you didn't have to be so perfect all the time.* She was drunk, distressed, and the perimeter between us had lowered. I might offer her advice.

"It went well," I said. "Big crowd. The food was good."

She blinked, seeming to remember that I wasn't a planned guest.

I looked away. On TV, a cubic zirconia replica of Elizabeth Taylor's wedding ring was selling for four payments of $39.99.

"Junk," Marina remarked.

I suddenly felt impatient with her wallowing. "I saw Philip this afternoon. He wants to talk to you."

She eyed my face, as if counting my pores. "Is that so? Did he tell you why I left?"

"Not exactly." I ran the toothpick along the seam of the couch cushion. "I heard a rumor . . . he was seeing someone. I assumed you'd heard it, too."

Her face gave nothing away.

"He told me what really happened. It's not as bad as it seems."

She laughed. "He's a liar."

"Give him a chance," I said.

"Oh, Finn." She sighed. "I won't get you on my side, will I?" She slumped back.

Too late, I noticed her real disappointment. She might have confided in me, but I'd shut her out.

"What happened earlier?" I said gently, trying to make up for it. "You sounded upset when you called. Is Amabel all right?"

"That depends on your definition. She's not hurt or deprived of anything. She is bratty, willful, and spoiled."

"I'm sorry. Kids have days."

Marina threw her head back. "That could be a yogic mantra. *Kids have days, kids have days.*" She released a deep, frustrated sigh, more of a growl. "You've no idea the time I've had."

After leaving the house, she realized she had nowhere to go. She couldn't go to a friend's; everyone knew about the party and would ask questions. Amabel limited her options. She was already whining.

Marina had felt absurd. The museum was just a few miles away. She could easily turn back. But the thought of facing everyone made her panic. Her heart was pounding, her palms sweating; she might have to pull over and be sick.

Soon it was rush hour, and traffic clogged around her. She took Amabel to an anonymous restaurant, the sort where ribs and burgers were the choices of entrée. Amabel refused to eat, then begged for ice cream, which made a mess. Marina couldn't hear herself think.

With no plan, she checked into the hotel. Told herself in the morning she'd decide what to do. But Amabel woke her at dawn for a day even worse than the one before. Marina did all she could. Took Amabel to the mall and bought her everything she wanted. They saw a movie and ate at the food court and petted the filthy puppies at the pet store. Back at the hotel, while Amabel was supposed to be napping, Marina took a shower. Amabel picked up the phone on the nightstand, called the front desk, and announced she'd run away from home. A manager came up, knocking with increased urgency until Marina answered the door, shampoo still in her hair. The manager was embarrassed, Marina humiliated. She retreated to the bathroom to splash water on her face. She counted to ten. When she put in her earrings one spun into the sink and vanished down the drain.

She called me from the hallway, hiding from Amabel as if she were the child.

Then, of course, Amabel fell asleep.

"You're going to say she was naughty because of the sudden change in plan. When I was a kid, we'd have loved this." She gestured at the hotel room, as if the plush sofa and textured wallpaper were the kinds of things kids went nuts for. Her eyes were red. She was wounded, not just irritated. "Why is she like this? What did I do wrong?"

"Maybe she picked up on your tension," I said carefully.

She laughed, her mouth turning down. "She was a great distraction from it." She ran a finger around the rim of her glass. "If you had any idea what I've been going through . . ." Her shoulders had folded inward like an umbrella.

"Talk to him," I said. "You can't stay here forever."

She nodded absently. "You're right."

I thought of Philip's hand in mine beside the pool table, the cozy intimacy I'd felt. Marina would enjoy the full warmth of his apology. I knew it, and I thought she knew it, too, and was putting on an act, making him suffer. She'd go to him when she was tired of being on her own, and make him grovel. So I didn't say anything comforting. I didn't tell her Philip had fallen apart in her absence, or the Senator was furious she'd left, or the party hadn't gone as well as it should have. I only sat and watched the TV, poking that greasy toothpick into my thigh.

A little white dog trotted onto the screen, dressed in a pink coat and booties. Pet raincoats, $19.99.

Marina flicked it off. "I can't handle any more absurdity." She rubbed her temples. "I've been having strange dreams. I'm in a classroom, drawing on an easel. There's a knock at the door. The teacher goes to open it. I can hear whispers from the hall, and all around me pencils keep scratching paper. There's no reason to be nervous, but I'm terrified. Then the teacher turns around and looks straight at me, and I know, I just know, something horrible has happened." She lifted her glass, but it was empty. "Why am I talking about this? I hadn't thought of it in years, until I dreamed of it."

I was staring at her, my mouth open. I closed it, my

teeth coming together with a click. She was talking about James, I thought, the moment she learned he was dead.

"You were only in high school?" I asked.

She didn't understand. "It was my college art class. It's not about the room, it's about the knock. The dread. I'm not describing it well. It's all falling apart."

She tipped the bottle over, but it was empty, too. She carefully caught a drip running down its side. "That was good wine." She touched the label. "It feels nice to talk like that. That wine is good. That TV was bad. The couch is gray."

"You should talk to him," I said, wanting to move on, feeling disloyal to Philip for listening to his wife's dream of his brother.

She shook her head. "I need Philip to listen to me."

Firmly, I said, "His side of the story is different from what you've heard."

With an effort, she opened her eyes and peered at me. Shut them again. "You don't know." The wine bottle slid off her lap.

I put it out in the hall with the plates. When I came back, she was breathing deeply. I shook her shoulder. "You should go to bed."

She roused herself. I went to the bathroom to give her a moment. Her solitary earring lay in the soap dish. A sapphire, large as my thumbnail.

I washed my hands to give myself something to do. When I came out, Marina was on the phone. "Drop the key at my room." Even drunk, she managed to sound aloof.

I gathered my purse, trying to be unobtrusive, already knowing she would regret our intimacy tonight.

She put the phone down. "I need you to help with Amabel tomorrow."

"Sure. Call me when you'd like me to come over."

"I'm treating you to a room. They're bringing up a key. Try to hop over before Amabel wakes up."

She cut off my thanks with a chopping gesture, then shut herself into the bathroom.

A bellman dropped off the key, and after he left I waited to say good night. There was a notepad by the phone, covered in pen sketches of a dog. Her coyote, I realized, the one in the backyard. She'd drawn him running, mostly, and once scratching his ear. The drawings were well executed. They made me pity her. She might have drawn them at night, sitting by the silent phone, focusing on the perspective of the cactus in the foreground and the mountains at the back, with no one to call and nothing to think about but Iris. Young, twitchy Iris, with her naked limbs, tacky clothing, candy smell: the opposite of herself in every way.

19

S unday morning was beautiful.

I woke freezing, tangled in starchy hotel sheets. I fumbled from bed and worked the air conditioner dial until the fan shuddered to a stop. The edges of the velvet curtains were curled and damp. I opened them, letting in milky early light. The sole hour of beauty the day offered before the heat set in. The grid of downtown streets and sidewalks was empty.

I dressed in my clothes from yesterday and went to get Amabel.

Marina was passed out on the couch, breathing loudly through her mouth. Amabel was groggy when I touched her shoulder, but within seconds, she was bouncing on the bed, asking about the party, if everyone had missed her, did I want to see her new toys. I got her dressed and left Marina a note.

"What's wrong with Mommy?" Amabel asked as I gently shut the door behind us. "She had her mouth like this." She flopped her tongue out.

"She's not feeling well. I heard you weren't very good yesterday."

She shrugged and took off running down the silent hallway, her footsteps heavy as hoofs.

I caught her as she spun for a second lap. "I've got a better idea."

The fitness center was empty. Amabel ran to the mirrored wall and struck a pose—hand on hip, the other held like a microphone to her mouth. She danced like someone three times her age, and I worried she watched too much TV, worried about the friends she had at school, worried nothing I could do would save her from the onslaught of growing up.

But then: "I'm hungry." Her gappy smile was pure kid.

A waiter in a crisp white shirt seated us on the patio, pulling out Amabel's chair, bringing crayons. She treated him with regal contempt. We ordered waffles that arrived on heavy white plates, soaked in puddles of strawberry syrup. The coffee came in a thin porcelain mug with a fat jar of cream that soured halfway through the meal. Little birds with hard brown beaks hopped across the patio, edging closer to our feet. Amabel cut a big wedge of waffle and let it fly in their direction. They scattered and reassembled cautiously to peck at it.

Amabel watched them, twisting in her seat. "How do animals live in the city?"

"Well, they have waffles for breakfast at the hotel. Then they fly up on the roof to sit in the sun. They swim in the fountain. And then it's time for bed."

She groaned appreciatively. "Finn, birds don't have bedtime."

"You're right."

She dropped another waffle square. "The babies get to sleep in a nest." She seemed jealous. I knew that afternoon she'd build a nest in her own bed, working her sheets to a tangle.

I ordered a coffee to go for Marina and picked up a newspaper at the gift shop. At the bottom corner of the front page, a photo of Gonzales led an article about his popular Twitter feed. Bryant would be annoyed. *Tweets aren't news,* he complained.

At our knock, Marina opened the door, releasing a fog of eucalyptus. She was scrubbed and pink. She wore her hair down, and it shone like polished wood.

Amabel barreled into her stomach to hug her, and Marina stiffened in irritation. She probably felt ill.

"You girls ready to hit the road?" Her voice was falsely chipper.

Amabel bounced around the room. "Can I ride with Finn?"

Marina shrugged her consent. She slid on sunglasses and marched out, leaving me to handle the logistics of Amabel and the bags. I'd expected her to act haughty for a while, to reassert her distance from me. I didn't mind. It was a beautiful day.

"Ocotillo Heights," announced Amabel as we pulled through the gates, pronouncing the name with an *l*. Bougainvillea grew wild over the road. Branches scraped my car, petals showering onto the roof. Giggling, Amabel stuck her arm out the window. The sun was cheerful as yellow cake.

Marina's taillights flashed at the final curve. The Senator's black car was pulled across the Martins' driveway. Marina rudely blared her horn. The driver backed precariously up the road, which climbed steeply for a few yards after the Martins' drive, and then petered out into an overgrown, dusty thicket. After Marina and I pulled in, the car eased back, like a gate shutting behind us.

"I wonder why your grandpa's here," I said.

Amabel blew a raspberry. "Can we play princesses?" She darted inside. Marina had already gone in.

I carried the suitcases into the laundry room and went through to the kitchen. On the island, a cutting board held slices of browning apple and an empty highball glass.

Voices carried into the kitchen. I crept down the hall. Sunlight streamed out the arched doorway of the living room. I hesitated outside, holding my breath.

"So it's true." Marina laughed, caustic. "You've known a month. And done nothing. Do you have any idea what I thought when she came to me? Do you have any idea what that felt like?"

"Please, let's not," Philip said. "I was protecting you. And Amabel."

"Spare me. You never thought of me. Of what this would mean for us."

"All I think about is you." To my surprise, he sounded as angry as Marina. "My entire life, everything I put myself through, is for you."

"That's what you tell yourself, isn't it? You never asked for this. As if you don't care, as if you're above it all."

Keeping my face close to the wall, I peered in. I could see half the room—the couch, the fireplace, the white canvas that had intrigued Iris. Marina perched on the couch, resisting the gravity of the feather cushions. Philip stood gripping the red womb chair, his back to me. His hair was wet and curling on his neck. His polo stretched over the broad muscles of his back.

He said, "You and Amabel can go away for a while. Take a few weeks. It will blow over."

"Go on vacation? Now? How would that look?" Marina's pale, hungover face was wounded and righteous.

They weren't facing each other. They addressed the empty space to my left, like actors on a stage. Eastern light poured through the huge windows behind them. Philip's silhouette was edged in light, Marina's face half shadowed and half illuminated, her hair gleaming like the surface of a swimming pool. Then I remembered the Senator was there, too. He must be standing on the other side of the room, by the bookshelves, out of my sight. I drew back, so I could hear but not see them. So I would not be seen.

"We'll pay her," Marina said. "She can't want much. She doesn't know anything about money."

"You're panicking. That's exactly what she wants. You're forgetting that she can't prove anything."

"The insinuation would be damaging enough," she said. "It could ruin us."

"She's bluffing. She's got nothing and she knows it."

"She has him, doesn't she? She heard it all from him in the first place."

My mouth was dry. I was waiting for Philip to say nothing had happened. Tell her the story that had comforted me: the harmless if stupid flirtation, Iris's aggression in the car. But already that story was fraying, like a shirt that looks good in the store and cheap in the daylight.

Marina, sensing weakness, became triumphant and condescending. "How many times did I tell you not to trust him? I never understood why you didn't cut ties with that loser, why you didn't—"

"He's my oldest friend!" Philip's voice rang clear now, but the snarl in it stunned me. "Not that that's worth anything to you. Clint won't say a word, I promise you."

There was a muffled thud from the corner of the room. Something dropped. I put my face to the door again.

"Wait a minute," a gravel voice said. "Just wait, now." It took me a moment to recognize it as the Senator's.

Marina half stood, but he protested, "No, don't get up."

He crossed the room, coming into my view. His sunburned scalp glared red over clouded features. He sank stiffly onto the couch beside Marina and drew a handkerchief from his pocket and pressed it to his forehead.

Marina watched him, concern tightening her lips. Oddly, she looked guilty.

The Senator's hand traveled to his lapel, reflexively straightening his flag pin. He cleared his throat. "You're acting like children." His voice was bitingly sharp. "It's bad enough that you lied to me. I can't stand this bickering."

"It's none of your business," Philip said, unmoved.

The Senator's tongue flashed across his lips. "Marina and I disagree with you. In fact, when the girl approached her, she called me immediately. I regret how badly I reacted at the time. I was in shock." He patted Marina's knee, and she stared at her feet. "Now it's time for us to come together and deal with this."

Philip didn't seem surprised by his wife's betrayal. He kicked a leg back and dug his toes into the carpet.

Marina leaned toward the Senator hungrily. "We'll pay her. Jim, don't you agree?"

"If we pay her, she'll never leave us alone." Philip spoke without intonation, knowing she wasn't listening.

The Senator didn't acknowledge either of them. His head was tilted thoughtfully. He inhaled deeply, ready to speak. I thought he might rise and pace to the windows, address them in his bombastic way as if from a stage. But he stayed seated, hands braced against his knees.

"You made a horrible mistake. And with such duplicity. I cannot imagine what you were thinking. It's inexcusable. I've learned more about this girl, where she comes from. And the things I've learned have turned my stomach."

Philip groaned, mutinous.

The Senator pointed at his son. "The fact of the matter is, we share a name. Therefore, in every way that matters, we share a future. You'll remember I told you much the same after your shameful car accident."

Philip let out an indignant cry and began to defend himself, or blast his father, I couldn't quite hear because Marina joined in, exhorting the Senator to side with her. The Senator sat with his head bowed, absorbing their words like blows, but his lips worked as though he had a pebble in his mouth, and I thought that he was holding in something very harsh, but wouldn't contain it for long.

I stepped away.

Fresh flowers bloomed in the foyer. Peonies again. I thought of Iris crushing the petals. *Are these real?*

If the story Philip told me was true, there would be nothing to pay off, nothing to anger the Senator so deeply. So Iris's version must be true. Pregnant. And the Martin name at stake.

I ran up the stairs. I wanted to see Amabel. I craved her face, her bossy voice, her simple goodness.

I knocked as I swung her bedroom door open. "You locking me out?"

The room smelled of pollen. The curtain blew out from the window and heat flooded in. Patrick the stuffed dog was splayed on the floor. The dresser drawers were pulled open, clothes trampled on the carpet. The bathroom door was closed. I called to her, "Do you need help?"

No answer.

I brushed Patrick off and tossed him on a chair. I went into the bathroom. She wasn't there. The pressure of the open window must have pulled the door shut.

I passed through the bathroom, stepping over the little wooden stool at the sink, into the playroom. Amabel wasn't there, either. The block castle we'd painstakingly built was toppled over, one skinny tower standing in the rubble. I called out to her again.

Silence.

I thought she was hiding. She often hid from me, giggling as I scratched my head and searched under pillows and inside shoes. She was mad at me for ignoring her—hadn't she asked me to play when we got home?

I checked Philip and Marina's bedroom. Unsupervised, she'd sneak to this forbidden place. But she wasn't hiding under the bed, or in the tub, or in the closet behind Marina's gowns.

She wasn't in the guest room, pulling feathers from the leaky duvet or curled in the wicker chair suspended from the ceiling by a chain.

"I give up!" I called.

Silence.

I ran down the stairs. I was anxious, but impatient. I still thought she was playing a game. There were a thousand places to hide in the Martins' house.

She wasn't in the poolroom. Not under the dining table, not in the pantry. I went out to the garage. Amabel liked to sit in Philip's car, fingers curled around the steering wheel, mouth revving a froth of spit. Or she'd ride her scooter down the street, leg pedaling furiously, wheels rasping. But the scooter was propped against the wall. The Senator's car still blocked the driveway.

She wasn't in the side yard, scraping her shins trying to climb the citrus trees.

These were her favorite places, but now I was furious I'd checked them first.

I was running across the sharp dry grass. I screamed, "Amabel!" and the shrill note scraped my throat.

She'd never gone to the pool by herself, ever. She didn't even like the water. Hated getting her hair, her face, wet. But I ran.

Grabbed the gate. It swung open. It wasn't locked.

Amabel's flip-flops were on the patio.

Her inflatable shark floated in the pool. Purple and pink striped, black plastic handles on the back; she liked to sit on it and kick her legs to paddle. I could picture her there, turning to me and waving. But now it drifted, riderless.

I couldn't see her at first. Then I did. She was in the water, behind the shark.

I meant to dive in but I must have been running because I hit the water with my legs bent. My kneecaps collided with my chest. I kicked, half swimming, half walking, too slow. My clothes dragged on my body. Amabel's face was in the water. I eased her over. She seemed to flinch when the sun hit her.

"It's okay," I told her. "It's okay."

I managed to lift her onto the patio. I leaned over her. Her face was blue. A trick of the light, surely.

"Amabel." I shook her shoulders. I waited for her to open her eyes, cough, spit up water. Nothing happened. I held my hand over her mouth. I couldn't feel breath.

The day kept running, artificially, like a film. I felt like I was in poured wax, moving slowly. Only my pulse was racing.

I shouted for help. What came out was, "Ammy! Amabel!"

I'd learned CPR, but confronted with her familiar face and delicate frame, I was afraid. I pressed into her chest, and her rib cage felt breakable. I blew into her mouth. Her lips were stiff, her nose slimy, her little round chin hard as bone.

Distantly I heard a door slam. A single, clear yell that echoed.

I counted. I remembered the importance of counting. I sobbed, shoved my fist against my teeth. *Shut up!* I had to count, to breathe into her.

The gate clanged, and they were there. Shadows over us. A confusion of voices.

Marina grabbed my arm. "You're hurting her!"

Any minute, Amabel would cough and push me away. *Stop it,* she'd say for herself.

The Senator's voice was too loud. He was giving someone directions. Philip stood at the periphery of my vision, saying, "Wait, wait!" to no one in particular.

My breath couldn't get into her. It was like blowing into a balloon that wouldn't inflate. I had plenty of air, too much, I was breathing like a marathoner. The sting of chlorine was in my nose, my mouth.

Marina was talking to Amabel, imploring, threatening. *What's wrong, what happened, get up.*

The Senator put his arm around her. "I've called an ambulance. They'll be here soon. Try to stay calm."

Amabel's swimming suit bottoms were inside out, the flounce of the skirt crumpled under the waistband. Her body jerked stubbornly, resisting air.

Once more I lifted my palms to her bird's chest.

"That's enough, I think," the Senator said.

There was a long silence. The day trickled in. Chirping sparrows. The shark rasping against the walls of the pool.

I brought a hand to my face. The sting wasn't chlorine but salt. Philip lifted me by the armpits like a child. I clung to him, my face pressed into his shirt, soaking the fabric.

Marina let out a hiss.

Philip pushed me away, gently. He hadn't hugged me back. He reached for Marina, but she turned away.

"Where were you?" She slapped me. Her ring scratched my cheek, a sharp diamond slash. "Where were you!"

Philip pulled her into him, murmuring quietly. They stepped away from me, arms around each other in a slow dance.

I sank to the deck beside Amabel. My hands hovered over her, forming a mute wriggling sign language. Gently, I squeezed the water from her hair. I remembered the box of cornstarch, rubbing it into her slippery, beautiful hair, the comedy of age on her baby face. Powder drifted over the kitchen floor, and we'd glided through it, taking running starts, Amabel's laughter maniacal.

The air filled with a shrieking sound. Marina's kettle. Amabel's fever. The dog pinned to her neck in the hotel bed. Her fist a microphone as she danced. A giant splash as Philip boosted her from the water. *I'm a mermaid.*

The noise got louder and louder. Sirens.

The gate slamming, radios crackling, shouting. The patio filled with people. I was pushed aside. Amabel was on a stretcher, tiny. A plastic cup over her mouth, cutting into her delicate skin. The Martins staggering behind, Marina's arm around the warm equator of Philip's stomach.

Somehow I was on the driveway watching the ambulance pull away.

A crowd of uniformed men stood about, aimless but alert. Two policemen seemed to be in charge. They talked with a fireman at the foot of the driveway.

The Senator went down to meet them, his head bowed. He looked as he did when taking the podium for a difficult speech. Solemn, weary, calm.

The men nodded deferentially at the Senator. They gathered in a triangle, conferring.

One of the cops had been nudged out. He noticed me standing alone. "Miss? Are you all right?"

I felt a surge of tears. I was still wet and shivering. I crossed my arms.

The Senator withdrew from his conversation and joined us.

"Are you the victim's sister?" the cop was saying.

The Senator put his arm around me. I felt protected and passive, like a doll to be handled. "Finn is a friend of the family. She was visiting today."

"Did you find the victim?"

"She dove into the pool," the Senator said. "She administered CPR until the paramedics arrived. She might have saved the girl's life."

The police officer tilted his head. "Are you able to confirm that for me, miss?"

The Senator's hand squeezed my shoulder, as if encouragingly. I whispered a yes.

In the cop's sunglasses, my hair was in snakes, my shirt clinging to my skin.

"Was anyone supervising the child?"

The Senator said, "She was supposed to be napping. She was an obedient girl. We never thought she'd wander."

"Is there a gate around the pool?"

"Of course." The Senator pinched the crook of his nose. "It's always locked. I'll show you. First, I'd like to send Finn home. She's had a shock."

"Sir—"

The Senator held up a hand. "I'll answer all your questions in time. If you need Finn, you can speak to her later. Please. We're all stunned here. I'd like to get to the hospital myself."

He put his hand on my back, lightly, and guided me to his car.

"It's too late," I blurted. My teeth were chattering. "Do they know that?"

The Senator sighed. "They have remarkable technology now. It's just a matter of getting there in time."

"But what if we waited too long?" My voice jumped at the end, a teary hiccup.

The Senator slowed. He took both my shoulders in his hands and bent so his famous face was inches from mine, enormous and craggy, its features distorted by the closeness. Capillaries threaded his nose. He was old, but far from frail; he looked cold and hard, like ancient rock. His grayish tongue wetted his lips before he spoke.

"I don't want you to think too much about this. There's nothing anyone can do now. Do you understand?"

I didn't. It was like the platitudes trotted out at a funeral—*she's in a better place now, she'll be young forever*—but spoken insistently, like an instruction.

"Accidents happen," he whispered. "We believe we're in control, but accidents do happen. That's what this was. It doesn't have anything to do with you. All right?"

I nodded.

"Good." He gave my arm another squeeze, and headed back to the house.

His driver materialized behind me. He wrapped a blanket around my shoulders and opened the car door. I stared after the Senator. He was stooped with exhaustion. Then he wiped his palm on his pants with a disgusted gesture. He must have gotten wet, touching me.

The driver cleared his throat, and I ducked into the car.

"Where did they take Amabel?" I asked.

"I don't know."

He didn't ask where I lived. He drove like a robot, quickly and precisely. It was too quiet. I couldn't even hear the hum of tires on the road. Cold air streamed from the vents. I sat cross-legged under the blanket. My feet were bare; my shoes must have fallen off in the pool.

We passed familiar fields, stucco strip malls, parking lots. People were everywhere, carrying shopping bags and talking on their phones. The tinted windows turned the sky a deep blue, as if it were beautiful.

The driver took me to Bryant's. Without speaking we rode up in the elevator. He had a key. The condo was empty and quiet. He followed me inside, filled a glass of water at the sink. Wrapped my fingers around it.

"Do you need a sleeping pill?"

I shook my head.

"You should." He'd removed his sunglasses. His eyes were small for his wide face.

I'd never really looked at him before. He'd probably gotten this job out of the military. His huge arms dangled away from his sides. He must wear a gun, though he hid it well. When we'd come in, he'd glanced rapidly around Bryant's great room, from the ceiling to the floor. Now his gaze was fixed on me.

I shrank away.

"Sleep is the best medicine." He took a silver case from his jacket pocket. Two blue pills the size of almonds clattered onto the counter. He watched as I swallowed one.

"Go on and sit." He tossed a throw pillow to the end of the couch.

I awkwardly lay down, balling myself up. I was wet and cold. I sensed the loom of the driver, but I lost the energy to worry. My eyes dropped, flung open, dropped. I fell and jerked up like I was going to fall into the pool. I thought I might vomit. My eyelids were too heavy. I couldn't move.

I heard the click of the door shutting.

I slept.

20

I woke feeling soggy. Someone was hammering on the door.

When I sat, my head throbbed. Dampness lingered at the small of my back, the nape of my neck.

Amabel had drowned.

I pushed the thought down and it bobbed up again, like an ice cube in a glass.

The knocking increased in tempo.

Marina stood at the door looking just as she had the day I met her. Clean and fresh in white linen, impossibly crisp. Tortoiseshell sunglasses, red lipstick, thin strips of gold dangling from her ears. Serene as a woman in an advertisement.

I thought: The doctors saved her! Of course. They'd

never let Amabel Martin die. Gasping, I reached for Marina's arm.

She leaned away. My purse dangled from her hand, and she held a manila envelope tucked under her arm.

"I woke you." Her voice was cool and flat. "Why don't you go freshen up?" She stepped inside and shut the door with a hushed click. "Go. I'll wait."

Sleep still dragged on me; I stumbled down the hall. In the powder room, I blinked at the papery face in the mirror. Bloodshot eyes, white flecks gathered at the corners of my lips. On my cheek, an angry pink puffiness rose where Marina's ring had scraped me. I splashed my face with cold water, swirling a palmful in my mouth. I pushed the damp tangles of hair back from my forehead. Never, I'd never leave Ammy alone again, not for a minute. I hurried back out.

Marina stood staring at the floor, still wearing her sunglasses.

"Are you all back from the hospital?" I asked.

Marina paused, as if someone might whisper the answer to her. Slowly, she set my purse on the bench. She pulled off her sunglasses and folded them in her hand.

When I saw her eyes, my hope evaporated. They were glossy, wide, restless. The eyes of a nervous horse. They roved the hallway, staring everywhere but at me.

I sank onto the bench. "They didn't save her."

She shook no tersely, a micro-motion, as if holding something balanced on her head. Her eyes swept my face and looked away, took in Bryant's cavernous living room. His ice machine clunked.

My fingers found the cut on my face and dug.

"I drove your car over." Marina cleared her throat. "The keys are in your bag. And your phone. I'm afraid it's broken. It fell in the pool."

My purse slumped beside me. Was Marina really apologizing for my phone? I heard myself murmur, "It must have been in my pocket." I swallowed the rest of the sentence . . . *when I jumped in.* The morning sun glittered off the subtle metallic wallpaper, and my eyes winced shut. But then it felt like my body was underwater, bobbing; ill, I opened my eyes and leaned forward.

"Finn?" Marina touched my shoulder. "Finn? You need to eat something. Those pills aren't good on an empty stomach."

I squinted up at her. "I only took one." There was something in her expression, her jaw; she was anxious, but I couldn't think why. The worst had happened. She should be despondent, or angry, furious, with me. "I'm so sorry," I said. "I was watching her. I always watched her."

She drew back, stiffening, and I braced myself—like yesterday, like her cry, her slap. *Where were you!* Instead, she took a breath, a deliberate, yogic inhale. Without meeting my eyes, she said, "That's not a road we want to travel." Again, her voice was calm. She sounded polished and impersonal, as if I were being laid off from a faceless corporation. Smoothly, she drew the envelope from under her elbow and held it out to me.

It was light, full of paper. "What is this?"

"Something for you. For your time with us."

My thoughts were delayed, meaning arriving long after speech, like an echo. "No. I don't want anything. I'm so sorry." I fumbled. The envelope dropped to the floor.

Marina inclined as if to pick it up, but instead laced her fingers together. "It will be better for everyone if we consider this chapter closed."

"What about the funeral?"

"There will be a small private gathering for Amabel. It will be easier that way. Trust me. It's for the best."

Already she was turning away, sliding her glasses on. Opening the door and shutting it behind her, gently.

For a long time I sat there. The sun played over the oyster-colored walls, the glinting textured wallpaper that so maddeningly reflected the light. I welcomed the pain in my eyeballs, the throbbing headache and thirst, tracking the layers of discomfort with grim satisfaction. Deserved, all of them.

Eventually I dug my phone from the bag. The plastic screen guard was puckered. The screen was crushed, a starburst that splintered my reflection. I never carried it in my pockets. It would have been in my purse, in the laundry room closet. Maybe I'd been carrying it and forgot, in the chaos. I didn't care. I dropped it into the bag.

I showered, a hundred gallons of steaming water pounding down my back. The waste of it was satisfyingly ugly. I dressed in Bryant's gym clothes. Gathered my damp things and buried them in the garbage, then scrubbed my hands.

I sat on the couch with the envelope, hopeful and afraid. Mementos of Amabel, maybe the drawings she'd made of our princess story. I eased the flap open, careful not to tear it.

Cash. I shook it out on the coffee table. Hundred-dollar bills, crisp and green. I sorted them into stacks of ten and made ten stacks total. I counted again. I hadn't made a mistake. Hands shaking, I stuffed the money back in the envelope. I'd never seen so much cash, not a fraction of it.

The bills were new, fresh, as if they'd gone to the bank that very morning. It was that important to them, the day after Amabel died, to give me money, to tell me they didn't want to see me again.

21

The imprint of the booster seat etched into the upholstery. A ghostly outline of the garage door opener on my visor. The tiny sunglasses in the glove compartment.

Amabel was everywhere.

My brain kept tripping over this new reality. It was not possible that what had happened had happened.

I pulled into a gas station. I expected everyone to stare, loss stamped on my face. No one noticed. I bought a cup of greasy coffee. Rotated a rack of sunglasses, tried on a few pairs, checked my reflection in the mirror. All ugly. I felt hideous for caring. I grabbed a random pair and paid with my credit card. Then I dropped into a mobile store and bought the cheapest phone, $200.

In less than an hour, I'd spent a quarter of what was in my bank account.

At home, I stashed the Martins' cash in my freezer, propped against a bottle of vodka. I lay in bed. I felt desperately lonely, clutching my empty, silent phone. I tried to compose a text to Bryant, but everything I typed out seemed pitiful, or false. Have you heard, where are you, please let me explain—

I erased them all. Obviously, he'd heard what happened. Hated me.

I should have gone straight to the pool when I'd found her room empty. It was the most dangerous place, I should have ruled it out before I checked anywhere else. I should have called for help right away.

I shouldn't have been listening to the Martins at all. Bryant was right, I should have kept out of their business.

When he finally called at noon I didn't dare answer.

I ran. Out of my apartment, down the ugly side streets, the sidewalks all to myself. The businesses in this area never got busy. A dollar store, money-wiring office, a self-operated car wash where looped black hoses dripped dirty water on the ground. After a mile, the streets gradually improved. Here was a McDonald's; after another four blocks, a Starbucks (though only a drive-through kiosk). I turned east, where a flat city park cleared a view of the Martins' mountain. The layer of smog over the valley obscured the base so it seemed to hover like a cloud.

I was soaked in sweat. I put my hands on my knees and gasped. A bee crawled across the curb inches from my sneakers. Its body was half crushed; I considered stepping on it, putting it out of its misery. I couldn't. I turned back.

At home, I had five missed calls from Bryant.

I showered again before I called him back. He answered immediately.

"Finn? Thank God. What happened to you?"

"You didn't hear?"

"Of course I heard. I've been calling and calling. Are you okay?"

I laughed. "No. I'm really not."

"I can't believe it. It's shocking. I don't understand how it happened."

"It was an accident," I said, disgusted by my lie.

"That's what Jim said."

I gathered my hair into my fist and tugged it. "Yes. He was there." He'd have told Bryant, I thought; told him how I'd failed.

"Hold on." The phone was muffled, but I heard voices. "Sorry," he said. "Finn?"

"When are you coming back?" I said.

"Well . . ." His voice was on tiptoes. "I got back this morning."

"What? I was at your place—you weren't."

"We're in emergency mode. I need to be here for Jim."

"Oh," I said.

"Don't sound like that."

"Like what?" I had my ear close to the phone. He sounded guilty, evasive. But I was the one who should be guilty. A bitter taste rose in my mouth. I dug in my purse for a mint and found a watermelon sucker, Ammy's favorite.

"Trust me, I know how it sounds. But things are up in the air right now. I just need to be here."

"Up in the air?"

"I don't want to discuss it on the phone."

We were silent a moment. I nibbled the ridge around the candy.

"I miss you." I hated the neediness in my voice. I didn't deserve comfort.

"I know," he said. "I hate the idea of you being alone."

I warmed, expecting him to promise he'd be over soon. But instead he said, "Why don't you fly home? Stay with your family for a while."

I bit down, and the candy cracked into shards. "Home?"

"Sure. You could use a change of scenery. Some time with family. Don't you think?"

"I don't know."

"I'd pay for your ticket, if you're worried about money."

"I want to be here." My voice was flat. I didn't have the energy to make up an excuse. It was all I could do not to snap: *no, never.*

I could hear Bryant breathing. I imagined him, suited and tied, in his sleek office, colleagues rushing in and out, the TV muted on his wall, its screen split into four to show several news channels at once.

His phone clicked with another call. "We'll talk about this later. I'll be over as soon as I can. Okay? I'll call you later."

"Wait. When did you find out?"

The clicking on the other line died. "What do you mean?"

"It's been a whole day, and we're just talking now." Saying it, I was sickened. It had been almost exactly twenty-four hours. This time yesterday, I'd been leaning against the living room door, or maybe heading up the stairs, moving so slowly, in the wrong direction. I brought my knuckles to my teeth.

Bryant was saying, "I knew you were sleeping at my place. I knew you were safe."

I pictured him stepping out of a conference room to take a call, his head bowed, his mind whirring, calculated, animated. He'd have been pleased to know I was safely asleep. Drugged, so I could rest.

"Call me anytime you need. I'll see you very soon. Tonight."

I wondered if he thought I couldn't hear his other calls. I tried to imagine the conversations he was having about Amabel. In terms of the campaign, the public image, the polls and the voters and the press. I wondered if he'd had a moment to think of Amabel. I wondered if any of them had.

"We're devastated. This loss is a tragedy. Our family is holding a private celebration of Amabel's life this week. We're truly touched by the outpouring of sympathy and love from our friends and neighbors. Please keep us in your prayers." The Senator held up a flat hand to stave off the roar of questions. Aides hustled him away.

Cut to news anchors, grave faces. "Senator Martin is canceling all appearances this week. No word on whether he's planning to suspend his campaign for reelection."

"What a tragedy, Kathy," the male anchor said. "If it can happen to the Martins it could happen to anybody."

She clucked sympathetically. "Our own Martha Michaels is on after the break with tips on keeping children safe around the pool."

The pool gate wasn't fancy. Wrought iron, about four feet high, bars woven in a diamond pattern, too small for a child to slip through. Blunt spikes ran along the top. When the gate was shut, a lock automatically snapped into place. To open it, you had to reach over the gate and down, maneuver a hinge. It was awkward, even for an adult. Ammy couldn't have opened it.

The clip of the Senator played again and again. The *Arizona Republic*'s website featured the awful headline. They showed a photo of Marina and Philip in a white hospital hallway, shielded by two Snoops. Marina stared at the floor, expressionless; Philip's mouth was open, face slack.

Philip and Marina didn't appear on TV. They made no statement.

Talking heads argued about what it might mean for the Martins. Might there be charges of neglect, endangerment? Thankfully, the conclusion was no; Sam

Klein, a lawyer who'd attended the gala, shut down legal ramifications, smoothly rattling off a series of bulletproof adjectives: "unthinkable, only in the most extreme and egregious case." Hearing them, I cringed; it had been egregious, it had been unthinkable. And my fault, not the Martins'. If they knew the nanny had been there, would they bring charges?

The Senator would hate that. A court case, the details of the family's life dredged up. No wonder he'd left me out of it, hustled me away.

Reporters got their hands on pictures of Amabel. Their favorite showed her with the Senator on the Fourth of July. His hand on her shoulder, her face paint echoing his flag pin. Jim wore a hundred-watt smile, and Ammy's lips curled dutifully, but her eyes slanted away, toward where I'd stood. I remembered the moment exactly—the crunch of dry grass underfoot, the weight of the water bottle in my hand. I could have told Marina about the redhead following Amabel right then. Saved her.

Four o'clock, five o'clock, six o'clock news. Helicopters circled the house, flying so low their cameras picked up the border of blue tiles around the pool. Caution tape sealed the gate.

Out front, reporters clutched microphones, their voices a strained mix of excitement and solemnity. Two

Snoops stood at the head of the driveway, guarding the house. Against the chatter, they were professionally blank.

The Martins were trapped inside. Avoiding the windows. Philip would be in the poolroom, not drunk enough yet, the blinds drawn. Marina would be in the bathtub, proving her strength by lying there vulnerable, in the light, in the water. She'd close her eyes and count her breaths, and through sheer willpower she'd grow deaf to the racket outside, and the silence inside.

And here I was wishing I were there.

On Friday, after Marina took Amabel away, I'd gone outside to tidy up the pool deck. I'd been carrying something, a juice box, some towels, back to the house. I couldn't remember the clang of the gate shutting behind me.

Closing the gate was a habit, unconscious, like buckling a seat belt. I wouldn't necessarily remember doing it. I could trust that I had. But it nagged at me. Ammy couldn't have gotten into the pool if it had been locked. And I couldn't remember.

22

I developed a tic. Open the freezer and check on the envelope. Pull it out, flip through the money, return it to the bottom shelf, with the frosty vodka bottle and the skinny microwave dinners. Shove it, deep as I could wedge it.

Why not a check? An official blue slip, Marina's graceful cursive on the line. Their accountant would deduct the expense next April. Instead I had cash, anonymous and bulky.

Marina had wanted to pay Iris, too. The idea floated in my head, drifted away. I couldn't summon any interest in Iris. My curiosity—strong enough to tie me to the living room doorway, away from Amabel—was gone.

After hours of watching the news, the sun glaring into my windows and filling my studio with itchy heat, I couldn't wait any longer to drink. In the fridge, I dug up a Diet Coke and bottled lemon juice whose origins I couldn't remember, and mixed them with vodka. With plenty of ice, it didn't taste too bad. (Remembering Amabel's cold, last winter, the cough syrup she gagged through, my advice to pinch her nose, drink it fast.)

Much later, after dark, there was a knock on my door. Disoriented, I got out of bed, surprised to see the TV on, the national news playing footage of a mudslide in some distant place, a scene I didn't recognize, though I'd been lying there watching the screen. I'd run out of soda and was nursing straight vodka.

I dropped my glass on the counter and lurched toward the door. The carpet rocked under my feet.

Bryant stood at my door, a briefcase in one hand, his tie in the other. He wore a suit, wilted from the day, oxford unbuttoned to his sternum. His face sagged with tiredness, and when he saw me stumble to the side, catch myself on the doorframe, his jaw tightened.

"I'm sorry I'm late," he said, coming in past me. "How are you?" He stopped at the threshold of the living room, arms dangling at his sides.

Bryant rarely came to my place—it didn't make sense, when his condo was so much more comfortable.

Whenever I'd expected him, I cleaned obsessively, lit candles, arranged everything just so. Tonight, it stank of stale laundry, alcohol, and fermenting misery. There was a backup in the sink where I'd dumped a moldy tub of yogurt under a stream of running water until the drain clogged, an inch of cloudy water sitting.

Bryant set his briefcase on the ground, laid his tie over it, the silk v's trailing over the linoleum. His body drooped. He obviously longed for his own bed, the high-thread-count sheets taut over the foam mattress, the air purifier humming along. But he shucked off his jacket and dress shirt, and in his pristine white undershirt reached his bare hand into the drain and moved it around until the clog gurgled free. He ran the water, scrubbing his hands. He wiped up with paper towels.

I muttered thanks and lay back down on the bed. Above me, the folded origami birds seemed to dive and swerve like a real flock. I shut my eyes.

"Are you as exhausted as I am?" Bryant was standing over me.

"Probably not." My voice was nasty. "I didn't have to work today."

He leaned to touch my back. "You've had too much to drink."

"I haven't had enough."

He sighed. "This is why I hoped you'd consider going home."

"It's just a drink, Bryant. I'm not hurting anyone." My voice had the defiant, idiotic tone of a teenager.

Bryant went back into the kitchen. I heard him going through cabinets. The suction of the freezer door opening. I scrambled up—would he notice the envelope?—but he only removed the ice cube tray, sighed because it was empty, and took it and a glass to the sink to fill them. He came back and pressed the glass at me.

"Here."

I sipped. The water was lukewarm, swimming with tiny gray flakes. It nauseated me. I put the glass on the floor, and Bryant moved it to the kitchen counter.

In a reasonable voice, as if we'd been discussing it all along, he said, "Finn, you're upset. You're grieving. And I'm swamped right now. It would be helpful to me if I knew you were with people who care about you. If I knew you weren't alone."

"I don't want to."

"Why not?" He tilted his head, patient.

"I can't leave." I dropped my eyes to my lap. The hem of my shorts was fraying, a crimped white thread trickling over my thigh. I tugged it, and a couple of stitches slithered open. "I want to stay. I want to be here. And we're together now, aren't we?"

"But look at you." He took my hand and softened his voice. "What if I called your parents? I could let them know what happened. I could coordinate everything."

"No!" I sat up. My hand had jerked from Bryant's.

He frowned, pulling his chin back.

"Sorry," I said. "I'm just upset."

"Exactly." He brushed hair off my face. "You're not thinking clearly."

My lower lip trembled. I clamped it firmly with my teeth. If I cried, I'd lose. "I want to be here."

"I'm only thinking of you, babe," he said. So softly. He kissed my eyebrow. "You don't have any obligations here. Why not? The weather would be nicer there, too. You could take the summer. Get back on your feet."

I searched his face. The summer? That was weeks. Had the Martins asked him to end things with me? Was this his way of extracting himself?

"Are you mad at me?"

"Of course not. That's not what this is about." He lay beside me and pulled me onto him. "I'm only trying to help."

I was ashamed of how comforted I was by his reassurance. By the warmth of his arm. I smelled salt on his skin, and the juicy faux fruit scent of my soap. We'd rarely been in my bed together. I remembered one afternoon, the fan oscillating across our bodies, music streaming from my laptop, he'd said he felt like he was back in college. He'd said it teasingly, happily. I'd told him how, when I first lived alone, I'd eaten a grilled cheese sandwich for dinner every night. We'd made sandwiches on my stovetop, ate them cross-legged in the tangle of sheets.

His hand stopped tracing my neck. He was pre-occupied. I followed his eyes to the TV. They were showing the Senator's statement again. He reached for the remote, and I expected him to unmute it, but he flicked it off. I supposed he'd seen all the coverage, too, had anxiously waited for everyone to move past scandal and blame, and toward tragedy and pity.

"They won't get in trouble, will they?" I asked. "For what happened?"

"No." He squeezed my elbow. "Don't worry about that. It was an accident."

The word lingered in the air like a bad smell. *Accident.*

Amabel sneaking down the stairs and out the door—the flash of glee she must have felt, evading me! Pulling the pool gate open and marching across the patio. The stones would have been blazing hot. She might have fallen in, stumbled more than jumped.

I cried out. Bryant grabbed me. "What is it?"

"It was awful." I was sobbing. Bryant held me, rubbing my back as I choked and gasped. How ugly it was to cry like this. Bryant murmured meaninglessly into my scalp. Finally, I stopped, ran out, really. I felt scraped raw.

"Tell me about it," he whispered. "What happened?"

It sounded like an invitation, to really tell him, to admit what I'd done. A charged silence opened; the air seemed to hum like I was in front of an eager microphone. I opened my mouth, felt my tongue poised on my teeth. Confess, you liar, I thought, just tell him!

"I was in the bathroom. It was only a few minutes. When I came out, Ammy wasn't there. I thought she was hiding." I told him about searching through the upstairs. I'd been too slow, stupid. I should have gone outside, checked the pool.

"It's not your fault. Anyone would have done the same thing." My head was tucked under his chin; his words pressed into the top of my skull.

"I should have been there."

"How many times did you leave her in the past, for a couple minutes? She never did it before. It was an accident." He traced circles on my back. He was being so nice. Ashamed, I closed my eyes.

"Finn?" He nudged me. "Do you know why Jim was there?"

I had dropped off a moment. I'd drooled on his shirt. I wiped it with my thumb. "No." The lie felt obvious, but he didn't seem to notice.

"How did you end up going there?"

"Marina called me." I told him about Marina's hotel room, dragging the memory forward as if it had happened months before. "Amabel was asleep by the time I got there. We went back to the house the next day. I took Ammy out for breakfast. We had a really nice morning." I thought of birds hopping at our feet. Amabel's delight when they pecked at her waffle.

"That's a good memory," Bryant said. "You were her favorite."

I shrugged.

"So." He stroked my hair, brushing it away from my eyes, exposing my face. "You didn't hear what Jim and the Martins were talking about?"

"No. I just told you." I pulled away and drew my knees into my chest. "Why? Did they say something?"

"I haven't seen them," he said. "Only Jim, briefly. It's just—I was curious. It's none of my business. I just wondered why they were all there."

"I think Marina called the Senator from the hotel and asked him to meet them at the house. I assumed they were talking about the girl."

"The one you mentioned to me, after the gala? Iris?"

I was surprised he remembered her name. That night he hadn't wanted to hear about her, had practically covered his ears.

"She hasn't contacted you again, has she?"

"No." What a relief to be honest.

"Good," he said. "But the Martins . . . you didn't hear anything?"

I shook my head.

He touched my back. "I didn't mean to make you go through it again. You should try to forget it. Just remember the good things."

"How can I forget? It's everywhere." I gestured at the TV.

"You shouldn't watch the news. They're being disgusting."

"Those photos of Amabel."

"It'll go away. Tomorrow, maybe the next day, it'll die down."

We both flinched at the phrase, and it ended the discussion. I took the opportunity to slip into the bathroom, where I ran the water and hunched over the sink like a gargoyle, mouthing horrible insults at myself in the mirror. When I came out, Bryant had folded his clothes on the floor and lay in bed with his phone, typing busily. He slid it away as I got into bed.

"You're still working?"

"Just making a note for tomorrow."

We lay side by side, staring at the ceiling. In our silence, I heard my neighbor return from his gas station job. His microwave beeped. The *rat-a-tat* gunfire of a video game started up.

"I'm sorry," I whispered. But Bryant was already asleep.

I was restless, bothered by the noises I usually tuned out, as though I were channeling Bryant's fussiness. I was thirsty, but Bryant was holding my hand.

Strange, how he'd pried about the Martins' conversation. He'd warned me to keep out of their business. Was he testing me, or was he curious to know for himself?

Stop thinking, stop thinking. I lay still, willing sleep to snatch me.

Iris was still threatening them, somehow. Maybe I should have told Bryant. I could have made it sound as if I'd heard them on my way upstairs.

Bryant was breathing quietly, the calm sleep only possible when you're sober, and innocent.

No, better to stay out of it, as he'd advised me from the beginning.

He rolled over, turning his back to me, his hand leaving mine.

I woke in the dark. The apartment was eerily quiet. Bryant wasn't in bed. I got up and padded around. He wasn't in the kitchen or bathroom. His clothes were gone. At the door, the chain lock hung open, though I was sure I'd fastened it.

I peered outside. The hall was lit with white bulbs beside every door. Insects swarmed in the glare. The doors were shut, all the way down the line. I stepped to the railing to check the parking lot. Bryant's car wasn't there.

I went back inside. He might have gone to work, or to his place to change clothes. But it was three in the morning. And he'd have left a note, wouldn't he?

My head throbbed. I swallowed three Advil with a bottle of water. I would just lie down for a second before texting him.

When I woke again, the apartment was bright. Bryant was beside me, deeply asleep. His clothes were folded just where he'd left them.

I was uncertain, unsettled. A dream? But the bottle of Advil was out, lid uncapped. I poured another two into my palm, and shook them like dice as I watched Bryant. The sunlight fell over him, and he rolled away from it, to the edge of the bed, like a man chased. I'd been dreaming, I thought, or half dreaming, that's all. I swallowed the pills, whose coppery shells had melted in my hand. When I went to the bathroom, I saw the chain lock was fastened as usual.

In the closet, I automatically reached for shorts and a T-shirt, realizing with a dull pain that I was dressing to be with Amabel. I didn't have the energy to take the clothes back off, to make some decision about what outfit my new routine required.

I made coffee, my machine noisily churning and releasing puffs of steam. Bryant stirred. He rubbed his face. Sitting up, he seemed lost, as if he had no memory of being here. He lifted the sheet from his legs and tossed it away from him. He buried his face in his hands and scrubbed it furiously.

"I made coffee," I said.

He looked up. His face was stiff, as if a mask had dried over his features.

"It's not good coffee," I said, nervous. "We could go out and grab some."

He shook his head. His lips twitched into a passable smile, fleeting, apologetic. "I can't." He grabbed his clothes and began to dress in jerky movements, pulling his pant legs on while seated and jumping to stand, tugging them up. "I've got to get home. Shower, change. It's going to be another long day."

Even when he turned, he didn't look at me. He ran a hand over his hair, pressing it flat. "But I'll call you later. We'll do something tonight."

He retrieved his shoes and stuffed his feet into them impatiently, crushing the leather backs. He knelt to tie them.

"I thought you might have gone home last night," I said.

He paused, glanced over his shoulder at me. "Huh?"

"I woke up in the middle of the night and you were gone."

His head dropped back down, and he slowly tugged the knots tight, twice. "I had to make a call. I went out to my car so I wouldn't wake you."

"I was worried," I said.

"I'm sorry. I didn't think you'd notice." He came forward and kissed my cheek, his jawbone hitting mine. His eyes darted away, locked on his wallet on the counter. He opened it and fished out a $20. "You get yourself that coffee."

I followed him out. He took the stairs at a run. His car was parked in the first row. There was no way I could have missed it last night. Maybe he'd gone for a drive, while he made his phone call. Rolled the windows down. It might have helped him stay awake.

He pulled out without waving goodbye.

If there was no chance the Martins would be blamed for Ammy, what was there to work on? For me, the election was about important but impersonal concerns. Immigration, taxes. Then I remembered Bryant's *just Latino* remark, and the Senator's charter flights, and Marina's manicured fund-raiser, and Philip's land deal. Bryant must be thinking about Amabel's death in those terms. No wonder he couldn't meet my eyes.

His crisp bill was still in my hand.

23

Nothing to do, get in the car, drive. I traveled on autopilot, staring at people I passed—women waiting for the bus laden with tote bags, a jogger with a stroller, a man and his Chihuahuas—both envying and disgusted by their ignorance.

Muscle memory took me north on the highway. I passed our familiar haunts, camp, stables, the bookstore with story time, the Froyo place with the tiny candy toppings.

At The Grove, a sign taped to the door read, CLOSED, SORRY FOR INCONVENIENCE. Not Philip's handwriting. No light illuminated his office window. I went back through the trellised arches, where flowers dropped dry, crumpled petals.

While I sat in the parking lot, Bryant called. He asked how I was doing, and I told him I was still in bed.

"You're lucky," he said. "I could sleep for a day."

"How long were you out last night?"

There was a silence. I dropped open the glove compartment to check the envelope. I'd been too nervous to leave it in my apartment. I didn't live in the best neighborhood, and a break-in wasn't unheard of, even in the daytime. I felt better when I could see it.

"Bryant?"

"Sorry. Just looking at my email. Listen, I won't keep you. Go back to sleep. Get some rest." He hung up.

I drove north, into a ritzy residential area. I got out of my car and crossed a parking lot into the long, triangular shadow of a church.

The Martins attended service here. I'd gone along once, when Ammy's friend's baby sister was baptized. Amabel stood to watch, and when the minister dripped water onto the baby's forehead, she let out an affronted shriek.

At this hour, the church was mostly deserted. A few women in cardigans came and went from a meeting room, chatting seriously. The chapel doors were closed.

The event schedule was posted on the wall by the bathrooms. It was a slow week, weddings not being popular in the Arizona summer. Along with services and prayer groups, there was an hour blocked off, discreetly labeled PRIVATE SERVICE. Tomorrow afternoon.

I copied down the time, not that I would forget.

Feeling like a thief, I drove into Ocotillo Heights. I expected helicopters overhead, lines of news vans, curious neighbors stalking the sidewalks. But the neighborhood was quiet. Not even a landscaping crew.

I drove up the hill and stopped at the hem of the Martins' yard. It was Eva's day to clean but her car wasn't there. The white brick house had never resembled a bunker so strongly.

I pulled up the road until my car was obscured by the overgrowth. I stepped out. The sky was chalk white, so bright it stung my eyes. Nothing seemed to cast a shadow, not even my legs as I strode up to the peak. The ground was red-brown dirt, tamped down in places and shaggy and loose in others, studded with clumps of rocks that were sharp under my flimsy sneakers.

I'd hiked up here once with Amabel. Her little legs had struggled up the slope, and she'd dropped to her palms and clambered like a goat until I shouted for her to stop. I was afraid she'd smash her hand into a black widow's nest. They were common out here, the spiders with their bellies like swollen blisters. Actually quite shy, afraid of humans, but in the bad habit of nesting in mailboxes and doorframes.

Spiders, scorpions, snakes. Coyotes. The Martins had built their house so close to so many dangers.

I reached the peak. The mountain at the horizon seemed flat as a stage prop. In the valley, the quilt of roads and buildings was dreamy and distant, beige and brown, without a speck of green.

I stood long enough that the birds resumed scrabbling and singing. My forehead and cheeks were tight and stinging from the sun. Shielding my face with a hand, I made my way down the ledge into the narrow ribbon of land behind the Martins' yard. The house loomed above. Its huge windows reflected the anemic sky. Perversely, I wanted to trip, sprain an ankle or a wrist, cry out weakly until someone emerged—or no one did, and darkness fell, and I'd be alone, the coyote moving toward me.

I came to the pool gate. The pool had been emptied. The concrete bowl was naked and white. Of course, I thought, they'd drained the bad water out. I gripped the iron bars. The metal scorched; I wanted to clutch it, punish myself, but my fingers reflexively snapped back.

I walked on. The ground was overgrown with sharp grass and prickling weeds that sliced my ankles. I stepped over cacti, big sections of them rotted out, new green growth bulging out of the brown. Ants swarmed over the ground, a living puddle.

Rounding a bend, I faced a line of trees a few yards ahead. They were thin and wispy, but their branches formed a natural barrier. Beyond them was the next yard, another private wilderness, another view unsullied by fellow human habitation.

Just before the trees, there was a disturbance in the air, a thickening and swirling. As I got closer, I realized it was a swarm of flies, hovering in a frenzy over a mound on the dirt. A smell hit me, slimy, putrid.

Some dead animal. A carcass, I thought, left by the coyote. But it was so large.

I edged forward, drawn toward it even as I was repelled. It blended in with the ground, tan and brown and yellow. It was him. Collapsed on his flank, snout fixed in a tight sneer, teeth digging into his lip. His eye was gone. His ear flared open like a shell. His legs jutted stiffly, paw pads worn white and cracked.

My shadow fell over his shoulder, and a mass of flies rose up, circling, exposing a dark patch of brown at his neck. Blood. The ripped fur around it was perversely downy and light, like dandelion fluff.

I backed away. I didn't breathe until I was past the house. Still, the rotten tang lingered in my nose even when I got back to my car, even as I drove down the hill.

The bloodied shoulder hadn't looked ripped, as if another animal had attacked it. It looked small, almost neat.

I was so preoccupied I didn't notice my flat tire until my car had sunk to one side and dragged over the ground, resisting the forward motion. I pulled over. The back tire was nearly flat. A long, straight slit ran through it. I must have driven over a sharp rock or glass when I pulled into the brush.

Sweating, I dug the spare tire from my trunk. I wished I smoked, since a cigarette might ease the carrion smell, which coated the inside of my mouth.

24

Bryant came by my apartment late again, found me lying in bed, sober this time. I hadn't wanted to lend any ammunition to his argument that I should go home. He said, "Let's go," taking me by the arm, and I felt the relief of being led.

At his place, he fixed me a whiskey with honey and asked what I'd done all day. I invented a long nap, grabbing coffee, going for a run. I told him about the bee I'd seen yesterday, wounded and crawling on the ground, thinking the detail made me seem honest. But he wasn't interested in the bee.

"The Martins are staying with Jim," he announced. "They can't stand being in the house."

"Oh," I said. "I thought they were there. The pool was empty."

"How did you know?" His eyes were sharp.

"The news," I said. "They showed the house."

"Right." He watched me carefully, cupping his hand around his own untouched drink. Why didn't I want to tell him? It wasn't a crime, walking around the Heights, outside the Martins' yard. But I dreaded the look he'd give me, and what he'd say, a blunter version of Marina's warning to stay away.

"Could I have another?" I pushed my glass over. Honey pooled at the base.

He sliced another wedge of lemon. I ran my fingertips over the marble bar. Amabel, holding a lemon peel over her mouth, bending it into a smile . . .

"How are they?" I said. "Marina looked so calm."

"She has a thick shell." He stirred my drink with a long spoon.

"And Philip?" He glanced at me, and I pretended to be absorbed in the gray veins of the marble.

"They're going on a cruise." He slid my drink over.

I blinked. "Philip and Marina?"

"Of course."

"Why?"

"It was Jim's idea. It will be restful for them. The same reason I thought you should go home. *Think*," he corrected. "I think you should go home."

I tipped back the drink. "Where are they going?"

"The Mediterranean. Greece, Spain. I can't remember. It'll be good for them to get away for a while. Over a third of marriages end after the loss of a child. They want to stay together."

"You looked up a statistic?" I was shrill. My glass struck the countertop. "Is that what they care about? Whether the Martin brand will survive?"

"Stop."

"You stop! You're acting like you didn't even know Ammy. You're acting like . . . a machine."

"That's not true."

"It is," I said. "Have you even cried? Do you feel sad at all?" I was so angry I felt shaky. Or maybe it was the whiskey. It sloshed in my empty stomach.

Bryant pushed back his hair, flushed. "I have to care. It's my job to care. We all can't just fall to pieces, can we? Can't just wander around the city all day, pretending like nothing's changed."

I threw my glass at the wall. It didn't shatter satisfyingly, but broke tidily in half. We both stared at it.

"Maybe it hasn't hit me yet." Bryant blinked at the wall. His eyes were bloodshot and hooded with tiredness. "I wasn't there. I only heard, and then everything moved quickly—maybe I wanted it to. I wanted not to think about it." He didn't look at me, and I thought he was embarrassed by his emotion. "Of course I'm sad. It's, it's—" He paused. Don't say *tragic*, I prayed. "Terrible," he said finally. "I'm sorry."

He came over and kissed the top of my head. My hair was flat and filmy from too much washing. I'd scrubbed it earlier, convinced the smell of the coyote had soaked in.

Bryant didn't even own a broom; he rolled out his slim vacuum cleaner. Waving him off, I swept the glass up with a piece of cardboard. I shook the pieces into his garbage can. Mixed in with spent espresso beans and energy bar wrappers was a tangle of shredded papers.

I envied his work. His access to the Martins. How easily he still spoke of them. Marina's shell. Their restful cruise. While I'd been cast out.

Upstairs, Bryant worked on his laptop in bed, fingers flying, while I brushed my teeth. When I got in beside him, he closed it.

"I don't mind if you work," I said.

"That's okay." He got up and put the computer in his bag. He came back carrying a prescription bottle.

"I got you these. To help you sleep." Bryant pressed the bottle at me, until I had to accept it.

It was a dose of the blue pills the driver had given me. The orange plastic case was unlabeled.

"Whose are these?" I said.

"I got them for you."

"I don't need them."

"You said you were having trouble sleeping. You need rest right now."

I tilted the bottle back and forth. I remembered the sick, lurching feeling of waking up in the morning after taking one, Marina's concern about my empty stomach. Were they all talking about my sleep together?

I put them in the nightstand drawer without commenting.

"What are you doing tomorrow?" Bryant asked.

I shrugged. The funeral was in the afternoon. "I'll figure something out."

"I'm going up to Flagstaff. Want to come along?"

I bit my lip, wishing I'd come up with a better reply. "I'll only be in your way."

"It's a pretty drive," he said. "You can be my chauffeur. I'm staying in a nice hotel. I'll be out all day, but you could enjoy it. Get room service. Watch movies."

"That's so sweet," I said. "But I'm going to stay. I'll keep myself out of trouble, I promise."

Dissatisfied, he shifted beside me. But our fight downstairs, and his apology, were working in my favor. He didn't want to start another argument. "If that's what you want."

As if he'd jinxed me, I couldn't sleep.

The Martins had parked in a forbidding row in front of the church. I slipped past Marina's car. She'd removed Amabel's booster seat, but the DVD player was still strapped to the back of the driver's seat. Had she lost heart halfway through her cleanout?

I stumbled, though the pavement was smooth. I was terrified to be here, my heart a stone longing for a sea to sink into. I'd spent the morning in my closet, trying on and taking off the dark dresses I had. They were all wrong: too short, too skimpy, too polyester. None of them was serious enough. I still had Marina's dress, the one I'd borrowed for the gala. I ran a lint brush over it and slid it on. In it, I looked dignified, grieving, stricken, not just someone crashing a funeral in a cocktail dress. I'd added a long black cardigan to disguise it.

I tugged the sweater around me as I walked to the church.

A pair of Snoops flanked the entrance. As I approached, one stepped forward. He wasn't the driver, but looked like a doll from the same box. He was tan, with narrow eyes and a soft, hairless hand that lifted into the air to stop me.

"I'm late." I made myself tearful, angry. "Don't you recognize me? We've seen each other at the gala, a hundred times."

He looked to his partner, and after a wordless exchange, a tough shrug, they let me pass.

The church foyer was cave-cool and empty. The sound of a piano playing seeped out the chapel doors. I stepped through.

A jewel box of stained glass opened around me. Polished pews fanned out from the dais, seating for hundreds, empty. A wooden cross, large enough to serve its ancient purpose, hung on the far wall. Below it was a coffin. So small. Amabel was mostly hidden. Only the lacy white puff of her dress showed, and a pile of roses. I couldn't bear the idea of having to walk past her, see her dear familiar face still with artificial calm. I wiped my eyes with the back of my hand. I was in danger of letting out a loud honking sob, when I wanted to be invisible.

The Martins sat in the front row. Intimately familiar and dramatically changed. Marina had chopped her hair into a sleek bob. She wore a charcoal gray suit I'd never seen before. Beside her was a small old man who wiped his face with a handkerchief. Her father, I guessed.

Philip sat on her other side, on the aisle. His elbow rested on the back of the pew; his body twisted away from the casket. He seemed ready to run for the exit.

I forced myself forward. Under my arm, I felt the

edge of the envelope through the flimsy leather of my purse.

Sensing a disturbance, Marina turned. Seeing me, she drew back, in surprise or anger. She wore more makeup than usual, lipstick overpowering her pale clenched face. She began to rise.

The Senator turned. He wore navy blue, held his military posture. After nodding courteously at me, he faced forward again. He touched Marina on the elbow. She scowled. But she turned back to the front, hair swinging.

Philip didn't move. He stared at some point on the back wall, not the minister, casket, or flowers. I wanted to sit beside him, hold his hand between mine. Warm skin in the cold church.

The music tapered. The minister stepped to the podium and shook back his billowy sleeves to open the Bible.

I slid into a pew. Enormous floral arrangements lined the aisle. Formal, stiff flowers, visibly expensive and throwing off a sickly smell. I would have chosen sunflowers or daisies, flowers that bounced when you swung them by the stem. Flowers Amabel would have liked.

The piano began to play, notes rippling loudly in the empty church. The minister sang, his voice obnoxiously strong. I couldn't hear the Martins, though they stood, and their mouths moved.

Ammy had been afraid of the dark. It had seemed fanciful—she enjoyed the drama of monsters in the closet and worked herself into real anxiety. Before bed, I tucked stuffed animals around her, a tight perimeter of fuzz and fluff, and she lay perfectly still like a mummy. I wanted to tuck her in now, fling away those prickling roses, the stiff lace. My face was hot and wet.

The Martins didn't cry. Didn't even flinch. They stayed fixed in position, listening politely, solemn and wooden. They didn't touch each other. They didn't slump. They'd always been masters of ceremony.

I'd never been one of them.

I dropped my head. An industrial gray carpet covered the floor, surprisingly ugly. My eyes wandered the maze of the herringbone pattern. The minister kept his sermon brief, impersonal, with none of the usual platitudes about angels and souls. When he called for a final viewing, the Martins filed past the coffin, each pausing, even lingering, but it was still over quickly.

I stayed hunched in place.

Teenaged boys in robes emerged to carry the casket out, and the Martins proceeded after it in a grueling slow march. I kept my head down.

I let several minutes pass. Or it felt as if I had. But when I went out into the lobby, Marina was waiting for me.

My feet stuck to the ground. She'd pinned a small square veil over her face. She approached me, her usual calm walk, her new haircut making her older.

"Finn." She held out a hand to shake. "How nice of you to come." A cool, peppermint voice. My own mouth seemed stuffed with cloth. I was surprised by her pleasant lie, after she'd been obviously displeased to see me.

"Nice service," I managed.

She murmured agreement. "We're going on to the cemetery, but I wanted to thank you for coming."

I laced my hands together, useless. "I'm going home, I guess."

"I heard that." She started for the door, and I went along. The Snoops, I saw, had left their posts, probably to go ahead with the Senator. "Back to Minnesota, was it?"

"Illinois," I provided automatically, though I'd only meant home to my apartment. I glanced at her profile, her lowered chin and stiff posture, and wondered why she'd assumed I'd meant the Midwest.

"It's a good idea," she was saying. "A change of scenery will do you good. Be with your family. Think about the future . . ."

"I heard you're going to Europe," I said.

A discordant shiver of tension grabbed her shoulders. She touched her veil to her nose. "Philip has never been to Greece."

Outside, the full glare of the sun stopped us both. We blinked in the light.

Marina unexpectedly took my elbow. "It's Wednesday. What would you have been doing Wednesday afternoon?"

"Riding," I said.

She crinkled her nose. "Those horses." Shaking her head, she laughed a little. "I was afraid of them."

"I didn't know that."

She released me. "Take care, Finn." Rubbing her ear, she trotted down the steps and into her car, pulling away as instantly as if she'd left it running.

25

I never thought of the past, but now it flooded back.

The smell of lilies, sweet, throat-coating. I carried two dozen wrapped in cellophane. Why is it always so sunny, the day of funerals?

The quiet lane was lined with cars, the shiny sedans of city friends, the dusty SUVs of the local set. The hose was stretched over the grass to water the maple. It had been a dry summer. Mrs. Everett doted on the roses, Mr. Everett on the trees.

The front door stood open, the screen shut against flies. The noise of conversation drifted out, subdued but strong, almost like a party.

I hesitated on the stoop. I hadn't been invited, after all.

Mrs. Everett's voice carried from inside. "It's open." Seeing me, a shutter fell over her face. In her black, she was years older than I'd last seen her.

Mr. Everett joined her at the door. She shooed him away. "Go to the gardens. I'll be there in a minute."

I watched him disappear, knowing his path so well. Down the tiled hall, past the carved banister and the closet under the stairs, which held rain boots and fishing poles, into the sunroom with its curved glass roof, and finally out to the flagstone patio, where the smell of mulch overpowered the roses. What I would have given to follow him.

Mrs. Everett stepped closer. The crosshatch of the screen was like a veil over her face as she whispered what she thought of me.

I left with my lilies. I threw them into the lake, from the pier outside the hotel. Technically I wasn't meant to go on the property. I'd been fired, allegedly for missing my shifts after the accident, but I knew the manager had heard what happened. His loyalty was with the Everetts.

The Swiss house in my photograph was, of course, the Everetts'. The girl in the picture was me, Natalie, after a work shift. Mrs. Everett snapped the photo casually, the end of a roll. She'd be furious if she knew I kept it in my wallet still. If she knew I told people I'd grown up in her house, perhaps she'd pity me.

Not long after I left, the Everetts sold that house. No doubt they couldn't stand the ghosts. The noise of the lake lapping at their pier all day and night; the catspaws rushing in on windy afternoons; the roar of motors and shouts of fun.

After Ammy's funeral, I drove. My spare tire droned loudly over the asphalt. I stopped by a liquor store and bought vodka, soda, a candy bar. I sat in the parking lot awhile, eating the toffee, softened in the heat, my teeth sticking together. Nobody else came or went. It was a Wednesday afternoon. I should be in a hot barn, pitying the horses as they trod their slow circle, shaking their necks to ward off flies. I started up my car and idled a minute, racking my brain for somewhere I wanted to go.

At home, I made a drink. I knocked a few ice cubes into the cup and drained it too fast for them to make a difference. I sucked the melting ice with its dregs of sweetness. It was only midafternoon, I had a long way to go.

Erica Everett had her back to me, the first time I saw her. She wore green shorts and blue sneakers with yellow stripes across the toes. Around her, moving close and away with the nervous energy of electrons around a nucleus, girls vied for her attention, whispered, giggled, tugged the ends of their ponytails over their lips.

The first track practice of the season, and winter clung to spring. The breeze cut through our flimsy T-shirts. I crossed my arms, trying to pass off my dejection as boredom. I'd moved from Chicago and missed the city. The suburbs were cartoonish, so much grass, such large garages, no sidewalk and nowhere to go if you did walk. I felt in my legs the pent-up energy of a month spent at home. We jogged around the track twice, warming up. Rows of pine trees, brown with winter burn, screened off the road. I'd spent my lunch hours loitering under those trees, kicking at the cigarette butts scattered over the dry needles like stubby bits of chalk.

The coach blew his whistle, and we lined up for the hundred-meter trials. Erica stepped up, and her posse followed. She faced ahead, her shoulders drawn in tension. I let my gaze settle on the pavement in front of me, the yellow paint of my lane number, 8, dissolving into the track.

At the whistle, we sprang forward. In seconds, most girls dropped behind me. The noise of feet reduced to a few sets. I ran so hard the air I breathed was hot in my throat. For a moment, I seemed to lift away from my life. I was angry at the rising lump of my mom's stomach while Caleb was barely one, her eager attitude toward Ted, the cramped house that smelled like diapers.

I sprinted past the finish, riding out my momentum. When I turned, I wasn't alone. Erica was close behind me. She'd dropped her hands to her knees, gasping.

I tapped her shoulder. "You don't want to lean like that. Put your hands on your head."

She looked annoyed, but she obeyed. She was four inches shorter than me, but absolutely domineering. Her neatly muscled legs were smooth as a doll's. A silver bracelet glinted on her wrist, and a slippery layer of peach brightened her lips. She occupied her body calmly, with grace, which set her apart from the rest of us, the arm-crossers, the hair-twisters, the nail-biters.

When she'd caught her breath, she said, "How fast are you?"

I shrugged.

"No one's ever beaten me." She eyed me. Then her friends surrounded her again.

But at the next practice, she joined me during the warm-up. We began running together on Saturdays. By the summer, we were inseparable. It was as quick, and lucky, as the flip of a coin. Erica picked me, just as Amabel had, the same queenly approval, and I'd been thrilled to go along.

When I showed Bryant and Ammy the picture of Erica's house, I never told them about the lake. But the house was on the shore, and all the best rooms looked out at the sweep of navy water freckled with tiny, wooded islands.

I hated thinking of the lake.

Erica and I did our homework in her frilled bedroom. We swam. Sunned ourselves on the deck. We went for rides in the family sailboat, and sometimes in the jaunty red speedboat, thrillingly quick and sleek. When I spent the night, I slept in a spare bedroom, the canopy bed piled with feather duvets, the dressing table lined with antique perfume bottles.

Her parents were as enchanting to me as her house. They loved me. Erica was irritated by them, secretive, private, standoffish. I was the same way with my mom and Ted, but when Erica acted that way I was genuinely shocked. Her parents were smart, generous, interesting. I happily helped with the cooking and cleaning up, if it meant hearing Mrs. Everett talk about the town houses she made over, the shows she saw. She was elegant, with dark hair and bright blue eyes. Mr. Everett was droll and sarcastic. He taught me to water-ski, let Erica and me drink beer on the boat.

At fourteen, Erica was sweet, curious, impatient. By sixteen, she was beautiful, cunning, and perpetually, lethally bored. I was content to be at her house, to swim with my now-expert crawl, to drop a ski and zip over the water on a single slalom, to paint our nails and drink endless Diet Cokes in front of the rec room's big screen. Erica roved her house as if it were a cage. She tried on every dress in her closet and left them on the floor. Turning up her stereo, she swallowed caffeine pills, which she claimed to be addicted to, and blew cigarette smoke out the window. Once, she climbed down the trellis to the yard, in the early evening, mosquitoes swarming over her legs, bruising her knees and cutting her palms, for no other reason than to see if she could.

We spent less time in the house and more time out, wandering, looking for something. If we found excitement—say, college boys invited us to a party—she'd want to up the stakes. Get drunk. Smoke something, and dance, with each other, then with boys, then kiss, then more, more. The next morning, waking with a dull hangover, she'd be bored, disappointed. Whatever she was searching for had eluded her again.

Her mother tried to enlist my help. When we were wiping dishes, or met in the hall while Erica took one of her endless showers, she'd casually ask how Erica was. *Is everything okay? She seems so unsettled.*

I pretended not to know what she meant.

Worse, she'd sometimes ask Erica, *Why can't you be more like Natalie? I doubt Natalie talks to her mother this way.*

Bewildered, I allied with Erica. What else could I do? I couldn't admit that what I most loved about Erica was her house, her family, her life. I had to pretend, even to myself, that I loved her, her wildness, that I was the same way.

Erica took up shoplifting. She goaded me until I did it, too. The first time: a green cashmere sweater was balled on the dressing room floor. When I tried it on, it turned my torso into a sculpture. I put my clothes over it, buttoned my coat to my throat, left the store. Alarms blared, and Erica held up her bag, politely slowing down. The clerks waved us on, unconcerned.

After that it was easy. Tights tugged from their cardboard sleeves. Tank tops crumpled up in my fist, springy and dense as tennis balls. Lipstick, perfume. What a rush, leaving the store, and even better, having the new things, which I scattered around my borrowed bedroom as if they were nothing.

Erica wasn't a good thief. She was overconfident, too blasé. One day, while leaning over a department store jewelry counter, asking the clerk to pull out this and that, pushing rings over her already-baubled fingers, Erica slipped a bracelet into her purse. Instantly, a security guard appeared behind us. He ushered us to a miserable basement office, where we had to empty our bags onto the desk.

We did fifteen hours of community service, picking up litter from the highway. Erica thought the whole thing was hilarious. I was humiliated, and furious with her for getting caught. Mrs. Everett's friendliness toward me dropped. For the first time, the Everetts knocked on Erica's door to remark that it was getting late, and maybe Natalie had better go home.

Home, to the bed and dresser pushed in a basement corner, because Ted said I wasn't around enough to need a proper room. The cheap carpet unrolled over the concrete floor, the brick walls painted a bluish shade of white. My mother had been upset about the stealing, but she'd been surprisingly quiet, saying only, "You don't have to do everything Erica does, you know."

Summer came. We were seventeen, one year from

freedom. I had my job at the resort, which gave me a good excuse to stroll over to the Everetts' every night.

In July, Erica met two brothers from across the lake. She claimed the charming, curly-haired elder, and I was left with the shrimpy younger.

On a Wednesday night, around ten-thirty, Erica and I picked them up in her speedboat. The night smelled richly of summer: motor oil, lake water, sunscreen, leather upholstery, glass cleaner. One of the mansions was having a party, and a reggae beat carried over the water.

Erica cut the motor, and we sat quietly awhile, passing a joint, listening to the waves slapping the hull. Apart from our lights, and a few windows onshore, the night was inky black. There was no moon.

"Turn off the lights," I said. "Let's look at the stars."

Erica reached and snapped them off, and our boat plunged into darkness. The stars glittered. They looked so close, as if we could walk up into them.

Erica and her boy disappeared into the nose of the boat, their usual routine. The brother and I stared for a while, finishing off the joint, throwing it into the water. He had a habit of slouching over his knees and rocking back and forth, an annoyingly insistent rhythm. I pretended to be mesmerized by the stars. I didn't know their names, and lost interest in searching for patterns.

I followed the swing of the satellites, reassured by their winking presence.

The noise of another motor carried over the lake, first loudly, then fainter. We were drifting in deep water, near one of the dark islands.

The scrawny brother set his slightly sticky hand on my shoulder and leaned in. His lips were soft, and he tasted like sour weed. I shut my eyes and gave myself over to kissing, feeling desired, at least.

I still heard, nagging as a mosquito, the whine of another motor on the lake.

When the boy reared up to make himself more comfortable on the bench, I stole a glance toward the nose. I couldn't see anything, but the occasional giggle slipped out. Nobody else was concerned. The boy above me was frowning in concentration, trying to work his way under my shirt. I lay back and closed my eyes, as if I could will myself into the sort of person who lost herself in the moment.

The noise of an engine got stronger. Louder. It didn't fade away. I opened my eyes. Erica reared up out of the nose and lunged for the steering wheel. Her face was open in a scream.

The force of the collision threw me airborne. A confusion of noise, and a light swinging in the dark, and no idea where I was until I hit water. The wet jolted me alert, and my body began to move, kicking, arms churning.

I was facing the shore, the party house. A few yards away, the speedboat was smashed up in big pieces. Shards floated across the water. Farther away, another boat had keeled over but stayed intact. It hung sideways, slowly sinking, its running light pointing up at the sky. It was huge, twice the size of Erica's boat.

I yelled for her.

Under the music, there were sucking noises as water filled the boats. I thought the engine might explode, the gasoline, and I kicked away. Erica must have been thrown in the other direction. I kept swimming, breathing so heavily I was already exhausted.

Three dark blots bobbed nearby. I called out, and they waited for me.

"Your lights were out," one said. He was a blank face and white teeth, shoulders bulging with a life preserver. "Your fucking lights were out!"

The other two were the brothers. They were silent with shock. The younger one let me hang on to him as we swam to the island. We sat breathless in the weeds, the curly-haired boy crying, the stranger swearing, the younger brother's teeth chattering. I alone stood and stared at the wreckage. "Where is she?"

We were rescued within minutes. The crash had

echoed around the lake, and a pontoon boat came over directly, honking, long loud blasts as it approached. The police arrived soon after. When I asked about Erica, they hushed me. In the ambulance, they hooked me up to an IV and I flipped off, pure blackness. Then it was the morning, a hospital bed, the police questioning me for an hour. Who had been driving? Were we drinking, doing drugs? Who had turned off the lights?

I pretended not to remember. *It was Erica's boat,* I kept saying. *Where is she?*

Divers went down for her in the morning. She'd hit her head in the crash, broken her neck.

I found myself at my mom's house. I spent the empty days wandering from TV to kitchen to bed. Caleb and Kyle trailed after me. Caleb was five, Kyle three. Sometimes I doted on them, invented games, made snacks, channeling Erica's energy and enthusiasm. But when I got tired I'd abruptly withdraw my affection, snap at them and retreat to my bedroom.

My parents conferred. I was making everyone miserable. My dad agreed to take me for the last year of high school.

My mom drove me. I stared out the window, lulled by the endless fields of plants I didn't recognize. Corn, and something low and bunched I learned later was soy. Cows roamed hilled pastures behind fences that seemed inadequate to contain them.

"Erica was a good friend," my mom said.

I tensed against her, dreading any words of comfort. She didn't know.

She sighed. "She was a sweet girl. But she was always wild, and a little bit dumb."

"What are you saying?" I was shrill, angry.

"Nothing against Erica. She didn't deserve that."

She glanced in the rearview mirror, rearranged her fingers over the steering wheel. Her wedding ring jutted up from her thin finger. Suddenly I took her in fully, as I hadn't, maybe in years. Her flowing, faux silk tunic and leggings, the pastel sandals, a hair band braceleting her wrist. She didn't seem related to me at all.

She sighed. "What I'm trying to say is, you're not like that. You're smart. You can choose to be wild or not, but you're the smart one. You know better. So be careful. Don't lose yourself again, following someone not as bright."

Her tone was mild. Her eyes were on the road, the vertical line between her eyebrows creased as always. Her lips pressed together as if rubbing in lipstick.

She might have hardly thought of what she was saying. She might only have been trying to give some last piece of parental advice before dropping me off, her duty done.

What I heard was: *You knew better. You were smart enough to know. You could have stopped it. You let it happen.*

Erica grew up around boats, Mrs. Everett told me, her eyes rimmed violet. She'd never have made such a mistake. It was my influence.

Turn off the lights. Let's look at the stars.

26

I sat on the kitchen floor with a glass between my knees. The smell of orange soda rose up. Ammy had loved orange soda. The flavor wasn't at all like oranges, the fruit—it seemed to be the color, liquefied. Acidic, neon, bilious. How did they get it so orange?

When the customary late-night knock came, I assumed it was Bryant. Back from Flagstaff and briefed on my funeral attendance and come to chastise me.

But it wasn't Bryant. Guy stood at the door. Hands in his pockets, kicking the ground. I hardly knew him, but in that moment he seemed deeply familiar and welcome. Someone tangled up in it, like me.

"I thought you might be alone." He looked me over. "Get dressed. Let's go someplace."

He drove a motorcycle. I climbed behind him. His back was damp with sweat from the ride over. His neck smelled like salt. A breeze blew under my dress.

How proud Erica would be of me. My hands didn't tremble as I held on. When we pulled into a deserted strip mall bar, I ordered a shot of tequila before I even sat down. We licked salt from our palms, swallowed, and then bit lime wedges. I coughed, painfully; the burn of the shot was like swallowing pool water.

I tapped Guy's wrist. "Something else." He asked for rum and Coke—easy on the Coke.

We slouched on barstools and watched the baseball game on TV. Whenever the ball flew in the air, I lost sight of it. Guy swore frequently, but when I asked who he was cheering for, he shrugged. "Nobody."

The bartender dropped off another round. I was wondering what this was about, wondering if Iris might come up behind me with her sickly smile.

"So," Guy said.

"So," I said.

"Were you there?" He sounded normal, which I was grateful for. I couldn't stand another careful, white-glove voice.

"Not officially."

"That sucks."

I snorted. "Sure."

"Sorry, I'm not good at this."

"No. It sucks. There's nothing else to say." I wrapped my hands around my glass. A grocery store sticker still clung to the wedge of lime on the rim.

"Was Iris there?" Guy kept watching the game, as if the question were casual.

"God. I knew it. That's why you came." I pushed my drink away.

He grabbed my wrist. "It's not the only reason. I haven't heard from her since Saturday. I'm worried."

"No, she wasn't there. Why would she have been?" I jerked away, standing up, and swayed alarmingly. "I'm sure Iris can take care of herself just fine."

"You don't know," he said. "She's gotten herself into some real shit."

"What are you talking about?" I was trying to tug my purse free, but it had tangled on the chair.

"Nothing. Listen, let's drop it." He held up his hands in surrender. "Okay? Stay. Please. I came here for you." His face was straight, without the usual smirk.

Heat washed over my face and neck. "How did you know I'd be alone?"

"I have a pretty good idea of what they're like. The Martins."

"Oh, really?"

"Yes." He nudged my chair out with his foot. "They're important. They're cold. You were in, and now you're out. Right?"

I slid onto the chair and took up my drink again. I didn't want to look at him.

"And," he spoke more softly, "you thought you were part of the family, didn't you?"

Sure he was mocking me, I glared at him. I wanted to say something dismissive—*it was just a job*—but the words died in my throat. I shrugged.

He patted my shoulder, fingers spread wide, the way you might touch a static globe.

"They didn't deserve you," he said.

I pulled away and wiped my eyes. They hadn't deserved me, that was true. My glass gave off a cloying tropical smell. I emptied it, shaking the ice to get the last drops.

We hunched over and resumed watching the game, as if the moment hadn't happened.

"What do you do?" I asked after a while.

He smiled with one side of his mouth. "Nothing."

"Come on. I need a distraction."

He shrugged. "I work at a golf course."

"But what do you want to do? You must have some plan."

He ground ice between his teeth. "Nope. Not every-one grew up hearing they can be a princess."

"You think that's how I grew up? Think again."

He hummed. "Sure."

"You don't even know me."

He held up a hand, probably afraid I'd cry again. "Fine. I'll play. Georgia. That's where I want to go. Someday. I'm in no hurry."

"Why Georgia?"

"When I was a kid I loved peaches. I'd eat them until I threw up."

"That's your reason?"

"Sure. I've never been there, so I can pretend it's per-fect. Smells good, nice and hot, and there's always a breeze over some peach trees. Perfect. What's your dream?"

The Martins' house flashed in my mind. The Everetts'. "I don't have one," I said shortly.

Another refill. The game had ended and a sports talk show started up.

"You can talk about it," Guy said. "It'll do you good."

I laughed, hard, like clearing my throat. The room wavered around me. I thought of the shimmering heat behind the Martins' house, the empty pool. The church. Marina's stiff anger; Philip's disregard. An offer, or an order, to go home.

"Go on," he said. "Tell me."

———

We were back on the bike. The road was empty. The breeze smelled like oranges. I stuck out my legs and flew.

Outside my door, I fumbled and dropped the keys. Guy let us in. I shut myself into the bathroom and threw up. The TV came on. I showered. The sour smell of vomit replaced with aromatherapy lavender body wash.

I came out wrapped in my towel. Guy lay on the mattress—there was nowhere else to sit. In the twilight glow of the TV, the apartment was a low-ceilinged cement cell. Suddenly, as if through Mrs. Everett's eyes, I saw how the minimal furnishings weren't chic but depressing. My careful little touches were obviously cheap—those paper birds! I'd been kidding myself.

"Sorry about this place. It's kind of a dump."

"Come here." Guy tugged me to sit with him. I clung to my towel. He put his arm around me. He'd taken off his shirt and wore only his jeans. His stomach was paler than his arms. His torso was broad, faintly lined with muscle.

He was watching a trashy crime drama. On-screen, a pretty woman picked a hair off the ground with tweezers. Drums thumped. Cut to a handsome man peering through a microscope.

"Do you think it was murder?" a voice off-screen asked.

"Either that or she impaled herself," the handsome man quipped, flashing teeth.

Guy brushed hair off my forehead. "Do you need a glass of water?"

My knees were tangled in his. He stroked my face with his thumb. I felt like a cat, leaning into his touch. I kissed him. He moved over me, his body pressing the length of mine. His keys were in his pocket, cutting into my leg. I held his elbow, tracing the hollow of his bicep. His lips tasted of salt. We were both sweating. The air conditioner must have cut out again.

He left my towel on longer than I wanted him to.

His body, more solid than Bryant's. Graceful, forceful. Moving me, lifting me at the hinges like a doll, under a knee, at my hips. He was unshy, his hand moving expertly down from my chest. We sat up together and he held my hips so hard the next day I'd still feel the place he'd touched.

In the morning, he was gone. No note. The smell of cigarettes and a fine layer of dust in my sheets the only evidence I hadn't dreamed it.

And this: a key on the counter. At first I thought he'd forgotten his, and then I recognized it as my copy of the Martins' house key.

I turned it over in my palm, until my skin was warm and smelled metallic. I wondered what they'd planned to do with it. My purse lay where I'd dropped it on the floor, the cash intact.

All morning, snatches of the night resurfaced.

My forearms on the sticky bar, running my thumb over the wood grain. Behind the shelves of liquor bottles, a mirror showed snatches of our faces.

Guy asking where my boyfriend was. Me, lip curled, telling him Bryant was traveling. *He's very important,* I'd sneered.

He asked what they were doing about Iris.

I told him Philip denied it. I said the Senator was furious. And Marina. It slipped out, like I'd been waiting for a confidant.

He listened, tracing the rim of his glass.

"Is she really pregnant?" I asked.

"What do you think?" He dug his wallet from his back pocket, and counted out cash.

The next morning, I couldn't remember his tone. *What do you think?* Sarcastic? Bitter?

Of course she is.

Or—obviously not?

The day passed in a pulsing hangover and a fever of self-disgust. I slept, chewed through a bag of potato chips, swallowed tonic water plain, adding tap water to stretch it. By dinnertime, I felt better. I drank a cup of coffee and noticed my thoughts were beginning to move in orderly patterns again. I was surprised to find myself ravenous. I scrambled the last of a carton of eggs (expired) until they were safely overcooked and rubbery. I settled in bed and watched the news. The star Diamondbacks player out with an injury. Another wave of heat coming our way, as if fanned by the wildfires in California. And, briefly, an update on the Martin Family Tragedy: Gonzales released a statement offering thoughts and prayers for Senator Martin and his family. He was formal and composed, reading at the podium, but when he finished, the reporters clamored, asking how this might affect the campaign, whether he would reschedule events . . . He waved them off. "It's not the time to think of that yet."

I snorted. They were thinking of it, all of them. Bryant would plan the Senator's next appearance to the last detail: the clothes, the flag pin, the words to say about Ammy. Eventually, Philip and Marina would join him again.

And Iris, what would she do next? She was obviously still involved, or Guy wouldn't be worried.

My sheets smelled like Guy. Cheap cologne, the sort that clung to everything, skunk spray. And smoke. *What do you think?*

I thought he was a liar, a fake, just like his sister. Taking advantage of Amabel to get to me. He'd fooled me, just like Iris had. Everything was her fault. She'd kicked off the chain reaction, bumped the domino, pulled out the pin that collapsed the wall.

Anger felt satisfying and right.

Googling Iris's cell number led me to dozens of websites offering her personal information for a fee. I clicked the first. The page prompted me to enter my credit card number and was littered with ads for miracle weight loss pills and searches to reconnect with high school classmates. No reassuring badge promised to protect my identity. I didn't have anything to steal, anyway.

Iris Jessica Jamison lived an hour south of Phoenix, in some town called Verde.

27

Though I'd never heard of Verde, I'd been there before. The town sat along the same desolate highway as the Sunset Motel.

My spare tire ground loudly as I drove. Uneasiness blunted my anger. Philip had come down here, to Iris's territory. I couldn't think why. All I knew was he'd lied.

The Verde exit was surreally familiar: a blazing truck stop, a billboard of a baby's arm grasping air ("Take my hand, not my life"). If I kept driving another five minutes, I'd be at the motel. I pulled off.

I drove down Main Street. Drugstores, diners, liquor stores, churches with Spanish masses, an ominous concrete hulk called the Treatment Center.

I've learned more about this girl, the Senator had said. *Where she comes from.*

My dad lived in a town like this, in Indiana. Replace the drab, flat desert in every direction with cornfields to the horizon, swap the stucco for aluminum siding. His house was a former farm. He played at country living with my stepmother, an artist who wove wall hangings and sold them online. My dad worked in the city, driving ninety minutes in each direction, so he was home late. He liked the deep country dark, the roof of stars like a colander overhead. Smoking a cigar, he walked the perimeter of the property, where the old post-and-wire fence still stood. Once, a carload of drunk kids swerved off the road and went through it, landing in the field ten yards away. They'd gotten out of the car and scattered, laughing, leaving spills of oil and vomit.

I hadn't thought of that in years. Remembering Erica seemed to have broken the membrane in my mind that had held apart my family, my old self. It wasn't a comfortable feeling.

My phone alerted me to my upcoming turn, and I snapped back to Verde. Over the bank, a sign flashed the time and temperature: 8:46, 99°. The sun had set without much drama, leaving a hazy purple sky.

I turned off the main drag into the grid of residential streets. Little ranch houses with pale gravel lawns.

The Senator's red yard sign sprouted everywhere, like a determined weed. I rolled my windows down to get a better look at the address numbers tiled on the houses. The air was still woolly with heat. No wonder there was no one out, not a kid on a bike, not a couple walking the dog.

I turned onto Iris's block, and a strong smell blew in. Smoky, with a chemical tinge, like someone burning trash. Iris's address was a white shoebox. Short and squat, as though it had been stepped on. The driveway bisected a yard of pebbles and terminated in a low carport. Beneath it, Guy's motorcycle leaned on its kickstand.

This wasn't the place I'd imagined for Iris, with her rich-girl style and spoiled manners. On the other hand, it suited her perfectly. Cheap and mean. Clearly, she wanted money from the Martins, and had nothing to lose.

I parked down the block, not wanting her to spot my car. My wheels sunk into the shoulder, and I hoped I wasn't risking another flat. Flipping my visor down, I studied myself in the mirror. In the last few days, I hadn't eaten much, and my face was thin and sharp. I looked a little like Iris. I felt slippery and dangerous. I stuffed the cash in my glove compartment and locked the car.

Outside, the fire smell was more intense, a sharp battery edge to it. All the houses were shut up tight against it, windows closed, blinds pulled, air conditioners droning loud as cicadas.

Walking up the street, I felt a ripple of giddiness. Of all the Martins, I was the only one who could do this: knock on Iris's door and challenge her.

Guy's bike slowed my momentum. A filthy rag hung from the handlebars, and I remembered the dust in my sheets with a flash between my legs, desire mingling with shame. I hesitated outside the side door, watching a spider crawl up the stucco and tuck itself under the doorframe. Then I heard a car coming, and instinctively stepped behind the bike.

It wasn't Iris's car but a glossy black sedan. It moved at the pace of a slow walk, its engine purring. Its windows were black as paint. I dropped lower behind Guy's bike.

After the car passed, my fear felt silly. I was worked up over Iris, that's all. I remembered her entering the Martins' house, how she couldn't stand still, how she'd touched things and fidgeted. It was nerves, the same I felt now, every hair on my neck at attention, my muscles itching to run. It was hard to think.

Iris might not even be home.

I slipped around the corner into the backyard.

At the end of the house, a window was lit. I moved swiftly toward it, jogging across a patio, past sliding doors showing a dark interior. Stepping off the brick, my sandals sunk into a bed of pebbles. They crunched underfoot, loud as a marching band to my ears.

An oleander bush grew beneath the window, covered in white flowers thin and crinkled as tissues. I crouched beside it, trying to slow my breathing.

My ears had been turned inward, to the rushing of my lungs, the frenzy of my pulse. Now, they opened to the night. Something scraped and rustled inside the oleander. Birds, I hoped. Through the window came the muffled sound of a laugh track.

Bracing against the stucco, I carefully raised myself, until I was half standing, half squatting at the window. My legs shook with adrenaline.

At first I couldn't see much. The blind was down, and the slats ran in stripes across my view. A beige carpet, a dark sofa, an accordion lampshade throwing brown light. Gradually, my eyes relaxed, and I saw better. A black coffee table. Bare feet propped up. Ankles porcelain white, toes siren red.

Iris.

I shifted to see her better. I had to press my face close to the glass. But it was bright inside, and dark out. She couldn't see me.

She was slouched on the couch, head thrown back against the pillows, chewing on the end of her ponytail. She seemed different. Her face was puffy. She hugged a pillow to her stomach, a Diet Coke balanced on top. She was definitely bigger, looser. Pregnant, I thought, she really is. My fist ground into the stucco.

My sandal slipped and I went down, scraping my wrist against the wall. The suddenness was jolting. I knelt, horrified, below the window, waiting for the blinds to lift, Iris to look out.

Nothing happened. The night continued its rustling, scraping business. I breathed again. I shook the pebbles from my shoes and eased myself back up.

Guy had entered the room. He stood across from the window, leaning in a door I hadn't noticed when I was staring at Iris. It was dark, presumably leading to a hallway. He wore the same jeans as the night before, fabric bagging in the legs. As usual, he was restless, shifting from foot to foot, biting his nails. I knew he picked at his calluses, too, the hard caps of blisters on his palm. I wondered what he'd done after sneaking out of my apartment. Whether he'd told Iris about me— whether they'd laughed.

But now they were ignoring each other, like any bored siblings would. She'd drawn her feet onto the couch and tucked them under her.

Guy turned to the door. He leaned a hand against the frame. And Iris stepped into it.

This was Iris. Her face wore a prissy grimace; her bright hair bulged in a tumorous bun on her head. Her short dress clung to her perfectly flat stomach. Apparently, her pseudo–maternity outfits had been for my benefit. A hard lozenge of anger wedged in my sternum. Her fault, all of it.

She was talking with Guy, their voices inaudible beneath the TV. I glanced at the girl on the couch. She now seemed obviously not Iris. I'd only seen who I'd expected to see. Her face was softer and plainer, her hair a paler red. She chewed her lip, anxiously watching Guy and Iris.

They were fighting, Iris's face lively with anger, or disdain. She reached up and pummeled Guy with her fists, landing blows on his shoulder and chest. He grabbed her hands and held them together, making her twist and flail against his grip. With a growling screech, she pulled away. She cradled her wrists to her chest, wearing a pout that could sell lipstick.

She was so fake. A conniving bitch, a despicable liar who'd destroyed Amabel.

Guy fell for it. He leaned down as if he were going to kiss her—instead he whispered into her ear. He ran his hands down her bare arms, to her hands, squeezed them. He went out into the dark hallway.

My heart was pounding. I remembered suddenly how I'd cried in bed, after we'd had sex, and he'd held me.

Iris approached the window, and I was too startled to duck. My face froze in a silent gasp. But she kept moving, sat on the couch. She curled her arm around the girl and spoke to her. The girl kept her eyes on the TV, and Iris raised her voice, angry, shaking her shoulder. The girl spun toward her, mouth dropped open.

Iris kept talking. The girl seemed frightened. She nodded, a nervous bob of the chin.

When Guy returned, he wore a backpack over a shoulder and gripped a duffel bag. His whole body was rigid.

Their anxiety was contagious. I glanced behind me. Total darkness had fallen, erasing the yard. Was the night always so quiet? In the silence, the smell of fire was more powerful.

When I looked back in, Guy and Iris were leaving, their fingers twined together.

I ran along the back of the house, the gravel slinging away from my feet. I squatted at the corner of the driveway. The bike waited. I waited.

When they came out, they were still arguing.

"Not worth the risk," Guy was saying.

Iris's laugh like a caw. "Wouldn't do it to me." Their feet scraped the pavement.

I peered around the corner. Guy was fastening Iris's helmet, her face tilting up. I could see the sharp jut of her chin, her little nose. Guy kissed her, not a passionate kiss, but a touch on the lips. A kiss that spoke of routine, of long familiarity.

How novel Guy had felt to me, and also nostalgic—the smell of Pert Plus and cigarettes, the crispy gel in his hair, the calluses on his hands. Like the boys I'd known as Natalie, and I'd fallen for it, as if I hadn't changed a bit.

Drawing back around the house, I sat, legs spread in front of me, dumb.

The bike's engine roared to life, and I knew without watching that Guy drove and Iris held on to him, her cheek pressed to his back. (The smell of salt, of oranges, the warm breeze.)

I listened to the bike ease down the driveway then gallop noisily up the street, until the sound faded to silence.

28

Everything, everything, she'd said was a lie.

I waded through a carpet of takeout menus and coupon clippers and junk mail to their front door. Cheap hollow metal, just like my apartment door. A motion detector light snapped on, accusatory.

Just a week ago, I'd thought nothing of letting myself into the Martins' house, wandering through the laundry room and setting up coffee in the kitchen, helping myself to a piece of fruit from the bowl. I knew the garage code. I knew where they kept the safe, which medicines were in the cabinet, the brand of milk they preferred. Somehow, that house had led me to this one.

Everything everyone had said was a lie.

I pressed the bell.

The door opened the length of the chain lock, and the Iris lookalike peered out. Her hair frizzed in a halo around her face.

"Hi." My voice cracked, brittle. I hadn't spoken all day. "Is Iris home?"

The girl shook her head.

"Really? She told me to meet her here." I pretended to check a watch on my naked wrist. The girl didn't notice.

"She's out." Her voice operated with a slight delay. A dreamy, serene monotone.

"Will she be back soon?"

She might have shrugged; the sliver of her face betrayed nothing.

"Well—" I turned away, as if about to leave, and hesitated. "Could I use your bathroom? Long drive home."

Her hand tightened on the doorknob, shrinking the angle of the open door. "I'm not supposed to let anyone in. There are creepers around here."

"Creepers?" I wished I could get a better look at her face. By the smell drifting from the house, I guessed she was stoned, and maybe drunk.

"Iris said to lock the door."

"Are you alone?" I winced. It was something a *creeper* would ask.

She stared at me, unmoving.

"I'm not a creeper. I'm a friend of Iris's. I won't be long, I promise."

Sighing, she jangled the locks and swung the door open. The moment I was inside, she pressed it closed and locked it again.

The smell was oppressive, skunky pot and incense battling with the fug of dog. I held out my hand to the girl and she put her palm in it, limp as a frightened rabbit.

"I'm Finn."

"Stacy." She crossed her arms over her belly. Her similarity to Iris was at once striking and submerged, like a watercolor painting of a photograph. She wore a loose black dress that made her skin pale as milk. On the top of her left foot, a tattoo scrawled, illegible cursive, festooned with flowers and hearts.

She studied me with the same curiosity. "Iris doesn't have many friends over."

"I know her through Guy. You're her sister?"

She nodded, reaching to toy with a gold locket on a slim chain.

"Older or younger?"

"She's my big sister."

I smiled, out of conversation. We were in a fusty, cramped living room. A pair of tufted armchairs flanked a mauve love seat, where a runty yellow-white dog was curled, so still it might have been dead. A glassed-in cabinet displayed dozens of porcelain statuettes: couples embracing, a baby angel sleeping on a swan, girls in white dresses. An archway opened into the dining room, where heavy furniture loomed in the dark. In the other direction was a narrow hallway lined with closed doors. The sound of the TV carried from the end of it. The little dead dog gave a wheezing snore.

"Well," Stacy said. "Bathroom's through here." She pointed down the hall and started that way herself. Her walk was languid, drifting, like her speech. She went into the last room without glancing back.

I lingered, waiting for her to be safely absorbed in the TV. My pulse was humming. I figured I had about five minutes.

I sidled down the hallway, into the first door. A bedroom, as garish and loud as Stacy had been plain and quiet. Green paint, pink bedspread, photographs covering a wall. I stepped closer, trampling piles of clothing. They were old pictures, Kodak prints, with red-eye smiles and shiny skin. Most of a boy, maybe sixteen, with a mop of blue-black hair and eyes the color of a new penny. Skateboarding, holding a guitar, smoking a cigarette and doing his best James Dean impression.

In one photo, he stood beside a girl in a prom dress. She was almost painfully pretty. Platinum hair, wide princess eyes, smile white as a fresh slice of apple.

She appeared again and again, in capris, bikini, pajamas. It took me a while to recognize her as Stacy. Not only because she was older, and no longer blond. She'd faded, somehow.

I moved on, having dawdled too long.

Next was the bathroom, medicine cabinet stocked with a half dozen prescription bottles made out to Stacy Jamison. Nothing I recognized, nothing to give a clue as to her illness, just warnings against using alcohol and heavy machinery.

The last room was across from the den, where a commercial blared. I hoped Stacy was stupefied on the sofa. I slipped in and shut the door behind me.

Iris's personality shouted through the room. In the pictures of fashion models pinned to the walls, the red silk sheets, the mirrored closet doors. Two closets, because this was the master bedroom. The en suite bathroom was ostentatious-nineties, pebbled glass and gold trim. The vanity was filmed with decades of dirt, the tiles rimmed with black mold. I picked through the drawers. No prenatal vitamins, no medications, no special pregnancy paraphernalia. A bulk box of tampons was stashed under the sink.

I moved on to the closets. One stuffed with clothes, so crowded they were pressed into wrinkles. When I rifled through the hangers, I noticed labels Marina wore.

The other closet was all bags and shoes. Here I was lucky. In a floppy leather handbag, I discovered a case of birth control pills, punched out to Thursday. Today.

I smiled, my lips stiff from disuse. Iris wasn't pregnant. Wasn't having Philip's baby, couldn't go to the tabloids and smear the Martins' name. I pocketed the case, pleased to imagine Iris digging through her things, trying to find it.

I went through her nightstand next, searching for a diary, a stash of ultrasounds—how long would she have kept up the charade?—or anything else she might have against Philip. I found a blue glass pipe, cigarettes, gum, loose coins. And finally, folded under a stack of concert tickets, a newspaper article, worn thin at the folds. Society fluff covering this year's Easter brunch benefit; Philip, Marina, and Amabel photographed in front of an ice sculpture.

I skimmed the article, my uncertainty returning. Why did Iris keep this—had she thought Philip looked handsome here? It was a nice shot of him. He held Ammy's hand, and she hid her face against his stomach.

I was so absorbed in the photograph that I didn't notice Stacy until she cleared her throat.

I crushed the article in my fist and braced for the torrent of fury I'd get from Iris.

Stacy tilted her head. "What are you doing? The bathroom's out there."

"I used the one in here."

"Why?" She seemed confused, not angry.

"It seemed—more private," I said. She was looking wonderingly at the paper in my fist. I rushed to the closet and ran my fingers down an embroidered sleeve. "I got distracted by her clothes. She has really nice things."

Stacy hummed. "She doesn't let anyone borrow them."

I studied her. Resentment? Envy? She was monotonous as a cornfield, and seemed equally wholesome and unsurprising.

"You done?" She flipped off the light and headed back to the den. I trailed behind. She flopped on the floor in front of the couch, stretching her legs. I hovered in the doorway, across from the window. I felt uneasy, as if now someone were watching me. On TV, coiffed middle-aged women argued drunkenly in the back of a limo.

Stacy uncapped a bottle of nail polish and bent her

knee under her chin. She slicked red over her toenails unsteadily.

"Where did Iris and Guy go?" I asked.

"Out." She was concentrating and didn't look up.

"Do you think they'll be back?"

"Nope. She's spending the night." She sighed. Polish had dripped onto the carpet. She didn't mop it up, but simply dipped the brush back into the bottle and swept off the excess. Suddenly, she said, "It's funny, because they're breaking up anyway."

"Really? She didn't mention that to me."

Stacy smiled. "It's a secret. We're going away soon. Finally."

"Really?" I said again. "Where are you going?"

She blew hair from her face. "Anywhere's better than here. I hope California."

"When are you leaving?" I was careful to keep my voice even.

"Soon," she said. "We're going to get some money."

"You're not packed," I said. Calmly, casually.

"We're traveling light," she said in a singsong, like she was quoting someone. She laughed softly.

I swallowed my anger. So Iris was still scheming. Traveling light, breaking up with Guy, anticipating money. I thought of the cash in my glove compartment. Was another envelope stuffed with crisp bills heading

Iris's way? For what? I still couldn't say what my own money was for; it didn't feel like severance, not the way they'd done it. It was for something else, and it made me as uneasy as the black window I was facing, as the old newspaper article in Iris's drawer and the key Guy left on my dresser.

Having finished one foot, Stacy stretched her leg and wiggled her toes. "So how do you know Iris again?"

"Through a mutual friend." I studied her. Maybe she wasn't as ignorant as she seemed. An actress, like her sister. "Maybe you know him. Philip Martin?"

She glanced up. Her lips were parted innocently, a dash between her eyebrows. "I don't think so."

"She's really close with him," I went on. "Actually, she's pregnant. I guess that's why she's breaking up with Guy."

I expected doubt, or concern. Instead Stacy froze, the brush lifted in midair like a conductor's baton. "She isn't! She would never!"

She bolted upward, kicking, the polish tipping over. Her body was bigger, stronger in motion. I put my arms out to defend myself, but she pushed past me and charged down the hallway.

I found her in the kitchen, holding the receiver of an old landline phone, her fingers spinning the rotary dial. Instinctively, I dropped my hand on the cradle, cutting off the call.

Her mouth opened to an O. Her face was red-streaked, puffy.

"I'm sorry." My voice was loud and angry. I took the phone away and hung it up.

Sobs shuddered in her chest. I was frightened of her emotion, of the noisiness in the silent house. It seemed that the whole town would hear. "Don't be upset," I said desperately, the way I'd begged Ammy to calm down from a tantrum.

In the cabinets, I found a sleeve of red plastic cups and filled one with tap water. Stacy took it from me, obedient, making a face as she sipped. She hiccupped.

I wished for Amabel. A piercing ache for the tiny tender gestures that made up our days. I wanted to pour her a glass of juice, coax tangles from her hair, talk her out of a bad dream.

Stacy was oblivious to my wince of pain. She wiped her face with the back of her hand, like a child. I noticed something I hadn't before. On her wrists, a thickening of the skin, purplish. Old scars.

She saw me see them. She wrapped her empty hand around her wrist protectively.

I looked away. Even in the spastic glow of the over-head light, I could see how filthy the place was. Little brown spots on the counter suggested cockroaches. My pity for Stacy was as instinctive and strong as my dislike of her sister. I wondered what her story was.

Stacy sniffled. "I'm sorry about that."

"Don't be. Why did you get so upset?" When she hugged herself without responding, I added, "I don't think she's really pregnant."

Her fingers traveled to the locket again, and she ran the heart along its chain.

"What did Iris say to you before she left? It looked like you were arguing."

Her shoulders rose defensively. "How did you know?"

Stupid, I thought. I should have asked whether Iris had ever been a waitress, why she was breaking up with Guy. Questions that wouldn't make Stacy tip her head to the side and frown at me. Suspicious, finally, of the stranger in her house.

A jangling screech filled the room, terrifying me before I realized it was the phone, its ring throaty and demanding. I grabbed Stacy's elbow so she wouldn't answer.

We waited through a dozen rings. When it stopped, the silence of the house intensified.

Stacy was leaning away from me, frightened. I let her go. "I'm so sorry. I never meant to upset you. I'm going now."

I went out through the dining room, my steps rattling the porcelain figurines. I shut the door behind me.

The night was a warm, dark mouth. No streetlights, no yard lights. The smell of fire was strong. I walked into it blindly. Rocks shifted under my feet when I went wide of the driveway. Finally my eyes adjusted, and I could make out the slanting mailboxes, and the chain link fences glinting in the moonlight, and the pale, crumbling edge of the road.

I started to jog, slow and noisy, scuffing the pavement. Stacy might be calling Iris on her heavy telephone.

Then I stopped. A black sedan had parked right behind my car. We were the only cars on the street, but the sedan was so close its nose kissed my bumper.

My eyes darted to the lit windows of the nearby houses. But they were all covered; I didn't see a face, even a shadow, moving. I pulled my keys from my pocket and held them between my fingers like claws, as my mom had taught me to do in parking lots at night. I wondered what exactly I'd do if I was attacked. Punch and prod with the little key?

A moth or fly or a ripple in the air brushed my skin. I ignored it. I walked quickly, holding my head high.

A light hit me in the face, a hot bright beam. I threw a hand over my eyes, but yellow spots flared in my vision. My keys fell to the ground with a distant jangle. Someone came toward me, a scraping sound like boots.

"Hey!" A man's voice, deep.

He grabbed my wrist, and I yanked away and stumbled, landing squarely on the pavement, the wind knocked out of me.

Once, years ago, I fell from a tree behind my mom's house. I hit the ground and suddenly I couldn't breathe. I wasn't in pain; I felt only panic. My lungs were disabled, unplugged. A few yards away, my mom dozed on a deck chair, heavily pregnant, oblivious. A can of Coke sat at her feet. I remember so clearly that precise shade of red.

After I fell on Iris's street, the light dropped from my face and slid down my body.

"Miss?" the man said. "Miss?"

I touched my mouth and tasted hot mineral pavement, the rasp of sand on my tongue. I sat back on my heels and slowly looked up. Shiny loafers. Dark canvas pants. Broad belt, heavy with the weight of a holstered revolver. A cop.

The morning after the accident, two police officers came to my hospital room. I was groggy, dazed. They told me Erica had died. Without pausing to let it sink in, they started in on their questions. I still remembered their formal posture, and the dull glint of their weapons, and their demeanor: distrustful, cold, robotic in their protocol.

At the sight of this cop, I felt a surge of old guilt and shame.

"Get up." He reached an arm down to me. It was bare, thick and veined, tattooed with an eagle grasping a machine gun in its claws. I stared at it, still catching my breath. He seized my elbow and hauled me to my feet. His fingers were hard as metal tools. When he released me, I brought my arm into my chest, shocked.

The cop was short, compact, with a weight lifter's torso. His head was shaved bald and looked shiny, almost plastic.

His flashlight trailed over me, my ankles, my legs, my midriff. "You don't have a weapon, do you?" The light reached my face and stayed a moment longer than necessary. My eyes stung.

"No," I said, trying to resist the impulse to lower my gaze, thinking I might seem guilty. Had Iris seen me in her yard and called the police?

He was chewing gum, snapping it in his jaws. He seemed keyed up, like he'd been bored and this was his fun. He was young, I thought, and new to this. Enjoying it. His flashlight flicked over my chest again before pointing at my car.

"This your vehicle?"

I nodded. The pain in my arm was sharp as a warning. *Be careful.* After Erica, I'd expected the cops to be on my side, and I wouldn't make that mistake again. I followed him, keeping my distance.

In the beam of his flashlight, my car looked abandoned, slanting over on its lame tire, dust coating its sides like talc powder. The cop stepped close to peer into the windows. I worried about the cash. But the windows were intact; no one had broken in.

"Is there a problem?" I asked.

He didn't answer. Stepping away, he set the flashlight on top of his car. Through the dark windshield, I thought I saw a siren perched on the dash.

"License," he said, extending a hand.

I dug out my phone. My credit card and ID were wedged in the case. "I was just about to move my car. If that's the problem."

He squinted at my ID. "Finn Hunt, 4411 McClintock." He threw his glance to me, like a dart. "Correct?"

I nodded.

"That across from the old car wash? Got, like, pink palm trees on the sign. Let me think." He snapped his fingers. "McClintock Village. Right?"

I stared at him.

His eyes glittered playfully. "A friend of mine lives there."

I swallowed. "Funny."

"Small world." He scratched his neck with the corner of my ID. "You might be neighbors."

I crossed my arms. My skin was covered in a film of dirt. It itched badly. His mocking smile seemed to suggest that he knew something about me. Maybe he was friends with Iris—maybe she'd asked him to mess with me.

He handed back my license. Then, as though settling in for a while, he leaned back on his heels and sank his fingers through his belt loops. The eagle on his forearm was spreading its wings. There was a ring around it, decorative, like a laurel. "Strange time for a stroll, Finn."

"I'm sorry?"

"It's dark. Late. No one's out." He gestured. "You noticed?"

"I just left my friend's house."

"Aha." He rose up on his heels, crossing his arms. "And where does she live? Or is it a he?" He flashed his narrow teeth.

I wanted to lie but didn't think I could pull it off. "She lives back there. The white house."

"And you parked all the way over here?"

I nodded.

"I'm surprised," he said. "After what happened, I mean."

He waited for me to pick up the bait. When I didn't he said, "A week ago someone set a car on fire. Right on the street. About this time of night. Lit the thing up." He chewed his gum. His gaze was over my head, on Iris's house. "Must have used a bucket of kerosene. Huge fire. Dangerous. Could have jumped to a house, easily. Could have leveled three or four of these shoeboxes. Pardon the expression." He lowered his eyes to mine again. "Iris Jamison is your friend, isn't she?"

I didn't nod; we weren't friends, and I was still absorbing his words.

"Her car was the one burned."

I hadn't wanted to take my eyes off him, but I couldn't help turning to Iris's house. It sat in darkness. No silver and white car in the port. The smell of fire filled the night. I thought of Stacy, peering out the chained door. *Creepers.*

"You're surprised," he said. "I'd have thought she'd tell you. She was real shaken up."

"Of course." I said, "I mean, of course she was upset."

"Really, she got lucky. Think if the car had been in

the driveway. If the fire had spread to the house." He shook his head. "We're taking it seriously. Gotta check out any strange cars after dark . . ."

I felt my shoulders relax. "I understand. I hope you catch whoever did it."

He smiled. "I'm sure we will." He reached up and shut off the flashlight. We were plunged into darkness.

Startled, I backed away. I heard a distant bark. It only made me feel more alone. "I'll be careful."

"Good." I could see his white, wet teeth. His dark clothes were invisible; his forearms, neck, and scalp were pale shapes. "That's all I need. I'll say good night now."

He moved to my car and took hold of the door handle. Unwillingly, I unlocked it. He opened the door for me, kept his hands on it as I slid in. I moved quickly, pulling my legs in fast, away from him.

"Drive safe." He almost whispered it. Then he was pressing the door shut, and I felt a rush of relief as my lungs untightened and my throat opened.

But he changed his mind and swung the door back open. He leaned down. "By the way. Your tire's looking pretty bad. I'd get it fixed if I were you. Can't be so careless." He clucked in disapproval.

I garbled a mouthful of agreement and apology, and he shut the door in the middle of it. I reached over and hit the lock. Hearing it, he smiled and rapped the window with his knuckles. I watched in the rearview as he strolled back to his car. I scratched my key at the ignition, finally slid it in, got the car started. I pulled forward, the tires spitting gravel. Behind me, the sedan glinted on the side of the road. Was he in it? I couldn't tell. I had to force myself to look at the road; my eyes kept leaping back up to the mirror.

I turned off Iris's street. Back to the main road, past the bank and the Treatment Center. I was tempted by the blazing lit-up truck stop and had to grit my teeth as I got onto the dark highway. I wanted miles between us.

Below my panic was a disgusted, smeary feeling.

29

I stopped at a gas station and locked myself in the bathroom. I wetted paper towels and wiped the dust from my legs. The paper dissolved in clumps. I remembered wiping Amabel's legs under the pink lights of The Grove's restroom. She'd spilled her milk. I could see her so clearly, her scraped knees and sleepy eyes. I saw myself speaking to her, my clean clothes, my calm. The image felt much more real than the moment I lived in. The girl in the mirror looked feral, eyes hooded and dark, lips cracked and purple. A bruise rose on my elbow, where the cop had grabbed me.

I leaned against the filthy door. It was only a jerk cop, I told myself. Put him from your mind.

I drove north without seeing the road.

Someone had burned Iris's car. I thought back to the last time I saw her driving it. Leaving the Martins' house. Days and days ago. The dented-up white panel in front, the dull silver sides, her arm holding a cigarette out the window. Someone had doused her car in kerosene and let it burn.

No wonder she and Guy were anxious. They must be hiding out somewhere, leaving her poor sister home alone.

I needed help. And I wasn't going back to my apartment tonight, absolutely not. McClintock Village. *Might be neighbors.*

Bryant's parking garage smelled luxuriously of oil and wax. The fleet of expensive cars seemed asleep under the low lights. I hurried between them, a creepy, jumping fear in the empty, echoing concrete.

When I stepped outside I felt safer. The courtyard was extravagantly lit with lamps and spotlights and glowing fountains. Sprinklers chattered, saturating the air with cool spray and the friendly smell of wet soil. After Verde, this was Oz.

Bryant opened his door, surprised. "Finn. There you are."

I rushed into him, wrapping my arms around his familiar narrow shoulders.

When I drew away, he looked at his hand. "You're covered in dirt."

"I'm sorry." I brushed at his shirt.

"It's fine." He headed back into the kitchen. "What happened? I called you a couple times. I was starting to worry."

I felt a kick of shame in my belly, like a flick of a belt. I'd avoided his calls all day. "I'm sorry. My phone died."

I trailed after him. He'd been working at the island. A paper bag of takeout was crushed on the counter, and a tumbler of bourbon sweated beside his laptop, which was opened to a spreadsheet dense with numbers.

"You've been back awhile."

"A few hours." He hit the sleep button, plunging the screen into darkness. "Like I said, I've been calling you."

"I'm here now. I really wanted to talk to you."

He hummed. A muscle in his jaw jumped. "I heard you went to the funeral," he blurted. "That's why you wouldn't come to Flagstaff, wasn't it?"

I was relieved. He was angry about the funeral, not . . . Not last night.

"Yes," I admitted. "I knew where they went to church, and figured out the time."

"Jim wasn't pleased. He thought it was disrespectful."

I flinched at the idea of the Senator complaining about me to Bryant. I looked at the floor. My legs were still mottled with dust from Iris's yard. Only yesterday, I'd worn Marina's dress to the church. I'd been so clean, so sad, so sorry. "You should have seen it. That big church and no one there for Ammy."

Remembering how Marina mentioned my going home, again I had the feeling they'd all discussed me.

"They shouldn't be upset I said goodbye," I mumbled.

He sighed. "Just don't lie to me. Please?"

I nodded, but my fingers crossed at my side, a gesture I'd taught Ammy. *I was crossing my fingers,* she'd crow, usually after she agreed to pick up her room or wash up for bed.

"Good." Bryant took his glass to the bar and refilled it, pouring me a drink, too. He sat on the couch, lying back against the cushion.

I joined him. My body stiffened on contact with the slick leather. The dizziness I'd felt, lying down here to sleep on Sunday afternoon. The silhouette of the Senator's driver looming over me, the too-soft sink of the cushions, the residual damp stickiness in the morning . . . I took a bracing swallow of booze. "I have to tell you something."

Bryant was already halfway through his drink. "Yes?"

"I went to see Iris today."

He rolled his head to look at me. His eyes were glossy. "The redhead?"

I nodded.

"I thought you were going to let it be," he said.

"No, listen." I told him how angry I'd gotten—how it was her fault. He protested, but I spoke over him. I explained that I'd found her address and decided to drive down. Confront her.

"I went around to look in the window a little. Just to see if she was home. She was there, with Guy. You remember . . . her brother. When they left, I rang the doorbell. Her sister let me in. She talked to me. She said Iris is still expecting money—that they're going to leave town."

Bryant bowed his neck, frowning. "That's all very convoluted." His glass had dripped on his pant leg, and he rubbed at the spot with a thumb.

In a leap, I thought: He doesn't know Iris's story. They didn't tell him.

"Iris threatened Philip," I explained. "She said she was pregnant, and it was his."

Bryant winced. The very idea sickened him. I rushed on.

"Tonight I found out she's definitely not pregnant. I have proof." I brought out the birth control pill case, set it on his coffee table. He stared at it, blinking. On the thick polished glass it seemed vulgar, like I'd tossed a hank of hair, or a dirty sock.

After a moment, he sighed. Rubbed his head with his hand, mussing his hair. "Finn, this isn't good."

"I know," I said. "I think she's still blackmailing Philip."

"No."

"Yes. It must be. Why else would she be expecting money?"

"No, Finn. Not Iris. You."

"What?"

"Listen to yourself! You're snooping around someone's house? You're breaking in, stealing things? What are you thinking?"

"You don't un—"

"They told you to keep out of it. I told you! It's none of your business. You'll only make things worse."

It was a slap. I brought my hand to my hair. "How could I make it worse?"

"Let's say she goes to the police, saying you broke into her house. Say it gets out that the Martins' nanny broke in. The media would go insane."

"Quit saying I broke in. I didn't. Stacy let me in."

"Stacy?"

"Iris's sister."

He slammed his glass on the table. "Now you've introduced yourself to her sister? What good can possibly come of this, Finn? Tell me, how will it help Philip?"

He was furious. I shrank back. "I thought—"

"No, you didn't think." He managed to control his voice, and spoke softly, holding my knee. "Listen to me. I can forgive you for going to the funeral, even if you weren't invited. You loved Amabel. Even the Martins can forgive that. But this kind of thing . . . This is really dangerous, Finn. You might get into real trouble. Trouble I can't help you get out of."

I wet my lips. "I know. As I was leaving, a cop stopped me."

He leaned forward, elbows on his knees. "For what? Trespassing?"

I shook my head. "More like . . . a warning. He told me someone burned Iris's car."

Bryant draped a hand over his eyes, as if he had a headache.

I fumbled into the silence. "You don't think Philip . . ." My voice failed.

He lifted his hand. His face was rigid with the importance of his words. "Listen to me. They're dangerous. Iris and Guy. They're criminals. Stay away from them. Don't go anywhere near them. Do you promise?" He followed my glance to the table. "Do you think these pills prove anything? Do you really want Philip to know what you did? Do you really think he'll be grateful?"

I shook my head. I was trembling. I'd never seen Bryant so angry.

The condo filled with silence. A current of air-conditioning raised the hairs on my arms. I'd been wrong. Bryant wasn't out of the loop; Iris's threat wasn't news to him.

"You're right," I said. "It was dumb of me to go there. I'm sorry. I don't know what I was thinking."

Bryant exhaled. "I didn't mean to yell at you. This just freaked me out." He rubbed the back of his head, not looking at me. "I'm going to shower." Standing, he reached and snatched up the pill case. He took it away with him.

I was left alone in the dark living room, the thick smell of leather in my nose, the dust of Iris's back-yard pressing into Bryant's upholstery. I swallowed the last of my drink, spilling down my front. I went to the bar and made another. My hands shook. I drained my glass. Had I eaten today? My knees felt weak, hollow.

I set the glass down and it rattled on the tabletop. I felt raw from Bryant's anger, but I told myself I deserved it. Not for going to Verde, but for Guy.

I climbed the stairs, my legs unsteady. The shower was running. I opened the bathroom door. Steam filled the upper half of the room. Through the glass partition, I watched Bryant rinse shampoo from his hair. Noticing me, he froze, as if afraid. Then I saw that he was crying. His entire face was red. Stricken, I stepped forward and touched him. His back was flushed with hot water.

"What's wrong?"

He turned his face into the stream and held it there, and then wiped his hair off his forehead. "Come here," he whispered.

I peeled off my shirt, stepped out of my shorts. I ducked into the shower, shivering. He put his hands on my shoulders and swung me under the stream. We kissed, his chin sharp.

"Just promise you'll stay away," he said.

I nodded. I didn't speak. He accepted it.

Then there was only the noise of the water, and the stamp of feet on tile, and the brief release I felt, like a valve turned until some pressure hissed free, only to be tightly sealed again.

In the small hours of the night, while Bryant slept, I lay awake. I was exhausted but my mind was frenzied. I held the facts awkwardly, unable to find a pattern, as though I'd been dealt too many suits in a losing hand of poker. Iris still expected money, enough to leave town. And she wasn't pregnant, though the Martins had argued fiercely. Someone burned her car. And Bryant was furious with me for getting involved.

He was right: it was dangerous for me to dig into Philip's secrets. But I sensed the risk wasn't what Iris or Guy might do. It was losing Bryant.

Imagine the alternative. I could stay at Bryant's place in the morning. I could get groceries delivered, work out in the condo gym, pass the daylight hours in the cool clean rooms. When he came home from work, I could be pleasant, pouring drinks, asking about his day. I'd study for the GRE. Time would pass, months; the election would keep him busy. Then, when it was over, and the Senator comfortably secured, there would be a pause. If I made it until then, we had a real chance together.

But I'd never know the truth.

I watched Bryant sleep for a long time. When I woke in the morning, he was gone, and I had a text from Iris.

Stay away from my sister.

I made Bryant's bed, folding the sheets into military corners. I dressed and brushed my hair and applied sunscreen. For once I felt completely calm and certain. I wouldn't pretend nothing had happened. I was involved.

30

Not yet noon, and The Grove was already hit by the lunch crowd. White-shirted elbows jutted from every booth. I made my way to the bar and wedged my shoulder in. "Tommy!"

The head bartender spotted me and passed off the bill he was tallying to a waitress. He shook his head as he came over, and I was afraid Philip had told him to send me away. Instead, Tommy took my hands in his smooth, fat ones. His wrist was still smudged with the stamp of whatever club he'd gone to the night before.

"Finn. My God. You must be a disaster. I was a disaster when I heard." His bright blue eyes were iridescent.

I was startled by my gratitude. He was the first

person to offer straightforward sympathy. "I was. I am." I couldn't help squeezing his hands longer than the polite moment he probably intended.

When I let go, he adjusted the bar towel over his shoulder.

"When did you reopen?"

"Today. They called us last night. I guess if you're closed too long, they're afraid the customers will forget about you. But listen to me going on." He lightly docked my chin. "What are you doing here? You should be with that gorgeous boyfriend of yours. He'll take care of you."

"Philip's not here, is he?"

"Not since it happened. You looking for him?"

"He asked me to pick up some papers from his office."

He flashed a coy smile. "Well, well."

I must have stiffened, because he shook his head and said, "Don't pay attention to me. Once I step behind the bar, flirting is a reflex." He tossed me a key. "Bring it back, huh?"

The other bartenders hustled around him, glancing at us curiously.

"One other thing. Did you ever meet a woman named Iris? Did she work here?"

"Doesn't ring a bell."

358 · KELSEY RAE DIMBERG

"She's about my age. Bright red hair. You couldn't miss her."

"Sorry. Lots of girls in and out of here, you know?" He flashed a wink, turned back to the customers, leaving me to wonder what he meant. Girls in the restaurant, girls with Philip?

I locked the office behind me and pulled open the blinds. Dust rose in the air. A dry-cleaning bag hung from a basketball hoop on the wall.

Philip's desk was bare apart from a leather pencil cup and a heavy lamp. The drawers were crammed and disorganized. One by one, I pulled them onto the rug. I was hunting for anything connected to Iris—a pay stub, a letter, a lipstick left behind. I found invoices, a blue zippered pouch jammed with receipts, takeout menus. Everything so chaotic I couldn't possibly keep it in the same position I found it in.

I was about to give up when I noticed the desk lamp was crooked. I lifted it. Under the base, I found a card printed with a setting sun. I opened it. A hotel key was tucked inside, the number 107 scrawled in pen.

I sat in Philip's chair and twisted, thinking. The air was stale and warm. I smelled cigarette smoke, but maybe I was imagining it. Across from me was a black office chair, tricked out with knobs and angled planes of supportive mesh. It had once sat in the Martins' office but neither of them had liked it. The night of Amabel's play, a long-haired stranger had sat there, arguing with Philip. The same man he'd visited at the Sunset Motel, days before Iris's car had burned. Had Philip given him cash, in that envelope? A payment for a fire? Philip might have wanted to scare her. Keep her from showing up all over his town like a bad penny. *We have to take steps.*

Remembering the man's seedy gaze, I thought he'd talk to me, if I acted nice.

I took the key, replaced the drawers, shut the blinds. If Philip heard I was there, I'd say I was trying to find him, that's all.

In the car, the ribbon of road vanishing under my tires, the pressure of the pedal under my foot, my grief fell into a stilled quiet, like a baby momentarily hushed. Telephone poles whipped by. My spare tire groaned noisily. I needed to get to a repair shop. I couldn't afford it. Not unless I dipped into the Martins' cash. But I couldn't start spending it, shearing off a hundred here and there, until it was whittled down to nothing. I still carried the envelope in my purse, touching it with my fingertips now and then, like an amulet.

Turning into the motel, I rolled down my windows.

The blacktop was soft as taffy. I felt as though I were driving through a dream. The quaint wooden sign. The empty parking lot. The green pool.

There wasn't a car in the lot. Strange. As I pulled closer, I saw a ribbon of yellow tape strung along the first-floor balcony. More tape crisscrossed one of the doors, a forbidding X.

I inched forward. There was the old Coke machine, faded to pink in the sun. There was the spot where I watched Philip's brief rendezvous, not with Iris, but with that man.

The taped-off door was the one the man had returned to. Number 107.

The day was silent apart from my shuddering engine. The motel seemed abandoned. I unbuckled and stepped out. The sun cracked over my skull and heat poured down my skin. My heels sank into the tar. I walked cautiously, waiting for a door to open, a police car to drive in. Nothing. Blinds were pulled down over the office window, where a sign read simply, CLOSED. I passed the soda machine, which groaned in the heat. At the taped door, some wild part of me wanted to swipe the keycard and see what happened. Instead I cupped my hands to the window. Curtains sealed off the glass, a thin crack between them. Through the murky darkness, I made out the white corner of a mattress.

I drew back and my face reflected in the dirty glass. Stark red lips, hoop earrings, blue silk blouse. *What's a girl like you doing in a place like this?* I imagined the long-haired man saying, if he'd been here. Instead there was silence.

I stopped at a diner down the road. I walked unsteadily across the lot and into the waiting area, where the glaze of sweat on my skin evaporated instantly in the air-conditioning. The waitress tipped her head at the tables, indicating that I could sit anywhere. I perched on a counter stool. She was quick to bring a glass of water, and I emptied it, the ice stinging my teeth. She offered a menu, but I waved it away.

"Can I have some toast? And maybe orange juice."

"Maybe?" She fanned herself with the menu, bored.

"Yes, orange juice."

She stuck the order paper through to the kitchen. Reaching back to tighten her apron, she chatted with an old couple perched on stools. A newspaper was folded on the counter beside them.

I leaned over. "May I borrow this?"

The man flicked his hand dismissively. They were intently discussing the heat.

The story was on the front page, below the fold: POLICE INVESTIGATE SUSPICIOUS MOTEL DEATH. The text box was a postage stamp, one line only: "The death of a man staying at the Sunset Motel continues to be considered suspicious, according to a source close to the investigation. STORY CONTINUES PAGE 8."

I flipped ahead. The story took up half of page 8, including a few photographs. One of the motel, obviously grabbed from its brochure. Much larger, a shot of a body on a stretcher, covered with a white sheet, feet jutting up like a mummy's. And finally, a mug shot, a grainy face staring out of a frame of long hair.

The waitress brought my juice. There was ice in that, too.

My palms were clammy. I wiped them with a napkin as I read.

Clint Davis of Florence, Arizona, was found dead in his motel room on Tuesday afternoon, when a housekeeper entered the room for a routine cleaning. The body was in the bathtub. Police were alerted immediately.

Investigators believed Mr. Davis had been dead between twelve and twenty-four hours. They hadn't ruled out the possibility of criminal activity. An autopsy would reveal more details, and was under way.

I counted back. He died on Monday, afternoon or night.

The motel owner said Mr. Davis had been staying at the motel alone for an extended period. He was a quiet, solitary guest.

Mr. Davis had previously served time for driving under the influence, drug possession, and violation of a restraining order. At the time of his death, he was serving probation for second-degree battery.

A neighbor at the Florence Mobile Home Village said Mr. Davis had no close relatives, apart from an estranged wife and daughter.

My toast arrived. A pile of white bread with a tablespoon of butter melting into a puddle at the center. I ate it with a knife and fork, the salt and fat quelling my nausea. The bread was soft and sweet as cake. I wolfed it down.

When I went outside, the sky was bleached as bones. I held the newspaper under my arm.

I paced the perimeter of the lot, but I didn't get any calmer. All I'd done was start sweating again. I stared out at the freeway, the semis dragging their cargo like shells. I recognized the name. Clint. That Sunday afternoon, Philip had said it, his voice emphatic, gripping the red chair. *Clint won't say a word.*

31

B ack in the car, drive. My phone's cool, robotic voice directed me to the house of a dead man. I concentrated on the unfamiliar road. I didn't want to think about the keycard in my purse, or the envelope I'd seen Philip pass Clint in the parking lot, or the acrid smell of smoke on Iris's street, or the sagging caution tape over room 107. Didn't want to think of the police who must be working on Clint's case. Digging through his suitcase. Finding the envelope from Philip. Reading Clint's call history, his texts.

The Florence Mobile Home Village sprawled along a six-lane county road. Across the street, an airport advertised skydiving. An airplane trundled down the runway and lifted into the air, its white wings almost invisible against the chalky sky. It flew directly over me, and I had the funny thought it was watching as I turned into the trailer park.

I parked outside the office, a trailer with a leasing sign out front. Its interior was decorated in the bland aesthetic of model homes, the air-conditioning shaking the leaves of the rubber plants, the beige walls yawning at the gray carpet.

"Up to three beds," the manager said, offering me a chair and a mouthful of teeth. "Or we have streamlined units for singles."

I had a line prepared. "Actually, I'm not here to rent. I'm a journalist. I was hoping you could tell me which trailer is Mr. Davis's."

"A journalist?" He looked me over. "There's no trouble, is there?" His worry wasn't concern; it was the worry of someone who doesn't want trouble, or late rent.

"Just checking on a few facts."

"Didn't know newspapers cared about facts anymore." He snorted. "Nineteen. Down on Palm Lane."

I drove over. The trailers sat in curved rows like an elaborate run of dominoes. I'd expected them to look transitory, but they were homey, ballasted with cheerful clutter: lounge chairs, lawn gnomes, flower patches, American flags, NASCAR pennants, grills, kiddie pools, bicycles.

Clint's address was unremarkable among its neighbors. No police cars guarding it or caution tape warding off the curious. I wasn't surprised; the manager hadn't known he was dead, after all. Somebody knew—the neighbor quoted in the article. I thought if no one was at Clint's, I'd walk around, try the nearby places.

But it was easier than that.

I climbed the steps to Clint's trailer. A bulky air conditioner hung from the window, girdled with duct tape. I rang the bell.

I'm Sarah Dewitt, I rehearsed. *A journalist. I'm writing about Clint.*

No—a reporter. Covering Clint's death.

"Hey!" A brusque, feminine voice.

I turned to see an enormous woman slowly closing the distance between us, hitching up a knee as if it hurt her. She was entirely pink: lipstick, blouse, capris. Her painted toenails were fat raspberries.

"What do you think you're doing?" She stood below me, holding the stair railing with a proprietary air. The part in her hair was sunburned to a rosy pink.

I tucked my purse tightly against my side and extended my hand. "I'm Finn Dewitt," I said, messing up my cover name. "I'm a reporter. Mr. Davis's death is my story."

It was a mouthful of garbage, delivered in a trembling voice, but she wrenched my hand up and down triumphantly, with a fierce smile. "I've been waiting for someone to show up. I'm Brenda. Brenda Argyle, like the plaid."

"You knew Mr. Davis?"

She glanced over her shoulder, at the empty street. "Let's speak in private." Moving past me, she dug out a set of keys. When she opened the door, stale, smoky air wafted out. She held it, waiting for me to go in first. Holding my breath, I went past her into the dim heat of Clint's kitchen.

The place was torn apart. Cabinets open and contents spilling onto the countertops. Drawers tugged out and emptied onto the floor. I crossed the linoleum, trying not to step on anything, and went into the living room. A recliner hunkered in a stare-down with a TV. The easy chair beside it had had its cushions ripped open, its ottoman flipped over, four feet in the air like a dead beetle. The braided rug on the floor had been pulled back and crumpled. A painting of a wolf hung askew on the wall.

In the closed-up space, the heat was oppressive and thick. Back in the kitchen, Brenda was trying to get the air conditioner on. When she slapped the unit with a flat hand, it sputtered to life.

"Hot as sin in here," she said, moving into the living

room. She sank onto the recliner. "It'll be nice and cool by the time we're ready to leave."

"It's okay," I said.

"You're lucky I saw you," she said. "I was just about to go to the grocery store, and then I looked up and there you were at Clint's. Have a seat." She swept her arm grandly, as if she owned the place.

I righted the ottoman and perched on its edge. The suede-ish microfiber immediately coaxed sweat from the backs of my knees.

"Did you know him well?" I said.

"Oh, sure. We go way back. Fifteen, twenty years. I don't think you'll find anyone who knew Clint like I do." Her smile was wolfish, with shiny brown-edged teeth.

"Perfect," I said, though I doubted her. She seemed too eager, too delighted by me. I wondered whether she'd dressed up deliberately, waiting for the news cameras.

"What do you think of this mess?" she said, grinning. "This is the police's version of investigating a man's murder." Her cheeks were flushed pink.

In spite of her superficial tone, hearing the word aloud chilled me. I swallowed dryly. "Are the police investigating the death that way? As a murder?"

"I doubt they'll bother." She fanned herself with a hand.

"Why would the police do this?"

"Looking for drugs, I'd bet. Probably found some, too."

"When were they here?"

"I didn't see. I only heard he died yesterday. I came right over and it was already a mess. But it musta been cops. Clint hadn't been here in more than a week." She squinted at me. "Who did you say you write for again?"

"Metro Digital," I invented. "I'm new."

"They would give this to the newb. Nothing sexy about an old burnout, eh?" Though her words were tough, she seemed suddenly tired and sad. Her skin was crisscrossed with faint lines, like linen. Her too-bright blush stood in ovals on her cheeks.

"What was he like?" I asked, sensing an opening, a lull in her conspiracy theorist's energy.

She twitched. "Huh?"

"If you help me get a sense of him—his past, who he really was, I could, uh, reveal the man behind the mug shot. For our readers."

She seemed amused. "The man behind the mug shot."

I nodded, trying to seem eager, like a reporter would be. "You said you knew him a long time."

She got so quiet I thought she'd lied. Maybe she'd barely known Clint, but was latching onto him for attention. To see her name—*Argyle, like the plaid*—in print.

"Were you close?" I tried.

Her eyebrows lifted. "Oh, yes. Even Clint would have admitted that by now." Her tone was bitter and fond at once—the tone of someone with baggage. I relaxed.

She jabbed the air. "There's a pack of cigarettes, top of the fridge. Could you?"

I fetched them from where they'd fallen on the floor. For a moment I lingered in the cool air conditioner stream. The items scattered on the tiles were startling in their ordinariness. Foil and plastic wrap, chopsticks in white wrappers, wooden spoons. Spilled out spitefully. Did people hide drugs in their utensil drawers? And if the police had been here, wouldn't the manager have let them in and heard that Clint was dead?

Back in the living room, Brenda lit a cigarette and coughed elaborately. "I quit ten years ago. Damnit." She waved the smoke away. "Oh, Clint. What can I tell you? Spend five minutes with his record and you'll get the basic outline. Always into drugs. Fighting. He had a temper. He didn't inspire much sympathy from the law. He wasn't a bad man but he seemed like one, plenty of times."

She'd regained her chatty tone, though she'd grown wistful. She drew deep, grand breaths from her cigarette and studied the wall, reminiscing.

"Mostly he had bad luck. Hurt himself playing football and got hooked on painkillers, real young. Worked construction awhile, too, which got him more hurt. His . . ." She paused, searching, and landed on the word. "His *issues* lost him both his wives. Not that either was any good. He was dumb enough to get the second knocked up. Had to pay child support for a kid he never sees. Saw," she corrected.

"Why was he staying at the motel?"

She nodded and pointed at me. "Exactly. There's no good reason he was staying there. Last week, he drops by my place, bag on his shoulder, and asks me to keep an eye on things. Wouldn't say where he was going. I assumed a trip—you know, away somewhere. Why would he stay in a fleabag motel down the road?"

So Philip could meet him without being seen at his trailer. I said nothing.

"Yesterday a neighbor came over with the paper. I couldn't believe it. Dead, in a motel down the road." She clamped her hand to her forehead. Her cigarette smoldered dangerously close to her wispy hair. "He wasn't a bad guy. He didn't deserve what happened to him."

"What do you think happened?" I asked.

"I went right down there after I heard," she said. "The motel wouldn't let me go in the room or see the body. But I hung out for a while. There were five or six cops. I heard them say the door'd been jimmied open. Like someone broke in."

"That wasn't in the paper," I said, uncertain.

She clicked her tongue. "Lazy reporters. No offense. I was surprised as hell to see one of you out here, doing legwork. Now it's paying off, though, isn't it? You've got something no one else has."

"Do you know the name of the cop who said that?"

She stubbed out her cigarette. "Some young cop, bald as a Marine and just as cocky."

"Did you hear how Clint died?"

She shook her head.

"It's possible he just died, isn't it? Got sick."

She narrowed her eyes. "Then why not say so and get it over with? Why tear through his place? Why all the secrecy?"

I couldn't answer. My forehead ached like a rope was squeezing it.

She scratched her chin. "I think he went there to hide from someone. I think they found him."

"Who?"

She shrugged. "Someone he owed money to, maybe. He ran with a tough crowd."

"Did you see him with anyone out of the ordinary lately? Did he mention any names?" My voice was high and nervous. I was praying—*not Philip, not Philip.*

Her face twisted, unfriendly. At last she said, "There were a couple girls here, one afternoon. Young girls, really pretty. But that was a month ago."

"Did he say who they were?"

"I didn't ask. I thought maybe—maybe he was paying them." She flushed.

I couldn't speak. Heat was running in waves over my skin. My forehead and the back of my neck beaded with sweat. My stomach churned and tightened and I clenched my teeth shut to hold in the nausea.

I stood, muttering about the bathroom, and ran out of the living room.

I stumbled down a dim hallway, where enough light seeped in through a window that I could see the bathroom door. I hurtled through and hunched over the sink. Nothing came up, just dry gagging coughs.

Two pretty girls. Iris and Stacy. If they knew Clint well enough to visit him, then maybe I was wrong that

Philip and Clint were allies. Perhaps Clint was helping Iris. But Philip had called Clint his oldest friend . . .

I felt I was missing something obvious. The longer I stayed in the trailer, the harder it was to remember Philip, my Philip, untarnished. How did he ever get mixed up with these people?

My nausea was subsiding. Running the water to let it cool, I splashed my face and pressed my wet hands to the back of my neck.

Philip had a key. I froze, hands dripping down my collar. Philip wouldn't have broken into Clint's room. My smile in the spotted mirror was deranged.

The bedroom door stood open. Tangled bedcovers, dresser drawers open and disordered, the closet spewing a mess of stuff. Someone had been as interested in Clint Davis's secrets as I was. I dug through his things with my toe, half-heartedly.

I was leaving the room when I stepped on something that cracked noisily. I bent to pick it up, and a paper fell to the floor. A photograph.

It was a picture of a woman. A girl. I shifted closer to the window.

It was Iris's sister, Stacy.

My thumb whitened. It was unmistakably Stacy. The beautiful, younger version I'd seen on her bedroom walls, silver-haired, smiling. Only here she was pregnant. The huge swell of her belly lifted, as though straining to get into the photo. A grin lit her face.

The photo had fallen out of a DVD case, some action movie. I opened it wide and found a few more photos stuck into the cover, and a strip of negatives. I took everything, snapped the case closed, and dropped it on the floor. My hands shook as I put the pictures into my purse. The clump of cash dug into my ribs like a gun.

I went out blinking into the living room.

"You done snooping?" Brenda asked.

I wondered if she'd seen me steal the photos. But she sat in the same position, a fresh cigarette smoldering in her fingers. She stubbed it out. "You want to tell me what you plan to do? Come on in, I don't bite."

Holding my bag close, I crossed the living room and stood in the threshold of the kitchen. My knees felt hollow and weak. "When Clint got married, the second wife, what was her name? Was it Stacy? Was she very young . . . blond. Pretty?"

"Ha!" Brenda drew back, her chin tucked up and in, as if she were stifling a belch. "In his dreams."

"I saw a picture in his room, of a pregnant woman. I wondered if it was his ex."

Her lips puckered. "What pictures? He doesn't have any pictures. He hates his ex-wife. His kid's grown.

Never calls him." She braced her palms against the recliner seat and stood, swaying a little. "I brought you in here, gave you my time. What are you gonna do next? You gonna write that article? You gonna find out what happened?"

I backed away until I felt the breeze of the air conditioner on my elbows. "Are you sure he didn't spend time in Verde? Or mention anyone named Stacy?"

"He might have done time in Verde, if that's what you mean. I can't remember where they had him."

"And Stacy?"

"You know how many women Clint mentioned to me? Dozens. He was one for telling stories. I can't tell you how many nights we sat right here and talked." She made it to the kitchen and leaned heavily against the counter. Her face was drooping, the menace slackened off. She took a deep breath of the cooler air.

The door stuck. I tugged it hard and it flew open. "Thanks for talking with me."

She snatched my hand. Her grip was strong and gelatinous as a sea creature's. "You've seen now, huh? You can write about what they did to him."

I agreed, pulling away. I was desperate to escape the claustrophobic tin rooms, to breathe fresh air and soak my head in sunshine. I tripped down the stairs and was swallowed up in the shimmering heat between the trailers.

Miles away, I pulled over to study the photographs. They were all of Stacy. Plump and blissful, like a pregnant woman in a magazine ad—if those ads had teenagers in them. She couldn't have been more than fifteen or sixteen. I flipped through.

Stacy posed in front of a tree, holding a grapefruit in her palms as though about to lob it. She wore a white baby-doll dress that flared over her belly.

Stacy dangled her feet in a swimming pool, a pink stucco wall behind her.

Stacy sat on a cream-colored sofa, legs tucked under, hands resting on a plump tummy. Her smile caught me. Radiant.

Stacy stood in front of a stainless steel refrigerator, eating from a container of ice cream, the only image in which she seemed unhappy. Her stomach tugged her red tank top upward to expose a pale seam of skin over her shorts. She looked ready to pop.

None of the photographs was of the house in Verde.

When I held the strip of negatives to the light, I saw more scenes of Stacy, always alone, always pregnant.

What was Clint doing with these? Hidden away like

dirty photographs. Had she been his girlfriend? But his yellowed body, the slouch of it—it was too grotesque. Stacy was so pretty, so well cared for, with her round happy face and the nice clean house.

But the photos weren't the whole story. I'd met Stacy. She was lonely, strange, something helpless about her that Clint might have taken advantage of.

Overhead, the sky was the color of dirty wool. Against it, three distant specks of fluorescence drifted downward. The skydivers' parachutes. How far could a person see from up there? Surely they could see north to the humped mountain where Ocotillo Heights over-looked the valley. And south, to flat, parched Verde.

My heart beat in quick, shallow beats, as though I'd taken some of Erica's caffeine pills. Anything might have happened to me in that trailer. Careless. The word was stuck in my mind. *Careless.* Where had I heard it?

I made a U-turn and headed south.

32

Guy's motorcycle wasn't in the carport. Trusting that I was in luck, and he and Iris were out, I left my car idling in the driveway and ran to the door.

When she opened it, Stacy wasn't thrilled to see me. She may have been hungover—she blinked in the light.

Instead of asking to come in, I invited her out for something to eat. "My treat," I added.

"I'll need to get dressed."

She left me in the living room. The infernal TV noise drifted down the hall. The little dog was still curled on the sofa, growling lazily, a yellow tooth hanging over its lip.

"Delilah!" Stacy clicked her tongue. She came in, fastening hoops through her ears. She wore a long-sleeved eyelet blouse, cuffs cinched over her wrist bones, hiding the scars.

"I like your shirt," I told her, and she gave me a sly look.

"It's Iris's. Don't say anything." She locked up behind us carefully.

"Do you and Iris share a car?" I asked, climbing into mine.

She cranked her window down and rested her arm on the ledge. "I don't drive."

"How do you get around?"

She shrugged.

As we pulled out, I saw a black mark scorching the road. "That must have been scary."

Stacy pulled a strand of hair into her mouth. "Someone started a fire. It was pretty big. Guy said we were lucky it didn't spread to the house."

"Does Iris know who did it?"

Shrugging, she lolled her head back and stared out the window. "Iris's car was crap anyway. She'll get a better one." She stuck her hand out and stretched her fingers through the air.

On the main street I pulled into a Denny's. It wasn't even four, but tables were already filling with early birds. Elderly, with an alarming array of maladies: walkers, canes, compression stockings, even an oxygen tank tugged impatiently across the tile like a naughty child. A waitress led us to a roomy booth by a window. Stacy fidgeted, pushing away her napkin roll and touching all the condiments, as if counting them.

I wondered why she'd agreed to come along. Boredom. Loneliness. Maybe one less meal to scrounge from her kitchen.

"Thanks for coming with me," I said.

To my surprise, she smiled. "I used to eat here all the time, with Jeremy."

"Your boyfriend?" I remembered the dark-haired boy with the mean eyes in her wall of photos.

Her lips wilted. "Yeah, I guess. He went away to college." She opened her menu and flipped idly through the pages.

"How old are you?" I asked.

"Twenty-one. I didn't go to college, though," she said, defensive. "I don't know what I want to do yet. I used to be a waitress, but I didn't like it." She bent the menu in her hands.

"I used to waitress, too," I said. "I was glad to stop."

She nodded, biting her lip, still twisting the menu. "And you're friends with Iris?"

"More like we have friends in common."

She seemed confused, but our waitress arrived, distracting her. She ordered a sundae with extra cherries. I asked for a club sandwich and Coke.

We sat, quiet. Overhead, a fleet of fans spun so fast their chains vibrated. Stacy scooped a piece of ice from her water glass and crunched it between her jaws. She'd been a silvery blond in Clint's photos, but that must have been bleach. Her hair was now a pale strawberry color, and since she wasn't even wearing makeup, I doubted she took the trouble to dye it. Though she was young, her face was tired and puffy. She was someone who stayed up late and slept in, got stoned, drifted from one end of her house to another, like a goldfish. The feeling of pity I'd felt last night, as she'd wept in her kitchen, resurfaced.

I opened my purse and took out the picture of Stacy in her white dress, under the grapefruit tree. I set it on the table between us. "This is a lovely photo of you."

Her chin crumbled. She picked up the picture with her fingertips, as if it might burn her. "Where did you get this?"

"From a friend."

Her lips dropped, rallied, dropped again. "I was fat," she managed.

"You're pregnant," I said. "You look happy. When was this?"

She bit her lip. "I was living in Tucson."

"You guys used to live in Tucson?" I kept my tone bright, as if the question were innocent, even pleasant.

A frown rippled over her forehead. "Just me. I went to stay for a summer."

"You're young to be living alone."

She put the photo down on the table but didn't take her eyes off it. "I stayed with a friend."

The waitress reappeared with our plates. They made a gritty sound sliding across the salt spilled on the table.

Stacy probed her spoon through the layers of cream and chocolate.

"Was the friend a man named Clint?" I asked.

She looked up, surprised and pleased. "You know Clint?"

"He gave me the picture," I lied. Her happy expression could only mean she liked him—and didn't know he was dead. "Was he the baby's father?"

She laughed, showing small, round teeth. "No way. Clint didn't like kids. But he was nice to me."

"He seems a little rough," I said.

"He's ugly," she said, "that's why." She scooped a cherry and ate it, her lips sticky.

I took a bite of a french fry, hoping the salt might calm my stomach. "So the father . . . He was someone else?"

Iris had been telling a slanted version of the truth. It wasn't her sneaking around with Philip. It was her sister. Stacy. Years ago, when she was so pretty it made your teeth hurt to look at her. And so young it surely broke several laws.

Waves of heat ran up and down my arms. I imagined Iris smiling at me, tilting her head. *And you thought you knew him.*

"Stacy? Was the baby's father . . . an older man? Named Philip?" I was holding my napkin in my lap under the table, wringing it and wringing it.

Stacy kept poking her spoon into her sundae, as if she couldn't hear me.

"How did you even meet him?" I whispered.

The ice cream slopped over the side, and she caught a drip with her thumb. She was frowning, annoyed.

"Stacy?"

She looked around, as if someone might be eavesdropping. She hissed through her teeth, "I never cheated on Jeremy. Not ever." Tears thickened her lashes. "He said he wasn't ready. That's all. So I had to go away."

"What do you mean, you had to go away?"

She looked out the window, biting her lip. Her body was rigid, and she blinked fiercely, quickly.

"I'm sorry." I touched her wrist. "Really. I'm sorry. I have a good reason to want to know."

I pulled a napkin from the dispenser and gave it to her. She dabbed her eyes. Blotches of pink stood out on her fair face.

Then it hit me, so clearly I seemed to have known it from the first time I saw her. I knew that face. I knew those eyes.

"Did you give up the baby?" The words floated between us. I wasn't listening for an answer. I was leaping forward, rushing into understanding, suddenly so obvious, suddenly so clear. "Because he wasn't ready?" Again I didn't need her to reply.

I couldn't unsee it. Their faces, small and round, the knobbed little chin, the wispy pale eyebrows, the small pink mouth.

The newspaper article in Iris's drawer wasn't about Philip at all. It was Amabel, her little pale red head against Philip and Marina's blond ones.

"The baby was a girl," I said. "With red hair. And blue eyes."

Stacy was flushed. She was blinking, confused, upset. She pressed her fingers to her sternum.

"You gave her up, didn't you? Someone adopted her." My voice sounded distant.

Ammy, dancing in the fitness room mirror; Ammy reaching out the car window to grab the bougainvillea; Ammy's imperial voice when we played with her dolls.

The Martins' daughter, their jewel, their heart; coddled and spoiled and loved. My Amabel. Stacy's.

The waitress appeared at our table, saw our faces, and melted away. The racket of the dining room was muted and fuzzy. Afternoon sun glared through our window and made everything overexposed.

"Stacy?" I said. "Please. This is important."

"I'm not supposed to tell anyone about it," Stacy said. "It was private."

"I'll keep it a secret. I swear."

She pulled a strand of hair over her mouth nervously. "How did you know?"

"I know her. The little girl. Was this five years ago? When you were sixteen?" I gestured to the photo, forgotten on the table. "You look like you were just old enough to drive."

"I don't drive. I couldn't learn. I was too big."

"It was five years ago, right? The baby was born in September."

A fat solitary tear rolled down her cheek. She let it run.

"Did you know who took her?" I asked. "Did you meet them? Was it a couple named the Martins?"

"The Hughes." She sounded certain. "They told me she'd be Becky Hughes. Look." She fished the locket from under her collar. She held it out to me and let me unclasp it. *Becky* was engraved inside. The heart-shaped charm felt heavy, like solid gold.

"What were they like? Was Mrs. Hughes blond, pretty? And Mr. Hughes, was he tall? Blue eyes?" I was describing the Martins like I didn't know them. And in fact I suddenly couldn't picture them. The couple on top of a wedding cake came to mind.

Stacy tugged the locket from my hand and tucked it back under her shirt. She pressed her hand over it. At last she said, "It was for the best." Her voice was mechanical. Her lips curled into a quick, grimacing smile.

I leaned back in my seat and let out the breath I'd been holding. Amabel was adopted. And so Iris had followed Amabel, and Marina had taken her away, and Philip had lied, and the Senator had stepped in. Because everyone, except for me, had been thinking about Amabel.

I felt exhausted. Scraped dry. The lie was so simple. If someone had only told me . . . I felt a phantom Ammy climb into my lap and pluck at my lips. *Smile. Why are you being boring?*

I was resisting tears, but a hot liquid ran down my throat instead.

33

I drove, gripping the wheel with both hands. My lips were dry. I worried the cracks with my teeth. Stacy didn't offer directions, and I was quickly lost, rambling down an access road on the outskirts of town. Desert stretched to the horizon, sand dusted with white gravel, cluttered with grayish scrub. Telephone poles relayed wires to nowhere. The road led to a shimmering pool of water, always receding as we approached.

Now and then I glanced at Stacy's profile. She chewed on her hair, her eyes rimmed with tears. Her shock at my knowledge of her baby seemed genuine. I didn't think she knew Iris was after the Martins.

A car emerged from the haze ahead of us. It was black and glossy, dazzling in the sun. It sped past, engine roaring.

I watched in the rearview mirror until it disappeared. "I think we're lost."

We retraced our steps down the long road, Stacy finally coming to life enough to gesture when I asked which way. Her house was almost a welcome sight. She let us in and moved quickly down the hall to Iris's room. The little dog raced around her heels, yapping. I trailed behind, worried Iris was home.

She wasn't. Stacy dug through her nightstand and retrieved a baggy of pot and a blue glass pipe. A shower of dry specks spilled onto the carpet. She led us to the den, where she settled on the couch.

We smoked, the noise of the TV drilling into my head. Stacy didn't seem to hear it. I wasn't used to smoking and coughed at the scorch in my lungs. Stacy smiled indulgently. Her hand kept traveling to her locket, fingernail tracing the seam.

"I was her nanny," I said at last. "Ama—Becky's."

Her face jerked up and became eager.

"She's beautiful." I looked at the ceiling. Fine cracks ran through the white paint like messy pencil lines. "She can already write her name. She loves to draw. Animals especially. Sunshines with smiles. She's a happy kid." I stopped, worried that would hurt Stacy's feelings, but she nodded, encouraging me to go on. "She lives in a big house, really pretty, with a big backyard." The pool appeared in my mind, afternoons in the blue water. I swallowed. Edited it out. "She loves riding horses. She's growing fast. She'll be tall."

"Do you have a picture?"

I reached for my purse. I had a thousand photos on my phone. It was in my hand before I remembered it was new. The cheap plastic felt light in my hand, and absurdly, the lightness seemed to reflect its emptiness. My old phone had been heavy with photos, videos, a million silly ordinary moments. Even texts, sent from Philip's phone, Amabel's distinctive emojis: koalas, mermaids, random letters carefully punctuated with exclamation points.

I hadn't cared that the phone was broken. Now it felt like a fresh loss. I wiped my eyes.

Stacy didn't understand. She watched me with a concerned look.

"I'm sorry," I said. "I don't have any with me."

She slouched back, her automatic, polite smile more tragic than distress would have been.

We sat in our own thoughts. Stacy snapped her locket open and shut.

"Can I keep the picture you have?" she asked.

I didn't know what she meant.

"The one of me in the yard. In the dress."

Something occurred to me. "You must have pictures, don't you? Ultrasounds, pictures of the baby before you gave her up?"

She shook her head. "It was private."

I leaned against the couch, and felt an unpleasant bit of knowledge slide into me like a bitter pill. Marina had broken my phone on purpose. She didn't want me to have all those private pictures, all those memories. They were hers, she owned them.

Iris's threat was fresh in her mind, too. Exposure. She'd want to contain all evidence of Amabel within the family.

"The woman who adopted the baby," I said. "What do you remember about her?"

"Mrs. Hughes," she supplied, in that automatic voice she seemed to use about the baby. Like she'd been given a set of flashcards to memorize afterward, the official story.

"Yeah," I said. "What was she like?"

"I don't know," she said. "She was nice."

I scowled at the useless adjective. "How did you know them?"

She looked away. "My mom knew them. She said they were nice people. That they would make the baby happy." She sounded guilty.

She dipped her chin down so her hair hid her face. I imagined Amabel on Stacy's lap, Amabel growing up in Verde, Ammy as Becky. Sticky-mouthed and bad-mannered and witness to difficulties Amabel never knew: lack of education, processed food, too much TV. Maybe limited by the inexperience of her parents and the whirlpool of their circumstances, but—maybe—alive.

"You were brave to give her up," I said.

Stacy shrugged. She dug her foot between the couch cushions.

"Will you tell me about it?" I said. "What happened?"

She was intent on her toes as they worked into the upholstery. "I was too young."

"Who said that?"

"Everyone. Jeremy. Iris. They said I was stupid. So I stopped telling people. I kept it a secret."

"How long did that work?"

"Until the summer." She told me she was sunbathing in her backyard when her mom unexpectedly showed up—hungover, it sounded like, wearing last night's slinky dress. Seeing Stacy's stomach, stretching the waistband of her bikini, her mother flew into a rage. Their argument carried on the duration of three or four cigarettes, and then her mother left again, grabbing her purse, swearing that she was gonna take care of this.

Stacy refused an abortion; by then it would have been late anyway. She was already five months along. Her mother should have noticed weeks earlier, but Stacy hid it carefully, draping herself in hooded sweatshirts or Jeremy's old T-shirts. And I got the sense, anyway, that her mother wasn't the noticing type.

After the argument, Stacy's mom was gone for days, a week, and Stacy assumed she was with her boyfriend, drinking, the usual routine. Instead, her mother came back with her hair newly cut and tinted auburn, a shiny professional job, unlike her usual at-home box dye. She wore unfamiliar clothes. A pencil skirt, a silky red blouse. Stacy asked if she got a new job. Her mother laughed. She said they were going on a little vacation, before the baby came. She helped Stacy pack a suitcase, and they drove, south, toward Tucson. They navigated into a suburb, dense with shopping malls and palms, everything nicer than Verde. They drove into a neighborhood of brand-new houses, pink and cream stucco, backyard swimming pools, boulevards heaped with black soil. But there wasn't anyone around. For Sale signs marked most yards. The tennis court didn't have a net. The recession was lingering like a bad cold, and developments were sitting empty all over Sun Valley. (Already, I was lining up Stacy's words against what I knew: I'd heard of a Tucson town house, sold at a loss before I worked for the Martins.)

Stacy's mother pulled up to a pink house. She let them in with a key. Inside it was cool and smelled of paint. She led Stacy upstairs, into a bedroom with a plastic bag still over the mattress and tags hanging from the drapes. As she unpacked Stacy's things, she explained that a nice family wanted to adopt the baby. Wasn't that good news? Stacy was much too young to have a child. She couldn't even imagine the work it would be, not to mention the expense. This was for the best.

While Stacy was still reeling from the idea, the doorbell rang. Her mother made her change into a stiff dress that made her look like a little girl.

As Stacy went down the stairs, a strange man and woman stood in the foyer. They watched her approach. Stacy couldn't meet their eyes; they were too intense. They introduced themselves as the Hugheses, shaking Stacy's hand, telling her mother how pretty she was, how healthy looking, as if Stacy were deaf. They moved to the living room, drank glasses of lemonade and carried on a conversation Stacy didn't follow. All she knew was, they wanted her baby. Every time Mrs. Hughes's eyes fell on her, they dropped to her belly. Her hands sometimes trailed over her own stomach, as if envious of Stacy's plumpness.

Finally, they left, taking with them their strange precise voices, as well as Stacy's mother's bizarre affectation.

"Thank Christ they're gone," she told Stacy. "I'm dying for a cigarette. Don't tell." She smoked it in the backyard, dangling her legs in the swimming pool, oval-shaped and blue as a lozenge. She said, "You'll be staying here awhile," as if the information were casual, even enviable. "It's comfortable, right?"

"Alone?" Stacy asked.

No. She'd have company. Her mother's friend, a man Stacy had known, peripherally, for years. Clint.

Clint was a lackadaisical caretaker. He went slouching out to the car and brought back food and rental movies and bottles of sunscreen. All Stacy did was lie beside the pool and eat. The summer reached its August peak and sloped into September, when the baby finally came. A midwife delivered her, a baby girl with tiny toes and perfect ears and waving fists. For a while, Stacy held her. The baby slept. Stacy traced her skin, her fine eyebrows, but then she drifted off to sleep with her cheek against her daughter's wispy scalp. When she woke, the baby was gone.

In days, Stacy was recovered enough to go home. Clint packed her things, and even drove her. By then, Stacy's mother had gone away. The family home seemed stuffy and ugly, and very silent. Stacy began her lonely season. In the summer, her leisure had been purposeful. She was growing a baby. Now, the empty days only mirrored her emptiness. School was down the road, but she didn't go back. Iris returned from L.A. to be with her, and the girls settled into their dreamy lives.

Stacy's muttered explanations were patchy in places, overly detailed in others, but between her lines I found I could imagine it clearly. How the Martins would have tucked her away, keeping her comfortable and concealed. How her mother, who sounded like an older version of Iris, managed to get rid of the baby and pick up some cash at once. How her sister swooped in, taking residence in the master bedroom, filling the closet with designer labels, carrying on a bored affair with Guy.

Because no matter that Stacy hadn't mentioned money, never mentioned money, it was obvious that they'd been paid. And when the money finally ran out, Iris wanted more.

I was exhausted. The late-afternoon sun poured into the room, turning the air hot and thick as soup. I felt as if I'd been sitting on the sofa for hours. I stood unsteadily. Stacy's head tilted in that curious look Amabel sometimes had. I put a hand over my eyes. I didn't want Stacy's face to invade my memories of Amabel.

"I'm going to go."

Stacy startled. Maybe she expected something in return for her story. Photos of Ammy, or at least those of herself, pregnant, which rightfully belonged to her. Instead, I dug the envelope from my purse. I pulled out a stack of bills, maybe fifteen or twenty of them, and dropped them on the coffee table.

Wide-eyed, Stacy leaned and pushed the stack off-kilter with a fingertip. The bills fanned out. "What's this for?"

"It's from the family." I tucked the envelope back in my purse while she gaped at me, astonished.

"Really?"

I mumbled, "Take care of yourself," and fled down the hallway and out of the house, the smoky afternoon air sharp as smelling salts in my lungs.

34

Twenty miles south of Phoenix, the freeway clogged with the crush of evening traffic. Everyone in a hurry, because it was Friday night. A ball game was beginning downtown, and restaurants were opening their doors to let air-conditioning spin over the patio, and bartenders were pouring sacks of margarita mix over vats of crushed ice.

The Martins spent their weekends like all the families in their circle. Occupying Amabel with carefully planned excursions, to the farmers market for locally grown strawberries, or to museums that taught scientific principles via clever toys, or children's birthday parties with catered lunches. A normal, happy family.

Amabel had been thoroughly a Martin, hadn't she? Mirroring Marina with her haughtiness and charming self-absorption, her beauty. And, like Philip, outgoing, curious, a little bit sneaky. Enjoying her secrets. Her fibs.

I wasn't concentrating on driving. Changing lanes, I nearly collided with another car sliding into the same gap. Brake lights rippled down the road. I pulled off downtown. A few aggressive salesmen were hawking parking for $20. Everything was filling up. I still had the hotel tag dangling from my mirror and so I parked in that garage.

I went into the hotel. Nobody stopped me from taking the elevator to our floor. I wandered the halls, trailing my fingers over the wallpaper. A busboy pushed a room service cart by me, silver lids rattling, and knocked at Marina's room. A round bald man answered the door in his swimming suit.

I tried to see past him, into the room where Marina had hidden Amabel from Iris. Of course by now it would be stripped of any evidence of them.

I went up to the rooftop bar. Though it was happy hour the bar was almost empty; the heat drove most people inside. But I wanted air on my skin, if only the dry breeze laced with dust. The bartender made my vodka tonic strong and retreated to the stripe of shade under the awning. The garnish tray made me hungry—cucumbers, cherries, oranges, lemons, limes, the color palette of Amabel's doll clothes.

Amabel Martin, adopted. From a little distance, it wasn't so bad. Stacy gave her a lovely face, the Martins gave her a lovely life. Maybe it hadn't been a secret at all. Perhaps a small, intimate circle knew about the adoption, but it was tacitly unspoken. The Martins were private people, after all.

But something gave Iris power over them. Otherwise her threat would be useless. They'd sue her, get a restraining order.

My phone lit up with a text from Bryant. Dinner?

I motioned to the bartender, and he brought me another drink. I asked for a few maraschino cherries, too, and he plopped them into my glass. Ammy had loved Shirley Temples, juice down her chin.

I wrote back, Sorry, going out with some friends. Then I turned off my phone.

The sky was beginning to pink, the light to turn syrupy. It would be a beautiful sunset in Ocotillo Heights. Marina had designed the house with a family in mind—the nursery, bath, and playroom running in a row. I imagined her readying the rooms for the baby, selecting the wallpaper with its evocative birch forests, the toxin-free wood furnishings, the Scandinavian textiles.

Marina and Philip would have driven south to collect Amabel, car seat pinned in the back, a bag of tiny clothes and cloth diapers and organic products ready to go. They'd have been momentarily stunned by the presence of the baby in their quiet twosome. Then weeks, months, of sleepless nights and bleary days, of feeding and changing and cleaning and calming, of first smiles and laughs. Amabel's cornflower eyes recognizing their faces, latching on and lighting up. It wouldn't have taken long for her to feel like their own. As if Stacy had never existed.

What about Clint?

When I emptied my glass, I was a little unsteady. I needed some dinner. I needed to decide where to go next.

At the garage, I took the elevator to the fifth floor. Stepping out, I didn't see my car where I thought I'd left it. Every space was full, and more cars drove swiftly up the ramp, aggressively hunting for openings. I started walking, keeping close to the parked bumpers.

A black sedan turned the corner, LED lights dazzling my eyes. Momentarily blinded, I stood still. The car sped up as it turned the corner and climbed the next ramp. Its engine roared.

A light beep nearly sent me out of my skin. A VW Bug was tailing me, wanting to take my spot. I made an apologetic gesture and hurried on. My car turned out to be just around the corner, crammed into a compact space.

I drove carefully down to the exit. The mechanical arm lifted. I eased out and idled a moment, orienting myself. The street was packed with cars and people, all streaming purposefully in the same direction, dressed in red and black.

Lights flashed in my rearview mirror. The black sedan was pulling up to the ticket booth.

Without thinking, I turned left, tires squealing. Pedestrians stopped to stare. I made another left, hoping to get to the highway. I wasn't familiar with the downtown blocks, and the streets were thick with baseball game traffic. As I slowed to decide where to go, the black sedan appeared behind me. It followed as I turned right, onto a one-way street solidly packed with cars. Bars lined the sidewalks, patios overflowing. Bros in baseball caps darted across the street, hopping as they ran, like deer. I longed to be out of my car; I could disappear into the crowd easily.

Left again. At the next intersection, two police cars parked diagonally, sirens silently flashing. An officer wearing an orange stick forced me to turn right. I wanted to roll down my window and tell him I was being followed, but in spite of my terror, it seemed foolish.

The black car kept close. The dark windshield gleamed, impervious. I felt horribly visible. It seemed as if the driver would be able to tell when my eyes lifted to the mirror, to see the sweat on my forehead.

All around us, the normal evening carried on. A scalper fanned himself with tickets. Vendors sold frozen bottled water. A ripping sound came from above: a Blue Angel warming up before the game. Traffic oozed.

When I came to the next intersection, I hesitated. Turn, or go straight? The black car nimbly slid into the left lane and zipped ahead. I watched it pull into a parking garage.

Just someone looking for a spot, failing to find one in the other garage, and trying elsewhere. I tried to laugh at myself—my hands had gripped the wheel so tightly my joints were sore—but my muscles didn't unclench.

I got onto the freeway and drove east. In spite of myself, I kept glancing into the rearview. I counted cars, tallying the colors. Most were white or beige, practical choices for the desert. But here and there someone had chosen black: a convertible, several SUVs, even a limo. Only now, tracking the cars around me, did I realize I should have looked at the license plate, so next time I'd know for sure.

Ridiculous, I told myself. There wouldn't be a next time. My knuckles were white on the wheel.

35

The football team was practicing. The stadium glowed. The campus was so quiet that the noise of commands and whistles carried to the library doors.

Philip had called Clint his oldest friend. And Clint had played football. Brenda had told me plainly, but it hadn't registered until, driving home, I passed the campus, and saw the stadium.

The library was deserted. I easily found the yearbook archive, and the volumes that covered Philip's student years. I remembered my first time reading them, new to working for the Martins, delighted to see Philip's evolution from eager freshman to confident captain. I paused at my favorite photograph, Philip carrying Tina on his shoulders, happiness plain on their faces.

No wonder I hadn't noticed Clint. He was younger

by two years, a freshman when Philip was a junior, kicker to Philip's quarterback. While Philip starred in candid shots splashed across the pages, Clint appeared only in a thumbnail-sized portrait, barely recognizable under a heavy cap of hair.

The following year, both boys appeared only in their individual portraits. Philip's accident had ended his season early, and under the shadow of scandal.

I checked the books for the next two years, but Clint had dropped from the team roster.

Decisively, I pinched the pages of Philip's football years and ripped them from their bindings. Then I replaced the books on the shelf, shoving them far back, until they dropped behind the others. Buried.

At the bank of computers, I pulled up the newspaper database. I'd read all the articles, until Philip's accident had imprinted itself on my mind. I seemed to have a sense memory for the events: the hot, dark night, the jarring tumble of the Jeep, the endless slide and echoing slam to a stop. But my focus had been trained on Philip and Tina like a spotlight. I'd nearly forgotten that one of Philip's teammates had been in the car with them.

My hunch was right. In the very first report of the accident, I read that Clint Davis had been riding shotgun. The article noted that he was hospitalized for his injuries but didn't provide details. Most of the

406 • KELSEY RAE DIMBERG

real estate on the page was devoted to Philip and Tina. Their team portraits were printed beside the photo of the crumpled Jeep. There was no picture of Clint.

Later articles mentioned Clint even more briefly. Many referred to him only as "the third passenger" or "Mr. Martin's teammate." He couldn't compete with beautiful dead Tina, or golden reckless Philip. Even the Senator was named more often than Clint.

Finally, in the university newspaper, I found more detail: FOOTBALL TEAM DOWN TWO PLAYERS AFTER ACCIDENT. Philip broke an arm. Clint broke three ribs and ruptured a disc in his spine.

This article included a photograph of the boys in practice uniforms, arms around each other's shoulders. Young Clint was unrecognizable. Handsome. Taller than Philip, with thick dark hair and a square jaw. Knowing he was only months away from the injury that would change his life, I found his smile poignant, unbearable.

I came across only one other significant reference to Clint: in the D.A.'s announcement that Philip wouldn't be charged.

He said there was no evidence that Philip had been intoxicated, and analysis of the accident didn't suggest unsafe speeding.

"Mr. Martin attested that the darkness, combined

with the sharp turns in the road, had made driving conditions difficult. The surviving passenger, Clint Davis, corroborated Mr. Martin's version of events."

Clint was the only witness. And he backed up Philip's story. Stuck with his friend. Maybe it was the truth. Maybe it wasn't, quite.

Chewing my lip, I looked again at the photograph in the school paper. Clint grinned at Philip, openly adoring. Philip faced the camera.

I printed the articles and cleared my history from the computer.

Clint's injuries were severe. He must have hated Philip. Philip, who was barely hurt, who got to leave Arizona and return a long-lost son.

Or Clint clung to the friendship of a powerful, rich man.

They must have kept in touch, or Clint wouldn't have wound up in a pink house in Tucson, waiting for a baby to come. Maybe they'd met, now and then. Gone for a drink. Talked softly about their old lives, scrupulously avoiding the present. Maybe, now and then, Philip gave him a little money. Helped him out.

Certainly he must have paid Clint to watch over Stacy.

Maybe, way back then, he even paid Clint to support his account of the accident to the police.

My oldest friend.

If Philip wanted help getting rid of Iris, there was no one more logical than Clint to ask for it. To help keep her away from the family. Scare her. Burn her car?

That loser, Marina had said, lashing out at Philip. *How many times did I tell you not to trust him?*

Brenda's dazed, forlorn face. The cramped trailer. The Sunset Motel key hidden under Philip's lamp. The tape drawn across the door.

Stacy's delight at my mention of Clint.

Collegiate Clint's young, naive grin, face turned to Philip, who didn't return his gaze.

Clint's hacking cough and gleaming eyes, and the way he and Philip glared at each other across the desk. Mired in a bond, maybe friendship, maybe something else. Water under the bridge. Muddy water.

On Sunday, Philip had reassured Marina. *Clint won't say a word. I promise.*

Two days later, Clint was found dead.

Before I left the library, I texted Iris. She knew the whole story. If Clint had been helping Philip, then Philip's words were in his defense. If Clint had been helping Iris, then the phrase had a different meaning.

36

I was at a crowded pool. I was looking for Amabel; I knew she was there, not drowned but hiding. I ran around lounge chairs, slipping on the wet stone. The water glittered. Blurred people splashed. I saw flashes of Amabel, over by the concession stand with a cup of lemonade, in line for the diving board—but I couldn't get to her.

I woke hot and breathless. An obvious dream, but the feelings had been vivid and physical. My mouth was dry as linen. Every light in my apartment was on. A bottle of vodka stood against the door, primed to topple if it opened.

I had a reply from Iris. Fuck off.

Please, I wrote back, offering money. If you tell me the truth.

I got up for a glass of water. I turned off the lights until only my bedside lamp glowed.

I lay back down, like Amabel before a nap. Something scratched at the door. Just my imagination. But my skin felt electric, as though even my pores were listening. The clicks in the walls. The drip of the kitchen faucet. Nothing unusual. Then the doorknob rattled. Not a forceful sound, but soft, as if someone had gently, slowly, softly, set their hand on it and twisted, testing for a lock.

My limbs were rigid. I held my breath. The faucet dripped. The lightbulb faintly buzzed.

I got up and approached the door on tiptoe. Through the peephole, I saw only empty space.

I grabbed the vodka bottle and went back to bed.

It was three. About the same time I'd woken up to find Bryant gone. The next morning, he'd seemed so strange. Stiff unhappiness in his face. And he hadn't liked my asking where he'd been, as if he'd hoped to escape notice.

Later that day, the maid found Clint in the tub.

I was being ridiculous. Bryant was squeamish about a paper cut. Not to mention his distaste for anything untoward. My sneaking around Iris's house, for example, looking through windows—he'd been shocked by that. It was low-class. Common. He was hardly capable of violence. My paranoia was only my midnight brain, hyperactive, exhausted, illogical.

At four I gave up on sleep. I ate a bowl of cereal. By then, the night was retreating, the dark lifting. I turned on a movie.

I woke to my door opening. The bolt scraped back and the door jolted to the end of the chain lock, catching with a metallic snap. Sun glowed in a bright ring around the blinds, as if angry to be shut out.

"Finn?"

It was Bryant. He stuck his fingers through the crack and fumbled around for the chain. "Are you here?"

I was already out of bed. "Hang on." To undo the chain, I had to shut the door, and for the moment it was closed, I had the impulse to throw the bolt again, to run for my desk chair and prop it under the knob.

Instead I opened the door, and he strode in. He wore sunglasses, pleated chinos, a tight black polo in stretchy athletic material. He ground his shoes into the mat. Strands of grass clung to his soles.

"Were you asleep?"

"Yeah," I said, hurrying ahead of him to move the vodka bottle away from the bed. I shoved it under the dresser.

"It's noon," Bryant said.

"You're joking."

"I was getting worried."

Turning my back to him, I tugged open the drapes. "I must have been tired. I haven't been sleeping well." I immediately wanted to snatch the words back, thinking he'd push those blue pills. But he didn't seem to notice. He was strolling around the room, picking up little objects: my keys, a hoop earring, a coffee mug, a framed snapshot from our early days. He held them inattentively and dropped them again.

"What were you up to yesterday?"

"I told you, I went out with friends. Are you looking for something?"

"Sorry, just curious." He picked up the dollhouse fishbowl and eyed the tiny, intricately painted goldfish behind the glass. "Which friends?"

"Some girls from my old job. No one you know."

He tipped the bowl over to see if the goldfish would come out. "And what did you do?"

"We went for drinks. We caught up. I haven't seen them in months. It was nice."

"You felt comfortable talking about Amabel with these people?"

"I didn't realize I wasn't allowed to mention Amabel to anyone."

We stared at each other. I looked at his hands, their clipped nails, his square strong shoulders.

"I listened to them talk, mostly," I said. "I wanted a break."

Bryant smiled without teeth, the way he did when he disagreed with someone but had to pretend otherwise. "I'm glad you got out." He dropped the fishbowl back on my nightstand. "Are you up for lunch?"

"Sure." I collected my cereal bowl from the floor and took it into the kitchen. I passed him, close enough to see how his skin shone lightly with perspiration. Veins threaded his forearms. He might have been in an ad for running shoes or sports drinks. He was sun-kissed, vibrant with health. Beside him I felt haggard.

"Were you golfing?" I asked.

He hummed. "It was a hundred and two at seven-thirty. I thought we'd cancel, but my partner is a fanatic. He's from Yuma. Doesn't faze him." He watched me rinse the dish, and as I walked by again he caught me by the arm.

I nearly jumped. He studied me carefully. My face braced against him, like a child holding her breath to avoid being seen.

He kissed me, lightly. I could feel his teeth shut behind his lips. "We didn't say hello," he whispered.

The corners of my mouth were dry as I smiled. I focused on the freckles scattered over his nose. Once, when I ran my finger over them, he'd confessed to using retinol creams to lighten them, because they multiplied in the sun and made him look childish. I'd loved that, his rare insecurity.

He glanced at his watch and said, "You should get dressed."

"Are you in a hurry?"

"I've got an afternoon booked solid."

I went into the closet to dress. All my clothes reminded me of Bryant. I still had the skirt I'd worn when we met, pale gray silk, even though the spilled water had left a mark that made it unwearable. And the dress I'd worn on our first date, and one of the shirts he'd lent me to sleep in, and the sweater he'd given me for our anniversary, when we exchanged keys. He'd never used his key before. We'd kept up the habit of knocking.

But I'd forgotten. Bryant had used his key before. Monday night, when he let himself back into my apartment.

After I dressed, I crossed the hall to the bathroom and brushed my teeth. My face was alarmingly bony and pale. I rubbed blush into my cheeks.

When I came out, Bryant was crouched on the floor beside my bed. My purse lay open at his feet.

"Your wallet slipped out," he explained smoothly, lifting my bag by the straps and holding it out to me.

I took it. Turning, I stuck my hand in and felt the edge of the Martins' envelope, the slippery surface of the photographs, the inky printed articles. Bryant couldn't have missed them. My wallet was at the bottom, flat against the fabric lining.

Bryant was watching me. "Everything all right?"

"Sure." I couldn't think of what to say. I zipped the bag and held it under my arm.

"Aren't you going to pack?"

"Sorry?"

"To stay over?"

"I thought you were busy today."

"What? I said we have a booked afternoon. You and me."

"I thought you said *you* were busy."

He looked at me like I was crazy. "Finn, I have the day off. We just talked about this. Couldn't you hear me? I was telling you, we've got that dinner tonight, and I want to be with you. I worry about you too much when you're alone. I want you to stay with me."

"I didn't hear you," I said. "I had the door closed."

He frowned, pressing his lips together. "Why do you sound disappointed? Is there a problem?" He looked hurt.

I rushed to say no, there wasn't a problem. I was glad. He followed me to the closet and leaned in the doorway. I felt his eyes on the clothes I chose, the shoes. When I brought only one new outfit, he said, impatiently, "That's it? You'll be doing laundry every day."

I didn't want to ask what he meant again. I felt wrong-footed. I stuffed more clothes into the duffel and zipped it. He carried it for me, his hand on my lower back as we went out. I locked the door and tested the knob. It made a tight, tense rattle.

We drove out to the fringes of the city, where an exclusive resort had transformed acres of desert into a lush, almost tropical landscape. Low, modern buildings scattered like archipelagoes in the midst of garden paths and swimming pools. In the main courtyard, an artificial waterfall thundered down a wall, and pastel fish drifted in the churning blue water. Presidents had stayed here; professional golf tournaments played out across the groomed green acres.

Bryant had arranged an afternoon in the spa. The front desk was expecting us. As we checked in, he slid his phone across the desk. "You, too," he said to me, grinning.

I pressed a protective hand over my purse.

"You'll get them back at checkout," the worker said. She was dressed all in white, her hair slicked back into a fierce tight knot. "We find that going phone-free re-laxes all the guests. And ensures privacy, of course."

I reached into my bag and fumbled for my phone. I had a new message from Iris: 4:00. Your place. With Bryant at my side, I could only reply hastily. I'll try.

He looked satisfied as I relinquished my phone.

A man and woman materialized from a door. They were also dressed in white, and their bodies were perfectly muscled and tanned and hairless. We followed our respective workers into the locker rooms, where my clothes and purse were sealed away in a locker, and I tied a creamy robe tightly over my nakedness and stepped into a pair of white sandals fresh from a plastic package.

"You'll start with our signature desert service," the woman said. "Follow me."

She led me into a courtyard, where a massive fire burned in a stone wall opposite a sparkling pool. A dozen women lounged on the deck, drinking champagne or goblets of water choked with lemon slices. Bryant sat, jangling his knee up and down. When he saw me, he leaped to his feet and lunged forward, smiling.

"Isn't this place great?"

"I thought we were getting lunch." I was suddenly hungry. Even the bright yellow lemons in the water seemed appealing.

"Sorry," he said. "Apparently this desert treatment is detoxifying, so they don't recommend eating until afterward. Don't worry, I have great dinner plans. It'll be worth it." He squeezed my hand.

The spa worker led us back inside, down a hall lined with unmarked doors. She opened one, unleashing a waft of eucalyptus. Calming music seeped from a speaker pod.

"This seems a little over the top," I said after she'd left.

Bryant touched the back of my neck. "Just relax. You're exhausted. This'll be good for you."

More strong, white-clad workers arrived. The desert experience began with burning sage. We were rubbed with coarse salt, then with shea butter and citrus, wrapped tightly in sheets, and left alone. The lights clicked off. There was a thin wet towel over my face. I shook it away. Bryant was lying perfectly still, cocooned. I watched him.

"How do you feel?" he said.

I considered quietly unbinding myself and slipping out. It was a fantasy.

"Fine," I said.

"I'm worried about you," Bryant said. "You haven't been looking well. Try to relax." I heard him breathing deeply in and out. "Finn? Is something on your mind?"

I was thinking of how he'd watched me as my skin was treated, as they spun me over and drizzled the warm puddled liquid on my back. I was thinking of my purse, the photographs, the cash, untended in the locker room. I was thinking Marina must have come here before, inhaled the burning sage and listened carefully as the workers chanted the litany of benefits—*healing, cleansing, purifying*—and believed them.

"This is nice," I managed.

When the treatment ended, my skin felt like expensive silk. Wrapped in our robes, Bryant and I sat by the pool and ate thin slices of watermelon. Parrots stirred in the trees. A fine net hung over the yard, keeping them in. A discreet sign warned against feeding them. They shuffled along branches, stretching their wings from time to time. I wondered aloud if they'd had their wings clipped—they weren't flying—but Bryant said they wouldn't need the net if they had. He wasn't concerned about birds. He dove into the pool and surfaced, floating on his back.

"Aren't you getting chlorine on your pure skin?" I called.

"It's oxidized, not chlorinated. It feels great." He took a breath and sank underwater, swimming slowly to the far side. When he emerged, I asked if he was ready to leave soon, keeping my voice casual.

"We've got massages," he said. "At five."

"What time is it now?"

He studied the sky. "It's probably four. We could sit in the sauna, if you want."

Iris would be at my apartment. She'd wait ten, maybe fifteen minutes. She'd be furious when I didn't show.

I excused myself for the bathroom and wandered the maze of doors and softly lit alcoves. In my borrowed robe and sandals, I felt like someone in a mental institution. When I reached the lobby, the desk clerk fluttered around me, apologizing that I'd lost my way.

"I need to make a call," I said.

But she clucked politely. *Impossible.*

"I can't have my phone?" I meant to sound authoritative, but I squeaked.

"To release it, we'd need you to check out. That is our policy."

"Listen," I said. "This whole day was sort of a surprise for me. I have to let a friend know I had a change of plans. Two minutes."

She shook her head. "The policy is for the guests' benefit. As small as it seems, we find it's a necessary rule in order to enable the appropriate state of mind for our services. The healing effects are simply not possible when a constant reminder of duties, schedules, contacts, is close at hand." She smiled, gently, tolerantly. "You're not alone. We frequently find people with spare cell phones in the sauna."

I retreated. Back at the pool, Bryant was swimming laps. His crawl stroke was tight, tense. He glided swiftly through the water. A breeze spontaneously rippled through the courtyard, and the fire popped noisily. Even the smoke smelled herbal. Boulders were heaped around the fire and the pool, as if we'd stumbled into a magical, private grotto.

I wanted to run, to clamber over the rocks and escape. I sat on a lawn chair. I lay very still. I was stuck here as long as Bryant liked. My new knowledge boiled inside me. Overhead, the net traced a faint crosshatch across the sky.

Suddenly hands dropped on my shoulders. It was Bryant. He laughed at my jump.

"You're tense," he said, squeezing, too hard.

I shifted away from his touch.

"What's wrong?"

"I just feel restless. I'm not in the right mood for this."

He flinched. "I wanted us to do something together. I feel bad. I left town, and you were alone, and we've been fighting . . . I wanted to reset." His hair was drying in waves. His expressive mouth was pulled to the side. "You're so unhappy. What can I do?" He took my hand and traced my palm with his thumb.

For a moment, I believed him. He was treating me so tenderly. He was only trying to help. The spa was probably costing a fortune. Taking the day off was costing more. The pressure of tears was hot behind my eyes.

"I'm just so tired."

"It's all right," he said. "I know you haven't been yourself. You'll be back to normal in a while. I'm not going anywhere."

One of the parrots leaped off the tree branch and coasted to the other side of the pool in one swift motion, like a tossed Frisbee. I thought if I were stuck here, I'd fly in loops around the net. Do laps, like Bryant. I wondered how long it took to break a creature of the habit of pacing.

A hundred years later, I lay stiffly on a padded table, my face plunged into a padded oval hole as my massage therapist wondered at the coiled tension in my back.

We were checking out at the desk when Bryant mentioned my car.

"What happened to your tire? It looked like you ran over a tree." He was signing the receipt and didn't look at me.

"I got a flat the other day. It's only the spare tire, it rides low." I was sodden with essential oils, even after I'd showered. My limbs glistened, slippery. I turned on my phone and found a dozen texts from Iris, increasingly irritated and finally outraged.

I texted back. Sorry, something came up. Tomorrow, same time?

Bryant was folding the copy of the receipt into his wallet. Would he find a way to expense it? Call it a client outing?

"It's not just low, Finn. The rim is all banged up. You must have been driving around on it. They're not meant for that."

He was lecturing me, his confident voice. I seized on it, glad to play dumb. "I didn't realize. I'll get it looked at."

"Already taken care of." He tapped his credit card against the counter, jaunty, and tucked it into his wallet. "I had a garage pick it up. It should be ready in a few days, they said."

"What? When did you do that?"

"Just this morning. As soon as I noticed it."

"Bryant, you didn't even ask me. I need it."

"Why?" he said. "You're staying with me now. You don't need a car. We'll just take it easy. I'll be your driver." He winked.

After that, the evening was blurred. We went to a restaurant, and Bryant ordered steak. The meat came on large plates, with no accoutrements. I was ravenous. We drank. Vodka, then wine. People dropped by our table. They were sorry about Amabel. They patted my back. They gave me strange glances, and then they left.

Then we were at Bryant's, and he was making nightcaps, stirring with a long spoon. And then I couldn't remember anything at all.

37

I didn't dream. A small, frantic animal had lodged under my armpit and was trembling, trembling, trying to get away. I jarred awake. Bryant's bedroom was bathed in calm moonlight. The air purifier sighed dreamily.

My phone buzzed, and I realized I'd been sleeping on it. The vibration against my skin had entered my dream, woken me.

It was Iris. Come down or I'll come up.

In the last ten minutes, she'd texted a dozen times.

I rubbed my eyes. I couldn't remember falling asleep. The last clear moment I had was of sitting on the bed, taking off my earrings, my bracelet, my rings, stacking them on the nightstand. A thick tiredness had come over me, and I remembered Bryant touching my hair, saying it was the spa treatment, it activated hormones . . .

He slept curled on the far side of the mattress, frowning.

I wrote back, I'm not at home. I'll meet you tomorrow.

I'm already here. Hurry up.

I swung my feet out of bed. A rush of dizziness, and I stumbled to the floor. I knelt, head down, blinking at the carpet. My forehead pulsed. I felt so groggy.

Moving slowly, touching the wall for balance, I crossed the room and pushed open the balcony door. In the courtyard below, a slim figure stood, dressed all in black. Her hand flew up, gesturing impatiently.

It was her. I stared down, dumb, and she shouted, "Finn!" Her voice rang.

I waved at her to be quiet. I spread my fingers. Five minutes.

Inside, I splashed my face with cold water, again and again, until I felt marginally more awake. Bryant roused, turning in his sleep. I waited in the doorway until he stilled.

In the kitchen, the bottle of whiskey still sat on the island. Bryant had rinsed the glasses. Had I had too much to drink? After Bryant made the whiskeys, we went out on the balcony and talked about—what? Next thing I knew I was sitting on the side of the bed. Removing earrings, rings . . . And Bryant had swung my legs into bed. How strange. Even drunk I was usually capable of showering, brushing my teeth.

I wasn't ready to face Iris. My head ached. My lips felt thick and numb. She wanted to catch me out; I knew it. On an impulse, I grabbed a paring knife from the block. I tucked it into my purse, the blade small and sharp against the envelope.

The night air was warm and fragrant with chlorine. The patio seemed empty, as if Iris had gone. Or I'd dreamed it. I crossed between deck chairs, hissing her name. In the center of the yard, a fountain bubbled noisily. Its blue-tiled floor was empty of coins.

At the lap pool, Iris stood with her back to the water. She wore a black sweatshirt, the hood pulled over her hair, and tight black jeans. Her face was sharp as a blade, her eyes enormous and bright as a nocturnal creature's. They swept over the patio and up to the balconies. Envious, I thought.

Snapping her attention to me, she gave a tight sarcastic smirk. "You went to Princeton?"

I crossed my arms over Bryant's shirt. "How did you know I was here?"

She rolled her eyes, but then there was a sound like a twig snapping, and she straightened, muscles drawn tight. "What was that?"

We both listened. Water churned. Otherwise all was silent. The noise didn't repeat.

"What's wrong with you?" My voice was a dry whisper. Iris's tension amplified my own. My skin seemed to crawl with invisible legs. I was so tired. The urge to sink onto one of the chaise lounges around us was as strong as lust. I pinched the inside of my elbow, telling myself to wake up. (I remembered telling Amabel to pinch herself, to test if she was dreaming, and the way that backfired, her pinching everyone, her friends, even Philip.)

Iris dug in her bag with uncharacteristic jerky gestures. She brought out a cigarette and flicked her lighter again and again before it took. After she inhaled, she calmed, or put on a better show of it, an actress seizing on her favorite prop.

"You have the money?" Her voice was low, harsh, and serious. No more girlish emotions, no more jabs.

"We're supposed to meet tomorrow. What are you doing here?" Now that she was before me, her hated foxy face, her cunning eyes, I didn't want to give her a thing.

"We were supposed to meet today, and you blew me off. I thought, best just to show up." She crossed her arms, seeming to shiver in the hot night. Her tone was suspicious, not angry. She didn't trust me. After how easily she'd manipulated me, her uncertainty was satisfying. I smiled, trying to put her acid sweetness in it.

She glanced up at the balconies again. "You said you wanted details. I'm sure Stacy's story was all over the place. Smart of you, by the way, to find her. How did you do it?"

"You're not the only one who can look up an address."

Her laugh was a caw. "Fair enough. If I were you, I'd have looked me up much sooner. But that's part of the fun of knowing you. Telling you stories, watching you jump at all the good parts." She exhaled smoke, dropped her cigarette, and lit another.

"Now I want the truth," I said. "How did your mom set up the adoption with the Martins?"

"Not adoption," she corrected, poking the air. "They stole her."

"Stacy said they had an arrangement."

She shook her head. "My mom did. Stacy, never. She didn't want to give it up. My mom didn't want to deal with a baby. So she bitched about it to a friend of hers, and he knew someone who wanted a kid. She was so pleased with herself. A rich family taking it off her hands? Win-win, right?"

430 · KELSEY RAE DIMBERG

Iris was a liar to her bones, but she was speaking differently. Without her usual drama. As if she didn't relish telling the truth, and spat it quickly.

"And the Martins? Why did they do it?"

She lifted a shoulder. "I can't tell you their side of it. I can guess. Stacy was beautiful. She used to be prettier than me. Healthy. Not very smart, but my mom probably lied about that." She glanced behind her, as if someone might be floating in the illuminated water. "All of a sudden I heard Stacy wasn't at home anymore. My mom wouldn't tell me where she was. In the fall Stacy came back with no baby. And my mom suddenly had a bunch of money. She took off. Left Stacy alone. She wound up in the hospital. Tried to kill herself. I had to come home to be with her."

Iris's staginess had crept into that last remark, an artificial selflessness. But the rest was real, I thought. It matched what Stacy had said.

"So blackmailing Philip was revenge?" I asked.

"We need money." Her voice turned reasonable and imploring. "You've met Stacy. She's broken. She needs someone to take care of her. My mom stopped sending anything back, we ran out of money . . . I didn't know what to do. Then I ran into Clint. He told me about the family. They were rich, the kid was spoiled, had everything. I thought they'd be happy to help us." She lifted her chin, daring me to protest.

"Clint told you their real name? Stacy called them something else."

She nodded. "He always liked Stacy."

"So he was helping you? Blackmail Philip?"

Her eyes flashed. "The opposite! He sided with them. The kid was in a good home; my mom had promised . . . When I didn't give up, he said I'd get what was coming to me. We started getting these horrible calls, threatening me, Stacy, our house. Then he set my car on fire. It was the middle of the night. We could feel the heat in the house. I got Stacy out of there . . . I couldn't tell her who did it. She likes him. I had to pretend it was strangers. Bad guys."

Creepers, I thought. Knowing Iris, there was an ulterior motive in lying to Stacy. Not wanting her to know she was blackmailing the Hugheses, for instance.

"I don't get why he helped you," I said. "Why'd he give away the name, just like that?"

She shrugged, but she was suddenly awkward, holding herself stiffly, as if in disgust.

"You didn't—?"

"I just ran into him, Finn. I'm not the one who'll sleep with anyone." She sneered.

My neck got hot, remembering how surprised I'd been, watching through the window as Guy took Iris's hand. "You mean Guy? I felt sorry for him. He seemed lonely. Talking about Georgia peaches."

She laughed softly, grinding her cigarette under her shoe. "You're lying. But still—you're funny. That's exactly how he is, deep down, under all his attitude. A little boy who just wants to crawl in your lap."

"I heard you're breaking up. Moving away. Where will you go?"

"Not Georgia."

The pool filter kicked on. By day it would have been a purr, but now it seemed like a roar.

Iris flicked a strand of hair from her forehead. "So. That good enough for you?"

"Do you have proof? You might still be lying to me. It's what you do best."

"I need money, Finn."

"Tell me first."

"The midwife." She was impatient. "The midwife put their names on the birth certificate. She made it like Stacy never existed." She threw her cigarette into the pool. "I have her name."

I let silence pass, watching her try to hold her pose. Then I shrugged. "That's it? No wonder Philip didn't pay you. I'm sure she'd never admit it. She'd go to jail."

She narrowed her eyes. "How can you be on their side, after everything?"

"You're the one who started this."

"You have no idea what they're like. Do you? Philip laughed in my face, even after I told him what Stacy tried to do."

Reflexively, I batted away that vision of Philip. "He'd never be like that. I don't blame him for not giving you anything. Who could ever trust you?"

"Ah, that's right," she said. "I forgot about your thing with him. It was funny, how miserable you were, thinking he was sleeping with me."

"I don't know what I was thinking. He'd never touch someone like you."

She shook her head. "Here's the Philip I know. When I met him, I pretended to want a job. He took me up to his office and shut the door. He kept touching me. Rubbing my arm. 'The trays get heavy, let me see your muscle,'" she said, making her voice deep. "He wanted to hire me to work the closing shift. 'You'll have to be up late.'" Her disgust was palpable. "When I told him who I was, you wouldn't believe how fast his pretty face got ugly."

I breathed through my teeth. "You're lying."

She stepped toward me, and I backed away. "I gave Stacy some money. I felt bad for her. Not for you. If you hadn't come around, Amabel would be alive. Your niece."

She jabbed her finger at me. Her nails were bitten to the quick. "That's not on me. Guy told me you were there. It was your fault."

I lunged toward her, furious, and she snatched at my purse. Her bony fingers fastened around the strap. I pulled back, but she had a better grip. She was ferocious, teeth gritted, the tendons in her wrists tight as cords. She was much stronger than me, and frighteningly determined, her tall frame bearing down. Her breaths came hard and fast, and utterly unself-conscious. My hands were sweating. The strap snapped, and she yanked the bag away with a triumphant grunt, dumped it onto the patio. The knife clattered out. She hooted. "A knife! Are you kidding?"

She picked it up and held it in front of her. The tip danced in the air between us. I didn't move. I kept my eyes on it.

"Did the two of you ever fuck? Guy and I argued about it. He thought yes. I had a feeling no. I think Philip was afraid of you." She was still amped up from our struggle, and her win, and she slashed the air with the knife, mockingly, giggling. Moving back, I stumbled and twisted my ankle. I caught myself on a chair.

Still smiling, Iris flicked the knife into the pool. She snapped up the envelope of cash from my scattered things. Opening it, she swore appreciatively. "Stacy said it was a lot, but I didn't know whether to believe her!" She stuck the envelope into the waistband of her jeans, dropping the hoodie over it.

I stepped forward again, caught her by the arm, but she shoved me, hard. I'd miscalculated my distance from the pool. The splash seemed like an explosion in the courtyard. I thrashed to my feet, gasping. The water was up to my chest. My clothes were immediately sodden and heavy. I dragged myself to shallower water.

Iris backed away, her face shadowed under the hood. "Watch out for yourself, Finn. Philip's bad news. You think you know him, but you don't."

"You're crazy." I didn't know if she could hear me. I was still breathless.

"Look at Clint," she said. Or something about Clint. She was already turning, beginning to jog, and then she vanished into the dark.

38

I was desperate to wash the smell of chlorine from my skin. When I entered the condo's gym, overhead lights flipped on automatically. A wall of windows exposed me to the courtyard. I moved quickly toward the bathroom. The hulking exercise machines cast strange shadows on the carpet. There was a trembling pressure in the air. I realized it was the motors, emitting a low, grinding hum I could just register.

I locked myself in the bathroom. There was a toilet, a waffled white curtain across a shower stall, a wire basket of folded towels. Everything smelled of bleach. After I undressed, I rinsed and wrung out my clothes and hung them up. I stood under the water for a long time.

The cheap hair dryer got the worst of the wet off

my clothes and hair. In the quiet when I'd finished, I was wincingly aware of how loud I'd been. The faucet dripped, echoed off the tile. I hesitated at the door, dreading going back out.

I quickly undid the lock and strode into the gym as if I weren't afraid. The lights flashed on. For a moment, my eyes faltered, dark blotting over my vision. I thought I heard a sigh. A rustle? When my eyes cleared, the room seemed normal. I made it across the courtyard, was pressing my pass to the door sensor, when I heard something for sure: the scrape of a deck chair against the patio. Iris? Guy? Someone else? I didn't wait. I slipped inside and pressed the door shut behind me.

Upstairs, Bryant's condo was dark and still. I kicked off my shoes and climbed the stairs quietly. He was in bed, turned away from the door, the sheet tucked under his arm. He didn't stir, even when I lay beside him. The sheets were cold and crisp. He ironed them, or had them ironed. Tentatively, I reached my hand under the covers until I touched his side. He still wore his boxers and undershirt. It couldn't have been him out there, I thought.

His skin was warmer than mine.

I lay awake. Everything ran together smoothly in my mind, until Clint's death.

Once Iris had extracted the Martin name from Clint, she'd gone to work. When I walked in on Philip and Clint in the office, they'd been plotting to keep her away. *Have to take steps.* Perhaps realizing how visible they were at the restaurant, they rendezvoused at the motel. Philip paid him. I could imagine Philip saying, *Don't hurt her, but*—. Clint made his phone calls. Set fire to her car. Then Iris had been afraid. When I'd met her after the gala, she'd no longer wanted to see Philip.

Days later, Clint was dead. Had Philip blamed him for Ammy? But he should have blamed Iris.

I reminded myself of the key—Philip wouldn't have broken into Clint's room. But the thought wasn't as comforting as it had been.

Beside me, Bryant slept, or didn't sleep.

In the morning, he pressed his nose to my cheek. A quick kiss before work? I didn't feel his lips. He might have been smelling the pool. I thought he whispered something.

I woke again later, and he was gone. A note on the island read: *Sorry, something came up. Home by 4.*

My head ached. I'd woken from the middle of a dream, something intense and unsettling, and tiredness clung to me, turned my head cloudy.

Ordinary signs of Bryant were scattered about the kitchen. The day's paper, already read and folded into a tidy roll on the island. A coffee cup with a drop trailing down from the rim. Our highball glasses. I tried again to remember the night before, what we'd talked about. I'd asked him something—about Marina? Everything was cloudy. I must have had too much to drink. The thing I most vividly remembered was the steak, dripping onto the white plate. And sitting on the edge of the bed, reaching up to unclasp my necklace, my arms so heavy, my fingers thick and clumsy.

I drank two cups of coffee. Bryant's fridge had been restocked with fruit, eggs, macadamia-nut milk, a pile of raw granola bars, some bottled cold-pressed juice. If he kept junk in the house, he'd told me, he'd eat it all. So he didn't. His self-control was exacting.

I chewed one of the soft, crumbling bars. I idly unfolded the newspaper. Beside the date was the weather: a yellow sun icon, high of 113. Bryant had left the paper open to the middle, a patchwork of half stories, continued from earlier pages. And, at the bottom, a headline.

MOTEL DEATH RULED ACCIDENTAL

I read it quickly. *Police closed their investigation of a man's sudden death . . . An autopsy determined the cause to be an overdose of painkillers . . . The discovery in-line with the scene . . . The death was the latest instance of the opioid epidemic . . .*

I rubbed my eyes with my fists. Clint, an addict, had died of an overdose. It hadn't even crossed my mind. I'd trusted Brenda Argyle, even though she was obviously eager to gossip. And Iris, a pure liar. *Philip's bad news.* She must have laughed all the way home.

I threw away the last of my breakfast. I went out onto the balcony. A worker in white overalls leaned a ladder against the palm trees and pruned dead fronds. Suspicion lingered like a toxin in my muscles. Bryant had left the paper just so, like a gift to me, wrapped up on the island.

I was still standing there, watching the palm fronds fall to the ground, when my phone rang. A local area code.

"Finn, this is Philip."

The reception flickered. "Philip?"

"I was hoping we could meet for lunch. Are you free?" He sounded calm and pleasant.

"Really?"

"I wanted to call sooner, but things kept preventing me. Are you up for it?"

We arranged to meet at The Grove at twelve-thirty. After we hung up, I went inside to dress, trying to decide if I was feeling excitement, or dread.

My taxi dropped me off fifteen minutes early. I lingered in the restaurant's garden. A wasp was bothered by my presence, and kept darting at me, its body a striped bullet.

Philip seemed to materialize in the tunnel of flowering trellises. He wore a pale linen suit and gold-framed sunglasses, as if already ready for his cruise. His face was tired but kind, the Philip I knew, though his hair was shot through with gray.

"It's good to see you," he said, kissing my cheek. He was clean-shaven, smelled of peppermint.

"I didn't expect to hear from you."

He took off his shades, and I saw how the skin around his eyes was thin and blue. "I wasn't comfortable with the way we ended things. I hope you understand it wasn't to do with you. Marina was upset."

"I shouldn't have shown up like that," I said. "At the funeral."

He brushed his hand in the air. "Enough. Let's go in, shall we?"

A hush fell as we crossed the dining room.

Tommy was at the bar. He took Philip's hand in both of his, as he'd done to me. "I'm so sorry. We all are. We're sleepwalking here."

Philip thanked him with a grimace, and I thought

later he'd have the manager tell the staff not to mention it. "I stopped in for lunch. Something light. And wine."

We went up to his office with two bottles. He closed the door, and I was uncomfortably reminded of Iris's story—how Philip sealed them in together, isolated from the restaurant. I hung back by the door. He shrugged out of his jacket and hung it from the basketball hoop. He loosened his tie, undid the top two buttons of his shirt. Reclining in his chair, he yawned until I thought his jaw might crack. "Are you going to sit?" His smile, how well I knew it, that sudden twitch, lips gathered slightly off to the side; the way he sometimes cocked his head first, like his smile was a weapon aimed at you.

I smiled back. I always did.

I perched on the chair opposite. Where Clint had sat.

"Did you come from business?" I asked.

He rubbed the back of his neck. "Just wrapping some things up. We're about to go out of town for a while."

"The cruise."

"You must think it's barbaric."

"No," I lied.

"It is, of course," he said. "But everything feels barbaric now, anyway." He poured the wine. He lifted his glass to me before we drank.

The wine was sweet and effervescent. Something harder would have been welcome. Something that stung. But I was nervous, and drained my glass.

"I've been wanting to apologize to you since it happened."

He winced. "You don't have to."

"I'm so sorry. I never should have left her alone, not for a minute."

"You can't watch them every instant. What, were you in the bathroom?"

This felt like the moment to confess, here in this quiet room, with Philip's newly gray scalp bowed. But the words stuck in my throat.

"You're not alone," Philip said. "The guilt. I hardly saw her this summer. I'd go past the playroom, peek at the two of you, and then—I'd keep going. It makes me sick."

"You were a wonderful dad." I swallowed. "Ammy adored you."

"And you," he said. "Now please, enough. It's not necessary between us."

I bit my lip. He was being too nice. He'd lost that blustering, talking-over quality I liked, that sideways, teasing slant on everything.

"Why did you invite me here?" I asked.

"Does there have to be a reason?"

I thought of Marina escorting me from the church, of Bryant lifting my legs into bed, of Iris backing away from the pool. *Watch out for yourself.*

"I think so."

He raised his eyebrows. "Not what I expected you to say." He lifted the wine bottle and filled my glass at my nod. "I heard you've decided against going back to the Midwest."

I pinched the stem of my glass, swirling the wine back and forth. "Honestly, I never planned to go back. Bryant suggested it, and apparently he told everyone that's what I was doing."

Philip smiled wryly. "You won't hold it against us that we asked about your plans, surely?"

I shrugged. "I guess not. But I'm not going home."

"Good. I have a better idea for you." He flopped his wallet on the desk and rifled through the bills.

"I don't want any money. You were already too generous."

He tossed a business card on the desk. "This is better."

I picked it up. *Meredith Willis, Director, Willis Design and Remodel,* etched in copper lettering on velvety gray card stock.

"What's this?"

"Friend of mine. You used to be in design, way back when, weren't you? I made a few calls. Meredith is looking to hire an assistant. She said it won't be a design job to start, but it's certainly a foot in the door. A major foot in a major door. Meredith's is one of the top firms in New York."

I ran my thumb over the raised lettering. "New York?"

"No better place to go when you're young. Phoenix is for old people."

"Does Bryant know about this?"

"You wouldn't give up an opportunity like this for that boyfriend of yours, would you?" His grin dropped when he saw my expression. "But seriously, New York and D.C. aren't so far apart. You know Bryant will be over there full-time after the election. Assuming all goes well, of course."

My stomach hurt. He hadn't told me. I wondered if he knew about this job prospect. Probably so. They all seemed to know everything about me.

"I don't think I can accept this." I pushed the card across the desk. "Even though I appreciate the gesture."

Philip's eyebrows lifted. "Why the hell not?"

I ran my thumb along the zipper of my purse. "It's a generous offer. But I think it's for the wrong reason."

Philip frowned. "This is one of those opportunities

that shapes everything else. Work. Life. Everything."
He pressed the card firmly back at me. "Trust me,
Finn."

I wondered what Philip believed shaped his life.
His brother's death? His car accident? Or just the
Senator, steering Philip through all of the accidents,
controlling the fallout, so that Philip would inevitably
land in this chair, would inevitably remark in a confident, self-mocking tone that "all would go well" in
November, that the Martin family would steamroll
along, inevitably.

There was a sharp knock on the door, and the waiter
entered without a pause. He greeted me by name as he
set down my plate, and asked if we needed anything
else. He bowed and went out.

Philip unrolled his napkin and shook it into his lap.
He took up his knife and fork and began eating with
relish. They'd prepared some kind of silver meat, a leg
bone jutting up like a flag, in a winey broth of veg-
etables.

The face of Philip's watch reflected the desk lamp as
he cut. "I can't sleep, but I've been eating like crazy."
He glanced at me. "Don't you like rabbit? It's not a
principle thing, is it? Rabbit is good peasant food."

He knew I'd be tempted to tease him about his fancy
peasant rabbit, his eating too quickly and too much.

He'd be confident he could charm me into accepting his favor.

"I went to Verde the other day," I said. "To confront Iris. I blamed her for— Anyway. When I was there I met her sister. Stacy."

Philip's chewing slowed. He washed the bite down with more wine.

"I just lost my child." His soft voice was reproachful.

"I don't care about Iris, or Stacy. I'm not going to tell anyone. I just want to know your side. Why you did it."

A frown flashed across his face—pain, or irritation. He tapped the table, his wedding ring making a hard clear knock.

I touched his wrist, imploring. I remembered taking his arm to climb out of the pool, and the way he'd smiled at me, the thousand drops of water on his shoulders glittering in the sun.

"All right." He sighed. "But this stays here. I don't want you telling that boyfriend of yours. Or anyone else. Agreed?"

I nodded.

His pale blue eyes, framed by dashes etched into the skin, appraised me. A muscle at his jaw tightened and released.

"We had to do it," he said. "It was our only choice."

"What do you mean?" I said. "You mean . . . Marina couldn't get pregnant?"

"We *were* pregnant."

I frowned. The smell of the heavy food was stultifying. "I don't understand."

He shifted in his seat. "It took a while. Years, actually, but it finally happened. A girl. We had a name picked out and everything. We were five months along. We went in for an ultrasound. Just routine. I remember, the doctor was talking to Marina while she watched the screen. All of a sudden she trailed off. She tried to cover it up. Told us she needed to run a few tests.

"We were there another hour, maybe longer. Waiting alone in that little room. Marina didn't realize—she was nervous, but it didn't occur to her how bad it could be. She hadn't seen the doctor's face. But I knew. The tests were only protocol. The baby was gone. Something genetic. It can happen, they said."

His fingers reached up and clamped his ear, a rougher version of Marina's tic.

"I'm sorry," I whispered.

He told me Marina was devastated. She stayed in bed. Refused to get dressed, to eat, even to talk about it. Sometimes Philip found her in the baby's room. They'd had it all set up, they'd been so sure. She'd sit in the rocking chair, foggy with misery.

"She made me promise not to tell anyone," he said. "She was humiliated. She felt it was her fault. Marina is complicated. She guards herself . . . you know. But I had to talk about it. I went out with an old friend, someone who didn't know anyone we knew. It was safe to tell him."

"That was Clint," I said.

Philip blinked. "Yes. I forgot you met Clint." He rubbed his jaw. "Well. A few days later, he called me up. He knew a woman whose daughter was pregnant, way too young. She was six months along. About the same as Marina had been. And the baby was a girl, like ours.

"I was excited. It seemed meant to be. We'd been trying so long, the idea of going through all that again made me sick. But I thought Marina might not agree . . . she might be upset if I proposed it." His voice had gone faint in his recollection. "I found a way to bring it up gently. She didn't say much at first. Then, after a few days, she came outside. She was so white in the sun. She wanted to take the baby."

It was difficult to imagine Marina falling into a stupor of grief. The Marina I knew would suffer silently, grimly determined. Hadn't she shown up at Bryant's the morning after Amabel died, with her lipstick on, her clothes pressed?

"I'm sorry," I said again.

His gaze was concentrated on a spot on the desk, where the paler oak was inlaid with a bow-shaped mahogany joint. "Gradually, I realized Marina meant for her to be ours. Not to go through formal channels but to . . . As if we'd never lost . . ."

He looked up, defiantly. "To tell you the truth, I felt the same way. Why not spare ourselves the spectacle of grief, all the pity? And we were right. From the minute we had her, Amabel was ours."

Something slid into place in my mind. Sunday afternoon, the Senator had been furious with both Philip and Marina. *You lied to me.* "That's why you didn't tell your dad."

Philip frowned, surprised. "My dad? Who told you that?"

"I was just guessing," I said.

Covering real anger with a sardonic eye roll, he said, "It wasn't anyone's business. You know Jim. He makes everything about himself."

"But it was so risky to hide—look at what happened with Iris."

"Iris is a bitch with no right to anything." He threw his napkin on his desk. "It's ghoulish, what you're doing. Running around, chasing down some girls who tried to ruin our family. Digging for dirt, after every-thing we did for you."

"Isn't that why you asked me here? And told me about this job?" I said. "Because I found out, and you were afraid I'd tell someone."

"I asked you here because we are old friends," Philip said. "Aren't we, Finn? If I respect you enough to answer your questions, I hope you'll respect our privacy. You'll forgive me for being so blunt."

He lifted the desk phone. "Tommy? Send up some coffee, would you?"

A dense silence fell. Philip was wounded and noble, twisting open the second bottle of wine.

"I don't want to hurt you," I said finally. "I never did. Iris was threatening the family. When Ammy died, I blamed her. I only wanted to find out who she really was. I had no idea how it would end up."

"You were told it wasn't your business," Philip said softly.

"It felt like it was," I countered. His cool expres-sion reminded me of Mrs. Everett, standing behind her screen door, looking at my lilies like they were ghastly.

The waiter returned. He moved silently across the carpet. He set down a French press ready to plunge, cream, sugar cubes. A plate of toffee bars, homemade, the edges unevenly cut and crumbling. He whisked away our lunches, stacking my untouched plate on top of Philip's.

When he'd gone, Philip uncapped the coffee and stirred the grounds. A rich, murky aroma rose. He poured a mug for himself and flipped the other over for me. "The usual way?"

I nodded, and he added a sugar cube, tossing it with his fingertips rather than using the tongs. He poured cream until the coffee was pale.

"We used to have coffee in the mornings together. Do you remember?" His tone surprised me: fond, nostalgic. "You'd make a pot and pretend like you hadn't been waiting for me to come downstairs. We'd sit on the balcony. You'd blush when I brushed your leg with my foot."

Warmth rose to my cheeks. Philip, gazing over the valley, the sun in the folds of his shirt, his cuffs pushed over his forearms, his feet bare.

"Amabel would play with her blocks on the kitchen floor," I remembered. "We'd leave the door open to hear her."

He grinned. "Bad nanny. Neglecting the child for the father."

A chill swiftly replaced the warmth in my chest. I sipped my coffee. Sweet. Philip held the plate of toffees to me, and I took one politely. My fingers were sticky.

"Were you and Clint really friends?"

He crunched a toffee. "Why do you ask?"

"He seemed so . . . different."

He laughed. "You sound like Marina. Clint and I knew each other when we were young. You don't understand what that means yet."

Of all the options I'd considered, the idea that the accident had brought them closer together hadn't occurred to me. I wondered what Erica might have become, if she'd lived. We might have been tossed from the boat together and swam to the shore, laughing, an adventure.

"Were you surprised?" I asked. "I'm sorry, I didn't mean to bring it up."

"What do you mean?"

My purse had slipped off my lap. I hoisted it up. "When he died."

Philip went absolutely still, like a deer. "What happened?" His voice was dry.

"I'm sorry," I said. "I thought you must have heard. He overdosed. In the motel room."

Philip ran a hand over his mouth, dragging the skin.

He didn't know. I quickly looked down to hide my relief. "He was addicted to painkillers since the car

454 • KELSEY RAE DIMBERG

accident. He overdosed on Monday or Monday night. The police just closed the investigation."

I hadn't meant to mention the accident, but Philip didn't seem to notice. In fact, he hadn't seemed to hear me at all. He was staring at the bow-shaped mahogany on his desk again, his face frighteningly blank.

Clint had sat in this chair, days before he died. Clint and Philip had hashed things out. Philip put him in the motel, paid him, trusted him to threaten Iris. For Philip, Clint was willing to commit crimes. Suddenly, I wondered how I'd ever suspected Philip. He needed that loyalty. He needed someone who traced back earlier than the Senator's influence.

Philip laughed. The noise made the hairs on my arms stand up. It was a wild sound, like a noise the coyote might make, pain and distress.

"Poor Clint," he said. "What a life." He lifted the wine and refilled his glass, though he was halfway through his coffee. "To Clint." He drank, spilling down his front. He wiped his mouth with the back of his hand. His eyes avoided mine, jumping when I came close.

Clint won't say a word. It had been a defense. The Senator was there, heard Clint's name, and understood that Clint knew too much.

The newspaper—folded just so on Bryant's counter.

The investigation was closed. I thought of the old article in my bag: D.A. ANNOUNCES NO CHARGES IN FOOTBALL PARTY FATALITY. The Senator had rushed home from Washington after the car accident, and within weeks, the case was closed.

I tried to choose my words carefully. "Did your dad know about the motel?"

"Motel?" Philip's eyes flicked to the base of the lamp. "As far as I know, Clint lived in a trailer park. He was always saying it was temporary. Ten years of temporary."

Philip's phone rang, startling us both. He silenced it without checking who it was. "What a mess. I won't be sorry to get away for a while."

I felt cold. "What do you mean, mess?"

"It's only an expression." He checked his watch. "It's getting late."

"It took the police a few days to decide Clint overdosed," I said. "At first they were investigating his death as suspicious. I heard a rumor that someone forced open the motel door."

Philip's face twitched. "A rumor? Where'd you hear that?"

"I saw you at the motel. I followed you." And then, realizing it as I spoke: "You had a key. You were keeping him there."

"What are you suggesting?" Philip said. "That I put a grown man in a motel room, and then killed him? My own friend?"

"No," I said. "You tried to protect him."

"Clint's been depressed a long time." Philip's voice was deliberate.

"He knew your secret. He'd given you up to Iris, maybe unintentionally, but still. He was dangerous to your family. To the Senator."

"If you're accusing—" He laughed, like it was absurd. "You're emotional. You're not thinking clearly." His voice was soft, but far from gentle. It held a tone of warning.

"I saw your face when I told you. You knew it wasn't an accident."

"That's enough!" He stood in a rush, chair spinning. Went to the window and yanked the blinds up. Dust motes exploded into the air. He was breathing so hard his shoulders rose and fell.

I felt dizzy, drunk, though I hadn't finished my second glass of wine. I stared at Philip's slowly spinning chair, willing myself to calm down.

He broke the silence. "The coyote came into the yard the other day, when we were emptying the pool."

I blinked, trying to catch up to this new thread.

"He was closer than I'd ever seen him. He was bigger than I realized. And yellow, like he had a disease. You were right, he was dangerous."

My dream surfaced, the coyote drinking from the pool, Philip petting him.

Philip's expression was ominous. "I went for my gun. When I came out, he was still there. Hunting in the brush. He only heard me at the last second. His ears flattened out." He turned to the window. "You wouldn't believe how loud it was. It must be the house, how it's over the valley. The pool guy was out front, packing up the hose. He came running, probably afraid I'd killed myself. I told him the coyote was going to hurt someone. We couldn't find the body. He must have dragged himself away."

I felt sick. "Why are you telling me this?"

He came back to the desk and stood over me. "You're a good girl. Let's go out on a friendly note. I'll say we should keep in touch. You'll tell me to enjoy my cruise. And then you'll go home and forget about this. You'll call Meredith. In ten years, you'll be a big-shot designer. You'll think of me fondly."

I protested, but he put his hand over my lips. "No, Finn." His face was close to mine. To my surprise, he didn't look angry, but afraid. "Don't. Take my advice. Get out of here. Get a fresh start."

He helped me up, held the door. Passing him, I felt heat coming off his chest.

I ran down the stairs, raising a metallic racket. The storeroom was quiet and empty. I could feel Philip at my back, lumbering with alcohol.

I pressed through the door to the dining room. The clamor of the lunch crowd enveloped me. Tables packed with women in sundresses drinking iced tea, businessmen in suits chewing steak. The normalcy of it returned air to my chest.

At the door, I slowed. Philip was gone. He'd vanished somewhere in the cavern of his restaurant. Or he hadn't followed me at all, but only watched me hurry away.

Walking through the garden, heat blazing up from the flagstones, I remembered the creature at the perimeter of the Martins' yard. Hollowed out and rancid. The disturbed air above it rippling and dancing, alive with flies. The dog we'd watched run and scratch and hunt, his fur painted with every color of the desert.

39

It took all my energy to channel that old Finn, to flirt and boss and cajole, whatever was necessary, until the auto shop agreed to repair my car immediately. I had to put it on my credit card. My bag felt hollow without the Martins' cash. Though I wouldn't have spent it anyway. Or so I wanted to believe.

For two hours, I waited in the auto shop, woozy with the smell of oil, a magazine unread in my lap. When I stepped outside for fresh air, the day was stagnant, heat lying heavy as a cat over the valley. The sky was stingingly bright.

I called the Verde Police Department. The man who answered the phone listened without interest as I told him I had information about a car fire. He put me on hold for someone whose name I couldn't catch. Minutes of country music followed—plus a recorded warning to call 911 if it was an emergency. A bus sped through a yellow light, trailing a swirl of dirt behind it like a cape. I chewed the inside of my mouth.

"This is Officer Mendez."

I introduced myself, awkward. "I'm calling with information on a fire in Verde. I believe it was last week. Iris Jamison's car was burned."

"Yes?"

"Well," I said. "I think I know who did it. His name was Clint Davis. He was staying at the Sunset Motel. He was also making threatening calls to Iris's house. I'm guessing that could be checked."

He was silent a moment. Then, "Miss? What was it? Hunt?"

"Right," I said.

"I'm having trouble keeping up. Let's take it slower. What connection did you say you have with this case?"

"It's complicated."

"Try," he said dryly.

"I was stopped outside of Iris's house by a policeman. He questioned me about the fire. How I knew Iris, what I was doing there, things like that."

He didn't speak, so I went on. "Like I said, it's complicated. I'm happy to come in—"

"You were stopped by an officer? When was this?"

"Thursday night. About ten."

"One minute." He put me on hold. When he came back, he said, "Miss Hunt, we don't have any record of that on our end."

"I didn't get a ticket or anything. I was just walking down the street, and he stopped me. He was under-cover. He drove a black car. He was short. Bald. He had a tattoo on his forearm. An eagle, with a gun in its claws."

"An eagle with a gun," he repeated. "A large tattoo?"

"Like a sleeve."

"Have you been to Verde, Miss Hunt?"

"Yes. I just told you—"

"We're a small town. We've got a small force. I know every person on it, and none of them is even a little bit like your description."

I sucked my lip. "But—"

"Did he show you any ID? Was he in uniform?"

"He had a gun. On his belt." Saying it I felt dumb. I'd fallen on the ground and looked up, and seen the dark clothes, and the heavy belt, and I'd assumed.

"Come on down and file a report, if you were threat-ened. But it wasn't an officer. That I promise you." He hung up.

I stared blankly at the sidewalk. Remembering the black car, its nose parked flush against my bumper.

The tattoo with veins rising under it. The menace in his smile. He wasn't a cop.

He was following me. I saw him in Verde, while I was driving Stacy. He'd chased me downtown, and I'd convinced myself I'd imagined it. Where else might he have tailed me? To the library? To my apartment?

He'd already known where I lived, what it looked like.

Last night, when Iris kept glancing around the patio, she wasn't afraid of Philip, or Bryant. It was him. A creeper, as Stacy would say.

A Snoop?

As soon as I thought it, I knew.

When I got to my apartment, Bryant was waiting in the lot. He wasn't surprised to see my car. He walked around it, kicking the tires. His sunglasses reflected the slate of the evening sky.

"We should get going," he said. "We have a dinner at eight." He was upset when I insisted on driving myself to his place. On the way, he managed to drop behind me, and whenever I lifted my eyes to the rearview, he was persistently at my back.

We were playing a game. I didn't know the rules, or if there were rules. I could only guess Bryant's objective. To keep me quiet? To persuade me I was over-tired, overemotional, overimaginative?

I was playing for knowledge. Evidence, something concrete.

While Bryant was in the shower, I stole his phone and looked through it. He'd never told me the password, but he had typed it in front of me a dozen times, his fingers flying quickly over the four numbers, the glass smudged darkly in four particular spots.

Nothing. He'd erased all of his texts, except for the thread with me. His email account required a password, which I didn't know. His photo album was sparse, a few snaps of roadside landmarks or rally crowds. There was a selfie of us from the Fourth, Bryant's arm outstretched, my cheek against his. I looked tired. I remembered feeling exhausted, after a day of Amabel and the Martins, of chatting with Bryant's circle. I'd had no concept of how deep exhaustion could cut. How little a person could live on.

We drove together to the dinner.

A dark restaurant, a private room, candles, tablecloths, a long banquet table with a dozen couples. It was an ordinary evening from my life before; now it was surreal as a dream. Bryant made his way around the table, touching shoulders, shaking hands. His smile. The same smile as when I'd met him, and he'd confidently touched my skirt, lifting it to see the spill, bringing the hem above my knees.

I waited for him to sit (Rick Leach, rosy with sunburn, practically tugged him into a chair). Then I sat on the opposite end, beside a girl I recognized. Rick's girlfriend, Meg, the girl with the lollipop. Fresh from a weekend in the Seychelles, she was sleek as a seal and so tan her face was darker than her blond hair. She smelled of coconut oil. Though I'd only met her once, she kissed my cheek as if we were close friends. She chattered quickly, not pausing for any response: I looked amazing, so thin, how had I lost so much weight, I had to tell her, she was such a whale. Had I come here with Bryant? She paused to look approvingly at him. Had I noticed how conservative men were better in bed? Nastier, she winked, isn't it ironic?

"I'm not sure," I said. "We're fighting now anyway."

She leaned in, intrigued.

"The Senator's involved in some shady stuff."

She waited, brows lifted. When I didn't go on, she said, "Who the fuck's the Senator?" She slumped back in her chair.

I didn't know what I'd been thinking. As if she'd

pass anything on to Rick. As if Rick would care. *The Senator's shady? Of course he is.* That's what these people would think.

The mojitos we sipped made me sugared and nauseated. Plate after plate of oysters came to the table, and Bryant and his friends slurped them down whole and tapped their lips with white linens.

I excused myself, picking up my bag.

I felt a touch on my back.

"Is anything wrong?" Bryant said.

"I'm not feeling well. I'm just going to head out. I don't want to spoil the night."

"I'll come with you."

I protested; he insisted.

In the car, he said, "I heard you had lunch with Philip today."

I studied his inscrutable profile. "I thought maybe you'd suggested it. I know you've been worried about me."

"That's a funny idea. I haven't seen Philip at all. He's been busy."

"You all seem busy," I said. "I've had nothing but time."

"Seems like you've kept yourself pretty occupied."

He knew I'd gone back to Verde. He must know the Snoop had confronted me. Had followed me.

I almost snapped back at him—*you were busy Monday night*—but I swallowed it.

The wheels splashed over wet pavement. A broken fire hydrant gushed water over the road. It pooled into a deepening puddle. There were no gutters to swallow it.

"What a waste," Bryant said. "We should call the city."

I hummed. I noticed a strange smell. Like shampoo. The car had been cleaned. No more folders in the back, no papers, not so much as a tissue. I dropped the glove compartment open. Maps, the manual, and a pair of gloves. I tugged them out. The fingers flopped over my bare knees. "What are these for?"

He looked at me, and the wheel jerked. "Please don't dig."

"What are they?"

"They're gloves." He set a hand on top of the wheel and flicked his eyes at me. "Can you put them back, please?"

I didn't comment. I put them away. But I understood, suddenly, where he'd gone that night. Someone had torn through Clint's trailer. Crept inside and progressed room by room, impatiently, kicking through clutter, searching for anything that might connect Clint to the Martins. The job required finesse, thoroughness, an eye for detail. Bryant's kind of thing.

"So," he said. "What did you talk about?"

"When?"

"With Philip."

"He gave me the name of a designer who's looking for an assistant."

"That sounds promising."

"It would be in New York."

We turned into the parking garage. The car plunged downward.

"I don't know if I'm going to take it. It feels off."

He accelerated around a corner. He sped into his spot and stopped fast. I jerked against the belt. "You sound so ungrateful." He got out of the car and slammed his door. I watched his figure move around the car to open my door. He was stiff with annoyance.

Getting out, I squeezed my arms into my sides so we wouldn't touch.

He grabbed my elbow and we walked. Our footsteps echoed. If the black car showed up, the Snoop, they might just push me in and that would be it. I thought, Bryant couldn't have known about Clint, he couldn't have participated. He shook children's hands at rallies; he remembered birthdays and anniversaries with unfeigned enthusiasm; he kissed the nape of my neck as he zipped up my dresses. He was good.

We got into the elevator. The TV screen inside flashed trivia questions.

Bryant didn't release my arm until we were inside the condo. When he did, he moved tensely, flipping on lights. He practically ripped his tie off. I wanted to go and set my hand on his back, to calm him: a reflex, from before.

"I should go," I said.

"No." He covered his eyes, then swept his hand over his head. "No. Please. I didn't mean to snap at you."

"It's not that," I said.

"Rick said he has money troubles," he said. "He's not giving anything. Next time, he said. He just likes being at the table."

I almost laughed. Donations, those little triumphs, felt far behind us. Unless he was making this up, an excuse for his anger.

"You want a drink?" He was already pouring. He carried the glasses into the kitchen. Under the work lamps, his skin was bright with sweat.

"I'd rather have water," I said.

"Have both. I'm making it your way." He squeezed in honey. He stirred manically with a spoon.

I thought: last night, in my drink, he gave me a sleeping pill. That's why I was so out of it.

He pushed the glass at me. He leaned against the

counter, holding his own drink in his palm. His legs were crossed at the ankle. He was wearing bright yellow socks with tiny white dots. A gift from me.

"Philip mentioned you were moving to D.C.," I said.

He looked up. "I wish he hadn't said anything. There are a lot of big *if*'s around that prospect."

"Were you going to tell me?"

His smile seemed sad. "At the right time. When it was certain."

I nodded. "Congratulations. That's what you've been hoping for, isn't it?"

"Yes. Probably." His shoulders sloped.

My drink was sweet and syrupy. I set my empty glass on the counter. "I'm going up." I moved ahead of him. The pills were in the nightstand drawer. I counted them. My hands were shaking. I accidentally dropped a few onto the floor. Twenty-two, twenty-three? Surely the bottle had started with thirty.

I was so tired. I slept soundly, but it might have been sheer exhaustion.

At five in the morning, my phone buzzed persistently. I'd set an alarm.

How many times had I woken up in this bed? Dropped my feet onto the wool rug and wrapped myself in a short silk robe Bryant had given me. Even this morning, even as my head ached and I held my breath with nerves, the room seemed calm, the Japanese-style bed wide enough to sleep a half dozen, the morning light filtered gray through the shade, the sighing of the air purifier. I was tempted to lie back down, pull the sheet to my eyebrows, and let sleep wash over me, not gentle but rough, like a tide.

Instead I dressed and went outside. The courtyard lights were still on, though the sky was light. Sprinklers soaked the grass. I passed the gym, where a bulky, shirtless man was running on the treadmill. In the parking garage, I took the stairs instead of the elevator, pulling Bryant's key chain from my pocket as I went.

The click of the remote echoed faintly. I ducked my head into the passenger door, and my body felt exposed.

The gloves were gone. The manual was there, and the maps. I tugged them out and shook the pages. Nothing. I stuffed them back. Moving faster, I checked every compartment, every seam in the leather. My fingers came away with a slight film, and the smell of shampoo. Every inch of the car was clean. The trunk was empty, though I knew Bryant usually carried an emergency kit: blanket, flashlight, first-aid supplies.

Frustrated, I slammed the trunk shut.

The elevator pinged. Instinctively, I darted to the front of the car and crouched. My back was against a concrete pillar, my body wedged between Bryant's car and an SUV. I should have run out, headed for the exit. I was trapped. I could hardly breathe.

The doors opened and someone stepped out, walking slowly. Heavily.

I dropped lower to the ground. My hand reached down and touched warm, greasy pavement.

Then, abruptly, the footsteps quickened. They moved away. A remote beeped, a door opened and shut, an engine shuddered on. I straightened. A sporty blue car was easing back from a space. As it pulled away, I saw the driver, a woman absorbed in poking her radio.

Time to go. I felt in my pocket for Bryant's keys. They weren't there. I'd sealed them in the trunk.

I rapped lightly on Bryant's door. I had a newspaper under my arm and a coffee cup in each hand. It was almost six. I hoped he was up.

I'd walked to the coffee shop two blocks from Bryant's condo. The place was swarming with crack-of-dawners on their way to work or the gym. Almost everyone idling around the barista counter was buried in their phones. I picked up a paper and idly twisted it in my hands as I waited. Soon enough the barista dropped two cups on the counter. I picked them up as smoothly as possible and headed for the door. A man held it for me. As I walked back, the coffee slowly heated through the cups, through the cardboard collars, and finally burned my palms. If I sped up, the liquid would spill from the lids, so I kept walking slowly, burning.

Bryant was dressed for the gym when he answered the door.

"I'm sorry," I said. "I was up early. I forgot my key. I'm such an idiot."

He frowned as I came past him. "I was worried."

I set the cups on the counter. "I got you a paper, too." Suddenly I saw the name scribbled on the cups. John.

Bryant took a sip. "What is this?"

"I must have grabbed the wrong order."

"It's not bad." He studied me. "You must have been up at dawn. I thought you liked to sleep in."

"I woke up. I can see why you like it. It's very private, so early."

He tilted his head. "Private?"

"I meant . . . peaceful."

We sat on the balcony. Bryant shuffled through the newspaper. I'd never noticed before how he didn't seem to read as much as to check. To check they got the right story, quote, facts. I put my feet up against the railing. The iron scratched my arches. The cloudless sky threw its fierce white glare. It seemed that the blue pigment had burned away in the heat.

Bryant sliced a peach, prying out the pit with the tip of the knife blade. When he passed me the plate, the knife spun off and clattered on the glass tabletop.

I jumped, spilling coffee.

Bryant pressed his napkin to my skin. "Did you burn yourself?" His hair smelled like almonds. He must have gone out in the middle of the night and gotten rid of the gloves. Why?

I pulled away. "I'm fine."

He was still leaning toward me. His eyelashes were thick as a child's. He set his hand on my leg. "Are you sure?"

I nodded.

"Good." He reclined. "I have the day off. What should we do? Sit by the pool?"

I smiled. He proceeded to eat the peach by himself, slice by slice.

"I'm going to hit the gym first. Do you want to come?"

I rubbed my face. "No—I'm pretty tired. I might take a nap."

He followed me upstairs and watched as I undressed and got back into bed. He stretched his hamstrings. "You could doze by the pool."

"I'd burn." His stare was making me tense. I lay flat on my back, holding the thin sheet over me. I watched him pull one arm across his chest, then the other.

I rolled onto my side. "Have fun." I shut my eyes.

He stayed a moment, but finally went downstairs. A minute later, he was back: "Where are my keys?"

"What?"

"My keys are missing."

I draped an arm over my face. "Where'd you put them?"

"On the counter. Like always. I can't find them." He opened and shut drawers. He picked up my purse from the floor.

"What are you doing!" I sat up.

"I've looked everywhere."

I grabbed at the bag. He surrendered it. He was angry, but I saw him bite his lip and control it.

"You didn't see them?"

"No," I said. "Maybe you locked them in the car." Avoiding his stare, I put the bag on the floor. "I'm going to sleep."

He stayed another minute, and then he left. I

knew he didn't believe me. He went downstairs and I heard him moving around the kitchen. Finally he went out.

I didn't have much time. I went right for his briefcase, tugging out the files. There had to be something. My hands were shaking. I checked the pockets of every suit, moving my hand swiftly in the cloth, finding folded tissues, pen caps, gum wrappers.

He'd left his wallet in the kitchen. The credit card slots were stuffed with IDs and security passes and cards. The billfold was stocked with crisp twenties, a school snapshot of his nephew, and a blank check. In the zippered compartment behind the credit cards was a folded sheet of paper.

I smoothed it over the counter.

Natalie Finn Hunt was typed at the top.

Below it was line after line of miscellaneous figures and notes. No details, no sentences. It would have been obscure, random, to anyone but me.

My mom's address.

My mom and stepdad's names and occupations.

The years my brothers were born.

Erica's address. Her parents' names. Their occupations.

The year I shoplifted, and the store.

The year Erica died.

The names of the boys who'd been with us in the boat.

My dad's name and address. His wife's.

"What are you doing?"

Bryant stood in the kitchen. He watched me with a flat, unsurprised look.

"What is this?" I didn't want to touch that paper anymore. I pointed at it.

He drew his lips to the side. "You know what it is."

"How long—?" I couldn't finish.

"Have I known you were Natalie? A few days."

I backed away as he came in. I ran into the counter. He picked up the paper. His tongue flicked over his lips. "It was pretty surprising. Most of this. I actually thought they might have been wrong." He laughed. "After a day or so, I realized I wasn't actually surprised at all. Things that had seemed strange suddenly made sense. The way you talked about yourself. It was like a story. Like a little girl telling a story."

I flinched. In spite of everything, shame spread like dampness over my body. I'd known this moment would come, and it carried in it every cringing lie, every anecdote told with my eyes on the ceiling, thinking of Erica's house, of washing dishes with her mother, of learning to drive with her father in the passenger seat and Erica lying in the backseat, shrieking with mock terror.

"You were so perfect," I managed. "I wanted to be perfect."

"I'm glad you're not going to deny it," Bryant said. "That shows some character."

"Are you?" I said.

He frowned. "Am I what?"

"Going to deny it," I said.

His face rippled with surprise, and then settled. "What do I have to deny?"

"The Martins adopted Amabel. Bought her. From Stacy. That's why Iris was after Philip. I'm not sure when you found out. At the gala?"

He didn't give a sign.

"The Senator found out that Philip's old friend Clint gave up their name to Iris. He was furious. He had you go through his trailer. To make sure there was nothing that tied him to Philip. That's where you were, when you snuck out of my apartment Monday night, wasn't it? Then the Senator had him killed, and shut down the investigation of Clint's death. As if it were an accident. You left the paper out for me."

Bryant had crossed his arms. He was listening to me with a relaxed, even interested expression.

"That's quite a story," he said.

"I have proof."

If he tensed, I couldn't see it. "What proof?"

"Clint burned Iris's car. If the police find out about that connection, they'll be forced to reopen their investigation."

He smiled. He shook his head. "I don't see why. Besides, who knows who burned her car? She might have done it, trying to get the insurance money. She has a record of her own."

"Stacy was pregnant. Iris and Stacy are witnesses."

"Witnesses? Iris was living in California. Stacy is confused." He stepped forward. "And you're a pathological liar. Calling yourself by a fake name. Telling people you lived in someone else's house. Someone who died. That sounds a little crazy, doesn't it? Who does that?"

I was breathing shallowly through my mouth. "Finn is my middle name. I was at Erica's house constantly. I did grow up there. Those aren't really lies. You're twisting them."

His laugh was harsh. "If they weren't lies, why tell them? Why not tell me you were close to a friend? Why not tell me your real name? I never knew you at all. That hurt me, Finn. I can see I got lucky, finding out when I did, but for a while I was shocked. I cared for you. I thought—well, never mind. After everything, you turned out to be a stranger."

"You're the stranger," I said. "I never thought you'd help them like this. I thought you were good."

"The Martins are good," he said. "Those people were blackmailing them. They were threatening them."

"They had some reason."

"Oh, spare me," he said. "You're being ridiculous."

"I'll go to the police."

"I wouldn't." His eyes were cold.

"Why not?"

"Don't be stupid, Finn. You stole from them."

I shivered. "What are you talking about?" Absurdly, I had a picture of Bryant picking up the dollhouse goldfish bowl from my nightstand.

"Things were taken from the Martins' house. Jewelry, mostly. Some art. Precious one-of-a-kind things." His eyes were dark pools. "Marina had some clothes missing. You were wearing one of her dresses at the gala."

"I borrowed that when we hosted the party. I'm going to give it back."

"You were alone in the house all afternoon before the gala. You had a few hours. It was like you jumped at the chance." He sounded genuinely disgusted. I couldn't tell if this was a threat or an accusation. He could say anything, and I'd never know what he believed.

"You know I'd never do that."

He shook his head. "How would I know that? I don't know anything about you, apparently."

A tear escaped my eye. I swiped it with the back of my hand. "I loved them. I loved Amabel. I'd never steal from them."

"But you've stolen before. Shoplifting. Petty stuff. It's on record. You're also known to befriend these . . . comfortable families. The Everetts. The Martins. You like to be welcome in their houses. Who knows how much else you took before they noticed."

"I shoplifted in high school. I was young. Stupid. It didn't mean anything." But my mother's words surfaced as I spoke. *Erica was always wild, and a little bit dumb. You're smart.*

Bryant was starting to lose his unruffled calm. "Come on, Finn. *Natalie.* You lie about everything. How could anyone ever trust you?"

I shook my head. "You've been dying to do this. Ever since Ammy. You wanted to get rid of me as soon as I was out."

"Do you really want to talk about Ammy?" It was almost a hiss. "I've been waiting for you to cry. To talk about her. Anything. You haven't said a word. No memories. No mention of missing her. And then"—he waved the paper in his hand—"then I understood. You were faking it the whole time."

My gut lurched. It was a sickening punch. Amabel and Bryant and me, lying on the blanket, looking up at the fireworks; Amabel and her sticky lemon-ice mustache; Amabel and her wild fueled-up wriggling as she led us onto the Tilt-A-Whirl.

I walked around him and began picking up my things. My purse. My phone.

"Finn." He caught me by the elbow. "Listen. You were there that day. Watching her. I'm sure the guilt is overwhelming. Instead of grieving, you're lashing out at the Martins. Inventing this . . . conspiracy." He was too close. His fingers twisted my skin. "It was only an accident."

The words sent a bolt of horror through me. I wrenched away. I moved for the door.

As though he didn't believe I was leaving, he came along, pressing his hand to my back. Coolly, he said, "You'll go your own way now. No one is going to press charges. This is kind. Believe me."

He corralled me into the foyer. I picked up my sandals, straps dangling from my fingers. I didn't want to kneel and put them on in front of Bryant.

He opened the door. "Take care of yourself, Natalie."

40

The long road to Verde burned past as if my anger were fuel.

I pulled into Iris's driveway. I pounded on the door and rang the bell until it echoed.

"Iris! Stacy! Hello?"

Not even a yip from the dog.

I went around back, crunching gravel. The patio blazed in the sun. I cupped my hands to the sliding glass door. The kitchen cabinets were thrown open, empty. On the floor were heaps of towels and rags, packages of plates and cups.

I looked in the den window. The TV was gone. The couch remained, stripped of blankets and cushions.

They were gone.

As I headed out of town, the black sedan appeared in my rearview mirror. When I turned onto Main Street, it followed. It crept along, never quite tailgating me, but sticking close. At a red light, the driver's-side window rolled down a few inches, and a plume of smoke emerged.

I got onto the freeway. I kept to the right lane behind a dusty van with a Jesus fish on the bumper. The sedan shifted left, crept through my blind spot, and pulled up beside my window. I faced forward. I held myself stiffly, determined not to show alarm. After ten, fifteen, twenty long seconds, he accelerated, pulled past me, and sped away.

I could picture him so clearly. The smooth forehead, the mean smile. The way he moved, the tight rough energy pent up inside him, unleashing in sudden, sharp movements. Grabbing my elbow. Bending his face to my window.

Was he the one who killed Clint?

Terror momentarily closed my throat. Then I fought it off. I wasn't like Clint. They wouldn't hurt me, surely. I couldn't just disappear.

The black sedan was far ahead, but not quite out of sight.

The Rolling Greens golf course was in a suburb south of the city, dense with McMansions built on the hem of the freeway, their tile roofs extending above the concrete sound barrier. The shells of new homes rose beside them. Apparently, demand for a freeway view hadn't been met. I wondered if this was one of Philip's developments. How much of Arizona did he own?

The golf course was a vast stretch of lawn so vibrantly green it seemed digitized. Imposing white pillars fronted the clubhouse. On an ostentatiously tall pole, the flag drooped like a handkerchief. The parking lot was nearly empty. It was too hot for golf.

I shielded my eyes and scanned the course. There was a lake in the middle, dark blue and boomerang-shaped. Periodically, the whiff of a golf club ruffled the still air. On a nearby green, a caddy dressed in white lifted a white flag from the hole. A quartet of men in sherbet-colored pants and caps ambled toward him, each holding a club like Mr. Peanut's jaunty cane. I knew exactly how they were talking—in that jocular, bullshiting, self-congratulatory way. I knew exactly what their homes were like, their wives, their cars, their social calendars. My lip curled against them.

I headed to the clubhouse. Inside the atmosphere was frosty in every sense—the temperature, my reception, the hair on every head. Some retirees wetted their dry throats in the lounge. In the pro shop, a worker ran a rag along the stale racks of polo shirts. He looked me over as I asked whether Guy was working. I had to admit I didn't know his last name, or even whether "Guy" was a nickname. I described him, blushing at the portrait my words painted.

The clerk smirked like he knew what I was really after. "If it's who I think, he was fired," he said. "Stopped showing up for work. So if you see him, let him know, won't you?"

He cast his glance over my head to greet a vast bald man in vast khaki pants, and hustled around me to direct him to the drivers.

I considered getting a drink at the bar, just for the pleasure of annoying them all, but I knew their voices would grate against me, like a too-small wool sweater on skin.

I didn't expect to see Guy again. I was the only witness left.

41

I set off on foot to find the grave. Flat shiny head-
stones ran in rows neat as cornfields. Their etchings
recorded only the parentheses of birth and death—life
itself abridged. I didn't see any as young as Amabel.

The grave was mounded up with fresh dirt, powdery
as cocoa. The stone was simple gray marble. *Amabel
Opal Martin,* the name a singsong.

I'd brought a bunch of daisies. I unwrapped them
from their crinkling plastic and scattered them over
the ground. She'd loved being buried . . . in sand at the
beach, under blankets. I imagined she'd giggle at the
tickle of the petals.

I sat on the stiff, parched grass. Once, picnicking
in the side yard, Amabel had found a brown lizard
crouched in grass like this. She held it in front of my

face. "You need to know lizards are friendly," she informed me. The lizard's amphibian eyes bulged in terror, its throat swelled and abruptly shrunk like a popped bubble-gum bubble. It wriggled and kicked, startling Amabel. She threw it. The body flew. She wiped her hand on the grass.

I'd yelled at her. She'd cried.

I should have been better to her. A million moments I'd been irritated or tired, not as patient as I could have been, not as kind.

A hawk wheeled overhead, pulling its shadow like a kite string over the flat ground. Somewhere out of my sight, a machine droned. Digging holes, maybe cutting grass. Around us, hundreds of American flags stuck out of the ground. I wondered if they'd been planted on the Fourth of July. I thought again of Amabel's bossy, proud face, her sneaker soles kicked up as she ran to the Tilt-A-Whirl, her fat, pretty teardrops when I didn't believe her about Iris.

All the miles I'd logged, the digging, the questions, I'd been distracting myself. Anything to avoid thinking about this. Anything to forget what I'd done . . . the pool gate open, my ear to the living room doorway, my darling Amabel alone. I'd been pouring out my energy, like a rat on a wheel, and it hadn't made any difference. I loved Amabel. I'd lost her.

"Once upon a time," I said quietly, "there was a beautiful girl. A princess. One day she lost something she loved very much. She was so sad. For days, she went around trying to learn what had happened. Then she found out something very wicked. Her friends had schemed with a very bad man. A sorcerer. They were lying, greedy. Even the prince."

I touched the stone. Hard, and gleaming hot in the sun.

"The thing is, the princess told some stories. She really only imagined that she'd ever lived in a castle. It was all make-believe. She wasn't actually a princess at all."

I shifted to sit, cross-legged. I plucked a blade of grass and ran it along my ankle, like Ammy had liked to do when I told her stories in the yard. We sat under the citrus trees, and drank fruit juice, and ran from the bees.

"The princess has to have a happy ending," I said. "Isn't that the rule?"

Amabel used to frown suspiciously if it seemed like the princess wouldn't wind up safely back in her tower.

"She'll get the sorcerer in trouble, of course. Then she might go away, find a new castle. She's still young and beautiful. She'll live happily ever after."

But how? Ammy would say. *What about the prince?*

I sat there so long the daisy petals had already begun to shrivel in the blistering heat. When I finally stood, my skin was mottled from the grass.

I called the Verde police from the parking lot. A procession of cars was just pulling in as I dialed, and when I was put on hold, I watched the mourners gather in the lot before making their way to the grave. Mostly they were old, humped and heavy. There was a young girl with them, maybe seven or eight, who couldn't be contained from romping across the grass.

The officer came on the line.

I explained who I was. I said I'd called earlier, about the car fire.

"Right," he said. "I remember you. The girl with the story about the detective."

I cleared my throat. "Well. I have the license plate of that man. He's followed me around. Threateningly. If you look into it, I think you'll find that he killed Clint Davis."

He sighed. "I don't think so. The Davis death was an overdose. Cut and dried. And the car fire, well, that was a group of kids. Caught them at it again late last night. Things get boring in small towns, as you can imagine. We find that people have all kinds of ways to invent fun for themselves. Calling in tips, for example.

The other day a woman came on claiming to have seen Elvis."

"But this man is following me around. Stalking me. You won't do anything?"

"You feel free to call the minute he breaks a law. In the meantime, I'd suggest the library. It's got shelves full of thrillers. Bye, now."

42

That night, the Senator was on the news. Not discussing Amabel's death, but speaking at a town hall. He stood onstage, dressed casually in belted khakis and a collared shirt. A banner behind him read, SENATOR MARTIN—*OUR* SENATOR.

"We're all frustrated by the economy," he boomed. "Some folks have been hit harder than others. Some of us are out of a home. Some of us out of a job. Some of us? Out of both." As he paused for effect, the cameras zoomed in. A microphone weighed down the lapel opposite his flag pin. He was swept up in his own words, perspiration glossing his forehead, his eyes glittering with fervor. "My opponent believes raising taxes on people is going to get us out of this mess. Myself, I don't like taxes." The audience began to cheer, and he raised his voice to continue. "I don't like financing a problem we shouldn't have in the first place." Applause overwhelmed him, and he ended on a triumphant shout.

The broadcast cut to an infographic. The Senator's approval rating had jumped eight points in the last week. Bryant must be pleased. Changing the slogan from "Your Senator" to "Our Senator" was subtly clever, just his thing. I sensed the tide turning, Gonzales unable to attack as hard, the Senator acting the part of brave, tragic figure.

I couldn't sleep. Every light was on. My neighbor stopped playing his video game at two-thirty, and the ensuing silence felt lonely and dangerous.

Keep busy. I sorted through my closet, weeding out clothes I could sell. Marina's black dress was tempting. Its designer label and mint condition could pay my rent for a month.

I found a Nordstrom bag crumpled in a corner. I didn't recognize it. It was surprisingly heavy. I brought it under the light and unknotted the handles.

Inside was a velvet pouch, the color of a shadow, thick and soft. I poured its contents onto the floor. A slim watch, diamond studs the size of dimes, a set of hairpins strung with citrine, a sapphire cocktail ring, a rose gold bangle hammered so thin it was nearly weightless. Marina's jewelry, all her favorites, the pieces she kept out in a tray in the bathroom.

For a moment I was confused, trying to remember how I'd brought the bag home—maybe Marina had put it in my purse by accident, instead of her own?

Then I remembered Bryant's accusation.

He'd mentioned more than jewelry, though: clothes and art. I went back into the closet and hunted, pushing aside hangers and kicking through piles of shoes. Item after item surfaced. Strappy green Manolo Blahniks, a leather handbag soft as cashmere, a wooden carving of a coyote howling at the moon, pitted and scarred with age. This last hidden at the back of my underwear drawer, perversely tangled in lace.

I lined everything up on the floor. My hands trembled, touching these familiar, coveted objects. If I had taken from them, wasn't this what I might have chosen? Exquisite and understated pieces; you'd never guess looking at it that the bag must have cost five or six thousand dollars, or the coyote carving was hundreds of years old, and probably should have been at the museum.

It was funny, how my instinct was to believe I'd done it. To feel shame and guilt. Hadn't Bryant been right about me? With the Everetts, I'd learned to cultivate generosity. There's always extra room in those big houses; there's a hole in every family, however happy. A pleasant, helpful outsider might slip right in. I didn't even need to steal.

It took me several minutes to remember that Bryant had a key to my apartment. What could be easier? He'd planted the items where I wouldn't notice them for a while. Knowing what I would want, which pieces might tempt me enough to keep them. And as soon as he knew I knew everything, knew I'd turned on them, he dropped this final threat.

If I didn't leave it alone, they'd accuse me of stealing.

Maybe it was also an incentive. Better than cash, because I couldn't get rid of it so easily.

It was ingenious, really. Bringing my story full circle. Once a thief, always a thief.

43

The next day, I packed the items carefully into a bag and returned to Ocotillo Heights. My gate pass still worked. I drove slowly up the tight road, catching glimpses of the opulent, familiar homes. I parked in the driveway and sat gazing up at the house.

By now, Philip and Marina had boarded the ship, unpacked their suitcases, joined the other passengers for cocktails on deck. They'd steeled themselves to marvel at the beauty of the Mediterranean coast, to eat and drink and admire old artwork. When they came home, they'd be themselves again.

Clouds knitted together at the horizon, and there was a charged, humid snap in the air. We were in for a storm, the first monsoon of the season. Back home, the end of summer brought coolness, a dry calm. Here, it brought the only extreme weather of the year, sudden furious storms, as though the desert were resisting the lessening of the heat.

The foyer glowed in the gray light. The vase that always displayed fresh flowers stood empty. I'd never seen it before—the lush bouquets had concealed it. It was beautiful, with tiny handles like ears and a faded, intricate design, blue over white. The porcelain interior was stained a deep reddish brown from the water. My fingers came away with a fine coat of dust. Eva must not have come for her weekly housekeeping. Already the house had a stuffy, closed-up feeling.

I went upstairs. I set the velvet pouch on Marina's dresser and arranged the jewelry on top of it. I took her dress to the closet. Though I'd patted it with a damp cloth and let it air over the shower, it still bore traces of my perfume.

The coyote was the only piece I left out of place. I set it at the head of the dining table, Philip's seat. I wanted them to know I'd been here, to see this proof of my integrity.

The kitchen window overlooked the yard. Reflexively, I avoided the sight of the pool. Coward, I thought, and I went outside to face it.

The wind had picked up, tossing handfuls of sand that hit the palm fronds with a gritty slap. The sky had darkened and lowered over the ground. I lifted the hinge of the pool gate and closed the gate softly behind me. As if my careful intention now made any difference. Reminders of Amabel were everywhere. In the chairs we'd used to support our towel forts, the paddle-shaped cacti I was afraid she'd run into, the shed stuffed full of floating toys.

Dirt and leaves had blown into the pool, mottling the bleached concrete floor.

As the storm gathered, the mountain rock beyond the backyard turned dark red. This was where the coyote had been shot. He'd dragged himself away, seeking protection in the cover of trees that were little more than a fence between mansions. I felt sorry for him. What chance had he had, in the Martins' territory?

I walked down the steps into the dry pool, daring myself to feel worse. In that instant, the air became water. Hot, soaking rain fell in drenching sheets. I ran inside, the bottoms of my sandals slick. I stumbled through the door, rain gusting in with me.

The storm would pass soon; monsoons were always dramatic but brief. I went to the living room to wait it out. The white furniture and walls were greenish in the storm light. The ceiling fan spun, the movement eerie in the still room. The pot Iris had emptied her cigarette into was angled toward me, like a raised eyebrow.

I'd expected to feel a righteous fury, returning here. Instead, I felt exhausted and sad. I stood at the window and watched the rain boil on the patio. Curtains of water obscured the valley below. I would never see that view again, and now I couldn't quite remember it. How much was the urban grid of rooftops and roads, how much rock and tree? I should have paid closer attention.

My toe hit something hard. Glancing down, I saw a patch of green sticking out from under the curtain. I picked it up. A book, bound in old fabric, *Call It Courage* in gilt letters on the spine. On the front page, someone had inscribed, *for James, from Dad*. I traced the text, wondering which James Martin had given it to which.

A clattering noise rose from the deck. The wind had blown one of the chairs into another. The powerful gusts drove rain into the window like handfuls of stones. On the glass, water pocked in droplets that ran together and flowed in ribbons. I followed one as it fell, merging and wending in a crooked path. It ran into another drop and paused, and at that precise spot I noticed a shape on the pane, a mark made from inside the house. A star, a starfish.

A handprint.

A chill ran through me, up my spine to the nape of my neck, as if cold fingers pressed my back.

The handprint was at shoulder height. Not a faint outline, not a smudge—a firm print. The oval fat of the heel, a delicately creased palm, whorled fingerprints. A large hand. Someone must have pressed the glass quite hard as he looked out, as though steadying himself.

I hovered my palm over it. Outside, I saw the patio, the dance of the chairs in the wind, rainwater spilling into the empty pool. I could see it all.

I swallowed hard against a sinking, nauseous feeling. I stepped back.

I dropped the book to the floor and ran.

I left Arizona that night, my car weighted with the few things I could fit.

Three hours north, I stopped at a diner. It was midnight, but coffee and eggs were served twenty-four hours. The only other customer was an old man soundly asleep over a plate of brown beans.

The women behind the counter didn't look at me twice. One read a magazine, the other balanced her checkbook. They wore kitschy gingham aprons. I might have to find a job in a place like this. Where would I end up? I'd vaguely considered the Northwest, far, far, from the desert.

The coffee gave me a sour stomach more than it woke me up, but I kept drinking. I was a little calmer now. I'd reached the mountains, lush with evergreens, the air cool with a damp astringent smell, like gin and mildew. In a while I might be able to pull over to the side of the road and get some sleep.

I waved off a third refill and went to the bathroom. The hallway walls were covered in framed photographs of notable patrons. A familiar face winked at me from the largest frame. I stumbled back, colliding with the bus cart, reaching to steady myself against it.

Senator Martin smiled out at me. He was sitting at the counter of this very diner with a group of men with slicked-back hair and white collared shirts. Everyone was laughing, mouths wide. The Senator's hand was lifted above the counter, about to slap it with amusement.

But something wasn't quite right, and as I leaned closer I saw it wasn't the Senator after all. The man's build was the same, same balding skull and broad forehead. Same charisma. But it wasn't Jim. A small placard under the picture identified him as the governor, fifteen years ago.

Washing my hands at the spitting sink, paying my

check, I couldn't stop shaking. The waitress noticed. "You okay, hon?"

Even back on the highway, I couldn't get the photograph out of my mind. What a shock it was, when the Senator's eyes flashed at me. Stared me down, as they had the last time I saw him, when I stood on the driveway in my soaking clothes, talking to the policeman. The Senator had fixed on us, his eagle eyes glinting. As he'd handled the policeman, I'd been grateful to him. I'd thought he was sparing me.

I still remembered the feeling of his hand against my back, guiding me down the driveway. *I don't want you to think too much about this*, he'd said. *It doesn't have anything to do with you.*

I'd thought he meant it as a comfort. Don't torment myself, blame myself. But he'd meant his words quite literally.

That afternoon, as they'd argued in the living room, Marina had been on the couch and Philip near the door, leaning on a chair. At first, the Senator had been out of my sight. Then we'd all heard a thump. He'd dropped something, interrupting the argument. He crossed the room, then sat on the couch beside Marina and joined the conversation.

Now I knew what he'd been doing, those moments before I could see him. He'd been standing at the window, holding an old book of his, or his first son's, the better son, the lost son. He looked out over the yard. Behind him, Philip and Marina bickered and sniped, but he didn't register their words. He'd had a shock, learning what they'd hidden from him. Of anything they might have done, this was the worst the Senator could fathom. Lying about family, about his own flesh and blood.

Philip was remorseless and dismissive, waving away his father's concerns like they were meaningless. Philip had never understood what it meant to be a Martin. Time and time again, he floundered, and his father fixed it, and received nothing but disdain for his trouble.

This time, the Senator felt defeated. The election weighed on him, his constituents abandoning him after decades of service, and now this . . . betrayal, there was no other word for it. He'd been lied to, by his own son, and, once again, he alone would have to bear the consequences.

He looked out at the clear sunny day. The valley that had been his home his whole life; the city he'd seen surge and grow through boom years, rebound from tough times. Had it ever been stronger than at this moment? Would no one acknowledge what a miracle this was, this metropolis on the sand? Nothing should flourish here, yet there wasn't a better place to live in the world. He'd always believed that. He still did.

To his surprise, the little girl came outside alone. She wore her swimming suit. She marched down to the pool, slipping through the gate with a sneaky wriggle. She was always so tiringly willful.

The Senator had a clear view of the pool. He watched as the girl wrestled an inflatable shark from the shed. On her own. Where was the nanny?

Amabel kicked off her sandals without anticipating the terrible, scalding heat of the pavement. She hopped unsteadily from one foot to the other, wrestling with the shark, taller than her, and ungainly.

The Senator's hand flew to the glass, instinctive, reaching out as if to warn her.

She lost her balance on the patio. Fell into the water.

The book fell from his fingers. It thumped loudly on the floor.

Marina and Philip turned, alarmed.

The Senator dropped his hand from the window, his blood racing, and turned. In the space of a heartbeat, an idea slipped into his head, like a paper airplane snatched from the air. Possibility. He unfolded it, pressed out its creases in his mind.

The girl would be gone. A terrible accident. Sweeping away the scandal of her hidden birth as if it had never happened. Banishing the threat of these other people, Iris and Clint, this scum who'd been bound up in the Martin name by his son's carelessness.

Marina and Philip watched him, worried. "Wait a minute," he said, a little breathless. "Just wait, now." He felt an easing, as though a finger that had been pressing into his chest had lifted.

He glanced around the room. His son was annoyed, Marina concerned. He spotted me, a sliver of my face at the door.

Marina began to stand.

"No, don't get up." His voice was firm, maybe a little gravelly. He sank stiffly onto the couch. A cold sweat prickled his scalp. He shook out a handkerchief and wiped his forehead.

He needed to start an argument. Keep them occupied. He reached with shaky fingers to the pin on his lapel, toyed with the familiar, reassuring shape, worn so many years. He remembered suddenly a phrase he'd used on James, sweet James, and Philip. He almost smiled.

"You're acting like children."

44

Clint was easy. No one would look too closely at his death.

Iris got what she wanted, money, and fled. She wouldn't come back.

I was the last loose end. They'd tried to pay me, but I wasn't leaving it alone. I was in Verde, in Florence; I was flinging accusations at Philip and Bryant, at the police. So the Senator dredged up my past. Easily poisoned Bryant against me. And if I hadn't gotten lucky and found the jewelry, I might be arrested by now, my fingers black with ink, my denials laughed off.

I drove until my eyes burned with exhaustion, the road as blurry as if my windshield had been smeared with Vaseline. I crossed through New Mexico, into Colorado. I was still in the mountains. Here and there, an unpaved road split off from the highway. Escape routes for runaway trucks, slanting uphill and ending in deep beds of gravel. I pulled into one, until the highway was out of sight. Pines towered around me, their branches thickly furred. I shut off my headlights and the trees vanished in a pool of darkness. The stars were so close up here, as if I could walk up into them.

I dreamed I'd kept driving, lost the road, crashed into a stand of trees. I dreamed of a hand reaching through my window. I dreamed I was awake in the car, listening with paralyzing dread to someone breathing in the backseat.

My eyes snapped open. It was dawn. Someone was outside, creeping at the tree line. I sat forward so fast my seat belt locked and I fell back.

Only a deer. At my movement, it leaped into the trees. Then it was just me, and bird cries in the thin air, and my skin buzzing with dread.

After that, I slept during the day, in rest stops or parking lots. At night, I drove, and when I was too exhausted to go on, I went to twenty-four-hour places, usually Walmarts. I'd wander the aisles, the unnatural white light overhead belonging to neither day nor night.

I saw dozens of black sedans. Parked at rest stops; idling behind me at gas stations; lurking in my blind spot outside an anonymous mountain city. My stomach twisted whenever I saw them, though the license plates were never from Arizona. I tried to tell myself that they couldn't know where I was.

One night, somewhere in Wyoming, I saw Philip and Marina again. I was reading the *Arizona Republic* homepage in the electronics department of a Walmart. They were the lead story: MARTIN FAMILY MAKES FIRST PUBLIC APPEARANCE SINCE TRAGEDY.

Marina and Philip waved from a stage. The Senator stood between them. His smile was craggy and triumphant. Our *Senator!* His lead in the polls had never been stronger.

He stood particularly close to Philip, gripping his son's shoulder.

Were they still plotting Philip's next six years, next decades? Schmoozing at parties, attending meetings, pressing flesh. Things Philip had grown good at. Things which, if he kept doing them, he might forget he hated, and only feel a gnawing, subterranean sense of loathing—for himself.

I bought a thick manila envelope, the kind that had held the Martins' cash. I wondered how much Iris had left. I had almost nothing, but my credit card still went through, town after town.

I took everything I had, the yearbook pages and

articles and photographs of pregnant Stacy, and sent them to my brother Caleb, who was good-natured and loyal and not particularly curious. *Hang on to this for me,* I wrote him. It wouldn't prove anything, but it was a comfort to think of it elsewhere. Safe.

My next letter took much longer.

Dear Philip, I began. *Please don't stop reading. I wouldn't write if it weren't important.*

I've always been a coward. I never told anyone about the boating accident, about turning the lights out to see the stars. Worse was what I'd done to Amabel. I couldn't stand the thought of anyone knowing. Especially Philip. Philip, who I'd always thought was like me.

If I told him only what his father had done, he wouldn't believe me. He'd think I was being spiteful, making up a story.

But if I told him my part, too—confessed my worst—he might believe me. He needed to know I'd listened at the living room door, ignoring Amabel. He needed to remember the afternoon himself, and realize my account was accurate. His father had stood at the window, dropped his book, kept them from getting up.

I told him about the handprint, though it would be gone by now, erased with a casual spritz of cleaning liquid and the neat flick of Eva's palm.

The Senator stood there, at the window. He saw her. He let her go.

He sacrificed Ammy for his career, I wrote. *His reputation. He cares more about his name than his family. He might get what he wants—from everything I've seen, he'll probably win. But you don't have to stand by him, or follow him, to keep the Martin legacy alive. He's sacrificed enough for that. Don't let him sacrifice you, too.*

I mailed the letter from a small town in South Dakota. I paid for rush delivery, and watched the postal worker toss the envelope into a bin like yesterday's newspaper.

I wound up in a stern, stony landscape. Cattle graze behind low post fences, their smell wafting for miles. People still ride horses here, meandering across the open fields, the way Amabel imagined she was riding: free, even as her pony made his circumscribed journey around the paddock. I see Ammy often, in the swing of a girl's hair as she runs to the playground, in the bossy intonation of a toddler's voice, in my dreams. I found a job in a restaurant, nothing like Philip's. I work the fryer, dropping in frozen breaded chicken breasts, watching the roiling cloudy oil. My hours are irregular, afternoon until past midnight, and I sleep in. That leaves me without much time to myself, which is the point.

I call myself Nat. The sound of the name, insignificant as a fly, pleases me.

Caleb asks what I'm doing here, if I'm bored out of my mind. For now, I'm fine. The air is clear and cold. I buy a suede jacket at the Salvation Army. It smells like bonfire smoke. The town's on the lap of a granite mountain, striped with mossy-looking black fissures. On my days off, I sometimes walk for five or six hours and never see another person. Once I saw a dog, large and fringy with a muddy coat, clambering up the rocks. For a moment I thought it was a coyote, but soon a man followed, picking his way with a walking stick.

The election comes in November, and the only surprise is to see the Senator alone at his victory party. I allow myself a glimmer of hope.

In January, I get an envelope. There's no return address, but my name's on it, and my exact address, down to the apartment number. Finn Hunt. A name from the past.

Inside, there's a photograph of a baby. He's wearing a white onesie. His legs are bent and splayed open, his feet curled. His spiky hair is black, his skin a caramel color. For a moment, I think he's Bryant's. I'm confused, hurt, like it's a postcard from a life I might have had.

I flip the photograph over, and there's writing on the back. *James Amado Martin. Our fresh start.*

Days later, I see the announcement online. Philip and Marina Martin are happy to announce the adoption of a son.

The article is breezy. It skims over Amabel's death—"happy news for the family, whose daughter tragically died in an accident."

In the picture, Marina holds James in her lap. She's beaming. Her fingers enclose his tiny fist. "We've given our son two lovely names. James, an old family name. And Amado, to honor our daughter, Amabel."

Philip stands behind Marina. Though his hands are on her shoulders, he seems caught in motion, his head turning away from the camera. His faint smile seems private, even sad. His hair is long again, waved back, the shine of it golden. I squint. He's wearing a flag pin on his lapel.

The Senator sits in a chair beside Marina, hands planted on his knees. "Nothing heals a family like a new baby. James carries a name that's been in my family for generations. We welcome him into the fold." He looks at me—at the camera—defiantly. He doesn't look happy, exactly. He's not flashing the smile he wore at his victory party, hands laced together over his head and beating the air. He looks stern, like that ancient snapshot of James Martin the first with his railroad crew. Like a man whose legacy will live on.

Acknowledgments

Thanks to:

Dan Conaway, my agent, for early belief and support. Your cunning insights made Finn sharper and the story more thrilling.

Kate Nintzel, my smart, savvy editor. Your edits brought the book to the best place.

Vicki Mellor, my UK editor, who went above and beyond with brilliant insights.

Vedika Khanna, Karen Richardson, Leah Carlson-Stanisic, and the teams at William Morrow and Pan Macmillan.

Maja Nikolic, Taylor Templeton, Andrea Vedder, and the team at Writers House.

Amy Schiffman at Echo Lake.

My teachers and classmates at USF and ASU, and especially to Lewis Buzbee, who dispatched pearls of wisdom exactly when I needed to hear them.

Much gratitude in memory of Lenore Brady, my inspiring mentor.

My early readers, especially John Flaherty, Leah Nuetzel, Peter Papachronopoulos, and Chris Hanks.

My family, and especially my parents, avid readers who encouraged my addiction.

Greg, my husband, for his unstinting support and faith from draft one. I couldn't have done it without you.